DEFINITELY
Maybe NOT
A DETECTIVE

DEFINITELY *Maybe* NOT A DETECTIVE

A NOVEL

SARAH FOX

BANTAM BOOKS
NEW YORK

Bantam Books
An imprint of Random House
A division of Penguin Random House LLC
1745 Broadway, New York, NY 10019
randomhousebooks.com
penguinrandomhouse.com

A Bantam Books Trade Paperback Original

ISBN 978-0-593-98425-3
Ebook ISBN 978-0-593-98426-0

Printed in the United States of America on acid-free paper

1st Printing

BOOK TEAM: Production editor: Abby Duval • Managing editor: Saige Francis • Production manager: Katie Zilberman • Copy editor: Brandon Hopkins • Proofreaders: Rachael Clements, Laura Petrella, Gabel Strickland

Book design by Alexis Flynn

Adobe Stock illustrations: AF DigitalArtStudio (footprints, magnifying glass), DDDART (heart binoculars)

The authorized representative in the EU for product safety and compliance is Penguin Random House Ireland, Morrison Chambers, 32 Nassau Street, Dublin D02 YH68, Ireland. https://eu-contact.penguin.ie

To Agatha Christie and all the storytellers
who made me fall for mysteries,
you had me at whodunit

DEFINITELY
Maybe NOT
A DETECTIVE

CHAPTER
ONE

It was happy hour, but murder was on the menu.

Death by daiquiri—or more accurately by cocktail glass—was seconds away from killing my new career as a restaurant server when my shift supervisor, Claire, swooped in and liberated the glass from my hands. She set it safely on the table while giving a smile to the sleazy middle-aged man who'd just doled out his fourth inappropriate comment about my body since I'd started serving him and his buddy twenty minutes ago.

I opened my mouth to give the creep a piece of my mind, but Claire was still in damage-control mode. She clamped an arm around my shoulders and steered me toward the back of the restaurant.

She spoke in a low, stern voice that contrasted starkly with the smile she kept on her face. "We don't dump drinks on our customers, Emersyn."

"Actually, I was planning to smash the glass over his head," I said, shooting a glare over my shoulder at my intended victim.

He winked at me, and my stomach churned.

"We don't do that either."

"You might want to rethink that policy," I said, seething.

Claire pushed me into the small employee break room. It was

empty, the fluorescent lights buzzing and flickering overhead. Claire took me by the shoulders and turned me around so we faced each other.

"I'm taking over your shift," she informed me.

I was about to protest when she cut me off.

"Chad wants to see you in his office."

My stomach sank. "Again? That can't be good."

Chad, the restaurant's manager, wasn't exactly an Emersyn Gray fan. I wasn't sure why. I hadn't mixed up all *that* many orders, and I'd only broken a few dishes. Okay, so maybe I knew why. I had to admit—to myself, not Chad—that I wasn't exactly a natural at waitressing.

Claire tipped her head toward the door. "Don't keep him waiting."

I gulped a breath of air, barely getting it past the lump of apprehension in my throat, and then started down the hall toward Chad's office.

Half an hour later, I sat on a park bench in the West Bronx, jobless for the second time in a month. I longed to drown my sorrows in a caffè mocha with extra whip, but I was painfully aware of the sorry state of my bank account balance. I couldn't afford to indulge in unnecessary treats. I also couldn't indulge in a pity party. Not for long, anyway.

I gave myself one more minute to stare morosely at the pigeons pecking at the ground beneath an oak tree. Then I heaved myself up off the bench and set a course toward home.

I'd almost reached the edge of the park when a familiar voice cried out with delight.

"Auntie Em!"

My spirits lifted even as my heart clenched. My seven-year-old niece, Livy, let go of her babysitter's hand and barreled toward me, her two strawberry blonde braids flying out behind her like kite tails. She launched herself at me so hard that she nearly knocked the breath out of me. I had to take a step backward to keep my balance as she wrapped her thin arms around my middle.

"Hey, Livysaurus." I kissed the top of her head. "What mischief have you been causing today?"

She giggled, releasing me and looking up at me with blue eyes so familiar that my heart clenched again. "I don't cause mischief. Mrs. Nagy bought me a hot dog from Alfonso!"

Alfonso was a hot dog vendor who often stationed his cart at the far end of the park. He always had a smile and a warm greeting for us whenever we saw him, even though I rarely bought his wares.

"Lucky you," I said to Livy before addressing my eighty-something neighbor, who'd just reached us. "Thank you, Mrs. Nagy. You didn't have to do that."

"It was my pleasure." She had a comforting voice, laced with a Hungarian accent. "I enjoy having a youngster around to spoil."

Zita Nagy and her husband had no children or grandchildren of their own. They lived in the unit next door to me and Livy, and they'd been a godsend over the last several months since we'd moved into the apartment building. They never let me pay them a dime for babysitting Livy, insisting that it was a treat for them, one that they always looked forward to.

"Well, I appreciate it," I said as we walked along the sidewalk at the edge of the park. "Thank you."

Livy held my hand and skipped along beside me. "I thought you had to work for hours and hours."

"I got off early." I kept my voice light, not wanting to let on that there was anything wrong. I must have succeeded, because Livy kept skipping happily.

"Can we have ice cream?" she asked, eyeing the ice cream parlor across the street.

"Not tonight, sweetie," I said with a pang of regret.

I felt even worse about denying her request when she accepted my response without protest.

"If you don't need me anymore tonight," Mrs. Nagy said as we neared a crosswalk, "I think I'll stop in at the corner store before it closes."

"Of course," I said. "Thanks so much for looking after Livy."

"Anytime, dear." She smiled. "Goodbye, Olivia."

"Bye, Mrs. Nagy." Livy waved as the elderly woman headed down the street.

We waited for the light to change and then crossed the road. Another few minutes of walking took us to the Deco Mirage, more often known simply as the Mirage. Back in its glory days in the 1920s, the building was a popular art deco hotel. It still boasted the geometric stained-glass windows, plaster detailing, courtyard fountain, and goddess statue in the lobby that could be seen in the old photos hanging on the walls in the entranceway, but some of the plaster had crumbled away and the fountain was no longer running. Moss had covered the stonework, obliterating many of the details of the mermaid sculpture. Inside the building, cracks ran through the walls and some of the windows were foggy, their seals broken. The building could have been a metaphor for my life. Once shiny and full of promise. Now crumbling, slowly but surely.

Or maybe not so slowly.

I looked up at the building with a sympathetic and self-pitying sigh. Then I reminded myself to be grateful for what I did have. My beautiful niece. A roof over our heads. And since we didn't live on the top floor, the leak in the roof didn't bother us much.

What had once been luxury suites had been broken into apartment units that had seen better days. For the last few decades, the building had catered to the fifty-five-plus community. Officially, it still did, but its low occupancy had left the landlord desperate for tenants. That was a good thing for me and Livy. The run-down building offered some of the cheapest rent around—at least within my niece's school district—and although most of the other residents were at least thirty years older than me, I tried to look at the positives: Grab bars in the shower—extra safety! Sweet elderly neighbors—free cookies and babysitting!

I spotted one of those sweet neighbors as soon as we entered the Mirage's lobby. Except Mr. Zoltán Nagy didn't seem quite so sweet at the moment. The man I'd only ever known as quiet and kind was currently chasing the building superintendent around the lobby, brandishing a croquet mallet over his head like a weapon.

I stopped dead in my tracks.

"Crazy old geezer!" the superintendent, Freddie Hanover, yelled as he dodged a swing of the croquet mallet.

Livy bounced up and down at my side. "Run, Freddie, run!" she cried, as if the men were playing an entertaining game.

Mr. Nagy let out a string of angry Hungarian as he took another swing at Freddie's head.

I was still frozen in place, wondering if I should intervene somehow or rush Livy up to the safety of our apartment, when the only other resident of the building under the age of fifty-five stepped off the elevator.

"Whoa!" Bodie Chase jumped back just in time to avoid getting creamed by Freddie and Mr. Nagy as they ran past.

It took Bodie approximately two seconds to assess the situation and jump into the fray. He grabbed the croquet mallet from Mr. Nagy and placed a hand on the elderly man's chest, bringing him to a halt. Freddie huddled by the elevators, glaring at Mr. Nagy as they both tried to catch their breath.

As for me, I breathed more easily. With Bodie on the scene, surely everything would remain under control. The thirty-year-old bartender from unit 505 stood over six feet tall and looked like he hit the gym several days a week. His hair was a more golden shade of blond than my own, and his eyes were as blue as a tropical ocean. Translation: He was built. And hot.

"Okay, gentlemen, let's calm things down." Bodie let the mallet hang from one hand. "What's going on here?"

"He threatened to confiscate my croquet equipment!" Mr. Nagy cried, his English more heavily accented than his wife's.

"You're always leaving it lying around the courtyard," Freddie shot back, still keeping his distance from Mr. Nagy. "I nearly broke my leg when I tripped on that metal hoop!"

Bodie turned those brilliant blue eyes my way and gave me a reassuring nod. "I've got this."

I mouthed, *Thank you*, and then pushed Livy ahead of me through the door to the stairwell.

"What did you do at school today?" I asked as we hurried up to the third floor. I didn't want her attention lingering on what we'd just witnessed, even if she hadn't quite realized that the men hadn't been playing a game.

Livy regaled me with stories about her teacher and classmates while we made our way to our apartment. Later, as Livy splashed about in the bathtub singing to herself, I flopped down on the couch and closed my eyes, a wave of exhaustion and defeat nearly crushing me.

The money that my brother, Ethan, had saved for his and Livy's future had been eaten up by his medical bills once he got sick with cancer and started his slow decline toward the end of his life. I thought that my niece and I would be okay financially after his death. Not well-off, by any means, but okay. Then my ex-boyfriend stole most of my savings, and my bad luck only continued from there. I lost my steady job as a copywriter thanks to financial restructuring, and now my career as a restaurant server was in the gutter too. I had rent to pay, a child to feed. I needed to get my life together, but it seemed like the harder I tried, the more it fell apart.

I allowed myself two minutes of distraction, thinking about Bodie Chase with his mesmerizing eyes and corded muscles. He and I had flirted—just a little bit—a couple of times when our paths had crossed and Livy hadn't been present. It would have been so easy to give in to the temptation to do more than flirt, but I needed to keep my life focused on Livy.

Besides, I couldn't trust my judgment when it came to men. I wouldn't have been in such a precarious financial situation if my ex hadn't run off with my life savings. I should have seen through him before he had a chance to leave me practically penniless, but in true Emersyn style, I'd remained clueless until it was too late.

So now I'd sworn off men, at least until Livy was older and I was wiser. If the latter ever happened.

Before my thoughts about Bodie strayed into X-rated territory, I forced myself up off the couch and reminded Livy to brush her teeth. After we'd read to each other from books of her choice, I tucked her in, kissed her forehead, and shut off the light.

"Sweet dreams, Livysaurus," I said, lingering in her bedroom doorway.

"Night night, Auntie Emersyn," she replied, as she did every evening.

My heart swelled as she snuggled beneath the covers with her purple dinosaur stuffie and closed her eyes. A surge of fierce love for my niece took my breath away. It was quickly followed by a wave of grief so strong that it nearly made me gasp.

I backed out of Livy's bedroom and shut the door all but a crack.

My life might have been a hot mess, and I was probably in grave danger of having my Competent Adult card revoked, but I knew without a doubt that I'd do everything in my power to keep that little girl safe, healthy, and happy. Which meant I needed a plan, and fast.

CHAPTER TWO

"What dish is best served cold?" My best friend, Jemma Ghosh, asked the question from across the small table in the busy coffee shop.

"Gazpacho?" I guessed.

Jemma rolled her eyes before removing a box from her oversize handbag and plunking it down in the middle of the table. "Revenge."

I took a sip of my caffè mocha—Jemma insisted on treating me—and eyed the box with a mixture of curiosity and apprehension. "I thought you were getting me ready for another job as a restaurant server."

"I'm not sure that's the industry for you."

I nearly shuddered at the parade of memories marching through my head: broken dishes, annoyed customers, an exasperated Chad.

"You might be right," I conceded. "But I need a job of some sort. And soon."

"Let's get back to my plan first," Jemma said, tapping the box with a perfectly manicured magenta fingernail. "After all, it's only partly about revenge and mostly about getting your money back."

That got my attention. "From Hoffman?" Hoffman Fisher, aka my ex-boyfriend, the snake who'd stolen my life savings.

Actually, it wasn't nice to call him a snake. There was no reason for me to go around insulting reptiles like that.

"You're going to scare him into returning every penny."

"I'm intrigued," I admitted. Then I eyed the box again, lowering my voice to a whisper. "But please tell me there's not a gun in there." The last thing I needed was someone calling the cops on us.

"Damn," my friend said. "I should've brought one of those too."

"Jemma," I said without humor.

"Just kidding. Sort of." She removed the lid from the box with a flourish. "Check it out."

I peered into the box, half expecting something with sharp teeth to leap out at me. Luckily, nothing stirred inside. The box held several stacks of identical business cards. Completely harmless, from what I could tell. I removed one from the box, running my thumb over the embossed lettering.

WYATT INVESTIGATIONS.

DISCRETION, EXPERTISE, RESULTS.

Below those words was a phone number.

"You hired a private investigator?" My gaze returned to the stacks of cards in the box. "And they gave you this many business cards?" Something wasn't adding up.

"It's not a real agency," Jemma said. "I made it up. Did you notice the name?"

"You used my favorite hot cowboy name." I had, on more than one occasion, described my dream man as a hot cowboy named Wyatt. I could picture him as clear as day. Dark hair, dark eyes, broad shoulders, washboard abs, a killer smile, and calloused hands that—

"Do I need to douse you with ice water?" Jemma interrupted my daydream.

"I was in the zone," I lamented, my fantasy cowboy fading into the ether.

"I know, hon," Jemma said. "But that zone is not PG, and we're in a public place. You were practically drooling." She rummaged around in her handbag and came up with a cell phone that she plunked down on the table next to the box. "Burner phone. So, if Hoffman wants to call the number on the card to see if it's the real deal, he'll get a legit-sounding voicemail message."

"Wow. You really thought this through." I was impressed, if not yet entirely sold on the plan.

"The phone and business cards are the perfect touches, right?"

I was thinking overkill—at least when it came to the number of cards. "How many are in there, anyway?"

"One hundred."

I fingered the card I still held in my hand. "I'm grateful and all, Jem, but you couldn't have just printed one on card stock?"

"Do I look like a stationery store? Besides, I had a fifteen-percent-off coupon." She paused for a sip of her latte. "All you have to do is give Hoffman one of the cards and tell him you've hired a private detective to gather enough evidence to take to the police and have him charged with theft. He'll be so scared that he'll be throwing your money at you."

"I don't know, Jemma." The thought of confronting Hoffman nearly had me breaking out in hives. Confrontation was not my strong suit.

Unless the confrontee was a sleazy man and I was armed with a cocktail glass. Hmm. Maybe I wasn't as anti-confrontation as I'd thought.

"The plan is foolproof, Em." Jemma shoved the box and burner phone toward me. "Not to mention it's the only one you've got."

She had me there.

Getting my money back from Hoffman wouldn't solve all my problems, but it would buy me time. Time to find a decent job so I wouldn't have to scrimp and save and take advantage of my neighbors' generosity. That's why I accepted the burner phone and box of business cards against my better judgment. How much stock could I put in my judgment, anyway?

Jemma dropped me off in front of the Mirage before speeding away in her red Camaro. I might have had a hint of car envy since I couldn't even afford an old clunker. Not that I needed a car in the city or wanted to deal with the constant street sweeping. I certainly couldn't afford to pay for a parking space, but I imagined that owning a vehicle came with a sense of freedom.

With the box of business cards in my arms, I started up the front steps to the Mirage, going over Jemma's plan in my mind.

"Afternoon, Emersyn!"

When I looked up to see who'd called out the greeting, I tripped and fell forward, landing on my knees on the steps. The box flew from my arms, and the business cards burst up into the air as the lid shot off, creating a cloud of white before fluttering down like a kaleidoscope of butterflies that had all simultaneously died mid-flight.

"I'm so sorry!" the same voice cried out. "I didn't mean to startle you."

I looked up to see Agnes Gao, a bespectacled, sixty-something Mirage resident, leaning out the window of her third-floor apartment, her short and graying black bob tucked behind her ears. She and her daughter owned a bakery two blocks away. She was a sweet lady, and occasionally brought Livy day-old treats that hadn't sold.

"No harm done," I assured her with a wave. Luckily, she was too far away to see me blinking away tears of pain. My knees throbbed, and I thought I felt blood trickle down my leg beneath my jeans.

As Agnes ducked back into her apartment, I scrambled around, collecting the fallen cards and dropping them into the box. After I'd picked up all the ones around me, I dusted off my hands and slid the lid back on. I didn't know if I'd retrieved all the cards, but I figured it didn't matter. With one hundred of them, I had ninety-nine spares, and I was pretty sure that card stock was compostable.

Once safely in my apartment, I cleaned up my bruised and scraped knees, using one of Livy's dinosaur bandages to cover a small cut that was oozing blood. Then I spent an hour online, hunting for jobs. None of the listings struck me as promising, but I bookmarked a couple to apply for anyway. It's not like I had the luxury of being picky.

When my eyes threatened to glaze over, I allowed my attention to stray. Even though it made me cringe, I brought up Hoffman's social media profiles. Just looking at the guy's selfies turned my stomach, but I needed to track his movements if I was going to put Jemma's plan into action.

When I saw his most recent post, from mere minutes ago, I jumped up from the couch. He'd posted yet another selfie—featuring his typical self-satisfied smile—with a caption stating that he'd just arrived at the Hickory Hill Country Club to play some tennis with his new girlfriend. She was the country club member, not Hoffman. Even the money he'd stolen from me wouldn't have covered the fees to get him into that exclusive club. No doubt he'd had dollar signs in his eyes when he met this woman and realized how loaded she was. Would he try to steal from her or keep the relationship going and milk it for all it was worth?

I felt sorry for her. Maybe I should warn her about Hoffman?

If I ran into her at the country club, I would, because that's where I was heading.

I still had a few hours before Livy got out of school. If I hurried, I could reach the club before Hoffman was done playing tennis.

On the train to Connecticut, I texted Jemma, telling her where I was going and why. She responded right away, demanding to know what I was wearing. Cringing, I took a quick selfie and sent it to her. Judging by her response, my worn jeans and V-neck T-shirt didn't qualify as country club attire.

I'll meet you at the club, she wrote back. *DO NOT GO IN BE-FORE I GET THERE.*

I felt relieved. I'd much rather have Jemma at my side than go it alone when confronting Hoffman. And the fact that she was willing to drive all the way up to Connecticut from her place in the West Bronx made my heart swell.

After the train ride, I had to hop on a bus to get closer to my destination. It dropped me off a short distance from the country club, and I figured I was lucky I didn't have to walk for miles. After all, how many members of the Hickory Hill Country Club would ever bus there? None, probably. If I had money to throw around, I would have been willing to bet that the only people who didn't use valet parking there were the employees.

I took my time getting to the club, not wanting to loiter awkwardly for long while I waited for Jemma. Even though I walked at the speed of a tortoise, there was no sign of her familiar red Camaro when I arrived.

I paced up and down in front of the semicircular driveway for a couple of minutes before Jemma's Camaro pulled up to the curb, windows down.

"Take the dress," she said, pointing at a blue garment on the passenger seat. "There's no way you can trick anyone into thinking you're a member looking like that."

I glanced down at my clothes. I knew she was right.

"Where am I supposed to change?" I asked. "In the car?"

I didn't see any other option. As much as I wanted to get revenge on Hoffman and get my money back, I wasn't about to strip down on the side of the road.

"Sorry, hon. I'm working at the salon this afternoon, and I'm cutting it close as it is." She leaned over and stuffed the dress out the window at me.

"You're not coming with me?" I asked in dismay. So much for backup.

"You've got this, Em," she said.

I jumped back just in time. She stepped on the gas and careened away from the curb. I watched her car disappear down the street and then turned to face the country club again.

If I wasn't going to change clothes out in the open, I really had only one option.

I hurried around the side of the ostentatious two-story clubhouse, where bushes and rhododendrons lined the stone wall that blocked most of the property from public view. I glanced about to make sure no one was watching and then ducked in among the foliage. Branches snagged at my hair, and I nearly screamed when I came face-to-legs with a spider dangling from a silken thread. I dodged the spider and worked my way deeper into the bushes.

When I reached the wall, I leaned against it so I could unzip and kick off my ankle boots. I wriggled out of my jeans and stripped off my T-shirt before pulling the blue dress on. I worked one arm into a sleeve before my hair snagged on a rhododendron branch. When I tried to turn around to untangle myself, more branches grabbed at my hair. I twisted and wrestled until I was hopelessly ensnared. The shrub now had a firm grip on both my hair and the empty sleeve of the dress. With the zipper undone, my entire back was exposed to the breeze, which sent unpleasant chills over my bare skin.

And was that something crawling up my back? With a gasp, I tried to whirl around. Pain shot along my scalp as my hair got pulled harder. I flailed—as much as I could under the circumstances—trying to swipe at my back.

"Get off! Get off! Get off!"

When I could no longer feel creepy-crawlies on my skin, I stopped struggling, out of breath. Working or not, I needed Jemma to come back and help me. But my phone was in the pocket of my jeans, which were on the ground at my feet. When I tried to reach down, the rhododendron yanked at my hair again, the pain making my eyes water.

"Okay, don't panic."

Despite my own advice, panic settled in to stay a while. My heart raced, and my thoughts spun in dizzying circles.

I couldn't believe this was my fate.

I was probably going to die here, trapped in the Rhododendron of Doom.

"You okay in there?" a male voice asked.

Yes, I was indeed going to die here. Of utter mortification.

CHAPTER
THREE

The man peering at me through parted branches could have stepped right out of one of my favorite romance novels. With his faded jeans and white button-down shirt, he managed to look both casual and chic. He had tousled dark hair, eyes that were nearly black, and light brown skin with a hint of a bronze undertone. From the way he was stooped down to peer at me, I knew he had to be over six feet tall. He had the top button of his shirt undone, and his sleeves were rolled up to his elbows, showing off his muscular forearms. I didn't fail to notice his broad shoulders either.

Yep. Right out of one of my fantasies.

Except this was more of a nightmare.

"I'm fine, thanks!" Edged with hysteria, my voice sounded unfamiliar to me.

"You sure?" he asked. "Because it looks like you've gone a few rounds with this rhododendron, and I hate to say it, but it doesn't look like you're winning."

With a grimace, I wriggled around, desperately trying to free myself. "I'm sure I can . . ." The sharp end of a branch just missed stabbing me in the eye, instead hitting right beneath it, drawing a hiss of pain out of me.

The mild amusement on the man's face morphed into concern. "Here, let me help you."

He pushed branches aside and maneuvered his way in behind me.

Great. Now he had a full view of my exposed back, including my fraying, totally-not-sexy beige bra. I didn't even like beige underwear, but this one had come in a pack of two with a cute pink one. Why couldn't I have worn the pink one? Or any of the other far cuter bras I owned?

Because this was the life of Emersyn Gray, that's why. Of course I had to meet a superhot guy while half dressed in the most unflattering way possible. The universe, which apparently loved to laugh at me, wouldn't have it any other way.

"The stegosaurus is cool, but I've always been more of an ankylosaurus fan myself," Mr. Hot-Cowboy-from-My-Dreams said.

It took me a second to realize that he was talking about the bandage on my knee, which, apparently, he'd had a good look at before moving around behind me.

"Why the ankylosaurus?" I was so used to talking dinosaurs with Livy that the question flowed out of me naturally.

"They were built like living tanks." With surprising gentleness, he freed each lock of my hair from the rhododendron's evil grip. "Plus, there's something Teenage Mutant Ninja Turtle–ish about them, and I was always a Turtles fan."

"Huh," I said with interest. "I can't say I ever made that connection."

He held the sleeve of the dress out for me so I could slip my arm into it. Then he zipped up the back.

I suppressed a shiver as his fingers brushed the base of my neck for the briefest and most tantalizing moment. Then I reminded myself that this was a nightmare, not a fantasy. A ridiculous farce of a nightmare, with me the butt of all the jokes.

Speaking of butts, I hoped the open zipper hadn't been so low that he'd caught a look at mine.

I brushed off said butt and ran my fingers through my tangled hair. I remembered at the last second to reach into the pocket of my discarded jeans and pull out the fake business card.

My rescuer squeezed out of the bushes ahead of me and then held the branches aside so I had a clear path out into the open.

"Thank you," I said, the words coming out grudgingly, not because I wasn't grateful, but because embarrassment was still overshadowing every other emotion.

"Anytime," he said with a grin.

I bit back a groan.

This was totally not fair.

His dark eyes twinkled with humor. Actually *twinkled*! And when he grinned, a killer dimple appeared to one side of his mouth. A mouth that probably knew how to kiss as well as my ultimate dream cowboy.

He cleared his throat, shattering my nascent daydream before it could really get started. And that's when I realized he'd caught me staring at his mouth. I quickly wiped the back of my hand over my lips, in case any drool had dared to escape.

Get ahold of yourself, woman! I scolded myself silently.

I stood straighter and fluffed up my hair. "Thank you for your help," I said, this time sounding rigidly polite rather than grudging.

"You know, there are restrooms inside," he said, his grin now bordering on infuriating. "Nice ones. With plenty of room for changing clothes."

"Not for people like me."

I turned on my heel, ready to march away with my head held high, but then remembered that I was currently barefoot. My cheeks flaming, I reached beneath the rhododendron and grabbed my ankle boots, probably giving the guy a clear view of my booty. At least it was fully covered by the dress. Although I needed to be careful not to lean *too* far. I had a few inches of height on Jemma, which meant that the skirt of the dress—already short on my friend—was perilously short on me.

I straightened up as soon as my hand closed around the black ankle boots. Not the footwear I would have chosen if I'd known I'd be wearing this dress, but it's not like I had any other options.

I wobbled precariously as I tried to jam my feet into the high-heeled boots on the soft grass.

"Careful," the man said, catching my elbow with a gentle but firm grip.

Tingles radiated up my arm, sparked by his touch.

The business card slipped from my fingers and fluttered to the ground. He picked it up before I had a chance. I saw curiosity on his face as he read the print before handing the card to me.

"You're a private investigator?" he said with a mixture of surprise and interest.

"No." I didn't offer any further response. As far as I was concerned, this encounter had already stretched on far too long.

I was about to turn away when he spoke again.

"I like the hair accessories. Very . . . earthy." That amused twinkle was back in his eyes.

My hand shot to my head, patting around. He reached out and snagged something from my hair, holding it up for me to see.

A twig.

"Doesn't quite match the dress, though." He dropped the twig and brushed dirt from his hands.

Strong hands that . . .

I would most definitely *not* imagine running over my body.

Nope, nope, nope.

I shoved all such thoughts aside.

"I appreciate your help, but I have somewhere I need to be." I strode off with as much dignity as I could muster, considering that the heels of my boots kept sinking into the soft ground.

When I made it to the driveway, walking became easier, and I regained some of my composure. Not that I'd had a whole lot to begin with.

I forced myself to keep my gaze fixed straight ahead. I didn't want the guy catching me looking back at him. He might have been easy on the eyes, but I hoped I'd never see him again. The crumbled ruins of my dignity wouldn't be able to handle it.

Besides, I needed to focus.

It was time to put Operation Make Hoffman Pay into action.

CHAPTER
FOUR

As soon as I stepped into the lobby, I could practically smell money. From the crystal chandelier above me to the leather couch and chairs in a sitting area to my left, everything shouted, *Expensive!*

To my relief, the woman behind the reception desk was busy talking to someone on the phone. I took out my own phone and stood next to the leather couch, pretending to type out a text message. I angled myself so that the woman wouldn't be able to see my grazed knees and dinosaur bandage.

As I fake-typed on my phone, I surreptitiously glanced around the lobby, assessing my surroundings. Next to the reception desk was a door that led farther into the building. It had one of those security pads next to it on the wall, the kind that require a card to be swiped. As I was beginning to panic—again—that the plan was going to fall apart before I'd even found Hoffman, two women dressed in tennis outfits, with bags slung over their shoulders, entered the clubhouse, chatting. They waved at the receptionist as they crossed the lobby. One woman produced a key card and swiped it. The green light came on, and the door's lock clicked. The women pushed their way through.

I knew this might be my only opportunity to get into the inner sanctum. I fell into step behind the two women, doing my best to appear confident, like I totally belonged.

As the door swung closed behind the women, I put a hand out to stop it.

"Excuse me, ma'am!"

I froze and looked toward the receptionist. The door clicked shut, the sound ominous to my ears.

"I'm afraid I'll need you to scan your membership card," the receptionist said.

I sent her what I hoped was a sheepish smile. "I forgot it at home, and I'm meeting a friend here for lunch."

"Perhaps you could text your friend and have them come meet you here in the lobby?" she suggested. Her tone was apologetic yet firm. A polite guard dog but a guard dog nonetheless.

"Oh . . . Um . . ." I desperately tried to pull myself together. "Sure, I can do that."

Crap, crap, crap.

I didn't know what to do. A voice in my head was shouting, *Abort! Abort!*

That sounded like a good idea to me. I'd just have to find Hoffman somewhere else on another day.

But then an arm settled across my shoulders, and the heady scent of fresh air reached my nose.

"It's all right, Agatha. She's with me."

The receptionist's face changed instantly.

"Of course. Nice to see you again."

The man who'd helped me out of the rhododendron flashed her a smile, and I swear she nearly swooned. "You too, Agatha."

He kept one arm around my shoulders as he swiped his card and pushed the door open. Then his hand moved to my back as I preceded him out of the lobby.

As soon as the door fell shut behind us, he removed his hand from my back, but I swear it left behind a glowing imprint. I could still feel the heat from his skin through the thin fabric of my borrowed dress.

A few paces away from the door, we drew to a stop.

"Thanks for that," I said, trying not to let on that I was annoyed that he'd now come to my rescue twice.

He grinned at me, his dimple making another appearance. I cursed the weakness in my knees.

"Now that we're partners in crime, do I at least get to know why you're sneaking into the club?"

"I'm here to meet someone," I said. After all, that was sort of the truth. Hoffman just didn't know I was coming to meet him.

"That's all you've got for me?" he asked, sounding disappointed. "Do I at least get to know your name?"

When I hesitated, he held out his hand. I eyed it like it was dangerous. It probably was, considering that simply thinking about his hands had nearly sent me spiraling into a steamy fantasy earlier. But I couldn't bring myself to ignore the offering.

I closed my hand around his.

I wouldn't have called the touch electric. It was more like a sizzle, a fiery one that held a dangerous promise of even more heat.

I swore his nearly black eyes darkened, and I knew he'd felt it too.

"Emersyn Gray."

My name came out sounding more breathless than I'd intended.

"Nice to meet you, Emersyn. I'm Wyatt."

Of course he was.

Suspicion cut through the fogginess in my brain.

"For real? Are you just saying that because of this?" I held up the business card he'd retrieved for me minutes earlier.

"Coincidence," he assured me. "My name really is Wyatt."

"Wyatt what?" I asked.

He released my hand and slid both of his into the pockets of his jeans. "Just Wyatt."

My hand felt cold in the absence of the heat of his sizzling touch. I tucked both hands behind my back, in case I got the crazy urge to reach for him. I cleared my throat and tore my gaze from his.

"I'd better get going." I took two steps and then stopped. "Which way to the tennis courts?"

He started walking. "I'll show you."

"I just need directions, not a guide." Despite my words, I hurried to fall into step with him, since he was already striding down the hallway.

"All right then." He held a door open for me, one that led outside.

I passed through it and found myself on a cement pathway, bordered on each side by flowerbeds full of colorful fall blooms. Ahead and to my right was the outdoor pool. One branch of the path led that way and another led straight. A third branch wound off to my left. I noticed a discreet sign indicating the direction to the tennis courts just as Wyatt pointed that way.

"Take that path, and you won't miss the courts," he said.

"Thanks."

I took about ten steps along the left-hand pathway before coming to an abrupt halt.

"*Emersyn?* What are you doing here?"

Even though I was at the club for the specific purpose of speaking with Hoffman, seeing him standing before me in his white shorts and polo filled me with a mixture of dread and anger. I fought the urge to turn and flee, made stronger by the presence of Hoffman's new girlfriend at his side. She had blonde hair and blue eyes like me, but that's where the similarities ended. She was shorter than me, slimmer than me, curvier than me. And dressed head to toe in what had to be designer tennis gear. Her gaze slid down my body, and a sneer tugged at her otherwise pretty features.

I silently cursed myself for not ripping off the dinosaur bandage.

I managed to speak with far more confidence than I felt. "I need to talk to you, Hoffman."

"I don't think we've got anything to talk about," he said with disdain. "And you're not even a member of this club. You shouldn't be here." He raised his wrist so I'd notice his ever-present Apple Watch on its orange strap. "I could call security and have you tossed out."

"You're not a member either," I pointed out, clenching my fists as the embers of my aggravation flickered into flames.

"But I am," his girlfriend sneered, "and he's with me."

Her haughty tone and the way she glared down her nose at me like I was a piece of trash made me seriously rethink my plan to warn her about Hoffman's character.

"So, I guess you won't mind if I tell everyone at this club the truth about you," I said to Hoffman.

"Try it, and I'll sue you for slander."

"It's not slander if it's the truth," I shot back.

Hoffman scowled at me. I stared back, not allowing myself to blink or waver in any way.

"Tiffany, give me a second," he said without looking at his girl-friend. He was too busy glowering at me to spare her a glance. "I'll deal with this."

Tiffany huffed but then flounced off toward the clubhouse, bumping my shoulder on her way past. I gritted my teeth and decided to get this over with as quickly as possible.

I held the business card out to Hoffman.

"I've hired a private detective. He's in the process of gathering evidence to take to the police. Evidence that will prove you stole money from me."

Hoffman didn't take the card. "Give me a break, Emersyn. You think I'm going to buy that story? The cops didn't charge me before, and they won't do it now."

I shoved the card at his chest and let it go. When it started to flutter down his front, he snatched it and cast a cursory glance at it.

"Give back every cent you stole from me, and I'll call off the detective," I said.

Hoffman glanced at the card again and let out a derisive snort. "Seriously? This is a joke. And not even a good one."

He crumpled up the card and threw it on the ground.

Defeat threatened to crush me.

But then Wyatt appeared by my side, radiating a calm authority that was both comforting and super sexy. "I'm Wyatt," he said, his dark gaze drilling into my ex. "Of Wyatt Investigations. I'm the detective Ms. Gray hired."

I barely managed to hide my surprise.

Hoffman glanced from the discarded business card to Wyatt. I nearly laughed at the expression of shock on his face. Somehow, I fought off the temptation.

"I suggest you listen to Ms. Gray," Wyatt continued. "I'm very good at what I do."

I waited a beat to let those words sink in before I spoke.

"Time's ticking, Hoffman," I said, feeling more confident now.

I turned on my heel and followed the path back to the club-house, holding my head high and not looking back, not even for a second.

CHAPTER
FIVE

Wyatt followed me as I made my escape from Hoffman, but once inside the clubhouse he was waylaid by two women who obviously knew him. I kept walking, not once slowing my pace. When I cast a quick glance over my shoulder, I saw the women fluttering their eyelashes at Wyatt while he watched me leave him behind.

Despite the way his gaze warmed my skin, even from a distance, I didn't break my stride. As grateful as I was for his help, I couldn't handle any more humiliation that day. I didn't want him knowing my embarrassing history with Hoffman, and I didn't need to be reminded of the way we'd first met.

Hot or not, Wyatt was now out of my life, and that was for the best. Even if the hopeless romantic in me was sobbing with disappointment.

Once through the front door, I made a quick trip back to the rhododendron to retrieve my clothes. I wasn't about to risk changing in the bushes again—who knew who would catch me this time—so I simply picked up my clothes and tucked them under my arm before making a beeline for the bus stop. Seconds after I arrived at the stop, the bus pulled up to the curb with a squeal of brakes and a mechanical sigh.

I thought I heard someone call my name as I stepped on board, but I stuck to my guns and didn't look back. I was committed to moving forward.

I closed my eyes during the bus ride, trying to restore a sense of calm. Not that calm was my default state. I wasn't sure that the plan was going to work out, but at least I'd given it a shot.

When I got back to the Mirage, I decided I should text Jemma with a mission report.

It was then, as I stood on the building's front steps, that I realized I was missing my phone.

I tipped my head back and let out a roar of frustration. Two startled pigeons flapped their way off the stairs and into the air.

"Smart birds," I said, watching them fly off. "Steer clear of Emersyn. My bad luck might be contagious."

With a sigh, I trudged into the Mirage. Jemma didn't work past six p.m. most days, so maybe I could use the burner phone to call her and ask her to drive me back to the country club that evening. I'd most likely lost my phone in the bushes out front, so chances were good that I wouldn't have to set foot in the clubhouse again. Although, with my luck, I'd dropped it in the inner sanctum. And it had probably hopped, skipped, and jumped right into the swimming pool.

But maybe my luck wasn't quite as bad as I thought. When I entered the lobby, I spotted Jemma perched on the padded bench near the mailboxes. She was leaning to the side, peering at a laptop sitting on the knees of a girl in a wheelchair. I didn't know the girl, but I'd seen her around the building a couple of times, whizzing past me as she rolled through the hallways. She looked to be in her midteens and wore her dark hair in multiple braids that were wound up into two buns on top of her head. She had warm brown skin and wore purple-framed glasses that matched her Converse sneakers.

When Jemma spotted me, she jumped up off the bench. "Emersyn! How did it go?"

"Not great," I said with a heavy sigh as I flopped down on the bench. "But I gave Hoffman the card. Then I went and lost my phone."

Jemma sat down beside me. "You don't need to worry about that." She held up the burner phone, which she must have fetched from my apartment with her key. "Someone already texted to say they found it. Although . . . if Hoffman has the business card, then he's the only person with the number for this phone." She frowned. "Maybe he's pranking us. He said his name was Wyatt. That's pretty fishy, now that I think of it."

I grabbed the phone. "Wyatt has it?"

"There really is a Wyatt?" Jemma asked. Her eyes widened, and she bounced in her seat. "Is he hot? Please tell me he's hot."

"No comment." I didn't want to talk about Wyatt or how we'd met.

"That means he's superhot," the girl with the laptop chimed in.

I narrowed my eyes at her. "Who are you? And shouldn't you be in school?"

Jemma answered for her. "Theodosia Harris. Her grandparents live in the building."

"I go by Theo," the girl added. "And I'm in a blended learning program. Half in-class and half online."

"I thought you were working." My statement, aimed at Jemma, came out sounding almost accusatory.

"I had a cancellation." Jemma snatched the burner phone back from me. "I can't wait to see this guy."

"You're not going to see him," I grumbled, wishing we could talk about something—anything—else.

"I might when he returns your phone. I'll ask him to bring it here."

"I don't want him knowing where I live!"

"Is he a creeper?" Theo asked, sounding a little too excited by the possibility.

"No, but . . ."

Jemma waved off my concern. "We can tell him this is my building, if that makes you feel better."

"Never mind," I said with a sigh. "Just don't give him my unit number."

She tapped out the Mirage's address and hit the SEND button. Then she checked the call log. "No missed calls or voicemail messages," she said with disappointment. "Hoffman hasn't tried calling the number on the business card."

"He tossed the card, so I doubt he'll ever be calling," I said. I realized now that Wyatt must have picked the card up off the ground. Unless he had a photographic memory, that was the only way he could have known the number for the fake detective agency. "And if Hoff bothers to look for Wyatt Investigations on the Internet," I added, "he'll soon find it doesn't exist, just like he already suspects."

Jemma let out an annoying buzzer sound. "Wrong! Theo here has been working her magic. She's a computer whiz. Take a look."

Jemma grabbed the laptop from Theo's knees and turned the screen my way.

I leaned in for a closer look at the page on display.

"A fake website for the fake detective agency?"

"A *real* website," Theo corrected me.

"I can't pay for that."

"Consider it an early birthday present." Jemma returned the computer to Theo. "Time to debrief."

"I'll take notes," Theo offered, adjusting the computer on her lap.

"That's not necessary," I assured her as I got to my feet, hoping to skip the mission debriefing, at least for the moment.

The look Theo shot me nearly froze my insides. It reminded me of the look I used to get from Mrs. Klein, my fifth-grade teacher, who still featured in my nightmares from time to time. I swallowed any further protestations and sat meekly next to Jemma, ready to recount every painful detail of my trip to the country club. The ones that followed my entrance into the clubhouse, anyway.

Nobody needed to hear about the Rhododendron of Doom.

CHAPTER SIX

By the time our debriefing session was over, Wyatt still hadn't responded to Jemma's text message, so she reluctantly left the Mirage. She'd finished her work as a hairstylist for the day, but she was attending a family dinner at her parents' place that evening, and her mom wanted her to arrive early to help with the prep work. Jemma invited me and Livy to the dinner, but I declined. Her parents meant well, but I knew they'd ask me about my now nonexistent job, and I didn't feel up to answering those awkward questions. Maybe that made me a coward, but I was okay with that.

As for Theo, she zoomed off in her wheelchair as soon as it became apparent that Wyatt wasn't going to show up anytime soon. Once I found myself alone, I made a quick stop at my apartment to change back into my jeans and then rode the elevator to the top floor and climbed a flight of stairs to the roof. I needed to gather my thoughts and get myself into a positive headspace before picking Livy up from school.

While Wyatt's presence shook him up, I was pretty sure that Hoffman would only return my money if it was pried from his cold, dead fingers. And even though I'd come close to murdering that sleazeball at the restaurant, now that I was out of the heat of the moment, I knew I didn't want to end up in jail. I couldn't be the parent Livy needed from behind bars.

It turned out that I wasn't the only one who'd decided to retreat to the peacefulness of the roof. Zoltán Nagy had beaten me to it. I spotted his balding head, ringed with white hair, as soon as I stepped out into the open air. There wasn't much of a patio up there. Just an expanse of concrete with two benches, all surrounded by a four-foot wall. But the sky was a beautiful shade of blue, and the air felt fresher up there than it did down on the street, where exhaust fumes and the pungent smell of marijuana often battled for dominance.

I hovered next to the bench where Mr. Nagy sat, a teacup and saucer resting on his knee.

"Mind if I join you?" I asked.

The elderly man smiled and patted the bench next to him. "I'd be delighted."

I sank down onto the wooden seat and let out a sigh as I watched a pigeon take off from the wall and soar across to the neighboring building.

"Troubles?" Mr. Nagy asked.

"Too many to name," I said with a wry smile. "But hopefully none that are insurmountable."

"Few problems can't be solved." He leaned down and reached beneath the bench. A second later, he produced a bottle of apricot pálinka.

He winked at me. "Especially when you've got the right fuel."

He added a dollop of the liquor to his cup of tea and then passed the bottle to me with an encouraging nod. I took a swig and nearly choked as the fruity liquid burned its way down my throat.

Mr. Nagy tapped the side of his nose as I handed the bottle back to him. "Our secret." He put the cap back on and returned the bottle to its hiding place beneath the bench.

"Has Freddie been giving you trouble?" I asked.

"Ah. You mean because I chased him."

I nodded. "Not that I blame you. Freddie's a jerk." I had choicer words to describe him, but I didn't want to use them in Mr. Nagy's company.

"He threatened to confiscate my croquet mallet!" he said, his ire rising. "I left it in the courtyard once—just once! So I left a hoop behind another time. I'm an old man, and he would rob me of one of my greatest pleasures. Croquet in the courtyard. It makes me happy. What's wrong with that?"

I patted his shoulder. "Nothing at all."

His anger seemed to drain out of him. "You are a good woman, Emersyn. You and Livy have a bright future."

An invisible weight pressed down on my shoulders. "I hope you're right about that."

He must have heard the desolation in my voice, because this time he was the one patting my shoulder. "If there's something you want in life, or something you want to change, go all out. Don't let anyone or anything stand in your way." He carefully rose to his feet, holding his saucer and teacup in one hand. "Now, I must get home before my wife comes looking for me. She'll be finished having tea with Agnes, and I don't want her discovering my secret." He nodded toward the spot where he'd stashed the bottle of pálinka and winked at me again.

Then he left me alone on the roof. Alone, except for a thousand thoughts, worries, and insecurities. They weren't great company.

I decided to take Mr. Nagy's advice and spent much of the following morning applying for jobs online and then hoofing it around the neighborhood, visiting any store with a HELP WANTED sign out front. Well, almost any store. There was one called Sugar Daddy with blacked-out windows. I gave that one a pass.

Unfortunately, that left me with only two other options. Not many people were hiring.

By the time I returned to the Mirage, my feet ached, and my stomach rumbled with hunger. For a brief moment, I allowed myself to fantasize about getting a panini from Agnes Gao's bakery. I should have known better. That made my mouth water and my stomach rumble harder, and all the while I knew I'd have to settle for a tin of orange segments or peanut butter on a slice of dry bread. I opted for the peanut butter but had to toast the bread to make it go down easier.

Once my stomach had quieted down, I mustered all the courage I could and checked my bank balance. At least Chad had paid me for my last few shifts at the restaurant. That meant I could hit the grocery store and restock the fridge before fetching Livy from school.

When I stepped out of the elevator, on my way to the store, I passed the lobby's trash can. The swinging lid was half open, with the bottom end of a bouquet of flowers sticking out. Roses, in fact. Some of the flowers were crushed by the lid, and a few petals had fallen on the floor.

Carefully, I extracted the bouquet. Why would anyone throw away such gorgeous flowers? Rejection, probably. Someone's attempt to woo their sweetheart clearly hadn't gone well.

I lifted the bouquet to my nose and breathed in the heavenly scent. A couple of the flowers were damaged, but if I removed those ones, I'd still have a beautiful bouquet. One I couldn't afford to buy for myself. And it wasn't as if there were hot guys lining up to give me gifts.

I returned to my apartment and put the flowers in water. That small touch brightened up the room and gave me a spurt of optimism. I almost had a spring in my step when I set off again for the grocery store. It felt so good to be out in the fresh air—as fresh as it got in the city, anyway—that I stopped at a small park and sat on a bench to bask in some October sunshine while enjoying my newfound positive attitude.

Unfortunately, my cheery outlook on life didn't last long. It deserted me once I reached the checkout counter at the grocery store.

Sure, I had enough money to pay the rent and buy groceries this month, but what about next month, and the one after that?

On the way home with my two bags full of provisions, I kept an eye out for HELP WANTED signs in shop windows. I hadn't walked this way during my earlier job search, and I spotted one in a clothing store's window and decided to walk in and apply on the spot. Except the store was closed.

I peered through the windows and knocked on the locked door, hoping someone might be around, but nobody emerged from the back of the shop. I told myself to remember to apply for the job at another time, and then I resumed my homeward trudge.

I'd almost reached the Mirage's front stairs when I drew to a stop on the sidewalk. A metallic green BMW convertible sat parked by the curb, its top down. It looked like it had just been driven out of the showroom, the car's paint gleaming in the sunlight.

Usually, Jemma's red Camaro was the sportiest car to stop on the street. I'd never seen this convertible before.

"Do you like cars as much as you like dinosaurs?" a man's voice asked from behind me.

I thought my body might short-circuit. The sound of the voice sent a tingling thrill over my skin while simultaneously making my heart stutter and my stomach sink. One-half of my brain screamed, *No, no, no!* while the other screamed, *Oh, hell yes!*

Slowly, I turned around.

Wyatt sat on the Mirage's front steps, looking casual and sexy and way too damn good to be fair. He wore a black T-shirt with his jeans today, and he was grinning at me, but in no way did that make me weak at the knees.

(Sometimes we just need to lie to ourselves, right?)

"What are you doing here?"

He'd caught me so off guard that the question slipped out of me before I could stop it. I knew full well that there was only one reason he was sitting outside my apartment building.

Sure enough, he held up my phone. "Returning this. You did tell me I could stop by."

I set my groceries on the bottom step and sank down next to him, not because I wanted to extend our meeting, but because my feet were desperate for a rest. (Another lie? Maybe.)

"What else did I tell you?"

One of his eyebrows quirked up in a quizzical way that was absolutely not sexy.

(I was on a roll.)

"My friend wrote the texts, not me," I explained.

"So you don't think I'm hotter than a jalapeño and . . ." He consulted his own phone. "Want to spice things up?"

My jaw dropped, and I made a grab for his phone, ready to kill my best friend the next time I saw her. Wyatt easily held the phone out of my reach.

He laughed. "Just kidding. She didn't write any of that."

I groaned. "Not funny."

"It was a little." His grin was infuriating and absolutely did not make him hotter than a habanero.

He handed me my phone, and I managed a grudging "Thank you."

Finally, his smile faded, and the butterflies in my chest—which I'd studiously been ignoring—acted more like normal butterflies rather than ones amped up on amphetamines.

"I hope I didn't cause any problems by pretending to be the detective you hired," he said with a hint of regret in his voice. "I heard the way that guy was talking to you, and wanted to wipe the smirk off his face."

He hadn't been the only one.

"I might have problems," I said, "but they weren't caused by you." Unless relentless butterflies qualified as a problem. Which they might, if they didn't get a grip and settle down. They were more than a little distracting. "If nothing else, I got a kick out of the look on his face when you introduced yourself."

"Like a deer caught in headlights," Wyatt said with a nod and a grin.

Agnes Gao interrupted us as she came up the steps. That was probably for the best. I was starting to enjoy our conversation a little too much.

"Hello, Emersyn," Agnes greeted, her gaze coming to rest on Wyatt. Clearly intrigued, she nudged her glasses higher on her nose. "Who's your handsome friend?"

My totally-not-a-friend stood up and offered his hand. "Wyatt. Nice to meet you."

Agnes's eyes lit up, and a knowing smile appeared on her face. "Of Wyatt Investigations?"

"What?" I blurted out. How could she even know about the fake PI firm?

Agnes ignored me. She was laser-focused on Wyatt. "My daughter and I own a bakery. We're thinking of getting a security system, but don't know where to start. Do you think you could help us out?"

"Absolutely."

I gaped up at him from my seat on the steps.

Agnes, however, beamed at him. "You can find me at Tasty Buns. Two blocks down." She nodded to the south.

"I'll be sure to stop by," Wyatt said, his smile practically oozing charisma.

Still beaming, Agnes gave him a finger wave. As she passed me, she leaned down and said in a giddy whisper, "I bet he's got some tasty buns!"

My eyes widened as she jogged up the steps with more vim and vigor than I'd ever known her to possess.

Wyatt laughed, so I knew he'd heard Agnes's parting words. For some reason, heat rushed to my cheeks. Definitely not because I was thinking about his buns.

I shot to my feet, gripping my phone in one hand. It was time to get this guy out of my life.

I was about to thank him again and send him on his way when a woman's scream tore through the air.

Wyatt and I spun around to look at the front door of the Mirage, which was still drifting shut.

The scream had come from inside.

By the time that thought had sunk into my brain, Wyatt was already running into the building.

I charged after him, leaving my groceries behind.

Another scream sent an arctic chill down my spine.

We ran toward it, Wyatt still ahead of me.

When he reached the open door of Freddie's office, he stopped so abruptly that I ran into his back. He put out an arm to keep me from passing him, but I leaned over it and peered into the office.

The pungent smell of alcohol hit my nose.

I drew in a sharp breath. The alcohol fumes burned my throat, and my stomach roiled. I was in danger of losing my meager lunch.

Because Freddie Hanover, the Deco Mirage's superintendent, lay on the floor of his office with his head resting in a pool of blood.

CHAPTER SEVEN

Agnes stood next to Freddie's body, her hands pressed to her mouth as she sobbed. My own body had frozen into a useless statue, with a cold-as-marble chill in my bones, but my mind had zipped into hyperfocus. A nasty wound on Freddie's head seemed to be the source of the pool of blood. A brown bottle lay smashed on the floor, shards of glass all around. I figured it was the most likely source of the alcohol fumes, although I couldn't see a label on the remains of the bottle.

"Is he . . . ?" I couldn't get the final word out, even though it was clanging in my head over and over again.

Dead. Dead. Dead.

Wyatt took a careful step closer to Freddie and crouched down to press two fingers to his wrist.

Agnes sobbed louder.

Her distress finally unlocked my frozen state. I sidestepped into the room so I could put an arm around her shoulders without stepping in any blood.

Wyatt straightened up, and the grim expression on his face answered my unfinished question. Not that I didn't already know the answer. There was an unnatural pallor to Freddie's face that was almost as good as a bright neon sign.

Dead. Dead. Dead.

Now that word flashed *and* clanged in my head.

"We don't want to disturb the scene any further," Wyatt said, gently ushering Agnes and me toward the door.

Murder scene, my brain elaborated. Because what else could it be? I didn't see how Freddie could have accidentally smashed a bottle over his own head. Although the shattered glass was closer to his feet than his head, so maybe the bottle hadn't caused his fatal injury. But he also wasn't near the desk or filing cabinet, so it didn't seem likely he'd struck his head during a fall.

Even though I screamed, *Don't do it!* in my head, I glanced over my shoulder on my way out the door. My stomach churned again at the sight of Freddie's lifeless body. The mixed smells of alcohol and blood didn't help either. I nearly closed my eyes in an attempt to block everything out, but then something caught the light, drawing my attention.

I stopped so abruptly that Wyatt bumped into my back. It was a testament to my level of shock and numbness that I barely registered the contact.

The office's fluorescent lighting glinted off little gold flecks dusting Freddie's shirt, near his left shoulder. The pretty sparkles seemed so incongruent with the rest of the scene that they held me transfixed.

"Emersyn?"

Wyatt's voice yanked me back to the here and now.

I gulped a deep breath and scooted out the door as an ominous weight pressed down on my shoulders.

The next hour or so passed in a blur. Wyatt called the police, and they descended on the Mirage like a swarm of uniformed bees. I was trying to comfort a still-sobbing Agnes when the cops swooped in and separated us. I provided my contact information and a witness statement to one of the officers before I started panicking about getting to Livy's school in time to walk her home. Fortunately, with mere minutes to spare, I was free to go. I looked around for Wyatt out on the street, but he and his gorgeous eyes—car! his gorgeous car!—had already disappeared.

I told myself that was for the best. Finding Freddie had shaken me to the core and left me wary. I didn't think I had it in me to deal with a Wyatt-shaped complication, no matter how hot and nicely muscled that shape might be.

As I set off at a brisk pace toward the elementary school, I almost called my parents in West Haven to ask them to take Livy for a few extra days, in addition to their upcoming weekend visit. I didn't want my niece catching wind of what had happened at the Mirage, but the police would likely be there for hours, if not for days, and it would be hard to hide the fact that something had gone on in the building. Still, as my thumb hovered over the screen of my phone, I ditched the plan and shoved the device back into my pocket.

If my parents found out that we lived in a building where a man had been murdered, they wouldn't be satisfied with taking Livy for a few days. They'd want to keep her for good. The mere thought of that happening nearly sent me nose-diving into a pool of panic.

Somehow, I managed to calm myself down before I reached the school, and I put on my best acting performance ever. Maybe I should consider a career in Hollywood? Livy held my hand, hopping and bouncing along beside me as we walked home, telling me all about her day and never once suspecting that anything was amiss. But even an Oscar-worthy performance couldn't distract her from all the police cars parked outside the Mirage.

Livy's blue eyes widened at the sight. "Is someone going to jail?" she asked with a mixture of worry and awe.

A stony-faced police officer stood at the top of the stairs, guarding the front door.

"The police are doing a standard safety check of the building," I fibbed. "Wait right here for a second, okay?"

I hated letting go of her hand in that moment, but I didn't want her to overhear my conversation with the officer stationed at the door.

Keeping one eye on Livy, who was now peering through the window of an empty police cruiser, I had a quick chat with the officer. He directed us to a side entrance, which we accessed via the narrow gap between the Mirage and the neighboring building. Using a stairwell just inside the door, I was able to get Livy upstairs to our apartment without running into more police officers or any other signs that something was wrong.

Livy seemed to forget about the police presence and whiled away the evening playing with her toys, while I surreptitiously checked every closet and every nook and cranny in our apartment for a lurking murderer. Once I was satisfied that we were killer-free, I did my best to relax, but I couldn't shake the dark cloud that seemed to be hanging over my head. It stayed with me through the night, which I spent mostly tossing and turning, trying without success to banish the image of Freddie's dead body from my mind.

There was still a police presence at the Mirage the next morning, but I managed to get Livy out the side entrance and off to school with minimal questions from her. My plan was to check out more online job postings once I got home, but I found several of my neighbors loitering out on the sidewalk. Rosario López, Bitty Dover, Leona Lavish, and Carmen Álvarez stood together, watching like hawks whenever a police officer entered or exited the building.

"What's going on?" I asked when I joined the group. "And how is Agnes? Does anyone know?" She wasn't present, and I felt a surge of worry for the woman. She'd been so distraught the day before.

"She's at the bakery," Rosario replied. "She wanted to focus on work instead of how she found Freddie."

Rosario lived on the third floor and worked as a bank teller. My best guess was that she was in her late fifties, but I didn't know her exact age. Short and slightly plump, she had straight, chin-length black hair that she always held back with a colorful headband. I'd also never seen her without a pair of whimsical earrings. Today's set featured dangling skeletons. An unintentional nod to Freddie's demise, or did she have a rather macabre sense of humor that I didn't know about?

Next to her stood Bitty, a tiny eighty-something woman with fair skin, curly white hair, and large, thick-lensed glasses. Every time I saw her, she wore a dress with a cardigan over it, even in the summer. Today, a delicate hummingbird brooch adorned her baby blue sweater.

"Any word on what happened?" I aimed the question at the group at large.

Leona Lavish of unit 412 clamped her bejeweled fingers around my arm. "Didn't you find the body?" She peered at me with violet eyes that were heavily lined in black and shadowed with purple powder. Her hair was dyed a shade of reddish orange that looked garish next to her pale skin. One of her false eyelashes was slightly askew, and I caught a whiff of alcohol on her breath.

The smell transported me with a jolt right back to the murder scene.

I gulped a breath of air.

"She doesn't want to talk about that," Rosario admonished, tugging Leona away so that she had to release her clawlike grip on my arm. I was pretty sure her ridiculously long, fake fingernails had left deep imprints in my skin.

"Nobody's been taken to the slammer," Carmen Álvarez informed me. She was an elegant eighty-something woman with short gray hair—always nicely styled—and beautiful deep brown eyes. She had the air of a former movie star, but her tongue could be as sharp as a razor. "At least, not that we've heard."

Leona pushed her way into the center of the group. Now well into her seventies, she'd once been a star of the long-running soap opera *Passion City,* and she never let anyone forget about that. Her career might have been in the past, but her theatrics were still very much a part of her daily life.

"Did I ever tell you about the time my character on *Passion City* was accused of murder?" she asked, a hand pressed to her generous chest. She had a Dolly Parton–like figure. Word in the building was that she'd had her plastic surgeon on speed dial until she lost much of her fortune to a divorce and a Ponzi scheme.

"Oh, God help us," Carmen griped. "Nobody cares, Leona."

As Leona let out an insulted gasp, I slipped away from the group, knowing that once those two women started squabbling, they could go on for hours. Sometimes even days.

Minnie Yang, another of the Mirage's residents, came scurrying around the corner of the building, short of breath. She was a slender woman with dark hair in a long pixie cut. Although she'd told me once that she was sixty-two, she could have passed for ten years younger, and at the moment she was moving even faster than she did on her daily power walks around the neighborhood.

"The police found something in the dumpster!" Her words came out in a gasp. "They're bringing it through the building!"

As a group, we surged closer to the steps. The cop stationed at the front door opened it for a good-looking blond man in a suit with an NYPD badge clipped to his belt. A detective, probably. A uniformed officer followed him, wearing blue gloves and carrying something wrapped in plastic.

The detective spared our group a brief, impassive glance before climbing into an unmarked car parked at the curb. The uniformed officer placed the plastic-encased object in the trunk of one of the police cruisers in front of the building. But not before I caught a glimpse of what the bag contained: a bloody croquet mallet.

CHAPTER EIGHT

"Oh, God."

I turned at the sound of the familiar voice.

Bodie stood a few feet back from our group, holding a black gym bag and dressed in jeans and a T-shirt that hugged his toned body. I was so used to him looking like the picture of health and fitness that it came as a shock to see him looking like he might faint.

Usually, the Mirage's female population flocked to Bodie whenever he made an appearance, but apparently the bloody croquet mallet had such a grip on their attention that nobody other than me seemed aware of the clearly squeamish, but still hot, bartender. Even with all the hoopla, I couldn't help but notice him. He always drew my gaze and set off happy fizzing in my chest.

I sat next to him on the stairs. "It's terrible, isn't it? A murder in the Mirage."

Bodie groaned and raised his head, his blue eyes radiating distress. "That's not the worst of it. Yesterday, when the cops asked me if I knew of any conflicts Freddie had with others, I told them how Mr. Nagy chased Freddie around with his croquet mallet. I didn't mean that I thought Mr. Nagy had killed him. It was just the only thing I could think of when they asked that question."

As Bodie's words sank in, I felt a bit faint too. "You think the police will believe that Mr. Nagy used his own croquet mallet to kill Freddie?"

He turned his troubled eyes on me. "I don't believe it, but if you were a cop, wouldn't you suspect him?"

I would.

Sure, Mr. Nagy was in his eighties, but I wouldn't call him feeble. He was a sweet, grandfatherly man, but the cops wouldn't know that. No, the police would look at the evidence.

The murder weapon.

Mr. Nagy's recent altercation with the victim.

I swallowed a burning lump in my throat and tried my best to sound positive.

"The police won't really suspect a sweet man like Mr. Nagy. Not for long, anyway." I gave Bodie's knee what I hoped was a comforting pat. "I'm sure everything will be fine."

I should never have said those words.

Why was it that I could easily manifest bad outcomes but never good ones?

Maybe I was doing it wrong, despite having watched about a gazillion TikTok videos on manifestation. Or maybe it was the fact that I could never keep the negative thoughts from creeping in and infecting the positive ones with their poison.

The words I'd spoken to Bodie left me with a heavy weight in my chest that compelled me to knock on wood every five or ten minutes as I sat in my apartment, combing through online job boards. Late in the afternoon, I'd just submitted my résumé and a writing sample to a company looking for someone to write blog posts about car insurance—a soul-draining job was better than no job at this point—when I heard a commotion out in the hallway. Thankfully, Livy was at a friend's house for an after-school playdate, so I didn't have to field any questions from her about why the police had descended on Mr. and Mrs. Nagy's apartment next door.

I stood in my open doorway, mouth agape as I watched uniformed officers file into my neighbors' unit. One officer remained in the hall, stationed just outside the door. I crept closer, but the officer blocked my way before I could go more than a few steps.

"Ma'am, please return to your apartment."

"But what's going on?" I asked, craning my neck to see around the very tall and very muscular officer.

"Ma'am." His voice brooked no argument.

I didn't know if he could really ban me from the hallway—legally speaking, anyway—but I also didn't want to press my luck. It didn't really matter, though, because I'd already caught enough of a glimpse through the open door of the Nagys' apartment to see that the police were searching the place.

I backed away, my legs having suddenly taken on the consistency of jelly.

It'll be okay, I told myself. *They won't find anything to incriminate Mr. Nagy.*

Except, my brain so unhelpfully reminded me, *they've already got the murder weapon that probably belonged to him.*

I returned to my apartment and was about to shut the door when Theo came cruising through it. I jumped back just in time to avoid getting my toes flattened.

"Shut the door," she commanded.

Her voice carried such authority that I found myself obeying before I even realized that I was being bossed around by a teenager in my own home.

By the time I decided that I wanted to protest her dictatorial attitude, Theo was already wheeling her way across the kitchen, which shared a wall with the Nagys' apartment, and appeared to be looking for something there.

Her gaze zeroed in on the air vent near the ceiling. She wheeled closer to it with an annoyed frown on her face. "Of course it's way up high." She glanced over her shoulder at me. "Get a chair."

I planted my hands on my hips, determined not to let her push me around. "Bossy much?"

She leveled a stare at me through her purple-framed glasses. "Don't you want to know what's happening next door?"

"I know what's happening," I said, feeling a hint of smugness. "The police are searching Mr. and Mrs. Nagy's apartment."

"I *meant* don't you want to know if they *find* anything?"

I was about to say that of course the police wouldn't find anything, but then I remembered how much the universe enjoyed proving me wrong. Besides, the truth was that I was itching to know what was going on in the next unit.

Grabbing the least rickety chair from the four arranged around the kitchen table, I dragged it over to the wall and stationed it beneath the air vent. I climbed onto it, but given the Mirage's high ceilings, standing on the chair still left me far short of the vent.

"The table," Theo suggested.

Actually, it was more an order than a suggestion, but I decided to pretend it was the latter.

Making as little noise as possible—I didn't need the police coming to investigate what we were up to—I dragged the table over to the wall, kicked off my shoes, and climbed first onto the chair and then onto the table, reminding myself to clean it before Livy and I ate dinner that evening.

I leaned in close to the vent, almost pressing my ear against the metal grate that covered it. At first, I couldn't hear anything other than muffled voices and cupboards opening and closing. Then a man's voice called out, "Sir! I think I've got something!"

Those words lodged a heavy stone of dread in my stomach.

There was a rustling noise, and then another man's voice. I had to strain to hear his words.

"What is it?"

The first man spoke again. "Looks like gold leaf."

"Get photos, then bag it."

A loud bang sent me dropping to the tabletop and then sliding to the floor in a heap, expecting to see a SWAT team bursting through my broken-down door.

Except the door was intact and Theo and I were alone in the apartment.

"What the hell?" I pressed a hand to my heart, looking left and right for the source of the noise.

"It's just a saucepan," Theo said, leaning over the side of her wheelchair to pick up the offending item. "You left it sitting on the edge of the counter, and I accidentally knocked it off. Kind of spectacularly, actually."

Great. I'd lost five years off my lifespan to a falling saucepan.

I took some deliberate deep breaths, trying to calm my racing heart.

"What did you hear?" Theo asked, apparently unconcerned by the fact that I'd nearly suffered a heart attack at the tender age of twenty-eight.

I scrambled to my feet, remembering what I'd overheard now that I'd recovered from my near-death experience. "They found gold leaf!"

Still shoeless, I dashed over to the door and burst out into the hallway, just in time to see the police leading a handcuffed Mr. Nagy out of his apartment. His balding head shone with perspiration, and all the color had drained from his face.

Mrs. Nagy lunged out of their apartment with a distraught wail that nearly broke my heart. The blond detective I'd seen earlier caught her before she could throw herself at her husband.

"No!" she cried with tears on her cheeks. "Not my Zoltán! He's innocent!"

As the uniformed officers led Mr. Nagy away, his wife collapsed into the detective's arms. He picked her up like she weighed nothing and took her back into the apartment. I tried to follow, but the officer on guard blocked my way.

"But Mrs. Nagy—"

"She'll get medical attention," the officer assured me.

Doors opened along the hallway, and curious heads poked out.

Theo had her chair parked in the entrance to my apartment. She gestured with her head that I should follow her, and then backed up, disappearing inside. I darted after her, not because I liked being bossed around by a kid, but because I knew that my neighbors would bombard me with questions if I didn't make a quick getaway.

After dashing into my apartment, I shut the door and leaned against it, my brain too numb to fully process everything.

Theo spun her chair around until she faced me. "Why'd they arrest Mr. Nagy over gold leaf?" Theo asked. "What's that got to do with the murder?"

"There was some on Freddie's body," I explained. "I was there when Agnes found him."

"I know you were." The *duh* was clearly implied. "That's why I came to see you. You took pictures, right?"

"What? Why would I do that?"

"Because that's what any competent investigator would do."

"I'm not an investigator! I'm a . . ." I trailed off, on the brink of an existential crisis. What was I? A jobless auntie? A hot mess? Yes and yes. But was I anything more than that?

"Next time, take pictures."

Theo's words managed to interrupt my rapid descent into panic-laced self-pity.

"Next time?" I echoed the two words with a mixture of confusion and disbelief.

"For now, write down everything you can remember about the scene. Every tiny detail." She wheeled toward the door as she rattled off those instructions.

"I already gave a witness statement to the police," I said.

"This isn't for the police."

"Then why would I do it?"

Theo swiveled her chair around until she faced me again. "Hello? Do you want to solve this murder or not?"

"Um, the whole detective agency thing is fake, remember?"

"So, you're okay with Mr. Nagy rotting in jail?" Disapproval hardened her voice and her eyes.

"I didn't say that!" I protested. "And of course I'm not. He's the nicest man I know."

"Exactly." Theo yanked open the door. "Remember, every little detail."

With those parting words, she was gone.

CHAPTER
NINE

For the record, I didn't follow Theo's instructions, because I'm an independent woman, one who doesn't take orders from kids, preteens, or teenagers.

At least, I didn't do it right away. It could wait until that evening. Until then, I planned to focus solely on my niece.

After walking Livy home, I set her up at the kitchen table with a snack of celery sticks and peanut butter while I helped her practice math. She didn't have any actual homework, but we'd started a routine back in the spring, doing math together once or twice a week. Sometimes I printed out worksheets from the Internet, and other times we played math-related games on my laptop. I tried my best to make each session fun and engaging. The whole point was to prevent Livy from developing negative associations with math like the ones I'd battled back in school. Ones I still battled, actually. The mere thought of having to do anything beyond basic addition and subtraction on the spot always triggered a wave of near panic, thanks mostly to an unfortunate experience in fifth grade when my teacher, Mrs. Klein, had berated me in front of the class for not knowing my times tables as well as she thought I should have.

My brother, Ethan, however, had loved math, and that was part of my motivation as well. I knew he'd want his daughter to succeed at the subject, if not love it like he did. So far, my strategy seemed to be working. Math was one of Livy's favorite subjects, right up there with art.

Today, though, she was struggling to stay focused on the addition maze we were working on. Then, when she got one of the equations wrong and found herself at a dead end in the maze, she burst into tears.

"Oh, Livysaurus," I said with dismay, running a hand down her glossy hair. "What's wrong, sweet girl?"

She climbed onto my lap and wrapped her arms around my neck, burying her face in my sweater.

Worry rushed in, like a quickly rising tide that threatened to surge up over my head. "Livy?"

She sniffled before speaking in a quiet voice. "Navneet told me she and her family are going out for dinner tonight because it's her dad's birthday."

"Oh." My heart sank.

"Daddy's birthday is in a few days, but he's not here. I wish he could come back from heaven."

"I know, sweetie. I do too." My words came out thick with emotion, and I fought against the tears burning in my eyes and the fierce grief in my chest.

Even though nearly a year had gone by since my brother's death, I didn't think a single day had passed that I hadn't felt like crying at least once, but I rarely allowed the tears to fall. I feared that once I started crying, I wouldn't be able to stop, and that wasn't what Livy needed from me.

I would have done anything to make Livy's wish come true. I would have traded my own life. But bringing Ethan back wasn't something anyone could do, so I needed to find some sort of comfort for my niece.

Memories of childhood birthday parties—mine and Ethan's—fluttered through my brain. Happy times. All in the past.

"Tell you what," I said as I stroked Livy's hair. "Why don't you and I bake your dad a cake on his birthday?"

"Can it be chocolate?" she asked in a tiny voice. "That's what he liked best."

"'Any cake that isn't chocolate is a wasted cake,'" I quoted, having heard my brother say that many times over the years.

"I like other flavors too." Livy looked up at me, her eyes shimmering with tears. Blue eyes, so similar to Ethan's. "But chocolate's the best."

I kissed the top of her head. "I think so too. And, yes, we can bake him a chocolate cake."

"With chocolate frosting?"

"Lots of chocolate frosting." I gave her a squeeze, and she smiled, just a little. "And for now, how about some mac and cheese?"

She nodded and climbed off my lap, running to grab a stool so she could help me make dinner. Within minutes, she was chatting away, telling me about the fun she had with her friends at school that day.

She was such a resilient kid, and she amazed and inspired me every day. She'd lost her mom as a baby and her dad at age six. If she could keep smiling after all she'd been through, I could get my life on track. I could find myself a steady job and succeed at adulting. Maybe I could even recall a detail of some sort that would help clear Mr. Nagy's name.

I spent extra time with Livy that night after I tucked her into bed, making sure she was sound asleep before I tiptoed out of her room. Then I grabbed a notebook and pen, curled up in my own bed, and wrote down everything I could remember about the scene of Freddie's murder. It wasn't a whole lot. The smell of alcohol. The broken bottle. The blood. The buzzing of the fluorescent lights overhead. The flecks of gold leaf.

Immersing myself in the memory became too much—I swore I could smell the blood and alcohol again. I slapped the notebook shut and tucked it away in the drawer of my bedside table. The exercise hadn't resulted in any new insights, and I didn't know how else I could help Mr. Nagy.

My gaze landed on the box of business cards I'd left on the floor by my closet. An image of Wyatt popped into my head, looking unfairly hot, his eyes doing that damn twinkling.

"Nope, nope, nope!" I told myself out loud.

I punctuated that statement by flicking off the bedside lamp.

As it turned out, thoughts of Wyatt—as dangerous as they were—would have been far preferable to the worries that plagued me all through the night. There was nothing I could do for my elderly neighbors, but knowing that didn't help me sleep.

It didn't take long to get the latest news the next morning. I heard it while checking my mailbox (empty except for flyers and other junk) down in the lobby. Mrs. Nagy was in the hospital, Carmen Álvarez reported as she collected the contents of her own mailbox. She'd collapsed from shock but was expected to return home soon. As for her husband, he was still in police custody.

I tried my best not to dwell on the Nagys' predicament, but my heart ached for the neighbors who'd been so good to me and Livy since we'd moved into the Mirage. Perhaps a job offer would have helped to distract me, but none materialized. I hadn't even been offered an interview.

Still, I was unwilling to accept defeat. That simply wasn't an option. Not with Livy to take care of, so I returned to my apartment determined to accomplish at least one goal: fix the leak beneath the kitchen sink that had been dripping water into Livy's blue plastic pail for the past couple of weeks.

A plumber I was not, but wasn't everyone an expert with a little help from YouTube?

CHAPTER
TEN

Carrying a handful of flyers bound for the recycling bin, I took a detour to the basement laundry room, where I'd left my clothes swishing in the washing machine. There was only one laundry room for the entire building, with four washers and four dryers. That might have been a sufficient—or at least passable—number of machines, if all of them actually worked. At the moment, we had two functioning washers and one dryer that actually dried. Of course, that particular dryer was already in use and had nearly thirty minutes left on the timer.

I shifted my weight from foot to foot, trying to come to a decision as my basket of wet clothes sat at my feet. I could come back down and use the dryer later, or I could hang up my clothes to dry in the apartment.

The buzzing fluorescent lights flickered, nearly extinguishing completely before valiantly fighting their way back to life. Something creaked elsewhere in the basement and . . . was that a squeak? Like a *rodent* squeak? Decision made.

I grabbed my basket and hightailed it out of there. Air-drying was better for the planet anyway. And staying out of a horror movie was better for my life expectancy.

Once I'd set up my two rickety laundry racks in the kitchen and had hung my clothes to dry, I turned my attention to my main goal of the day. I opened the cupboard under the kitchen sink and peered inside. The dripping water plunked into the nearly full bucket with a slow but steady beat.

Did I need a wrench? I wasn't sure. Some of the rings on the pipes looked like they could be tightened with my bare hands, but there were other parts that looked a little trickier.

Fortunately, being an independent woman, I had my own tool-box, complete with basic tools. It was a gift from my dad when I moved into my first apartment after I graduated from college.

With a wrench in hand, I felt like I could conquer the world. One leaky pipe would be no problem. But before I had a chance to wriggle my way under the sink, someone knocked on the door. Jemma, as it turned out.

"Aren't you working today?" I asked as I returned to the kitchen, still armed with my wrench.

"I start in an hour, but I wanted to come by here first." She held up the burner phone. "I forgot to leave this with you."

I sat down on the floor with my back to the sink and lowered myself onto my elbows. "I don't suppose Hoffman called?"

I had low hopes for the success of our plan.

"Not Hoffman . . ."

I scooted backward until my head was in the cupboard, below the pipes.

"What are you doing?" Jemma asked.

"Fixing the leak."

"Why didn't you get Freddie to fix it when he was alive? That thing's been dripping for weeks."

"Have Freddie in my apartment alone with me?" I suppressed a shudder. "No, thanks. The guy was a sleazebag. Besides, I've totally got this."

"Maybe you should leave your plumbing ambitions for another time. And do you really want your place looking like a lingerie store?"

"Someone's already using the only working dryer," I explained as I examined the pipes.

I heard a sigh from Jemma, and then her heels clicked as she crossed the parquet floor.

"I'm going to do you a favor, hon," she said from somewhere across the room.

Rustling noises followed. I was about to ask what she was up to when someone knocked on the door. Somehow, I managed not to bump my head as I maneuvered myself out of the cupboard. Jemma had left the apartment door open, giving me an instant view of Wyatt standing there, looking like a living advertisement for Hotties "R" Us.

I dropped the wrench with a clang.

Wyatt glanced down at himself. "Do I look that bad?"

A high-pitched, hysterical laugh escaped from me as I struggled to get to my feet. I didn't even care that I probably looked as ungainly as a hippopotamus, because all I could think about was my colorful array of underwear on display on one of the two laundry racks.

"No! Of course not! You don't look bad!" I was babbling now, but I couldn't stop the words from spilling out of my mouth. "You look hot!"

Wait—did I really say that out loud?

My cheeks heated. "No, not hot!"

"No?"

My face flamed. I whirled around and took in the sight of the laundry racks. One had jeans and tops draped over the bars while the other had nothing but a few pairs of socks hanging from it.

Jemma cleared her throat, and my gaze bounced over to where she stood near the bathroom door, a slight smirk on her face. I knew in that moment that my bestie had saved me from mortification.

Jemma's smirk transformed into her most charming smile as

she crossed the small living room to greet Wyatt. "Definitely hot," she said as she offered him her hand.

I stifled a groan. I really had said it out loud.

"I'm Jemma."

Wyatt shook her hand. "Wyatt."

"Oh, I know." She released his hand as she eyed him up and down. "It's nice to finally meet you. I'm so glad you could make it."

"Hold on. What?" My brain scrambled to piece things together. "You knew he was coming?"

Jemma held up the burner phone again and gave it a little wiggle. "Wyatt has something he'd like to discuss with you, so I arranged a meeting."

"Is this a bad time?" Wyatt asked. "I didn't realize you weren't expecting me."

"What could we possibly have to discuss?" I asked instead of answering his question.

Jemma pressed the burner phone into my hand. "As much as I'd like to stay, I need to get to work. I'm sure the two of you can get along fine without me."

"Nice to meet you," Wyatt said as Jemma sailed toward the door.

"Likewise," she said with a smile. As soon as she was behind Wyatt, she fanned herself and mouthed, *So hot!*

Then she was gone.

And I was alone with Wyatt.

CHAPTER ELEVEN

"Is there a problem with your sink?" Wyatt asked.

He stood just inside the door that Jemma hadn't bothered to close on her way out. That was for the best, I realized. I didn't need to be alone in my apartment with a man I'd met only twice.

I eyed him with suspicion, searching for potential signs of homicidal mania and definitely not admiring his perfectly tousled dark hair or the way his forest-green T-shirt hugged his impressively toned torso and biceps. "You're not a serial killer, are you?"

"I accidentally drove over a box of Froot Loops once, but I didn't think that was much of a loss. I'm more of a Corn Pops kind of guy."

I crossed my arms over my chest, but neither my suspicious stare nor my lack of reaction to his joke seemed to faze him.

He came farther into the apartment and crouched down in front of the open kitchen cupboard. "Hmm. Hopefully it's an easy fix. Do you want me to have a go at it?"

I snatched the wrench up off the floor before he could close his fingers around it.

"No, thank you. I've got it."

He must have noticed the hint of frost in my tone, because he straightened up and backed off a couple of steps.

I tapped the head of the wrench against the palm of my left hand. "What is it you wanted to discuss?"

He gestured at the pipes under the sink. "Don't let me keep you from your task."

Gripping the wrench handle so tightly that my fingers hurt, I smiled—although it felt more like a grimace—and sat back down on the floor, maneuvering myself under the sink again. The bottom edge of the cupboard dug into my spine, but I decided the pain might help to keep my mind sharp. I nudged the plastic pail aside so I could shift closer to the pipe and got rewarded with a drop of water hitting me square between the eyes.

"I have to admit, I'm a little confused," Wyatt said as I wiped the water off my face.

You're not the only one, I felt like saying. I'd planned to do this job with the help of YouTube, but now I had an audience, and I wasn't about to let on that I needed video tutorials to help me fix a simple leak. But what, exactly, was I supposed to do?

"I was hoping to talk to whoever's in charge of Wyatt Investigations," he continued, "but I thought you were a client, not an employee."

"I'm neither, actually."

The light in the cupboard dimmed as Wyatt moved closer. He leaned down to peer in at me. "Are you sure you don't need help? I'm pretty handy."

Oh, I bet you are! my traitorous brain purred. Not out loud, thankfully. I'd already met my daily quota of self-humiliation.

"I'm fine, thanks," I grumbled.

Unfortunately, he kept watching.

"You turned the water off, right?"

"Of course." I glared at him.

"Sorry."

Thankfully, he straightened up so he could no longer see what I was doing. Or not doing.

How the heck was I supposed to turn off the water?

I started fiddling with random rings and valves. Surely it couldn't be that difficult to figure out.

"So how do I get ahold of who's in charge?"

"In charge of what?" I couldn't remember what we'd been talking about. I was too focused on trying to recall which rings and valves I'd already turned and in which direction.

"Wyatt Investigations."

I huffed out a sigh. "Wyatt Investigations doesn't exist. It was a ruse to scare my ex into returning the money he stole from me." Hoping I now had the water turned off, I started unscrewing one of the rings around the pipe. "You need a private investigator?"

That added a hint of mystery to his already intriguing persona.

"No, I'm looking for a job."

So much for the mystery.

"You want to work for a private eye?" Somehow that didn't strike me as a typical job for a member of the Hickory Hill Country Club.

"I have a background in security."

I had trouble picturing a rich guy like him guarding a bank or working as a bouncer at a nightclub.

"Well, unless you're looking for an imaginary job, I'm afraid I can't help you."

I gave the ring a good twist.

A jet of water erupted from the pipe, hitting me right in the face.

I let out a garbled yell as I flailed and sputtered, trying to free myself from the onslaught of water. I was vaguely aware of Wyatt diving into the fray. He reached into the cupboard, right through the stream of water, and . . . did something. Whatever he did, the jet of water mercifully cut off, leaving me gasping and blinking rapidly.

I managed to shimmy a few inches out from under the sink. One of Wyatt's hands closed around mine, and he pulled me to my feet before I even knew what was happening. I came to a stop right up against his chest, one hand pressed to his pecs.

It took a good three seconds for my shock to wear off. Then I realized I was molded against his deliciously solid body. Beneath my palm, his soaked shirt was plastered to his chest, revealing the dips and planes of his sculpted muscles. His body heat seeped into my chilled skin, beckoning me to move even closer. I tipped my head up to find his eyes smoldering like hot coals, ready to burst into flame.

He inclined his head toward mine, bringing his mouth tantalizingly close to my ear.

My breath hitched and my fingers dug into the waterlogged fabric of his shirt.

"Pretty sure you didn't turn off the water," he whispered.

I pushed off from his chest, taking a step back that was as abrupt as my return to reality.

"I *meant* to, but you distracted me." I crossed my arms over my chest, suddenly realizing that my own T-shirt was clinging to me in a very revealing fashion. I was wearing a bra, but still. My shirt was white, and Wyatt-with-no-last-name didn't need to be getting an eyeful of my assets.

"You find me distracting?" The light in his eyes danced with humor.

"Only when you talk too much," I grumbled.

He laughed, and I feared he saw right through my lie.

I wasn't sure why he got my hackles up, but maybe it was because he affected me more than any other man I'd known, and that knocked me off-kilter. Or maybe it was the fact that he'd now swooped in to help me three times. I wanted to prove—to myself more than anyone—that I was a fully capable, self-reliant adult, but I felt like I'd been failing at that over and over again.

Silence fell between us, and the air practically crackled with electricity.

I averted my gaze from his body, not wanting my thoughts to stray into spicy territory.

A steady drip, drip, drip caught my attention. I glanced down and realized that I was standing in an ever-growing puddle as droplets of water rained slowly but steadily from my sodden clothes.

"Can I get you a towel?" Wyatt asked as he looked down at the puddle. The humorous glint in his eyes had dimmed, although it hadn't disappeared completely.

"Please," I replied, deciding I could assert my independence when I wasn't in danger of soaking the area rug that stood between me and the bathroom. "And get one for yourself too."

He'd fared better than I had, given that only his shirt was drenched while I looked like I'd been dunked upside down in a pool from my head to my knees. It didn't seem fair that he could stand there as if artfully sprayed with water for a sexy photoshoot while I resembled a drowned rat.

"From the closet by the bathroom door," I added as a shiver racked my body.

He kept his gaze on me for another second before turning in the direction I'd indicated. His shift of attention brought me a sense of both relief and disappointment. Which made no sense! My brain was seriously messed up.

We need to have a chat, I told my brain. *You can't be letting a man affect you like this. Remember what happened the last time you got involved with a guy?*

I didn't have a chance to continue my internal lecture.

Because when Wyatt opened the closet door, my freshly laundered underwear tumbled out and hit him like an avalanche of lingerie.

CHAPTER TWELVE

"Close your eyes!" I screamed like a crazy woman.

To hell with the area rug, I decided the split second before making a mad dash for Wyatt.

A purple bra had landed on his head, one cup dangling in front of his face. He brushed it aside before I could reach him. A cross between a whimper and a burst of hysterical laughter escaped me as I snatched the bra out of his hand. It matched the purple thong resting on his left shoulder. I grabbed that too and started plucking damp and brightly colored underwear—well, brightly colored except for that one beige bra—off him like my life depended on it.

I spun around, lunged into my bedroom, and dumped everything on the bed. I took half a second to make sure I didn't have any underwear still clinging to my clothes, and then I bolted from the room, slamming the door behind me. I snatched a towel from the open closet and shoved it at Wyatt's chest. Then I grabbed his arms—barely registering the feel of his corded muscles beneath my hands—wrenched him around, and shoved him toward the open apartment door. I didn't ease up until he was out in the hall.

"Sorry! Thank you! Sorry!" I babbled before slamming the door and sagging against it.

"You have reached a new low, Emersyn Gray," I said once I'd caught my breath.

Could life get any more mortifying? If so, I didn't want to know about it.

Through my haze of humiliation, I managed to remember that I was still dripping water all over the floor. Shivering, I realized that I was freezing.

And the drop in my body temperature had nothing to do with Wyatt's absence.

Not at all.

Muttering an array of curses under my breath, I stomped back over to the closet, grabbed two towels, and took them into the bathroom. I struggled out of my wet clothes and dried myself off before wrapping myself in one of the towels and fetching fresh clothes from my bedroom.

Dry now and fully dressed—but without a shred of dignity left—I emerged from my bedroom and dug the oldest towels out of the closet to use on the kitchen floor.

"Stupid rippling muscles," I groused as I sopped up the puddle. "Ridiculous twinkling eyes. Infuriatingly luscious hair."

That I long to run my hands through.

"No!" I reprimanded myself. "No, I don't. Absolutely not."

And I totally wasn't the least bit disappointed that Wyatt hadn't stripped off his soaked T-shirt in my presence. Not even a little bit. Nope, nope, nope.

I paused when I heard footsteps and voices out in the hall.

Familiar voices.

I abandoned my cleanup and lunged for the apartment door, yanking it open. I nearly flung myself out into the hall but stopped right before hitting Wyatt's chest.

He stood there, fist raised to knock, holding my towel—blush pink—and wearing a perfectly dry, heather gray T-shirt.

"Why are you still here?" I pointed at his shirt before he could reply. "And where did you get that?"

"I'm heading to the gym later, so I had a spare shirt in my car. But I thought I should bring back your towel."

"Oh. Right. Thanks." I was about to take the towel from him when I remembered why I'd opened the door in the first place.

I squeezed past him so I could get out into the hall. Our arms brushed against each other, skin against skin.

If there was an electric sizzle in the air, I was perfectly capable of ignoring it.

At least, I was at the moment, because I was far more interested in the fact that Agnes Gao was currently holding Mrs. Nagy by the arm and leading her into the apartment next door.

"Mrs. Nagy!" I exclaimed with relief so immense that I forgot about any sudden desire to plaster myself against Wyatt.

"Hello, dear," Mrs. Nagy said with a weak smile. She then disappeared into her apartment, Agnes still supporting her.

Since neither woman made a move to shut the door, I took that as an invitation to follow them inside.

"Are you okay?" I asked Mrs. Nagy as she lowered herself into a worn old armchair.

Even as the words came out of my mouth, I saw that she looked pale and appeared to have aged five years overnight. Concern prickled beneath my skin.

"I'm all right," she said, attempting a stronger smile. "Just worried about my Zoltán."

Agnes shook her head sadly. "He's still in custody."

"He didn't kill Freddie." Tears brimmed in Mrs. Nagy's blue eyes. "My Zoltán would never kill anyone."

I knelt on the floor next to her chair and took her hand. "I know that. The police have got it wrong. They'll figure that out soon."

I hoped with soul-deep desperation that I'd spoken the truth.

"Sorry," Wyatt said from the open doorway. He stood there, still holding my blush-pink towel. "Should I put this in your apartment, Emersyn?"

"Wyatt!" Agnes's face lit up. "Perfect timing!"

I jumped up and grabbed the towel from Wyatt. "He's just leaving."

Agnes didn't seem to hear me. She took Wyatt by the arm and tugged him over to stand in front of Mrs. Nagy. Then she dug a crumpled business card out of her pocket. My stomach sank when I recognized it. She pressed the card into Mrs. Nagy's hand.

"Wyatt of Wyatt Investigations," Agnes declared with a radiant smile. "He's a private detective."

"Actually—" Wyatt began.

"*Actually*," I cut in loudly, "Wyatt Investigations is *my* firm."

"Oh, perfect!" Agnes exclaimed before I could say anything more. "You can work the case together!"

She looked at us like we were avenging angels, there to save the day.

"I'm sorry," I said, wondering how to explain the whole Wyatt Investigations thing succinctly, but my thoughts stumbled to a screeching halt when I saw the glimmer of hope in Mrs. Nagy's eyes.

She smiled, the expression no longer weak. "Emersyn, I didn't know you were a private detective now."

"Technically, I'm not," I said.

"It's a new agency," Agnes chimed in with an understanding nod. "But we're not worried about licenses or certifications. You can get those later. You don't need them to clear Zoltán's name."

"Er . . ." I glanced at Wyatt, wishing he'd clear up the obvious confusion.

He, however, seemed completely unbothered by the hot water we were rapidly sinking into.

"You'll help her, won't you?" Agnes asked Wyatt, beaming at him expectantly.

"Actually, he's—"

"Please," Mrs. Nagy implored.

I made the mistake of looking at her. Those kind blue eyes of hers shimmered with tears.

"Please help my Zoltán," she begged. "Please, Emersyn."

That request coming from a kind, elderly lady would have been difficult to deny. But Zita Nagy was a kind, elderly lady who also happily provided me with free babysitting for Livy, who kept my niece supplied with homemade cookies, and who'd welcomed us into the Mirage community with open arms when we'd moved in last year.

That made her request impossible to turn down.

Which is why, despite my grave misgivings, I heard myself saying, "Of course I'll help you, Mrs. Nagy."

CHAPTER
THIRTEEN

Dread filled my veins like slow-setting cement. I numbly accepted Mrs. Nagy's effusive thanks and listened to Agnes's assurances to her that Zoltán's legal problems were practically already solved now that I was on the case.

I returned to my apartment in a daze, not realizing until I stood in the middle of the kitchen that I was clutching the slightly damp blush-pink towel to my chest like it could somehow save me from the ridiculous promise I'd made to my sweet neighbor.

"What the blankety bleep have you done, Emersyn?" I asked myself out loud.

"Sounds to me like you secured our first case."

I whirled around to see Wyatt standing in the open doorway.

What was it with this guy and doorways? If there was an open one, he seemed to be in it. Filling it with his tall, sculpted frame.

"*Our* case?" Had I really heard right?

"My name is on the business cards," he pointed out.

"They're fake business cards! It's all fake!" I was getting dangerously close to shrieking.

"I'm not fake," Wyatt said, the picture of cool composure. "I'm pretty sure you're not. And you did tell Mrs. Nagy we'd help her husband. Are you going to break that promise?"

I'd reached my limit for the day. Maybe for the week. I needed time to think, to sort out . . . everything.

Still clutching the towel, I said, "I need time. And space."

Wyatt didn't budge. "Meaning?"

"It's not you. It's me." That was probably true.

He raised an eyebrow. "Are you breaking up with me?"

"We're not together," I pointed out.

"Exactly."

This conversation was not helping my muddled and over-whelmed state.

He must have caught on to that, because he finally vacated the doorway.

Once out in the hall, he turned around. "I'll let you know if I come up with any leads."

"Sure. Okay. Thanks," I said on the off chance that my agree-ment would send him on his way.

Thankfully, it did.

I shut the door and locked it for good measure. I hoped I'd now seen the last of Wyatt.

Well, the sensible, wise part of me was hoping. And maybe that was a very small part of me, but it still existed somewhere deep inside.

"Forget about him," I muttered to myself.

Easier said than done, perhaps, but I was going to give it my best shot.

While I cleaned up the mess of wet towels on the kitchen floor, I considered my next move. As foolhardy as it was for me to prom-ise to help Mrs. Nagy and her husband, I'd made the commitment and absolutely could not go back on it. So now I had to figure out how to solve a murder.

Easy peasy lemon squeezy, right?

I preferred the romance genre when it came to books and mov-ies, but I'd watched a couple of reruns of *Bones* with Jemma a few years ago. Of course, I'd mostly watched for David Boreanaz, not the plot. And come to think of it, I couldn't remember how they'd solved any of the crimes except that they'd used some fancy-schmancy scientific techniques that were way out of my league.

Maybe not so easy peasy then.

Even though I still had no idea how to clear Mr. Nagy's name, the next morning my day got off to a decent start. Bright and early, I applied for the job at the local clothing shop after finding the posting online. As I was in the midst of doing that, I received invitations to interviews for two copywriting positions I'd applied for. That buoyed my spirits. Copywriting wasn't my dream career, but I had experience in the field, and I wasn't about to be picky at this point.

After walking Livy to school, I spent the rest of the morning preparing by looking up practice interview questions on the Internet and coming up with answers that I hoped sounded intelligent. Then I donned a pantsuit, made myself presentable, and rode the subway into Manhattan.

I arrived fifteen minutes early for the first interview, with butterflies dancing in my stomach. Not the pleasant kind that I got when I encountered Wyatt or Bodie but the sort that made me want to throw up. Nevertheless, I took some deep breaths to center myself and walked into the office.

Five minutes in, they revealed that they wanted someone who could work overtime—in the office—on evenings and weekends, with little to no notice. As soon as I mentioned that I had a child in my care, the interviewers lost interest in me.

I told myself that the next one would go better. I showed up ten minutes early for that interview, only to be told that they'd already offered the job to another candidate but would keep me in mind for any future openings.

I absolutely did not cry when the receptionist gave me that

news, but my eyes burned as I trudged back to the subway station, thinking of my dwindling bank account and how I was going to take care of sweet Livy. Could I ask my parents for financial help? Sure, but that would earn me a lifetime of disapproval from my mom. I would do it for Livy's sake, but only as a last resort.

I honestly didn't know what I was doing wrong. Every time I tried to get my life back on track, I discovered that those tracks were broken or washed out or didn't exist at all.

I clamped my eyes shut as I sat on the train. No crying. No pity party. Optimism was the way to go.

I cast around in my mind to find a positive thought.

At least I had time to figure out how to keep my promise to Mrs. Nagy now?

Sure, I'd go with that.

Except, by the time I got back to the Mirage, I still had no idea how to fulfill that promise.

As I approached the building, I checked the time on my phone. My heart lurched when I realized that school was already out for the day. Then I remembered that my parents were picking Livy up at the elementary school and taking her to their place for the weekend. The panicked fluttering in my chest morphed into an ache. Being my niece's full-time caregiver had definitely required some adjustment, but it hadn't taken me long to get used to having her around. She'd been living with me for eleven months now, and whenever she spent a night or two away, I felt like an integral piece of me was missing, like there was a gap in my soul.

She'll have fun, I reminded myself.

She'd be happy and well cared for, and my parents needed time with her as much as she needed time with them.

Besides, I could use the weekend alone to apply for more jobs and figure out how the heck I was going to keep my promise to Mrs. Nagy. Maybe the police would figure out their mistake, release her husband, and drop the murder charge before the weekend was over, but I couldn't count on that happening.

As I walked through the front door of the Mirage, I was contemplating a Google search for tips on solving murders. I reached into my purse for my phone, but then all such thoughts flew off into the ether when I saw Wyatt walking my way, carrying a peachy orange box that I immediately recognized as coming from Agnes's bakery, Tasty Buns.

"If there's chocolate mousse cake in that box, you could be my hero," I said as we met in the middle of the lobby.

He opened the box to reveal half a dozen scrumptious-looking mini cherry cheesecakes. "I'm destined to disappoint."

My mouth watered at the sight of the desserts. "Hardly."

When I raised my eyes to Wyatt's, my stomach did a funny flip-flop that had nothing to do with cheesecake.

I cleared my throat, trying to do the same to my suddenly fuzzy brain. "Are you here to see me?"

"Actually, that's a bonus. I had a meeting with Agnes about the security system for her bakery." He nodded at the box in his hands. "The consulting job comes with some perks."

The elevator doors parted, and Bitty Dover stepped out with Leona Lavish, who wore a floor-length, sparkling black gown and what looked like several pounds of glittering costume jewelry. Bitty, on the other hand, wore a demure gray-and-white dress with a pink cardigan and a single strand of pearls.

"Emersyn!" Bitty waved at me like I might somehow miss seeing her there. "Just the person we need to talk to."

"Agnes told us that you're on the case, and we have intel to share," Leona added as they hurried across the lobby toward us. Well, Bitty hurried while Leona sort of glided with her chin up and her chest thrust forward, like she was making a grand entrance onstage. That's the way she walked pretty much all the time.

"I see you're dressing the part," Bitty said with approval as she took in the sight of my pantsuit. "My dear cousin Princess Di always said that's the first step to success."

I looked down at my clothes and was about to explain that I'd come from unsuccessful job interviews, but Leona didn't give me a chance. She'd already turned all her attention to Wyatt. Frankly, I was surprised that she'd noticed me at all, and I definitely *wasn't* surprised when she took hold of Wyatt's arm and pressed her ample bosom against it while gazing up at him with her false eyelashes fluttering wildly.

"And who's this?" She practically purred the question.

Wyatt smiled, and he did a good job of it, but I still suspected that he'd forced the expression. "I'm Wyatt."

Once again, he supplied no last name. What was up with that?

"The private detective!" Bitty exclaimed with delight. "Agnes told us that you run the PI agency with Emersyn."

"That's not quite—" I tried to say, but Leona cut me off.

"Darling, you can be my private eye anytime," she said to Wyatt in a sultry voice.

"You have intel?" he said, a little louder than necessary.

Bitty nodded. "About Freddie. We figured you'd want to know if he had a beef with anyone."

"Absolutely," I said, as if I'd planned to ferret out such information all along.

"Leona and I heard Freddie arguing with Rosario López a few days before he died," Bitty divulged.

Although I wouldn't have thought it possible, Leona pressed herself even more snugly against Wyatt, forcing him to shift the bakery box to one hand. "That's right. We did."

"What were they arguing about?" Wyatt asked.

He took a subtle step back, but Leona moved with him, all the while stroking his biceps.

"We're not sure," Bitty replied. "We heard their raised voices but couldn't make out any actual words."

"How often do you work out, darling?" Leona's voice dripped with desire.

Although I was tempted to gag, it pleased me to see a slight crack in Wyatt's composure. He shot me an alarmed glance before regaining his laid-back, confident demeanor.

"Had they argued before, to your knowledge?" he asked Bitty, ignoring Leona's question.

"I'm really not sure," Bitty admitted. "And I'm sorry, but I've got to run. I've got a dental appointment."

With a wave, she pushed out the front door.

Leona ran a finger down Wyatt's chest. "How about we go up to my apartment, and you can conduct a *very thorough* investigation?" She followed the suggestion with an over-the-top wink.

Wyatt stepped back and raised his hand to cover a cough, which I suspected was itself a cover for nearly choking.

I took pity on him then. After all, he'd helped me out three times. The least I could do was save him from Leona's clutches.

"Sorry, we've got plans." I grabbed Wyatt's arm and yanked him over to the elevator with me.

Luckily, the doors parted as soon as I pressed the button, and I quickly jabbed first at the number three and then at the CLOSE DOOR button.

Leona clutched one hand to her chest and raised the other to get our attention. "I'll ride with you!" she cried, a frightening sort of desperation in her violet eyes.

She was two steps away when the doors closed.

"Oh, thank God." Wyatt shoved the bakery box at me. "Here. Take all the cheesecakes as a token of my gratitude."

I removed one mini dessert from the box before pushing it back into his hands.

"Consider us even." I took a bite of heavenly cherry deliciousness and let out a moan of pleasure, nearly sagging against the wall. Agnes and her daughter were baking magicians.

I was about to take a second bite when my eyes met Wyatt's.

The heat in his gaze nearly stopped my heart.

I licked a bit of cheesecake filling from the corner of my mouth before realizing what I was doing. Wyatt's eyes tracked the movement. My fingers dug into the soft dessert, and I had a sudden urge to lift those cheesecake-covered fingertips to his lips.

The elevator dinged, and the doors parted.

Theo was stationed right outside with her arms crossed over her chest. She fixed me with a cool stare and said, "It's about time you showed up."

CHAPTER
FOURTEEN

Theo wheeled halfway onto the elevator, which was just far enough to reach the bakery box held in Wyatt's hands. She flipped it open and took a mini cheesecake, unfazed by the closing elevator doors, which bumped the wheels of her chair before opening again.

"Thanks," she said to Wyatt as she set the dessert on her lap. Then she backed up and inclined her head toward the hall. "Come on."

I followed her off the elevator and waved at Wyatt as the doors closed fully, with him still on board.

"Who's the hot guy?" Theo asked as we made our way down the hall.

"Nobody." The word came out mumbled since I'd just taken another bite of cheesecake. Which immediately took me back to that heated moment I'd shared with said nobody on the elevator. I took another bite, hoping the explosion of cherry flavor would distract me from those thoughts.

No such luck.

Theo stopped outside my door.

"Why were you waiting for me?" I asked, holding the remains of my cheesecake in one hand and digging through my purse for my keys with the other.

"Because we've got a murder to solve?"

"We?" What was it with everyone thinking this was a team sport?

I opened the apartment door and let Theo zip through ahead of me since she seemed determined to invite herself in.

"The whole building is talking about how Mrs. Nagy hired you to get her husband out of jail."

"She didn't hire me," I said. "She asked for a favor, and I agreed, no compensation involved."

"Well, nobody else is going to hire us if we don't solve our first case successfully."

"*Our* case?"

Theo glanced around the apartment as if looking for something. "Where's the murder board?"

"Um . . . I don't have one."

Theo rolled her eyes and nudged her glasses up. "Every murder investigation needs a murder board. Have you not watched any mysteries?" She didn't wait for an answer. "We'll take care of the board later. For now, let's start with the victim. We need to search Freddie's apartment." She punctuated that statement by taking a big bite out of her cheesecake.

"Oh, no," I objected. "We're not breaking into anyone's apartment."

Theo inhaled the rest of the cheesecake and licked the last bit of pink filling off her thumb before reaching into the pocket of her jeans. She pulled out a small rectangle of thick paper. "I'll call your boss and get him to help."

As she produced a cell phone in a purple case from a bag hanging on the back of her wheelchair, I stepped closer and got a good look at the business card in her hand.

"Where did you get that?" I asked as soon as I saw the words WYATT INVESTIGATIONS written in glossy black ink. "And what do you mean by my 'boss'? I'm the one in charge, okay?"

"Everyone says you're working with Wyatt from Wyatt Investigations. If you're in charge, why is his name on the card and not yours? Hey, was Wyatt the guy on the elevator?"

"Yes, but it's not really *his* name on the card."

She scrunched up her nose in a way that was utterly adorable, although I suspected she wouldn't want me saying so. "His name's not Wyatt?"

"Okay, it is," I conceded, "but the agency wasn't named for him *specifically*. Just . . . Wyatts in general."

Fictional hot cowboy Wyatts, anyway, but I didn't deem it necessary to share that detail.

"So he's not working the case?" Theo asked.

"Definitely not."

She heaved out a long-suffering sigh.

"And neither are you," I pointed out.

She leveled a stare at me that sent ice creeping through my veins.

A jumble of words bubbled out of me. "I mean . . . technically . . . it's . . . um . . . just me on the case."

She didn't let up on the stare. "Do you even have a job? Like, a real one?"

"Not at this exact moment," I hedged.

"Would you honestly say that you have your shit together?"

"That question requires a complicated answer. You see—"

Theo was already wheeling her way to the door. "I'll start with Freddie's apartment. *Someone's* got to keep this PI agency from going under."

I dropped my purse on the couch and took two steps to follow Theo. Then I dashed back and grabbed my phone and keys before chasing after her.

"You know the agency isn't real, right?" I had to jog to keep pace with her.

"It is now."

She zoomed off down the hall, leaving me in the dust.

"I'm really not sure this is a good idea." I hovered next to Theo, my gaze darting up and down the hallway like an erratic Ping-Pong ball.

She kept her focus on the lock she was currently trying to pick with the help of a set of slender metal tools. "No risk, no reward."

"When the risk is five to ten in the slammer, I'm not sure any potential reward is worth it." I wiped a bead of sweat from my hairline. The hallway I was keeping an eye on seemed to waver and tilt. Was I about to faint? I clutched one of the handles on Theo's wheelchair. "I think I'm having heart palpitations."

"Get a grip. We're investigating, not carrying out a jewel heist."

I suspected that masterminding jewel heists would be right up her alley.

I swallowed hard and reminded myself of my promise to Mrs. Nagy. That helped me to gather some courage. Or maybe it was recklessness. Either way, at least I no longer felt like I was about to pass out.

"Do you even know what you're doing?" I whispered as time ticked along and Theo kept wiggling tools inside the lock.

"I spent my lunch hour watching online videos about how to pick locks."

"Couldn't you, like, join the library club or something?"

The withering glance she shot my way made me clamp my lips together. Although, after a few more nerve-racking seconds of expecting to get caught, the need to chatter took over again.

"Where did you get those tools, anyway?" I asked. "Isn't it illegal to have them?"

She shrugged and kept working, leaning in closer to the lock for a better view. "I bought them at a flea market last year. I figured they'd come in handy eventually."

"Isn't that a bit of an odd thing for a fifteen-year-old to buy at a flea market?" How many kids even went to flea markets these days? I thought it wise to keep that second question to myself.

"I was *sixteen* last year," she said with a distinctly frosty edge to her voice. "I'm *seventeen* now."

I winced. "Sorry."

"I suppose it's hard to guess a young person's age when you get old."

"I'm twenty-eight!" I protested.

"Exactly."

I planted my hands on my hips, ready to defend my status as a totally-not-old person, but she looked up at me with a self-satisfied smile and turned the knob. The door swung open.

"Never underestimate Theo Harris," she advised before wheeling into Freddie's apartment.

CHAPTER
FIFTEEN

As much as I didn't want to enter the dead man's apartment, I relished even less the prospect of getting caught lurking in the open doorway. So I slipped inside after Theo and quietly shut the door behind us. Theo was already on her way across the living room, but I stood in the entryway, taking stock of my surroundings.

Freddie's unit had a layout similar to the one I shared with Livy, except it appeared to have one bedroom instead of two. The entryway was barely big enough for a small closet, and it would take me only two steps to reach the kitchen, which was open to the living room. On the far side of the apartment, two doors stood open, and I could see from my vantage point that the left one led to the bathroom and the right one to the bedroom.

I advanced a few paces and took in the sight of dirty dishes piled in the sink, drawers left half open, and clothes and empty take-out containers strewn about the apartment. Maybe some of the mess was left behind by the police searching the place after the murder, but I had a feeling that Freddie was responsible for most of it.

"Hey, check this out," Theo called from the living room.

"Keep your voice down," I chided in a whisper as I scooted around a ratty armchair to join her by the coffee table.

She ignored my admonishment and pointed at something on the scuffed parquet floor.

I leaned down for a closer look. "A false eyelash?"

It was smooshed up against the leg of the coffee table and barely visible from more than a foot away.

"Probably not Freddie's," Theo said. "But we shouldn't make assumptions. Check his bedroom closet."

"You think he was a drag queen?" I asked as I wandered toward the bedroom, ignoring the fact that she was bossing me around again. I hesitated at the door, not keen to wander into the bedroom of a man I'd considered a sleazeball.

"The longer this takes, the more likely we are to get caught," Theo pointed out.

That got me moving.

The air inside the bedroom had a stale quality to it, and the curtains were messily drawn across the window, leaving a narrow, uneven gap in the middle. Pale daylight seeped in through the crack, providing just enough illumination for me to see by. I picked my way over a pile of dirty clothes and eased open a set of bifold doors. The closet held a couple of pairs of pants, two sweaters shoved onto a shelf, several empty metal hangers, and an old pair of work boots.

"Anything?" Theo asked from the doorway.

"No women's clothing." I eased the doors shut again.

Theo was already turning around. "So that eyelash didn't belong to Freddie."

I glanced toward the drawer of the bedside table, but there was no way I wanted to know what Freddie kept there, so I scurried after Theo. "Maybe he had a girlfriend."

"If he did, she has terrible taste."

I couldn't argue with that.

"You'd better bag it," Theo said with a nod toward the eyelash.

"I don't have a bag."

"Then put it in your pocket."

"I don't want to touch it. What if the person who wore it had pink eye?"

Theo let out another heavy sigh and fished a packet of tissues out of the bag hanging on the back of her wheelchair. She handed one to me and snapped a photo of the eyelash before I carefully picked it up with the tissue and tucked it in my pocket.

"Keep searching," she ordered.

"What, exactly, are we looking for?" I asked, wandering around the living room. My gaze skipped over a chess set—all its pieces in their starting positions—and the red toolbox I'd seen in Freddie's possession on more than one occasion.

"Anything that might tell us why he was killed. Evidence that he owed someone money, threatening notes, things like that." She pulled up in front of a battered bar cart. "The guy sure liked his booze."

I joined her by the cart. An array of bottles cluttered the three levels, with a couple of dirty glasses among those on the top shelf. The collection included vodka, whiskey, tequila, and rum. The contents of most of the bottles were running low, although a dark brown one with a yellowing label declaring it to be whiskey was still three-quarters full.

We both lost interest in the alcohol and moved on in opposite directions. I drifted over to a bookshelf that was home to only three actual books—military fiction by the looks of them. Otherwise, the shelves held odds and ends, like nails and elastic bands, a framed and faded photo of a red Corvette, and a silver trophy with no inscription.

I reached for the photo but froze when Theo snapped, "Don't touch anything without gloves!"

"I already touched the closet doors!" I reminded her.

"So wipe them off." She held out a pair of purple disposable gloves.

"Why didn't you say you had these?" I accepted the gloves and started pulling them on.

"I forgot, okay?"

I heaved out a sigh that sounded uncannily like Theo's earlier ones. Maybe they were contagious.

With my purple gloves on, I reached for the framed photo again. I checked the back of the frame and even peeked between the backing and the photo itself. No clues appeared, and there wasn't even any writing on the back of the picture.

As I set the frame back on the shelf, my elbow bumped the silver trophy. Before I could catch it, the trophy toppled off the shelf and fell to the floor with a crash, breaking into three pieces on impact. I stood frozen, expecting someone to pound on the door, demanding to know who was in Freddie's apartment.

I looked up to meet Theo's wide-eyed stare. Five full seconds ticked by before she spoke.

"And you thought *I* was being too loud?"

I dropped to my knees and gathered up the pieces of the trophy. I thought I'd broken it, but as I handled the parts, I realized that they were meant to come apart. It wasn't an ordinary trophy; it was a cocktail juicer and shaker disguised as a trophy.

Relief flooded through me. I hadn't harmed the silver cup, and no one would ever know that I'd touched it. With all the pieces put back together, I carefully returned the trophy to the shelf and stepped back, reluctant to touch anything else.

Theo was rifling through the open mail, empty take-out containers, and other junk on the coffee table, so I moved into the kitchen. On the counter was a colorful flyer advertising plastic food-storage containers with a brand name I'd never heard of: Grub Tubz. I spared it little more than a glance and peeked into the cupboards, where I found three different sugary cereals, mismatched dishes, and a half-empty box of pasta.

I shut the last cupboard door. "Anything?" I asked Theo.

"Nothing." She sounded disappointed.

I was experiencing a bit of a letdown myself. I hadn't really expected that we'd find anything earth-shattering. The police had likely gone over the place with a fine-tooth comb, and it wasn't likely that Freddie would have left a note or sign pointing us to his killer. Even so, it would have been nice to find something to suggest that he'd owed money to a bookie or had wronged someone so severely that they'd want him dead. Since no such clue presented itself, all I had to go on was the information that Bitty and Leona had shared that morning.

Although I nearly told Theo about the fact that the ladies had overheard Freddie arguing with Rosario, I stopped myself. If Theo knew about that, she'd no doubt want to break into Rosario's apartment next. I, on the other hand, wanted to go home to my own unit. My nerves were shot after one round of breaking and entering. I didn't think I could handle another in the same day.

Thankfully, Theo had given up on our current search too, so I peeked out into the hall. The coast was clear. We hurried out of Freddie's apartment, closing the door quietly behind us, and stripped off our purple gloves before heading for the elevator.

"We need to find out if Freddie really did have a girlfriend," Theo said as I pressed the button on the wall. "The murder could have been a crime of passion."

"Aren't you coming?" I asked when she didn't follow me into the elevator.

"I've got an appointment to get to, and I'm supposed to meet my grandparents out front. We'll reconvene later."

CHAPTER
SIXTEEN

The answer to my internal question of what my next investigative steps should be came to me the following morning. Not because I had a light bulb moment, but because I received an email from Minnie Yang. She'd sent it out to all residents of the building, or at least to those of us who had email addresses, inviting us to a cocktail party that she and her partner, Yolanda Antonopoulos, would be hosting that evening as a sort of celebration of life for Freddie.

Although I had no affection for our building's deceased superintendent, I didn't need to be a detective to know that the gathering presented a golden opportunity for learning more about the dead man and what my neighbors thought of him. Of course, I hoped that the person responsible for killing Freddie didn't live in the building, but there was also a chance that the other residents would know about shifty characters who'd been hanging around or any recent suspicious activity.

I texted Jemma to see if she wanted to come along—I'd already filled her in on my foolish promise to Mrs. Nagy—but she declined, preferring to spend her Saturday evening doing pretty much anything else. I couldn't blame her. What did it say about my life that I was spending my Saturday evening hanging out at a party for a sleazy dead guy? I didn't want to ponder that question too deeply.

I wasn't sure what to wear to a cocktail party held in honor of a murder victim, but after standing in front of my open closet for several minutes, I settled on a dark gray dress that I used to wear to work when I had an office job. I tied my hair back in a sleek twist, applied a bit of makeup, and slipped into a pair of black heels. All in all, I thought I looked appropriately somber, as well as professional and competent, good qualities for a private detective running her own agency. Not that I was a detective.

The elevator delivered me to the second floor, where the door to Minnie and Yolanda's apartment stood open. I hadn't quite known what to expect in terms of attendance. I didn't think anyone in the building was close to Freddie, unless his mystery lady friend lived at the Mirage. In fact, I was pretty sure he'd never been popular with the residents. Trying to get him to fix things or simply to maintain the common areas was like trying to extract teeth from a cranky crocodile. So I was a little surprised when I entered Minnie and Yolanda's apartment to find well over a dozen people already there.

Discreet speakers piped quiet jazz music into the high-ceilinged living room, and the kitchen peninsula had been turned into a temporary bar. Bodie stood behind the counter, pouring champagne for Leona and Agnes. Leona was leaning so far over the counter that she was practically sprawled on it, and the neckline of her sparkly purple dress was so revealing that a wardrobe malfunction seemed imminent. No doubt she was flirting with Bodie. He seemed to be taking it in stride, though. He probably had women of all ages throwing themselves at him regularly.

My gaze lingered on him as I admired his strong profile. Maybe he sensed my presence, because he looked my way, and our eyes locked. He sent me a private smile that made my heart flutter. Then Leona put a hand on his arm, and he dragged his attention away from me.

Still standing near the door, I scanned the room, noting that I recognized everyone in attendance. They all lived at the Mirage. Rosario stood with Yolanda and Carmen, apparently chatting about a large painting on the wall, which had Minnie's signature in the bottom corner. I'd hardly ever spoken with Yolanda, but I'd chatted with Minnie on a few occasions and knew that she was a professional artist. The canvas that currently held the women's attention was mostly covered in a bronze, textured paint, with what looked like the slim trunk of a birch tree running from top to bottom on an angle. A few black and silver brushstrokes broke up the bronze background, but otherwise there wasn't much to it. Of course, I knew next to nothing about art, so maybe it was a complicated piece that took weeks to make. I really had no idea.

Leona had finally left the bar—and Bodie—to speak with Mr. and Mrs. Harris, who I figured must be Theo's grandparents. Theo, however, wasn't present. She was probably at home with her parents. After all, she didn't live at the Deco Mirage. At least, that was my understanding. But I didn't actually know much about Theo.

As Mr. and Mrs. Harris left Leona to speak with another Mirage resident, I took over the floor space they'd vacated.

"Hey, Leona," I said as I fished the false eyelash out of my clutch. I'd transferred it from the tissue to a plastic baggie. "I found this in the building the other day and wondered if it might be yours?" I wasn't about to say exactly where I'd picked it up.

Leona peered at the baggie and then waved a hand through the air dismissively, the many rings on her fingers glinting. "Darling, I don't wear false eyelashes. I'm one hundred percent au naturel."

It was a good thing I wasn't drinking any champagne. I probably would have choked on it.

"Besides," Leona continued, "there's no point in returning it to its owner. Nobody wants to wear an eyelash that's been lying about, touching who knows what."

That I could agree with.

Nevertheless, I returned it to my clutch. I didn't think Theo would be impressed if I tossed our only piece of evidence in the garbage. Not that Theo was the boss of me.

I snapped my clutch shut. "You know how you and Bitty overheard Freddie arguing with Rosario?"

"Of course I do, darling. My memory is as sharp as Esmeralda's tongue."

"Esmeralda?" I wondered if that was a Mirage resident I'd yet to meet.

"My character on *Passion City*." Leona's voice had taken on a slight edge, as if I'd insulted her.

"Right," I said quickly. I'd never seen a single episode of *Passion City*, but I didn't think it wise to mention that. "But you really don't know what they were arguing about?"

Leona fluttered her fingers in the air. "Oh, who knows." She touched the jeweled necklaces at her throat. "Although it might have had something to do with pets."

"Pets?" I really needed to stop echoing what people said to me, or I might end up being known as the Mirage's resident parrot.

"Yes, I think that's it." Leona's forehead twitched, as if it would have scrunched up in thought if not for her most recent dose of Botox. "They argued several times, you see. I remember once Freddie was upset that Rosario had more than the allowed number of pets in her unit." Her attention drifted across the room, and she squeezed my arm with her clawlike fingers. "Excuse me. I promised I'd tell Yolanda about the time I had a guest role on *Miami Vice*."

She glided across the room, leaving me alone with my pathetic piece of evidence shut away in my clutch. Leona's eyelashes were about as real as the color of her violet eyes, but had she lied out of vanity or because she'd guessed where I'd found the clue?

Agnes had moved on from the bar to chat with a small group of residents gathered by the dining table, which held an array of finger foods, including some dainty petits fours and chocolate-topped profiteroles, which I suspected had been provided by Agnes and her daughter.

I smiled and said hello to several people as I slowly cruised past the dining table, snatching up a petit four on my way by. The delectable, two-bite dessert was long gone by the time I reached the bar.

"Quite the shindig, huh?" Bodie leaned his muscular forearms on the counter as he spoke to me. "Goes to show that nothing draws a crowd better than free food and booze."

"Yolanda and Minnie are providing the drinks?"

"They supplied a few bottles of champagne. When those are empty, the bar closes."

"It was nice of you to help out with the party."

"Don't go thinking too highly of me," he warned. "Yolanda's paying me fifty bucks to hang out here for an hour or so. I'm still paying off my student loans, so even with two bartending jobs, I'll take any extra money I can get."

"I hear you," I said. "My life lately seems to be all about finding a job and paying bills."

And now, apparently, solving a murder.

Bodie filled a champagne flute. "Then you'd better make the most of the free food and booze while you can. Besides, you deserve a break. You work too hard."

I bit back a sardonic laugh. "I don't even have a job."

"At life," he clarified. "You're always working hard at life. Taking care of Livy, looking out for your friends and neighbors."

"Thank you." My words came out quietly as he handed me the flute, but I was thanking him for far more than the drink. He viewed me in such a positive light. I wasn't sure I deserved it, but I appreciated it all the same.

I leaned against the bar as I took a sip of champagne and surveyed the room, remembering why I was there. "Do you think Freddie had any real friends?"

While a few people present, like Theo's grandparents, wore suitably somber expressions, most seemed to be enjoying themselves, as if they were at a festive gathering rather than an event held in honor of a man who'd been murdered.

"Maybe down at the pool hall," Bodie said with a shrug. "He hung out there a lot. I only know because it's two doors down from the bar where I work."

Across the room, Rosario tipped her head back as she let out a loud laugh in response to something Carmen had said. She certainly didn't seem to be in mourning. Even more interesting was the fact that I could tell from across the room that she was wearing false eyelashes.

"How's everything?" Minnie asked Bodie as she joined us at the bar.

"All good," he assured her. "We've still got two bottles of bubbly."

Minnie patted his hand. "Thanks so much for your help, Bodie."

He flashed her a grin. "My pleasure."

"Did you know Freddie well, Minnie?" I asked before she could drift away.

She fiddled with the gold cuff bracelet on her left wrist. "Oh, no. I never spoke to the man. Well, except to say hello maybe." A slight smile wavered on her face before she scurried off to Yolanda's side.

"Did you talk to Freddie much?" I asked Bodie once we were alone.

He leaned his forearms on the counter again. "From time to time. We weren't buddies or anything, though."

I wondered if I was being too obvious about my questioning. I didn't think I should advertise the fact that I was investigating the murder. Although Agnes had probably announced the news to half the building already.

"I just realized I hardly know anything about the man," I said, hoping that would explain my curiosity if Bodie didn't already know that Wyatt Investigations—meaning me and only me—was on the case.

"Probably for the best," he said. "The guy was a bit of a sleazebag."

Don't I know it? I thought.

I glanced at Bodie and silently cursed myself for the next thought that ran through my head. Should I consider everyone who knew Freddie as a suspect, including Bodie? He struck me as too genuine and kind to be a murderer, but then how well did I really know him? He hadn't lived at the Mirage all that long.

"Were you in the building around the time of the murder?" I asked, hoping I sounded casual. "Did you see or hear anything out of the ordinary?"

"I wish I could say I knew something that would help the cops find the killer," he said with a slight frown, "but I was at work."

"In the morning?" That struck me as odd. The bar where he worked wouldn't have been open at that hour.

"I was helping the assistant manager with inventory," he explained. "I take whatever overtime I can get." He straightened up. "And I'm really glad I took on that shift, because the cops didn't waste time looking at me as a suspect once they confirmed my alibi."

"They thought you were a suspect?" I said with surprise. Even though I'd wanted to eliminate him from my list of suspects, I'd never considered him a real possibility and therefore hadn't expected the police to either. "Why would you kill Freddie?"

"I wouldn't, but I was arrested a couple of years ago after I tried to break up a fight at a nightclub. The charges were dropped, but as soon as the detective in charge of the murder case found out about the incident, he was knocking on my door. I hope he's got some real suspects now."

I hoped so too, for Mr. Nagy's sake.

Bodie's blue eyes focused on something over my shoulder. "Huh. I didn't know Freddie would have any friends like that."

I turned around and froze, my champagne flute at my lips.

Wyatt had just entered the apartment.

CHAPTER SEVENTEEN

"What are you doing here?" I demanded after steamrolling my way over to Wyatt.

"You really cut to the chase, don't you?" he said. "Never waste any time with greetings or small talk."

My parents had drilled politeness into me as a little girl, but sometimes my brain overrode that setting. Wyatt's words, however, racked my inner child with guilt.

"Hi. How are you? And how did you even find out about the cocktail party?" I said it all in a rush, hoping to assuage the guilt that was quickly getting overridden by curiosity.

Wyatt's slow grin awakened the butterflies that had been slumbering in my stomach. His dimple appeared as he looked at me with amusement. "Zita mentioned it."

So now he was on a first-name basis with Mrs. Nagy?

I narrowed my eyes. "You've seen her since yesterday?"

Even I hadn't seen her since I'd made my foolhardy promise to her, and I lived right next door to the woman.

"She called me." Wyatt slid his hands into the pockets of his tailored suit pants. He wore a cobalt blue suit with a white dress shirt, but no tie. He'd left the top two buttons of his shirt undone, and his dark hair was artfully tousled. "Agnes gave her my number," he continued, looking perfectly relaxed and at ease. "Zita called to thank me for taking on Zoltán's case with you."

"And you're here because?" I couldn't seem to stop myself from acting prickly around him.

He glanced at all the people present, several of whom were not-so-subtly watching him out of the corner of their eye. "A room full of potential suspects and sources of valuable information. Isn't that why you're here?"

"But why do you care about suspects? You don't live at the Mirage, and you've never met Mr. Nagy. You'd never even met his wife until a couple of days ago."

"True," he conceded. "But she reminds me of my late grandmother, and did you see the look in her eyes when she asked for our help?"

The impossible-to-ignore pleading. I'd seen it all right. Just the memory of it tugged at my heartstrings.

"Besides," Wyatt continued, "I've always wanted to be a detective. Blame it on my childhood obsession with the Hardy Boys."

"Huh." I sized him up. "And which one are you? Frank or Joe?"

"I'd like to think I'm a little of both." He grinned, looking oh-so-casual and oh-so-good. "Should we work the room?"

A sense of satisfaction brought a smile to my face. "I've already got what I came here for."

I threw back the last of my champagne, set the empty glass on the nearest side table, and strode out the door.

I made it two steps into the hallway before Agnes called me back.

"Emersyn! Will you try a profiterole before you go? It's a new recipe of mine. My daughter and I are thinking of selling them at our bakery, but we want to get some feedback first."

By the time she got those words out, she had an arm around me and was ushering me back into Minnie and Yolanda's apartment.

So much for my grand exit.

I let Agnes steer me over to the food table because if I couldn't have my perfect mic drop moment, I could at least have more free food. I tasted one of the chocolate-covered profiteroles while Agnes watched with anticipation. The heavenly pistachio and Irish cream filling made me sigh with happiness, much to Agnes's delight.

While I didn't have to lie about how delicious the profiterole tasted, I struggled to stay focused after the first bite because my traitorous gaze wanted to follow Wyatt around the room. At the moment, he was chatting with Bitty and Yolanda, but as I watched, Leona slipped in between them, latching on to Wyatt's arm.

Serves him right, the prickly part of my brain grumbled.

The rest of me felt sorry for him. I tried to silence that part but without success, so I turned my back on Wyatt and focused my full attention on the profiteroles.

Once Agnes was satisfied that I was absolutely sure about my glowing review—I had to eat three profiteroles for her to believe me, though that wasn't exactly a hardship—I slipped out through the open door. This time, my exit definitely lacked any drama, but at least it was more successful.

I'd just stepped into the elevator when I realized I had no idea how to carry out the plan that had formed in my head. It made perfect sense to take advantage of the fact that Rosario was currently at Freddie's wake/celebration of life/cocktail party by searching her apartment. The reports of her multiple arguments with Freddie had shot her straight to the top of my admittedly short suspect list. The problem was that I didn't have Theo with me, and I had no idea how to pick a lock.

I dug my phone out of my clutch, hoping to consult YouTube.

The elevator doors had nearly closed when a hand shot in to stop them.

A very masculine hand.

The doors parted, and Wyatt stepped into the elevator.

I dropped my phone back into my clutch. "Couldn't you have taken the stairs?"

"Why?" He'd had a grin on his face when he first appeared, but that expression fizzled away, and he suddenly looked stricken and decidedly less at ease. "Do I make you uncomfortable? I didn't mean to make you uncomfortable."

"I'm not uncomfortable!" Okay, so I was a little, but he wasn't responsible for that. Unless you could say he was responsible for the thoughts in my head. Thoughts that involved his buttons flying off as I ripped open his shirt to reveal his sculpted chest and abs.

"Are you sure?" It was the first time I'd seen him worried, and there was something endearing and adorable about it. Which only made him hotter somehow.

"Positive." Did I sound a little breathless? I hoped not. "You're fine."

Oh, so very, very fine, a voice in my head piped up.

I fanned myself with my hand. "I'm just a little warm. I think it's the champagne."

Yes, that had to be it. The alcohol had gone to my head.

To my relief, the elevator dinged, and the doors parted. I stepped out into the hallway, relieved to be able to put a little more space between us.

"Okay, I'm glad I didn't make you uncomfortable," Wyatt said, sounding as relieved as I felt. He followed as I started down the third-floor hallway. "But can I ask why it is that you hate to like me?"

"I don't hate to like you!" I protested. "I don't know you well enough to hate to like you or to like to like you."

"Really?" His good-humored disbelief irked me. "Because I seem to make you cranky. Unless you're a cranky pants by nature?"

"I'm not a cranky pants!" I stopped in the middle of the hallway and crossed my arms over my chest. I wasn't as annoyed with him as I was with myself. I always seemed to go on the defensive in his presence, and my habit of protesting against every second thing he said grated on my nerves.

He stood there, watching me expectantly. Clearly, I wasn't going to get rid of him easily. And maybe I owed him an explanation, if not an apology.

I let out a resigned sigh. "Okay, so I've been a little grumpy with you. But that doesn't have anything to do with liking you or disliking you. It's just . . ." I took a second to figure out how to explain my jumbled feelings, or some of them, anyway. "I don't like being a damsel in distress, and even though we've barely known each other for five minutes, you've already had to help me out of scrapes on multiple occasions."

Wyatt nodded. "That's a blow to your independent nature."

"I guess that's a good way of putting it." I uncrossed my arms and approached the door to Rosario's apartment.

I knew full well that there was more to my irritation and defensive attitude. What I'd told him was true, but there was also the fact that I felt this crazy ridiculous attraction toward him that was so incredibly inconvenient at this point in my life. Add to that the fact that he'd seen me in awkward and embarrassing situations several times already. He probably thought I was an amusing hot mess, and knowing that awakened lingering vestiges of humiliation, which then got me as prickly as a porcupine facing off with a mountain lion. He didn't need to know about all that, though.

"Are you going to knock?" Wyatt asked.

I realized I was standing there, staring at the three gold numbers on Rosario's door. "No." I didn't offer any further information.

"It's just . . . this isn't your apartment, so . . ."

I glanced at him. The knowing, amused glint in his eyes raised my porcupine quills again.

"You know exactly why I'm here," I said.

He slid his hands into the pockets of his pants. "I've deduced that you learned something at the cocktail party that made you decide to search somebody's apartment while they're otherwise occupied." His smile was a little smug. "I've also deduced that you don't know how to get inside without a key."

I fought against the urge to remain prickly. The sad fact was that he was absolutely right, and I was running out of time. The cocktail party might wind down at any minute.

"Do you know how to get in without a key, Sherlock?" I asked with only a slight edge to my voice.

His grin widened. "And here I thought you might never ask."

He reached into an inner pocket of his tailored suit jacket and removed what I thought at first was a wallet but then realized was a small carrying case for lock-picking tools.

First Theo and now Wyatt. Was lock picking a common skill that I'd somehow missed learning in school?

Wyatt slid out two of the tools and handed me the case.

He paused before getting to work on the lock. "If I'm going to help you with breaking and entering, I think it's only fair that you acknowledge we're investigating this case together."

Several emotions flew into an instant wrestling match inside of me. I didn't want to need his help yet again, and I didn't want to keep fighting my attraction to him, but I really wanted to keep my promise to Mrs. Nagy. To do that, I needed to get into Rosario's apartment. And as much as I didn't want to admit it, the foolish part of me wasn't the least bit disappointed about the prospect of spending more time with him, even though I knew I should remain wary of him. After all, he'd been at the Mirage around the time of the murder, and he'd now inserted himself into my investigation. Was it really because of his grandmother and his lifelong desire to be a detective? Or was he hoping to steer the investigation in a direction that pointed firmly away from him?

I had no clue what reason he'd have to kill Freddie, but that didn't mean he didn't have one. I'd have to stay on my toes if I was going to have anything more to do with him.

Wyatt waited, the tools held loosely in one hand. Those darned coal-like eyes of his flickered with amusement, and I feared he could see all the different thoughts spinning around in my head.

"Fine," I said eventually, knowing we couldn't afford to waste any more time. "We're on the case. Together."

CHAPTER
EIGHTEEN

Wyatt, it turned out, was even more skilled at picking locks than Theo. I had only a few seconds to admire the deft movements of his strong hands before he had the door open. That was probably for the best, since my mind was tempted to stray into X-rated territory, imagining what else those skilled hands could do.

It's the champagne, I lied to myself again. *Blame it on the champagne.*

I handed the tool case to Wyatt and slipped into the apartment, but not before glancing up and down the hall to make sure no one was watching. It was a good thing that the Mirage didn't have security cameras in the hallways. In fact, the building had only two cameras, one in the lobby and one outside the rear door that led to the alley. I wasn't even sure if they worked.

Wyatt followed me inside and quietly shut the door behind us. My fingers tapped nervously against my leg, and I had to fight to still them. Maybe it was for the best that Wyatt and I were working together—at least for now. With two of us to share the task, the search would take half the time, and I definitely didn't want to spend a second longer than necessary in Rosario's apartment. I really wasn't good at breaking laws, or even rules. Sure, I'd sneaked out of the house a few times as a teenager, but I'd always required a couple of swigs from Jemma's flask of liquid courage before I could actually climb out the window, and that was only partly because I had a terrible fear of jumping from any height greater than about four feet. Not that we'd ever jumped from the second-story window, just from the tree outside the window.

"So, who lives here, and why are they a suspect?" Wyatt asked in a low voice.

I gave him the lowdown on Rosario as I pulled on the purple disposable gloves I'd stashed in my clutch. Wyatt watched with what I thought might be respect. He, I observed, hadn't come so prepared.

"What kind of pets does she have?" Wyatt asked, surveying the kitchen and living area. "I don't see or hear any."

"Huh," I said. "I'm not actually sure. I've never seen her walking around with a dog or taking a cat to the vet or anything like that." I slid open a kitchen drawer, took a peek inside, and shut it again.

Stopping in front of the combination fridge/freezer, I opened the fridge and studied the very ordinary contents. Would Rosario's penchant for expensive ketchup tell me anything about her persona as a possible killer?

Doubtful.

I shut the fridge and yanked open the freezer.

I stumbled backward and slapped my hands over my mouth, suppressing a scream that instead came out as strangled garbling.

Wyatt was at my side in an instant. "What's wrong?"

Too horrified to form coherent words, I simply pointed at the freezer. The door had drifted shut when I'd let go of it, so Wyatt opened it warily and got an eyeful of what had freaked me out. Inside the freezer, between a pint of ice cream and a bag of peas, Rosario had a stash of frozen mice and lizards.

Wyatt seemed a little surprised, and maybe slightly disgusted, but he remained calm.

Me? Not so much.

I stumbled out of the kitchen and collapsed onto Rosario's couch. "Is she a psychopath? A serial killer?"

"A serial rodent killer?" Wyatt shut the freezer.

"Those could be trophies."

"She only kills owners of rodents and reptiles and freezes their pets as trophies?" He sounded more than a tad skeptical.

I shot to my feet. "Maybe! How would I know how a psychopath's mind works?"

"Interesting . . ." Wyatt now stood with his back to me, staring at something on the living room floor, over by the wall.

My curiosity overrode my lingering disgust and my annoyance with Wyatt. When I reached his side, I saw what had caught his attention.

A hand-drawn portrait of Freddie lay on the floor, half hidden behind a credenza. It was a good likeness, done in pencil by a skilled hand. At least, that was the impression I got. It wasn't easy to tell for sure, considering that holes had been pierced through his eyes and other parts of his face.

I raised my eyes to the dartboard hanging on the wall above the credenza. I tugged out one of the darts and picked up the paper. The point of the dart was a match for the size of the holes in the portrait. Someone had used Freddie's picture for target practice.

"Well, that's"—I struggled to find the right word—"freaky."

"I'd agree with that assessment," Wyatt said.

He took a picture of the dart-pierced portrait with his phone, prompting me to do the same before I set it back on the floor where we'd found it. I realized that Theo would want pictures of the frozen mice and lizards too. Not that I reported to a seventeen-year-old. If she wanted photos of frozen dead things, she could break in and take them herself.

I imagined the scathing way she'd look at me when I didn't supply her with photos of everything. I cast a sidelong glance at Wyatt, who was now searching the drawers of a nearby desk.

I absolutely could not ask him to take the frozen-dead-things photo for me.

You're an independent woman, Emersyn, I told myself. *You're brave, not squeamish.*

Or you can at least fake it till you make it.

I straightened my shoulders, mustered all my courage, and returned to the kitchen. I got the freezer door open, but I couldn't bring myself to look inside again. Instead, I turned my head away and scrunched my eyes shut while I blindly snapped several photos. Then I opened my eyes a crack to check the results on the screen without actually looking at the subject matter too closely.

Good enough, I decided with a shudder before I slammed the freezer door shut.

I spun around when Wyatt let out a low whistle.

He stood in the doorway to what I assumed was the bedroom. "I think I found the pets."

He ventured across the threshold, and I crept after him, entering the dimly lit bedroom with cold apprehension slinking along my skin.

"Oh, this keeps getting better and better," I said, fighting the urge to run screaming from the apartment.

Several large glass tanks lined the walls of Rosario's purple-and-black-themed bedroom. Inside each tank was a snake with red, black, and yellow stripes. The biggest was maybe a little less than two feet long. Still, that was two feet too long for me.

I took a step back. "Are those things deadly?"

Wyatt moved closer to the tanks to study their reptilian occupants.

I, however, stayed put. Although I didn't suffer from ophidiophobia, I didn't exactly love reptiles and felt no particular urge to get up close and personal with them. Besides, I had to put a hand to the doorframe to hold myself steady. I was feeling a little wobbly all of a sudden, and it didn't have anything to do with the champagne.

No, it had everything to do with the fact that I was now imagining one of Rosario's snakes escaping, slithering its way through the building, and harming my sweet, beautiful niece. I'd once read a news story about a child getting crushed to death by a boa constrictor. And what if these things were venomous?

I clutched the doorframe harder, worried I might be about to lose my profiteroles all over Rosario's parquet floor.

"Well, are they?" I prodded, desperate for him to respond.

He took a close look at the last snake and shook his head. "Nothing to worry about. They're harmless."

"How can you be sure?" I demanded, not at all ready to simply trust his word. "They're so . . ."

"Scary looking?" Wyatt finished for me. "They do look similar to coral snakes, but these guys are scarlet kingsnakes. They aren't venomous, and they're harmless to humans."

I would have sagged against the doorframe with relief, but I wasn't keen to show any further signs of weakness in front of Wyatt.

"Are you a closet herpetologist?" I asked.

He laughed. "I went through a snake-crazy phase in my teens. Anyway, this explains the frozen mice and skinks in the freezer."

I released my grip on the doorframe and wiggled my fingers to get the feeling back into them. "Snake food?"

He nodded.

I backed out of the bedroom, so ready to be done with this whole search thing. I'd had enough surprises and adventure for one day. Probably for the entire year.

But, of course, the universe disagreed with me.

Wyatt had just joined me in the living room when we heard voices outside the apartment door.

CHAPTER
NINETEEN

We scrambled out onto the fire escape and shut the window behind us in the nick of time. When I chanced a peek through the glass, I saw Rosario enter the apartment along with Agnes. I quickly pulled back out of sight.

Wyatt was already making his way down the rickety metal staircase. He reached the lowest landing, where a drop ladder had to be released to extend down to the alley. Instead of bothering with the ladder, he crouched down and then jumped from the landing to the ground. He did it with such grace and agility that it was as if he jumped from heights on a regular basis, like maybe it was part of his hot-guy training regime.

Admittedly, the ladder looked like it would clatter when dropped, causing a commotion and probably drawing a crowd. Not something we wanted to do. We couldn't exactly explain why we were on the fire escape without lying, and at the moment, I couldn't even think up a good lie to explain it.

Still, my muscles were already starting to freeze up at the thought of having to make that jump. I slipped out of my shoes since high heels and metal grating do not mix well. Then, gripping my shoes with one hand and the railing with the other, I crept down one step, then two.

I stopped.

"What's the matter?" Wyatt whisper-called to me from the alley below.

I gulped and crept down to the lowest landing. Then I backed up one stair.

"I think I'll go another way." I tried to sound casual, but my voice came out more high-pitched than normal.

"Hang from the edge, and I'll help you down," Wyatt said.

Sure, that's exactly what I wanted. To accept help from Wyatt *again*.

"Thanks, but I'm good! I need to go up anyway! See you later!"

I scurried up the fire escape, crouching at certain points so I wouldn't be visible through any windows. When I made it to the fifth floor, I paused, mapping out the building in my head. If I'd guessed right, that would put me at . . .

I peeked through the nearest window.

Yep. Exactly where I thought I was.

I glanced downward. Wyatt still stood in the alley, looking up at me.

The last remaining threads of my dignity required me not to appear foolish to him. I needed to look like I was absolutely not panicking or doing something ridiculous.

So I tapped on the window and waved through the glass.

I couldn't blame Bodie for looking surprised to find me outside his window, but his shocked expression lasted a mere second or two. Then he was at the window, raising the sash so I could climb in carefully, making sure not to rip my dress or get myself into any unladylike positions.

When I had my feet safely on the floor, I leaned out the window, waved at Wyatt—who was still watching me—and then ducked back inside.

I smiled at Bodie. "Thanks."

"You could have used the door." Bodie hooked his thumb in

that direction. "I know the people in this building like to gossip, but we're both adults."

"That's not why I'm here," I rushed to say as my face flared with heat.

Then I saw the laughter in his blue eyes and the twitching of his mouth.

My shoulders relaxed, and a relieved breath whooshed out of me.

"I'm kidding," he said, confirming my suspicion. "But why were you out there?"

"Let's just say I wanted to escape an awkward situation."

Bodie took a look out the window as he lowered the sash. "One involving that guy from the cocktail party?"

"You could say that."

"Hmm." He dragged his gaze away from the window. "Come on in. All the way in, I mean." He turned and headed for his kitchen.

I took one last peek out the window—to see Wyatt finally walking off down the alley—before I followed Bodie.

"Why 'hmm'?" I asked as I set my shoes on the floor and slid my feet into them.

He opened the fridge and looked at me over the door. "Sorry?"

"You said 'hmm' like it meant something."

"Nah. It's nothing. Can I get you a drink?"

"I'm good, thanks," I said. "Drink-wise, anyway. Curiosity-wise, not so great. You can't say 'hmm' like that and not tell me what it means."

He shut the fridge without taking anything from it. "Look, I barely know you, so I'm not going to tell you who you should or shouldn't date. It wouldn't be my place to do that even if I did know you well."

"I'm not dating Wyatt." The statement came out more emphatically than I'd intended.

"Oh, okay." His expression relaxed. "My mistake. That's proba-bly for the best, though."

"Why do you say that?" For a panicked moment, I wondered if Bodie knew of some evidence linking Wyatt to Freddie's murder.

He gestured toward one of the barstools by the kitchen's penin-sula. I shimmied my way onto it while he leaned his forearms on the counter, like he'd done at Yolanda and Minnie's apartment ear-lier. The stance drew my attention to his tanned, muscular arms, distracting me from my worried thoughts.

"You know," he said, "he probably has a fancy car, a penthouse suite, a country club membership. Those guys are always players."

No evidence of murderous traits then. That came as a relief, though skepticism quickly followed.

Bodie caught sight of my raised eyebrow. "Okay, I know what you're thinking. I'm a thirty-year-old bartender. Probably a player too, right?"

He'd guessed correctly. I didn't have to tell him that.

"There's more to me than meets the eye."

"Care to share?" I asked, intrigued.

He grinned, though I thought I detected a shadow of sadness in his eyes. "One day."

I shoved aside my disappointment. "I guess the cocktail party is over?"

He shrugged as he opened the fridge. "There were still people there, but the bubbly ran out, so my work was done." He smiled again, this time without any sorrow. "And Minnie slipped me a twenty-dollar tip on my way out." He looked in the fridge. "Are you sure I can't get you something to drink?"

"I'm sure, but thank you." I slipped off the stool. "And I won't impose on you any longer. You weren't exactly expecting me to drop in."

He shut the fridge, turning his full attention to me. "Maybe not, but I can't say I'm unhappy about it."

Butterflies stirred in my stomach. "No?"

"As the only two adult residents of this building under the age of fifty, we should hang out more."

"That would be good. Except I don't have a whole lot of free time. Definitely not free nights. Well, rarely, anyway."

"Because of Livy?"

I nodded. "Unless she's with my parents, I can't really have a night out. Mrs. Nagy loves to babysit, but I don't like to keep her up late at night, and now that . . ."

"I know." Bodie sank down onto the couch. "I hate what she and her husband are going through. I wish I hadn't told the cops about the croquet mallet incident."

I hesitated but then sat down beside him. "You just told the truth. The police would have found out about it eventually anyway. Especially if that security camera in the lobby works."

"Still . . . I wish I hadn't been the one to tell the cops, you know?"

I nodded. "I can understand that." I stood up again. "I should really get going. I didn't mean to interrupt your day."

Bodie got to his feet and touched a hand to my arm. "Hey, feel free to interrupt my day anytime."

I smiled at him, the sincerity of his words warming my heart and my cheeks.

His blue eyes held mine captive, and the air between us practically crackled with intensifying electricity. My breath hitched.

A glint of light caught my eye. I looked away from Bodie, and the electric energy vibrating in the room faded.

Something sparkly lay beneath a leather recliner, one corner peeking out far enough to catch the light streaming in through the window. I picked it up and saw that it was a dangly earring, about three inches long and encrusted with diamonds and emeralds. Real or fake, I didn't know, but it was pretty. And it most likely didn't belong to Bodie. He'd never actually denied being a player, and now I wondered how many women he had traipsing through his apartment each month.

"Looks like somebody lost this," I said, handing the earring to

Bodie while avoiding his eyes, embarrassed that I'd felt flattered by his apparent interest in me moments earlier.

He held the piece of jewelry in his palm. "I'm glad you spotted this. It should get my ex off my back."

"Your ex?"

"We broke up weeks ago, but she's been hounding me about a lost earring ever since," Bodie explained. "I'll drop this off at her place. Maybe then she'll finally stop texting me. Thanks, Emersyn."

A thread of tension eased inside of me. "I spotted it by luck, but I'm glad I was able to help."

His story had a ring of truth to it, so maybe he wasn't a player after all. I was willing to withhold judgment on that point.

I left his apartment with a smile and some parting words, glad that my fear of heights had led me to Bodie.

CHAPTER
TWENTY

"You really need to give me your number," Theo said as she approached Jemma and me the next day. "I've got better things to do than spend my time looking high and low for you."

My bestie and I were seated on the wide rim of the Mirage's decrepit and empty mermaid fountain, enjoying the few rays of October sunshine reaching us there in the courtyard. I'd just filled Jemma in on the previous day's escapades when Theo interrupted our conversation without a shred of contrition.

I could have told her that I had no obligation to report my whereabouts to her, but who was I kidding? It was easier to hand my phone over, so I did.

"We've been debriefing," Jemma told her. "Rosario's a solid suspect. We need to find a way to serve her up to the police on a platter."

"I need details," Theo said as she sent herself a text from my phone.

She handed back the device, and once again, I relayed what I'd learned at the cocktail party and what Wyatt and I had found in Rosario's apartment.

"He can pick locks?" Theo said, impressed, when I reached that part of the story. "He's more than just good looks then. He'll be a great asset for the agency."

"The *fake* agency," I stressed.

"It's not fake anymore," Theo countered. "We've got a phone number, a website, and you're investigating. How much more real could it get?"

Jemma shrugged. "She could be getting paid to investigate."

Theo waved off that detail. "Once we've got this pro bono case under our belts, the money will roll in."

I decided not to shatter her crazy fantasy. She was just a kid, after all.

I continued with my story of searching Rosario's apartment and finding the dart-pierced portrait of Freddie. As I'd predicted, Theo demanded to see photos, so I passed my phone to her again.

When I got to the part about the snakes, Jemma made a face.

"I can't stand reptiles." She gave a dramatic shudder. "I'm so glad I wasn't with you."

"Wyatt told me they're harmless," I said. "I sure hope he's right about that."

"He knows snakes?" Theo said, looking thoughtful. "I'll add that to his file."

"He's got a file?" I asked with surprise.

"So do you."

What? I did not like the sound of that. "I want to see mine."

Theo gave an unconcerned, one-shoulder shrug. "It's confidential."

"It's my file and my agency!" I protested.

"Take it up with HR."

"There is no HR!" I shot back.

Theo gave me a smug smile. "Nope."

"All right, children," Jemma broke in. "Let's focus here." Her eyes took on a dangerous glint. "So, Em, what else happened while you were alone with Wyatt?"

"Nothing." I shrugged in what I hoped was a nonchalant way. "We searched the place and got out of there."

Jemma shook her head with disappointment. "What a wasted opportunity, Em."

"If you're so into Wyatt, why don't you make a move on him?" Even as I grumbled those words, my stomach twisted at the thought.

"I'd never do that to you, hon."

I didn't get the chance to argue that she wouldn't be doing anything to me.

"Besides," she continued, "I've got DeVaughn, and he's keeping me plenty happy."

Theo leaned forward with obvious eagerness. "Who's DeVaughn?"

"He plays for the Jets," Jemma said, referring to the NFL team. She brought up a picture of him on her phone.

"Whoa," Theo said with appreciation when Jemma showed her the photo. "He's smokin'."

"Right?" Jemma smiled at the photo before shutting off the screen of her phone. "Now, back to Emersyn," she said with frightening determination.

"Not back to me," I countered. "Whatever might be going on with my love life—"

"Or lack thereof," Jemma said out of the corner of her mouth.

Theo snort-laughed, and my traitorous bestie joined her.

I raised my voice to drown out their snickering. "Isn't that my own business?"

Jemma patted my knee. "Not when you're in need of help, hon."

"I don't need help!"

"You haven't been on a single date since you broke up with Hoffman," Jemma pointed out unnecessarily. "And that was *months* ago."

"I've got Livy to raise now," I reminded her. "I need to focus my attention on her, not dating. Besides, I don't want men cycling in and out of her life."

Jemma put an arm around my shoulders and gave me a squeeze. "And I commend you for that, Em. But raising a kid doesn't mean you can't have a love life. You don't have to introduce any men to Livy in the early stages. Plus, if you're completely fulfilled in all aspects of your life, that will only benefit Livy."

"And you've got two hotties to choose from," Theo added. "Bodie's got a thing for you."

"No, he doesn't," I protested.

Okay, so maybe he'd given me that impression when I made my impromptu visit to his apartment the day before, but I was feeling defensive now that Theo and Jemma were teaming up on me, so I wasn't about to agree with anything they said.

"He asked the elderlies about you," Theo said.

"Ooh, do tell," Jemma prodded, not that Theo needed any encouragement.

And if I were completely honest, I really wanted to know what, exactly, Bodie had asked about.

"He came by to fix a leaky pipe while my grandparents were hosting bridge night," Theo explained.

Jemma smacked my arm with the back of her hand. "You should ask Bodie to fix your pipe."

I crossed my arms. "I fixed it myself."

Nobody needed to know that I'd done so with the aid of a YouTube tutorial, after I nearly flooded the apartment and Wyatt swooped in to save the day.

"Then unfix it so you can ask him," Jemma suggested.

The door that led into the front section of the building opened, and the blond, broad-shouldered detective I'd seen on two previous occasions stepped out into the courtyard. He wore a gray suit and carried a tablet in one hand. He paused for a split second, taking in his surroundings, and then strode over our way.

His presence distracted Jemma and Theo enough that they stopped hassling me about my love life. I'd never been so happy to see a cop.

"Ladies," the detective said, his piercing blue gaze passing over each of us in turn. He tapped the badge clipped to his belt. "Detective Callahan, NYPD. Do you all live in the building?"

Jemma and Theo pointed at me and said in unison, "She does."

"With my niece," I added, and realized that probably didn't matter to him.

"My grandparents live here," Theo said.

"And Jemma's my best friend," I said, indicating my BFF. Again, I realized that probably wasn't relevant to the detective, but something about his sharp blue eyes made me want to blurt out all my secrets, not that I had any. Well, not many.

Jemma gave him a little wave and a smile. "Jemma Ghosh. How can we help you, Detective?"

Callahan woke up the tablet and turned the screen our way. "Do you recognize this person?"

The photo on the screen looked like a slightly grainy still from the surveillance camera in the lobby. It had caught a person dressed in jeans and a black sweatshirt with the hood pulled up as they walked across the lobby, from the direction of the front doors.

We took a closer look at the screen, all of us shaking our heads.

"No. Sorry," I said. From their fair-skinned hands, I could tell that the person was white, but that was it.

"Is that the murderer?" Theo asked, a light of excitement in her eyes.

"A person of interest," the detective replied. "We're hoping to speak to them to see if they have any information that would aid us in our investigation." He swiped the tablet's screen to bring up another photo taken from the surveillance video. "How about this woman? Does she look familiar?"

"That's me," I said right away.

Detective Callahan didn't appear at all surprised, and I suspected he'd figured that out before asking the question.

He shut the tablet's case. "You found a bouquet of flowers in the trash can."

I nodded. "Roses."

"Was there a card attached to the bouquet?"

"No," I replied. "I took a quick look in the trash can, but I didn't see one there either."

The detective produced a business card from the inner pocket of his suit jacket and offered it to me. "If you remember anything related to the case or have any information to share, please get in touch with me."

I accepted the card. "Of course."

He gave us a nod and continued on his way across the courtyard, disappearing through the next set of doors.

Jemma snatched the business card from my fingers.

"Detective *Thomas* Callahan?" she read with obvious disappointment. "I was hoping his name would be Thor."

"He's totally a Thor," Theo agreed.

"Not according to his card," I pointed out.

"Thor can be his code name," Theo decided.

"Why does he need a code name?"

Theo didn't bother answering my question.

Jemma pressed the card into the palm of my hand and curled my fingers around it. "Keep that safe. We'll come up with some information you can share. Hopefully you can meet with him in person. Privately." She waggled her eyebrows.

"Why are you trying to set me up with every man under the age of forty?" I asked. "We don't even know that he's single."

"No wedding ring, at least," Theo said as she retrieved her laptop from the backpack hanging from the handles of her wheelchair.

Jemma gave her a nod of approval. "Always look for the ring."

I crossed my arms. I seemed to be doing that a lot lately. "I'm actually perfectly fine without a man in my life."

Jemma patted my knee. "Of course you are, hon, but a little spice in life is even better. And that cop is super spicy."

Theo's fingers flew over the keyboard of her laptop. "Maybe

we'll have better luck identifying the person of interest from the actual video footage."

"Okay, but how can we get ahold of that?" I worried I might already know the answer. "I'm not breaking into Freddie's office. Besides, the cops probably took his computer."

Theo dismissed my concerns without glancing up. "All the footage is on the cloud."

"Always look on the cloud," Jemma said with a nod.

"Got it!" Theo turned her laptop so we could see the screen.

The date and time stamp on the footage from the lobby revealed that it was from right around the time of the murder. Sure enough, the person in the black hoodie strode into view carrying a bouquet of roses and disappeared off camera about four seconds later.

"How did you get that?" I demanded.

"Child's play," Theo said, offering no further explanation.

Maybe it was best if I didn't know the details.

The figure walked back into view after about sixty seconds. Whoever it was, they dumped the bouquet of roses in the lobby's trash can and jogged out of sight, heading deeper into the building again. The still Detective Callahan had shown us must have come from a point in the video after the mystery person got rid of the roses.

"The flowers," I mused, mostly to myself. "Why suddenly dump them and take off like that?"

"The flower bearer didn't run out of the building," Jemma said. "So the intended recipient probably didn't chase them away."

"Maybe the flowers were for Freddie, but then . . . what?" My theory fizzled away before it gained any steam. I directed the next question at Theo. "Is there any footage of this person leaving the building later?"

Theo fast-forwarded through the video. I was the next person to appear. I found the roses, disappeared, and then returned to the lobby without the flowers. After I left through the front door, an elderly couple who lived on the ground floor entered and took the hall to the right, which led to their unit. A while later, Agnes entered the building. Soon after, Wyatt and I ran in through the main door, in response to Agnes's scream.

"What about the back door?" Jemma asked.

Theo searched on her laptop but then shook her head. "Looks like that camera hasn't been working for a while."

"So, there's no evidence that this mystery person left the building before the murder," Jemma said.

"Which means they could very well be the killer." Theo brought the first video clip up on the screen again.

"Could it be Rosario?" Jemma's question was laced with doubt.

I shook my head. "Not the right build or skin tone." A sickening lump grew in the pit of my stomach. "Can you play it back again?"

Theo did so.

"Stop it right there," I said as the person disappeared off camera. "Back a few frames." When Theo got to the right spot, I said, "There!"

I leaned in closer to the screen, not wanting to believe what I was seeing.

"What is it?" Jemma asked.

Peeking out from the left sleeve of the person's hoodie was an orange wrist strap, one I recognized as an Apple Watch. That confirmed what I'd already surmised from the individual's familiar, loping gait.

I sat back, the world tilting around me.

"Em?" Jemma prodded with concern.

"The person of interest?" I said faintly. "It's Hoffman."

CHAPTER
TWENTY-ONE

"A thief *and* a killer?" Jemma said with amazement. "And here I thought he couldn't sink any lower."

"Um, hello?" Theo waved at us. "Who's Hoffman?"

"Hoffman Fisher, Emersyn's ex," Jemma explained. "He wormed his way into her trust, got hold of her passwords, and drained her bank account."

Theo gave me a pitying look. "Wow. You really know how to pick 'em."

"Hey, he's *one guy!*" I objected. "It's not like I have a history of dating criminals."

"No . . ." Jemma drew the word out. "But there was that guy who told you he was an accountant."

"What was he really?" Theo asked, a little too eagerly if you asked me.

Jemma was also enjoying the conversation too much, if her smile was anything to go by. "A professional clown."

Theo laughed while I shuddered. I wasn't a fan of clowns.

"Maybe Thor is the right match for her," Theo said to Jemma. "A cop would make a good change."

I didn't give Jemma a chance to agree or disagree. "We're not setting me up with anybody, remember?"

They ignored me.

"Wyatt's got this hot, mysterious vibe going on," Jemma said, "but there's something super sexy about a good-looking cop."

"Can we please stay on task?" I begged.

"And don't forget Bodie," Theo said to Jemma.

Jemma's smile turned wicked. "Couldn't if I tried."

I threw my hands in the air. "Seriously?" I stood up, ready to walk away, but Jemma grabbed my arm and tugged me back down again.

"What are we going to do about Hoffman?" she asked. "You should probably call Thor."

"And tell him what? That Theo hacked into the surveillance footage?"

"Say that you think there's something familiar about the person in the photo after all and you'd like to see the video to confirm your suspicions."

Theo took in the sight of my worn jeans and T-shirt with a critical eye. "Maybe wear a different outfit when you meet up with him."

I jumped to my feet again but didn't stalk off, even though the temptation was there. I had too many worrisome thoughts swirling around in my head, and I needed to talk them out.

"Maybe Hoffman came to the Mirage to break into my place and steal more from me," I theorized.

"What have you got left to steal?" Jemma asked.

I decided to sidestep that question. "Maybe Freddie caught him trying to break into my apartment." I considered what I'd said. "Except that doesn't explain why Freddie was killed downstairs. Unless Hoffman followed or chased him down there after Freddie caught him."

"All speculation," Theo said.

I bristled at her dismissive tone. "What else have we got?"

"It's not about what we've got now," she said with a confident smile. "It's about what we're *going* to get."

I didn't much like the sound of that.

At least I didn't have to worry about picking a lock or otherwise forcing entry into Hoffman's apartment. That was about the only bright side I could see as I stood outside my ex's door that afternoon. I couldn't entirely blame Theo and Jemma for what I was about to do. They might have been the first to voice the plan to search Hoffman's place, but it had already been forming in my head at the time. Sure, I could have gone straight to Thor—Detective Callahan—and given him the spiel that Jemma had suggested, but I wasn't quite ready to throw Hoffman to the wolves.

Not that I'd voiced that out loud. Jemma would have shipped me off to therapy if I'd so much as hinted that I might not want to turn Hoffman in to the cops. I had no positive feelings left for the guy, but the thought that I could have dated a murderer, even if he hadn't yet killed anyone while we were together, threatened to chip away at my soul. I wanted to know if there was any more evidence against him before I talked to Detective Callahan. Or maybe I simply needed time to come to terms with the extent of Hoffman's villainy. Whatever the true reason, I'd ridden the subway to Longwood in the South Bronx and hoofed it the rest of the way to the three-story brick building where Hoffman had lived since before I met him.

Fortunately, our breakup had been so abrupt that I'd never returned the key he'd given me back when we were still starry-eyed with each other. When I was starry-eyed, anyway. I was no longer certain that he'd ever felt that way about me. I'd probably been a mark right from the beginning.

My already fragile self-esteem crumbled a little more with that thought, so I tried my best to shove it into the dark, cobwebby shadows at the back of my mind.

Before leaving the Mirage, I'd taken a page out of Hoffman's own book and pulled on a black hoodie. I'd paired it with black cargo pants that I dug out from the back of my closet. Before disembarking from the train, I'd pulled up the hood to hide my face from any surveillance cameras at the subway station, local businesses, and residences. Big Brother was everywhere, as Theo had reminded me before she'd zoomed off to her grandparents' apartment.

Once inside Hoffman's building, I jogged up the stairs to the top floor. I made sure I was alone in the corridor and then slipped the key into the lock, hating the slight tremor in my fingers. I wasn't cut out for a life of crime, and I definitely wasn't cut out for flying solo in a life of crime. My sidekicks had abandoned me. Theo because she had to help her grandmother prepare Sunday dinner, and Jemma because she had a date with DeVaughn.

My brain shoved Wyatt to center stage in my thoughts and shone a spotlight on him. I could have invited him along, since we'd agreed to work the case together, but Wyatt felt like a dangerous complication, one I didn't think I could handle in my life. So I lassoed my thoughts of him with a mental rope and, with great effort, dragged them out of the spotlight.

I slipped into Hoffman's apartment and quietly shut the door behind me. Thanks to his love of documenting every moment of his life on Instagram, I knew that he was currently off enjoying an extended weekend in the Hamptons with Tiffany. Hopefully that gave me plenty of time to search his place without getting interrupted by his sudden return. I didn't need a repeat of what had happened at Rosario's place.

I paused inside the door to pull on my purple gloves. To my right was a door that led to the bathroom, and the cramped kitchen was to my left. I bypassed both rooms as well as the door to the bedroom. I wasn't sure if I could bring myself to go in there. Partly because I didn't want to face memories of intimate moments shared with Hoffman and partly because I wasn't keen to find any evidence of what he'd been up to with Tiffany. Although I doubted he ever brought Tiffany to his place. The building was old and outdated and in serious need of TLC. It also smelled perpetually of Thai curry due to a neighbor's obsession with the dish. Plus, cleaning was not something Hoffman bothered to do very often.

That certainly hadn't changed, I observed as I reached the living area and took in the sight of take-out containers strewn about the room along with empty beer cans and the occasional item of clothing. Tiffany probably lived in a penthouse apartment when she wasn't weekending in the Hamptons. Hoffman might not be the sharpest tool in the shed, but even he would know that the sight of this place would probably be enough to make Tiffany dump him.

I worked quickly, wanting to get out of there as soon as possible. I didn't want to get caught, and simply being in Hoffman's place, being surrounded by his belongings, filled me with memories that now made me cringe and question my judgment. Hoffman was fairly good-looking, and he talked a good game, but now that I knew the guy behind the façade, it was hard not to feel ashamed that I'd ever fallen for him.

"Ugh," I said aloud as I carefully looked beneath a pile of stained take-out menus.

It wasn't the mess that had grossed me out, though. It was my memories and the effect they were having on my feelings of self-worth.

I paused my search and rolled my shoulders, blowing out a breath that made my lips wobble. My version of shaking it off. It helped enough to allow me to refocus on my reason for being there.

I made quick work of the living room and then forced myself to peek into the bedroom. It looked much the same as I remembered: rumpled sheets, an iPad on the bedside table, jeans and T-shirts strewn about.

What got me was the smell. As faint as it was, Hoffman's scent hung in the air and sent another rush of shame through me. I backed out of the room and turned my attention to the kitchen. I hadn't made it far when I spotted something on the counter, sitting between the coffee maker and the microwave. I picked it up carefully with my gloved fingers, recognition and dread forming a hard lump in my stomach.

It was a label from a bottle of whiskey, with bits of broken brown glass stuck to the back of it. If I recalled correctly, it was similar—if not identical—to the label on the open bottle of whiskey that Theo and I had found in Freddie's apartment. If Hoffman had taken the label from the smashed bottle in Freddie's office—which might have been broken in a struggle right before the murder—that would explain why it had bits of broken glass clinging to it. But why the heck would Hoffman bother taking the label?

I didn't know the answer to that question, but I did know that the label connected Hoffman to the murder scene.

I tugged off one glove so I could use my phone to snap several pictures of both sides of the label. With that done, I decided I didn't want to press my luck. I eased the apartment door open and peeked out into the hall. The coast was clear, so I got the hell out of Dodge.

CHAPTER
TWENTY-TWO

Hoffman now shared with Rosario the dubious honor of being my prime suspect. Maybe he'd even edged Rosario out of that spot. After all, my neighbor might have hated Freddie with a dart-throwing passion, but Hoffman was the one caught on video near the location of the murder, and he was the one with the label that had likely been taken from the scene of the crime.

As much as I wanted to talk my findings over with Jemma and Theo, that would have to wait. When I got home, I barely had a chance to change out of my burglar outfit and do a rush job of tidying the apartment before my parents showed up to return Livy from her weekend at Grandma and Granddad's house in West Haven.

As soon as I opened the door in response to their knock, Livy threw herself at me, wrapping her skinny arms around my waist and pressing her face into my stomach. My heart nearly exploded.

"Hey, sweet Livysaurus!" I said brightly, running a hand down her strawberry blonde hair. "Did you have a good weekend?"

She nodded and released me, immediately bouncing up and down on the balls of her feet. "We went to the nature center and saw turtles and lots of cool stuff, and then we had ice cream!"

I smiled at her excitement. Nothing made me happier than seeing her happy.

"Lucky girl," I said, giving her another hug. "I guess that means you don't need the chocolate ice cream I put in the freezer for to-night."

"No, it doesn't!" She wriggled out of my arms. "I always need ice cream!"

I laughed. "Darn. And here I thought I'd get to eat it all myself."

She gave her head an emphatic shake. "No way!"

My mom broke in, speaking to Livy. "Honey, why don't you take your things to your bedroom? Granddad will help you put your new books on your shelf." She gave my dad a pointed look that sent apprehension thrumming in my chest.

"Let's go, sweet pea," my dad said, taking Livy's hand and carrying her bag.

My mom shut the apartment door with a quiet thud.

"What's wrong?" I asked with trepidation.

"Nothing's wrong, Emersyn." Despite her words, the tone of her voice warned me that I wouldn't like what she was about to say next. "But your father and I have been talking."

"About?" My mouth had gone so dry that I barely got the word out.

She adjusted the strap of her purse on her shoulder and lowered her voice. "I think you'll agree that Olivia has to be the top priority for all of us."

"She is."

"She has such a wonderful time when she stays with us," my mom continued, as if she hadn't heard me.

"Of course she does. You're great with her."

"I'm glad you agree."

"Because?" I prodded, even though it felt a bit like poking a poisonous snake.

"Because your father and I think it would be best for Olivia if she came to live with us full-time."

I grabbed the corner of the kitchen counter, desperate to steady myself as the floor tilted beneath me. For a second, I wondered if we were experiencing an earthquake, but then I realized it was just my personal world that had tipped on its axis.

"But I'm her guardian." Shock gave my voice a vague quality that sounded unfamiliar to my ears.

"Don't you think it's best to change that?" my mom asked, as if she were discussing something as ordinary as changing the curtains or the wall color.

"No!" The word came out forcefully even though I could barely breathe. "Ethan wanted *me* to look after her."

Hurt flashed in my mom's pale blue eyes. Then they turned flinty. "Your brother was very ill at the time."

"He still knew his own mind."

Livy burst out of her bedroom, my dad following behind at a slower pace.

"Daisy's so happy to be home!" she told my mom and me, hugging her purple dinosaur stuffie. "Auntie Em, what are we having for dinner?"

I tightened my grip on the edge of the counter and forced myself to smile as naturally as I possibly could. "Spaghetti."

"Yum!" She tugged on my dad's hand. "Granddad, Auntie Em makes really good spaghetti."

I blinked back the tears that threatened to well up in my eyes.

"I'll have to get her to make it for me sometime then," my dad said.

Somehow that made the urge to cry even stronger.

At first, I thought my dad was as oblivious to the tension in the air as Livy was, but then he glanced warily between my mom and me, and I knew he was aware of what we'd been discussing.

Under other circumstances, I would have confessed to my dad that my spaghetti sauce came from a jar, but those words shriveled up inside of me. Serving meals from a jar might count as another strike against me in my mother's book. Just another reason why Livy should go and live with them.

"Granddad and I need to leave now," my mother told Livy. "Do we get hugs?"

Livy threw her arms around each of them in turn, and I had to swallow another lump of emotion. Simmering beneath it, deep in my chest, was a growing anger and sense of protectiveness.

As my parents made their way out the door, Livy waved and called out, "Bye, Grandma! Bye, Granddad!"

My mom directed her frosty gaze at me and said, "We'll talk more later."

I shut the door and tamped my feelings down to be dealt with later—maybe.

Then I smiled at my niece and said, "Let's get that spaghetti ready."

I held back my tears all evening and managed not to smash anything out of anger, even though the temptation arose swiftly and fiercely on more than one occasion. By the time I tucked Livy into bed, my heart and head both ached, but the threat of tears had disappeared, leaving me weary and defeated.

I crawled into my own bed and hid beneath the covers, my stomach roiling. I couldn't even convince myself that my mom would change her mind over time, because I knew from twenty-eight years of experience that when she set her mind on something, stopping her was like getting in the way of a speeding freight train with no brakes.

So many emotions swirled inside of me that I had trouble separating one from another. I could recognize the fear, though, fear that Livy would be ripped from my daily life. I'd loved that little girl so much right from the day she was born, but since I'd become her guardian and had taken care of her each day, my love for her had grown to the point that my heart often felt like it could burst right open. I loved her so much that it physically hurt at times.

Of course, that meant I always wanted to do what was best for her, even if it pained me. But wasn't it best for her to be with the person my brother had wanted her to live with? Yes, Ethan had been ill when he'd made his wishes known, but although cancer riddled his body and was slowly leeching the life out of him, his mind was still working at full capacity, and I didn't doubt for a minute that having me be Livy's guardian was his true wish.

But what if he could see you now? a cruel voice whispered inside my head. *No job, almost broke, and an all-around hot mess. Would he still think you're the best guardian for his daughter?*

I burrowed my head deeper into my pillow, trying to silence that voice, but its words echoed in my brain, working their way into my heart, my bones, every part of my being.

The tears that my anger had held back for hours finally rushed free, spilling out onto my cheeks and soaking into my pillow. I was about to give in to full-out sobs when my bedroom door creaked open and a narrow beam of light danced around the room.

"Auntie Em?" Livy's voice sounded tiny and frightened.

I sat up like a shot, quickly wiping away my tears as the beam of her small flashlight danced away from me. "Livy? What's wrong, sweetie?"

"I'm scared."

Those words nearly ripped my heart in two.

"Can I sleep here with you?" she asked, a tremor in her voice.

"Of course, baby girl."

At those words, she clambered up onto the bed, crawling over my legs until she reached a spot where she could burrow under the blankets. She had her pink flashlight in one hand and her purple dino stuffie tucked under her other arm.

I took the flashlight from her and shut it off before setting it on the bedside table. Then I snuggled down with her, wrapping my arms around her.

"You're safe, Livysaurus. Did you have a bad dream?"

I felt more than saw her shake her head.

"Then what's wrong?"

She spoke in such a tiny, quiet voice that I had to strain to hear her. "I don't want you to die, Auntie Em."

"Oh, sweetie." I fought off another wave of tears. "I'm not going anywhere."

I knew I couldn't guarantee that I'd be around for a long time—my brother hadn't made it to age thirty-two, and Livy's mom had died in a car accident at an even younger age—but my niece needed that promise, and I wasn't going to hold it back from her.

"But Grandma asked if I wanted to live with her and Grand-dad. When I came to live with you, it was because Daddy died. So if I have to live with them, does that mean you're going to die?"

I hugged her tighter, grief and anger and heartbreak whirling in a fierce storm inside me. How could my mom bring Livy into this? How could she place a cloud of uncertainty over this little girl's head when what she needed most of all was stability?

I wanted to scream and cry and never let go of my niece, but instead I pressed a kiss to her temple.

"Grandma only asked you that because she loves you so much and would like to have you with her all the time. Not because I'm going to die."

"Promise?"

My heart squeezed. "I promise."

Livy fell silent for a moment. I thought she might be drifting off to sleep, but then she spoke again. "Auntie Em, I love Grandma and Granddad, but I really love you too."

The ache in my chest nearly stole my breath away. "I know, sweetie. And we all love you. So much."

"But I want to stay here with you. Will Grandma be mad?"

I kissed her head. "She won't be mad at you, sweetie. Not one bit."

She tightened her hold on her stuffie. "And you're not mad?"

"Of course not. How could I be mad at my sweet little Livysaurus?" I tickled her, and she giggled, the sound soothing my soul. "Do you think you can sleep now?"

She nodded and nestled her head against my shoulder. "Just don't leave."

"I won't leave," I promised.

I shut my eyes and fought back yet another wave of tears.

CHAPTER
TWENTY-THREE

If the zombie look were in style, I would have been the height of fashion the next day. I spent the night holding Livy while I endured wave after wave of mixed emotions that left my mind and heart in far too tumultuous a state to get more than a few minutes of sleep here and there. While getting Livy ready for school, I moved about as fast as molasses in January. I got her there just in time, and I counted that as a win.

When I got back to the Mirage, I wandered the hallways like a lonely ghost. I absolutely did not want to focus on my own troubles, so I figured I should work on keeping my promise to Mrs. Nagy. The problem was that I didn't know what to do next, and I didn't have my team around to help me out. Jemma was working and Theo was at school, so I wouldn't see them for hours, if at all that day. My fingers itched with the temptation to text Wyatt, but I resisted. After the bomb my mom had dropped on me, I needed a Wyatt-shaped complication in my life even less than before.

As I wandered down the third-floor corridor, the sound of voices drifted toward me. I turned a corner and saw that the door to Rosario's apartment stood open. When I reached it, I peeked inside. Rosario sat at a card table with Carmen Álvarez, Leona Lavish, and Bitty Dover.

The four women were in the middle of a card game, and there were two bowls of snacks on the table, pushed to the corners to leave a clear space in the center.

"Your turn, Leona," Rosario said. She had a pad of paper and a pencil on the table beside her. Her silver pineapple earrings swayed whenever she moved her head, and her chin-length hair was held back by a stretchy band of blue fabric.

With a flourish, Leona set a card face up in the middle of the table. "Ten of clubs, darlings." She fiddled with the jewels at her throat. "You know, when I was on *Passion City,* I had this sizzling casino scene—"

"Your turn, Bitty," Carmen said loudly, bulldozing Leona into silence.

I think everyone else present appreciated that. I certainly had no desire to know what Leona had been up to on a blackjack table, even if it wasn't for real.

The former soap opera star glared at Carmen, but then she caught sight of me hovering in the doorway.

"Emersyn, darling," she trilled. "Do tell us what delicious dirt you've dug up on Freddie."

"Oh." I continued to hover. "I didn't mean to intrude."

Carmen waved off my apology. "You're hardly intruding. Draw up a chair. I'm sure we'd all like to hear how the investigation is going."

The other ladies nodded and murmured their agreement.

Wincing, I crossed the threshold into the apartment. I grabbed a spare chair from the kitchen and pulled it up so I could sit between Rosario and Carmen. As I did so, I glanced toward the credenza, but I couldn't tell if the dart-pierced drawing of Freddie was still behind it.

"Does everyone in the building know I'm looking into the murder?" I asked.

"Probably not everyone." Leona sighed and drew the cards in the middle of the table toward her while Rosario marked down the scores.

I suspected they were playing Hearts.

Carmen tipped her head to one side and made a sound of disagreement. "I'd say pretty much everyone."

So much for my hope to fly under the radar.

"I'm afraid I might end up disappointing everyone," I confessed. "Mrs. Nagy most of all. I don't think I'm cut out for this detective stuff."

"You just need to remember what my dear cousin Princess Di used to say." Bitty sat up straighter before quoting, "'Nothing is impossible. The word itself says, "I'm possible!"'"

"Wasn't it Audrey Hepburn who said that?" Carmen asked.

Bitty's lips formed a thin line. "Perhaps Audrey took it from my cousin."

All the other ladies rolled their eyes as they pushed their cards toward Rosario. Bitty liked to remind everyone at every opportunity that she was related to the late Princess Di. I didn't know if it was true or not, but Bitty seemed convinced.

Carmen turned her sharp eyes on me. "Do you have any suspects?"

"Um," I hedged, with a subtle glance at Rosario, who was now shuffling the deck. "I'm not sure I should reveal any details at this stage."

Leona tossed the end of her gauzy scarf over her shoulder. "Decent delivery, darling, but next time perhaps inject your words with a little more authority."

Leona didn't just love telling everyone about her former television roles, she also enjoyed dishing out acting advice. It didn't seem to matter if the recipients—like me—weren't actors.

Although maybe I needed to try acting more like a detective. Fake it till you make it and all that.

"Speaking of the murder," I said as the ladies started another round of the card game. "Were any of you in the building the morning that Freddie was killed?"

"Ooh!" Leona exclaimed with relish. "Are we all suspects? I wouldn't mind being questioned by that dishy blond detective."

"Oh, for God's sake, woman." Carmen's tone could have out-scorched the sun. "Take a cold shower and play a card."

"I was at the pharmacy, picking up my prescriptions," Bitty broke in. "Before that, I had breakfast with my granddaughter. By the time I arrived home, the police were everywhere. I do wish my granddaughter would carry herself with more poise. I mean, *really*. Rings in her nose and studs in her eyebrows! It's not really a look befitting our status as relatives of the Spencer family. I wanted to give her my hummingbird brooch so she could add some sophistication to her appearance, but I haven't been able to find it." She looked a little distressed as she fingered one of the buttons on her cardigan.

"You lost that too?" Rosario asked. "Did you ever find the cameo necklace you misplaced?"

"Not yet," Bitty replied, her gray eyes troubled, "but it must be in my apartment somewhere."

Carmen steered the conversation back on track. "I was home all morning. I didn't leave my apartment until I heard the sirens and saw the police cars out on the street."

"What about you, Rosario?" I asked, hoping the question sounded casual.

She played a card. "I was out all morning. My sweet little Zeus was under the weather, so I took him to the vet. They were already behind, so we had to wait nearly half an hour before we saw the doctor. I came home to find the police crawling all over the building."

"Zeus being . . . ?" I prompted, wondering if she'd admit to the type of pets she had in her unit.

"A snake, dear," Carmen answered for her. "Why on God's green earth anyone would choose a snake as a pet, I really don't understand."

"We'll all be crushed to death in our sleep!" Leona exclaimed, pressing bejeweled fingers to her chest. "Oh, the peril!"

"Scarlet kingsnakes are harmless," Rosario said sharply.

I wondered if the other ladies thought Rosario had only the one snake or if they knew she had several. Leona must have at least suspected that there was more than one reptile, considering the arguments she'd heard between Rosario and Freddie.

"What time did you leave the building?" I asked Rosario. "Did you see anything suspicious on your way out? Somebody hanging around the lobby maybe?"

Another round of the game had ended, so Rosario pushed her cards over to Carmen, who shuffled the deck.

Then Rosario considered—or at least pretended to consider—the question. "I didn't see anyone. And I must have left around nine o'clock in the morning because Zeus's appointment was scheduled for nine-fifteen."

I made a mental note of that information. I'd have to get Theo to check the video surveillance footage to confirm the time of Rosario's departure.

If, in fact, Rosario was telling the truth, then she had an alibi for the time of the murder, leaving the spotlight of suspicion shining fully on Hoffman. I wanted her to have a solid alibi because I didn't want the killer to be someone living in the building with us, but the thought that Hoffman could very possibly be a murderer still set off a squidgy feeling in my stomach.

I thought about the eyelash Theo found in Freddie's apartment. Keeping my eyes on Leona, I asked, "Do any of you know if Freddie had a woman in his life?"

Leona let out a gusty laugh that was more than a little over-the-top. "Freddie wasn't much of a head turner, although I suppose some people do have to settle for less than movie-star good looks."

It was clear from her tone that she didn't consider herself such a person.

I glanced around at the other ladies. Carmen rolled her eyes, but it was Rosario who caught my interest. She pressed so hard while marking down the latest scores that the end of the pencil snapped. I noticed a hint of pink in her cheeks as she made a sound of frustration and jumped up to fetch a pencil sharpener from across the room.

Interesting.

I really would have to check out that alibi because, at the moment, I wasn't sure I bought it.

"Rosario," I said once she'd returned to the table, "I got the impression that maybe Freddie was . . . special to you."

Her eyes grew almost comically wide. "Where—what—why would you think that?" she sputtered.

"I don't know." I pretended to be confused. "I thought I heard someone say you were seeing him."

"Pishposh!" Carmen gave a dismissive flick of her hand. "Rosario has more sense than that."

Rosario nodded as if both agreeing with and thanking Carmen for her support, but her cheeks had turned a brighter shade of pink, and there was a fearful, hunted look in her eyes.

"Did anyone have any conflicts with Freddie in recent weeks?" I asked, wondering if Rosario would admit to her arguments with the victim. "Anyone you haven't already mentioned," I added quickly when I saw Leona about to speak, her eyes fixed firmly on Rosario.

Leona snapped her mouth shut and appeared to be giving my qualified question some thought.

"There was that incident with Minnie," Bitty offered.

Carmen dealt the cards. "But Minnie wouldn't hurt a fly."

"Oh, I wouldn't be so sure of that." Rosario picked up her new hand of cards and fanned them out. "Our sweet Minnie definitely has a dark side."

CHAPTER
TWENTY-FOUR

Leona gasped. "Not darling Minnie!"

Bitty piped up. "As my cousin Princess Diana used to say, 'In order for the light to shine so brightly, the darkness must be present.'"

Rosario glanced up from the cards in her hand, confusion drawing her slim eyebrows together. "Wasn't that Sir Francis Bacon?"

"It was," Carmen confirmed with a regal nod.

Bitty's voice took on an acerbic tone. "He was probably quoting dear Diana."

"Bacon died in the seventeenth century," Carmen pointed out, her words positively caustic. "Are you suggesting he was a time-traveling quote thief?"

"What exactly do you mean?" I jumped in, directing the question at Rosario in hopes of stopping the brewing argument in its tracks. I really didn't feel like sitting there listening to the women bicker all day, especially now that Rosario had dangled that potentially tasty tidbit of information in front of me.

Fortunately, Bitty simply huffed before studying her cards. Carmen flicked her eyes heavenward and then did the same with her own cards.

"Oh," Rosario began as she and the other ladies each passed

three cards to the player on their right. "She bottles up her feelings until they explode out of her."

"Like the time she smashed her former neighbor's sunglasses after he left the dryer full of lint for the seventh time in a row," Bitty said.

Rosario nodded as she rearranged the cards in her hand. "Exactly. I tried to give her a healthier way to release her emotions, particularly as they related to Freddie."

"Okay, but what sort of feelings did she have about Freddie and why?" I asked.

"You know Minnie's an artist," Carmen said before asking, "Who's got the two of clubs?"

"That's me," Leona announced, placing the card face up in the middle of the table.

"Right. I've seen some of her work," I said.

"We were all at Shanahan's Suds one evening last week," Carmen continued, referring to a pub located a couple of blocks away. "Freddie had a few drinks in him."

Bitty played a card. "When didn't he?"

"He started ridiculing Minnie's work," Rosario said. "Loudly. Everyone in the pub heard him."

Leona gave a dramatic shudder. "It was ghastly!"

"Was Minnie there?" I asked.

"Oh, yes," Carmen replied.

Rosario clicked her tongue. "Poor thing. She sort of shrank into herself, and her face turned red. I got her out of there, but she was already so humiliated and angry by that point."

I felt a pang of sympathy for Minnie, until I reminded myself that she might have killed Freddie. "So how did you help her release her emotions?" *And did it involve a croquet mallet?* I added silently.

"We played a game of darts." Rosario selected a card from her hand and added it to the small pile in the middle of the table. "With Freddie's face as the board."

Bitty sighed and drew the trick—which contained the queen of spades—toward her.

Rosario made a note on the scoresheet. "Minnie drew a great likeness of Freddie, and we pinned it to the dartboard. You should have seen her hurtling the darts. She got him right in the eyes."

That explained the hole-riddled portrait. But had Rosario enjoyed the game as much as Minnie? Had she found that she still had some simmering anger that the darts hadn't cooled?

Checking on Rosario's alibi really needed to be my next task.

Now I had to add Minnie's name to my suspect list. Maybe throwing darts at Freddie's portrait didn't give her enough of a release. Maybe her anger had bubbled over later or had been reawakened by further comments from Freddie.

In my mind's eye, I saw a furious Minnie grab Mr. Nagy's confiscated croquet mallet from Freddie's office and swing it at the super's head.

I winced.

Minnie wasn't a tall woman, but she probably could have reached Freddie's head with the mallet. The angle of the blow might give the police an idea of the assailant's height, but I didn't have that kind of evidence to work with.

I stood up from my seat. "Thanks for talking with me, ladies. Enjoy the rest of your game."

They all called out their goodbyes as I left. I'd made it only a few steps down the hall before Rosario called my name. I turned back to see her rushing after me.

"Emersyn," she whispered when she reached me, "did you have a specific reason for asking if Freddie had a woman in his life?"

"Oh . . ." I tried to think of a way of answering without letting on that I'd been in his apartment.

Rosario solved the problem by not giving me a chance to respond. "It's just . . . I'm hoping you and your colleague can be discreet."

"You and Freddie were . . . ?"

Rosario's cheeks flushed. "It wasn't serious or anything, and it didn't last long because he was a jerk about my snakes, but I'd rather the other ladies didn't know."

I couldn't blame her for that, especially after Leona's comments.

"Did you lose a false eyelash recently?" I asked.

The question took her by surprise. "Yes, actually. I did have one go missing."

"I don't think there's any need for the other residents to know about you and Freddie."

She relaxed with relief. "Oh, thank you, Emersyn."

Leona called out Rosario's name from inside the apartment.

She glanced that way. "I'd better get back to the game."

"Rosario," I said to stop her from leaving. "Which vet clinic do you use?" When I saw her puzzled expression, I quickly added, "I'm thinking of getting Livy a pet."

She smiled. "South Paws. All the doctors there are fabulous. I hope you find the killer soon!" She hurried back into her unit.

Did she really want me to find the murderer?

Only if she wasn't the culprit.

With a plan taking shape in my head, I pulled out my phone on my way to the elevator.

A notification alerted me to a new text message.

From Wyatt.

Ready to compare notes?

I stopped in the middle of the hallway, staring at the message, my thumb hovering over it.

No, I typed out.

Then I deleted that and wrote, *Yes.*

My thumb hovered over the SEND button.

Then I deleted that word too.

I shoved my phone back into my pocket.

Clearly, my brain wasn't up to the onerous task of responding to a simple text message.

Although maybe the real problem was that nothing to do with Wyatt felt simple.

Not that anything in my life felt simple at the moment.

Once seated on my couch, I took out my phone again, but this time to search for the address for the South Paws Veterinary Clinic. It was located within walking distance of the Mirage. Ignoring Wyatt's message—which seemed to call to me like a siren singing to a doomed sailor—I sent a text to Theo instead.

Then I killed some time by looking at online job boards, which didn't exactly help to boost my mood, and by doing some actual cleaning rather than just the rushed tidying I'd done before my parents had brought Livy home the day before.

As I put away the cleaning supplies and stretched out my back, my thoughts threatened to stray into dangerous territory again. I scrunched my eyes shut and forced the thoughts, and all their accompanying feelings, into a dark corner. I'd become quite good at that over the past year or so.

The door buzzer sounded, putting me instantly on edge. Had my mother decided to show up unexpectedly in the hope of gaining an edge?

I pressed the intercom button. "Yes?"

"Package for Emersyn Gray," a man said.

With relief, I buzzed him into the building.

I opened the door to wait for him, wondering what could be in the package. I didn't recall ordering anything recently. It wasn't like I had money to spend on any extras lately.

I darted back inside to check my phone. Nope. No emails about orders being shipped.

The delivery guy appeared in the open doorway, so I set aside my phone.

"Emersyn?" he asked as he approached.

I smiled. "That's me."

"Sign here, please." He held out his e-signature device.

I signed with my finger, and he jutted his chin at a box leaning against the wall next to the door. "It's all yours."

I peeked around the doorframe and saw how big the box was. "But—"

The delivery guy disappeared into the stairwell at a jog.

"What the . . ." I stepped out into the hall and stood staring at the box that had to be five feet wide and nearly four feet tall. The package was probably only four inches deep, but still. I hadn't ordered *anything* recently and certainly not something the size of . . . whatever this was.

I checked the shipping label. Sure enough, it had my name and address on it.

With a few grunts and a colorful word or two, I maneuvered the cumbersome package into my apartment and sliced it open with a box cutter.

There was no note inside telling me who'd sent the parcel, but I didn't need one.

As soon as I saw the large whiteboard and the accompanying markers and magnets, I knew exactly what it was meant to be:

A murder board.

I sighed as one name came to mind:

Theo.

CHAPTER
TWENTY-FIVE

"We're done here." Theo slid her laptop into her backpack, which she then hung from the handles of her wheelchair.

"Ready, Livy?" I asked my niece.

She slurped up the last of her chocolate milk and bounced out of her chair. "Ready!"

I helped her into her coat, and the three of us left the café that was conveniently situated two doors down from South Paws Veterinary Clinic.

Outside, Livy ran ahead a short distance, picking up a bright red-and-orange maple leaf that the blustery wind had carried from somewhere other than the treeless street we were on. The gray October day called for a jacket, but I'd left the Mirage with nothing more than a sweater.

In accordance with our text exchange, Theo had met us at the café with her computer so she could try to hack into the vet clinic's security camera footage to confirm—or shatter—Rosario's alibi. I'd asked her ahead of time not to mention what she was doing or why when Livy was around. So we'd simply told my niece that Theo was working on a project.

"Any success?" I whispered to Theo while Livy was ahead of us.

"Of course." She shook her head as we continued along the

sidewalk. "Someone should tell the clinic that their system has a whole list of vulnerabilities. Their security is like Swiss cheese."

"But did you get what we need?" I pressed.

"Rosario was there when she said she was. She wasn't anywhere near the Mirage when Freddie was killed."

That was some progress, at least.

I scratched Rosario from my mental list of suspects.

That left Hoffman and Minnie.

"So, about your ex," Theo said. "If you want, I could hack into his bank account and get your money transferred back to you."

"You could seriously do that?" I asked, shocked and a little awed. "What are they teaching you at that school of yours?"

Her smile had a mischievous tilt to it. "I learn the best things *outside* of school. And, yes, I can totally do it. Tonight, maybe, if my parents aren't hovering."

"Not so fast," I said. "I can't let you do that. It's illegal."

"It was illegal for him to steal from you."

"Sure, but I'm not having you break the law on my behalf. Thank you," I added firmly, "but it's a no."

As much as I wanted and needed my money back, that was an easy decision. I didn't want Theo getting into serious trouble for trying to help me. As soon as Hoffman realized that the money had been taken from his account, he'd know that I was somehow involved. He'd probably spin a good story for the police—with him as the sole victim—and Theo and I would end up behind bars while he remained free as a bird.

"Fine," Theo muttered, clearly disappointed.

Thinking of Hoffman and my suspects in general reminded me of the surprise I'd received earlier.

"A package arrived for me today," I said. "One I didn't order."

"Good." Her frown morphed into a smile. "Now we're real detectives."

I was pretty sure that a badge or license would make us real detectives, not a murder board.

"We can't keep it in my apartment," I said, my voice low. "I don't want Livy seeing it." Or my mother, for that matter.

"Then we'll stash it in the laundry room."

"We can't leave our murder board where anyone and their uncle could find it!"

"Well, we definitely can't have it at my grandparents' place. They've got no clue what I do when I'm out of their sight, and I want to keep it that way." As Livy skipped back to join us, Theo whispered, "Stash it under your bed. She'll never know."

Livy held up the leaf for me to see. "Look, Auntie Em. Isn't it pretty?"

"It's beautiful, sweetheart."

She took my hand and continued to skip as I walked and Theo wheeled.

"Theo, why are you in a wheelchair?" my niece asked.

"Livy," I scolded, "it's not polite to ask things like that."

"I don't care," Theo said with a shrug. "I was born with something called cerebral palsy. It makes my legs not work a hundred percent."

"But they work a little?" Livy asked.

"A little," Theo confirmed.

When we turned the corner, I spotted Wyatt sitting on the front steps of the Mirage. He was hard to miss. So was his metallic green car, parked half a block away.

"Oh, shhh—sugar." I barely caught myself before swearing in front of Livy.

"What's wrong?" she asked, looking up at me.

"Nothing," I said quickly.

Theo grinned in a way I could only describe as wicked when she noticed Wyatt. "Should I leave the two of you to debrief alone?"

"Definitely not."

Wyatt got to his feet when he saw us approaching. An olive-green military-style jacket hugged his delicious frame.

It would be even better to see him out of it, and everything else, the evil part of my brain piped up.

"Shush." I realized I'd spoken out loud when Theo sent a curious glance my way.

Livy giggled. "We're not talking."

"Hey," Wyatt said to the three of us, saving me from having to explain that I was shushing myself. He focused his coal-dark eyes on me. "I was hoping we could chat, but you didn't answer my text message."

"Right," I said. "Um. I wasn't sure about my schedule." Which wasn't a complete fib. It wasn't impossible that someone could have called me, offering me an interview that very day.

He raised an eyebrow. "So you're not avoiding me?"

"Why would I be avoiding you?"

Next to me, Theo only half succeeded at smothering a snicker. "Answering a question with a question. Classic avoidance."

"Who are you?" Livy asked, looking way up at Wyatt.

Standing two steps up as he was, he towered over all of us.

"I'm Wyatt."

I didn't fail to notice that he hadn't provided a last name. Again.

Suspicious. Maybe he belonged on the murder board, but I really hoped he didn't.

Wyatt descended the last two stairs. "Who are you?"

"Livy. It's short for Olivia. Emersyn's my auntie."

Wyatt's gaze flicked my way as he smiled at my niece.

Theo moved closer. "We haven't officially met yet. I'm Theo, and I'm in charge of administration at Wyatt Investigations."

"She's got a file on you," I said before he had a chance to comment.

In the space of a single second, his expression morphed from surprised to worried to curious. "Can I see it?"

"You'll have to ask the HR department." I smiled as I echoed what Theo had told me earlier.

Before Wyatt had a chance to question my statement, a noisy truck rumbled by, making further conversation impossible for several seconds. A damp gust of wind sent dry leaves hurtling down the street, and a few drops of rain pattered down around us.

"Let's debrief inside," Theo suggested once the truck had passed us. Actually, it sounded more like an order than a suggestion.

She took the ramp off to the side of the staircase, and Livy ran that way with her. Wyatt and I took the stairs. I deliberately hung back a pace so he wouldn't see me as I desperately ran my hands through my hair, hoping I didn't look like too much of a mess. I hadn't bothered checking my reflection in the mirror before running out the door to meet Livy at her school.

Once I pulled out my keys and unlocked the Mirage's front door, Wyatt held it open for the three of us to pass through before him.

"Auntie Emersyn, can we play hide-and-seek?" Livy asked once we were in the lobby.

"Oh, hon, I don't know," I said, hating to disappoint her. "This might not be the best time."

"I love hide-and-seek," Theo said. "I'll play."

Livy jumped with excitement. "Yes! And you too, right, Auntie Em?"

"I need to talk to Wyatt, sweetie," I said, "but maybe after."

Wyatt grinned at my niece. "We can multitask. Who's it?"

"I am!" Theo declared.

I stopped Livy before she could take off at a run. "This floor only, okay? And Freddie's office is off-limits."

I hadn't yet told her that Freddie was dead, and I didn't want her seeing any bloodstains that might still be on the floor.

"Don't worry," Theo said. "The office is locked."

Did she know that because she'd tried the door? Had she picked the lock and snooped inside? Did I even want to know?

Livy slid her arms out of the straps of her backpack. "Can you hold my bag, Auntie Em?"

"Hang it on the back of my chair," Theo offered. "It'll fit over my bag."

"Thanks!" Livy hooked her nearly empty backpack on top of Theo's.

"Better get ready to hide," Theo advised us. "I'm counting to fifty." She placed her hands over her eyes and started to count out loud.

Livy let out an adorable squeak and took off at a run, heading down the corridor to the right. I skirted around the lobby's marble goddess statue and took the hallway leading into the wing that had once housed the hotel's ballroom, restaurant, and kitchen. Those spaces had since been broken up into apartments and a common area, but thanks to previous games I'd played with Livy, I knew of a place where I could hide.

I realized that Wyatt was keeping pace with me. "What are you doing?" I asked.

"Same as you," he replied.

I opened a door.

Wyatt peeked over my shoulder into the dark cubbyhole of a space. "What's this?"

"It's the old dumbwaiter shaft, but the dumbwaiter's long gone, so it's empty now." And the bottom of the shaft was right in front of me.

Fortunately, the shaft had housed a full-height dumbwaiter, so I didn't have to stoop to get through the narrow door. I slipped into the small space and reached for the doorknob. I almost got a handful of Wyatt's jacket instead.

"This is my hiding spot," I said as he followed me in.

"How can we compare notes if we're in two different places?"

I was about to shove him out into the corridor when I had second thoughts. I probably shouldn't trust him alone with Livy when I barely knew him and had no evidence to prove that he wasn't a killer, even though I really didn't think he was one. And how could

I make sure he wasn't alone with my niece if I didn't know where either of them was?

In my moment of hesitation, I heard Theo call out, "Ready or not, here I come!"

Wyatt squeezed in next to me, and I pulled the door shut. As soon as the darkness closed in around us, I seriously questioned my sanity.

CHAPTER
TWENTY-SIX

The old dumbwaiter shaft was so narrow that there was barely room for the both of us in there. My right shoulder was touching Wyatt's chest, and my skin suddenly felt more sensitive, as if every square inch of it were aware of his proximity. My fingers twitched with the knowledge that his hand was likely mere inches from mine, well within grasping distance.

This, I knew without a doubt, was a terrible idea.

And not just because I couldn't prove that Wyatt wasn't Freddie's killer.

I had serious doubts about his possible guilt—call it a gut instinct—but no doubts at all about the fact that I found him ridiculously attractive.

The urge to flee wrestled with the temptation to move closer to Wyatt. My flight response got the upper hand, and I grabbed the doorknob and tried to turn it. It wouldn't budge. I rattled it and shoved my shoulder against the door, but it remained stubbornly shut.

"Did you lock this thing?" I asked.

"I don't have a key. And why would I do that?"

I ran my fingers over the doorknob. Sure enough, it wasn't the kind that could be locked from the inside. It was just plain old stuck. I gave it another jiggle, to no avail.

"I'll have a go." Wyatt's hand searched for the doorknob and found my fingers instead.

I sucked in a breath at his touch and let go of the doorknob. Wyatt's hand fell away from mine.

"Sorry," he said.

"S'okay." I barely recognized my breathless voice as my own.

He turned the doorknob and gave the whole door a good shake. Theo's voice drifted down the hall. "I'm going to find you!"

I grabbed Wyatt's hand to stop him from rattling the door. "Shh!"

I wasn't sure why it felt so important to not let Theo find us. Maybe I wanted to prove to myself that the seventeen-year-old wasn't better than me at everything in life.

We fell still, listening for any signs of Theo's approach. Silence rang around us, making me hyperaware of my every breath, and Wyatt's too. When I realized I was still holding his hand, I dropped it like a hot potato. My heart absolutely wasn't thudding in reaction to the feel of his skin against mine.

A few more seconds ticked by.

"Should we continue?" Wyatt asked.

"Continue what?"

My brain—probably delirious—shouted possible answers at me. *Holding hands? Getting acquainted? Smooshing closer until our bodies are plastered together?*

Maybe it was my imagination, but the temperature in the cubbyhole seemed to shoot up several degrees.

"Debriefing," Wyatt replied.

"Oh." My shoulders, which had inched up toward my ears, lowered. From relief or from disappointment, I wasn't quite sure. "Right. Sorry. It's a little hard to think while . . . um . . . playing a game."

"Not a multitasker then." I could hear the amusement in his voice.

"I can multitask! It's just . . ." I huffed, not wanting to disclose the real reason my brain was more scattered than usual. "Never mind. You go first."

"All right." Wyatt shifted slightly in the darkness. "Freddie has a criminal record. Fraud. Dealing in stolen goods. But nothing from the past five years. He spent a lot of time at the local pool hall and various bars in the neighborhood. Some of his acquaintances are of questionable character, but so far, I haven't come across any recent conflicts with any of them. However, Freddie was seen meeting a man on a couple of occasions in the days before he died, a man no one I've talked to has been able to identify. One of those meetings took place at Shanahan's Suds."

I was a little annoyed with myself because it hadn't occurred to me to study Freddie as a person outside of his role as superintendent of the Deco Mirage.

Some of that annoyance came out in my voice. "How did you find out all that?"

"By asking around. And I called in a favor or two from former associates."

"Associates?" I echoed with suspicion. "What kind of associates?"

"I've got a background in security, remember?"

"What, exactly, does that mean?" I still had trouble picturing him as a bouncer or security guard.

"I worked for an executive protection agency."

It took a second for my brain to translate that into something more familiar. "You mean a bodyguard agency?"

"I guess you could call it that."

I wanted to ask why a rich guy like him, with a fancy car and a country club membership, worked at all. Maybe it was to fend off boredom. Or maybe he liked the pop stars and supermodels he probably got to work with.

Thinking about him associating with gorgeous female celebrities made me painfully aware of how ordinary I must seem in comparison. I tried to move away from him, but my back hit the rough wall, and something sharp jabbed into my skin near my right shoulder blade.

"Ow!" I tried to get away from the offending object but ended up pressed against Wyatt. "Sorry!"

I inched away from him, wary of what might be behind me. I was glad it was too dark for him to see my flaming cheeks. Embarrassment had sparked the fire in my face—and the rest of me—but not by itself. Even in the fleeting moment of contact, I'd noticed how perfectly our bodies fit together.

I will not think about that! I will not think about that! I repeated in my head.

Maybe it wasn't such a bad thing that the pain in my back was providing a distraction.

"What happened?" Wyatt asked.

"Something jabbed into my back." I tried to reach over my right shoulder with my left hand but came up short. "I think it might still be in there. Oh, God. Maybe it's a scorpion! Is it a scorpion?"

I had to put all my energy into not panicking.

"Not too likely here in New York." Wyatt woke up his phone, bathing us in blue light. Then he switched on the flashlight app. "Is it all right if I take a look?"

Even though I'd moved away from him, there were still only a few inches separating us, and I had to tilt my chin up to see his face. He held my gaze as he waited for my answer.

"Yes," I said, telling myself that my heart was galloping simply because of whatever venomous creature might be latched on to my back and absolutely not because of the man sharing my personal space.

I gathered my hair over my left shoulder and drew in a shaky breath as Wyatt moved so close that I could have nestled my face into the crook of his neck. I inhaled his scent, which reminded me of fresh air and the great outdoors. It left me lightheaded.

"Can I . . . ?" Wyatt asked, the hand not holding his phone now hovering close to my neck.

It was simply my overactive imagination thinking I could feel his body heat against my skin, right?

I nodded and used my left hand to slide my loose, wide-neck sweater down my arm, exposing my right shoulder and part of my upper back. The air buzzed between us, and my every breath suddenly felt amplified. I tried to turn but could move only a few inches. Wyatt's chest touched my shoulder as he leaned in close to get a look at my back with the aid of the light from his phone.

This time it wasn't my imagination. I could definitely feel the delicious warmth of his body seeping through my thin sweater.

"Hmm," he said in a way that set off alarm bells in my head. "Maybe I was wrong about the scorpion thing."

"What?!"

He laughed, and I felt the rumble of it in my arm, which was still pressed against his chest. "Just kidding. It's a splinter."

"That was so not funny," I grumbled.

"Sorry," he whispered, not sounding at all contrite. He spoke the word so close to my ear that his breath tickled my skin in a way that sent a shiver through my body, one he couldn't have failed to notice.

I heard him inhale deeply, like he was breathing in my scent. Then his warm fingers touched the skin on my back, lighting a fire along my spine.

"I think I can . . ." He paused, and I felt the tiniest sting by my shoulder blade. "Yep. Got it." He ran his thumb over the spot, and the heat simmering in my back shot through my bloodstream, invading every part of me. "No blood," he declared. "It just pierced a layer or two of skin."

"Thank you," I whispered. I hadn't meant to speak so quietly, but his touch had snatched my breath away.

He shut off the flashlight app, but his phone still gave off a bluish light.

I let my hair fall down my back as he shifted the sleeve of my sweater up my arm, his knuckles grazing my skin. He caught a lock of my hair as it swung into place and let it slide slowly through his fingers. I looked up at him, my chest rising and falling faster than normal. He met my gaze and his night-sky eyes seemed to glow with blue fire in the light from his phone.

All the nerve endings near the surface of my skin buzzed like they were overloading.

I could have sworn electricity crackled in the air around us. I half expected to see sparks as Wyatt's phone went to sleep, plunging us into darkness.

"Emersyn." His voice was jagged with desire.

The sound of it untethered me from my misgivings and hesitancy.

I slid a hand up around his neck and pulled him down toward me. Except I didn't need to pull him, because as soon as my fingers made contact with his skin, his lips were there to meet mine, at first with gentle brushes and nudges, then with heat and hunger that stoked the flames burning inside me.

Something hit the floor with a thud, but neither of us paid any attention. I tangled my fingers in the hair at the nape of his neck.

Wyatt's hands slid down my sweater as he changed the angle of the kiss, sending me right to the edge of a chasm that was nothing but him. Nothing but us. I silently cursed the knitted strands of yarn between us, but then my sweater rode up and his fingers grazed my lower back, skin against skin. I gasped against his mouth, my eyes fluttering open. Our gazes locked in the darkness, fire on fire, then our lips found each other again. Wyatt deepened the kiss and tipped me over the edge of that chasm.

Light flared around us.

For the briefest of seconds, I thought we'd exploded like a supernova.

Then Wyatt let me slide slowly out of his grasp, and I landed with a jarring thud back in reality.

Theo sat outside the now-open door, grinning like a Cheshire cat. "Found you!"

CHAPTER
TWENTY-SEVEN

Flustered, I raked my fingers through my hair and adjusted my sweater. "We were just . . ."

My gaze bounced to Wyatt and away again. I couldn't look him in the eye without remembering the feel of his hands on me, without reliving the mind-blowing kiss that had left my lips tingling and my brain scattered. I could still feel trails of fire on my lower back where his fingers had run over my skin.

Theo smirked at us. "Debriefing?" she finished for me.

I stepped out of the cubbyhole. "Um . . . yes." I scowled when Theo's smirk didn't disappear. "Took you long enough to find us."

She spun her wheelchair around. "I knew where you were ages ago, but I thought you might want a little more time for *debriefing*."

Wyatt retrieved his phone from the floor—the cause of the earlier thud, I presumed—and closed the door to the dumbwaiter shaft as he joined me out in the hall. His arm brushed against mine, sending sparks through my bloodstream that nearly overloaded my brain.

I scurried after Theo, who was rolling swiftly toward the lobby.

"Have you found Livy yet?" I asked.

Wyatt followed us with his long, easy strides, but—for the sake of my still-fuzzy brain—I refused to look his way.

"We're already on our second round of the game," Theo replied. "But I'm pretty sure I know where she's hiding."

Theo cruised through the lobby, heading for the hall that led back toward the courtyard. She stopped outside the first of two indoor phone booths, relics from the Mirage's heyday as a glitzy hotel in the 1920s. She opened the door and peeked inside. By that time, I'd reached her side and could see that the booth was empty.

She rolled up to the next booth. This time, when she opened the door, giggles burst out.

"Found you!" Theo declared in triumph, reminding me of the moment she'd found Wyatt and me.

I begged my cheeks not to flush, but they ignored me.

Livy sprang up from a crouch and darted out of the booth. She ran for the lobby, Theo following in her wake.

My cheeks warm, I shut the door to the phone booth, looking anywhere but at Wyatt.

"It's your turn next," he said.

His words startled me into facing him. "But I initiated the first kiss!"

A slow grin took shape on his face, and heat flashed in his eyes. "I'm happy to take turns with that too, but I was talking about sharing information."

Now my cheeks weren't just on fire, they'd been inhabited by two suns, each burning hot enough to destroy the entire solar system.

"Ha!" I tried to sound amused, but the sound came out crazed. "I knew that!" One look at his grin and I could tell he saw right through me. "Okay, so I didn't," I confessed in a rush. "But . . . um . . . where were we?"

"The dumbwaiter shaft."

"I meant in our conversation!"

The laughter in his eyes told me that he'd known that full well. I walked briskly toward the lobby, trying desperately to get my brain functioning properly. "Never mind," I said as Wyatt walked with me. "Rosario López, aka Snake Lady, was on my suspect list—as you know—but she's got a solid alibi. I've got two other suspects: Hoffman Fisher and Minnie Yang."

"Minnie Yang hosted the cocktail party, right?" Wyatt said.

"She and her partner, Yolanda."

"So she lives in unit 211."

I stopped short. "Right above the dumpster. She could have disposed of the croquet mallet in two ways. Either she took it out into the alley and chucked it, or if she was worried about the security camera—which doesn't actually work—she could have taken it back to her apartment and dropped it into the dumpster from one of her windows."

"What's her motive?"

I resumed walking again, and Wyatt kept pace with me. "Freddie publicly ridiculed her artwork. She was humiliated and furious enough to use his portrait as a dartboard."

"I thought that was Rosario."

"They both played the game, for Minnie's benefit."

"Isn't Hoffman your ex?" When I glanced at Wyatt in surprise, he explained, "I heard you call him by name at the country club."

Another incident best forgotten.

Like that kiss.

Which I feared I'd never be able to forget.

I also feared that I was now doomed to compare every future kiss against that one and have them fall woefully short of measuring up.

Unless those future kisses were also with Wyatt.

My eyes strayed to his lips, and I had to force myself to look straight ahead again.

Livy bounced into view, providing me with a distraction that I desperately needed. She was using the padded benches in the lobby as a parkour course, with Theo cheering her on. Normally, I'd tell my niece not to jump on the furniture, but I thought it admirable that I was even still breathing, considering the state of my mind.

"Why would your ex kill Freddie?" Wyatt asked, and I appreciated that he kept his voice low enough that Livy wouldn't hear him. "Did they know each other?"

"Not that I'm aware of, but Hoffman was in the building around the time of the murder. And remember that smashed bottle at the crime scene? There was a label from a bottle of the same color in Hoffman's apartment, with broken glass stuck to the back. Freddie has an intact bottle in his apartment with the same kind of label."

"You were at your ex's apartment?" Wyatt asked. "Not that I'm judging."

"Not for *that*," I said quickly, hoping to set him straight. "He doesn't know I was there."

Livy took a flying leap off one of the benches and ran over my way.

"Auntie Em, look what I found." She opened her hand to reveal a cuff link.

The round fastener was studded with a three-by-three grid of square gems in shades of blue and green, with four tiny diamonds spaced evenly around the edge.

I'd seen the cuff link before, along with its matching partner.

A wave of queasiness crashed through my stomach at the memory. Overpowering cologne. Clammy hands on my arms.

My skin crawled, and anger simmered inside me.

"That was Freddie's," I said, my voice faint.

Livy tipped the cuff link into my palm. "You can give it back to him."

Light from the overhead chandelier—which was missing at least a quarter of its crystals—glinted off the cuff link, revealing the initials TR engraved into the silver.

Theo joined us. "His initials were FH, not TR."

"Maybe he inherited them." My voice still sounded weak. I gave myself a mental shake and spoke normally as I addressed Livy. "Where did you find it, sweetie?"

"In the phone booth."

I glanced back that way. "Freddie must have lost it."

"But we can give it back," Livy said again.

I rested a hand on her head. "We'll make sure it gets to the right person."

"What would Freddie have been doing in the phone booth?" Wyatt posed the question that was on my mind.

As a group, we moved in that direction. I tucked the cuff link into the pocket of my jeans, hoping that hiding it from my sight would rid me of the memory it triggered.

Wyatt opened the door to the phone booth, and we all stared inside. The booth was constructed from wood, with a window making up the top half of the door. What looked like the original plaque remained above the door, with the word TELEPHONE emblazoned on it, but the actual phone itself had been removed, leaving the narrow space empty.

Livy pointed at the back corner. "It was right there. On the floor."

I still couldn't think of any reason why Freddie would have been in the phone booth. Had he been hiding from someone? If so, why?

I stepped into the booth and gazed around. When I looked up, I noticed a water stain on the ceiling. I pointed it out to the others. "That's probably why Freddie was here." I looked down by my feet. The wooden floor was also marred by a water stain. "Water was leaking from somewhere up above. It dripped down and probably started trickling out into the hall, drawing Freddie's attention to the booth."

Livy squeezed inside with me. "Let's see how many of us can fit in here!"

"I'm not sure that's such a good idea, hon," I objected as gently as I could.

"Come on, Wyatt," Livy pleaded.

Theo nudged him with her elbow, her smile matching the evil light in her eyes. "Yes, Wyatt, you join Emersyn in there. You two seem to like sharing small spaces. Livy and I can occupy ourselves elsewhere."

"Nope! We're all coming out!" I scooted Livy out ahead of me.

In my haste, I knocked my elbow on the back wall of the booth. I heard a click from somewhere close behind me. Then Theo drew in a sharp breath.

I spun around, and my eyes widened.

Where seconds ago there had been a wall, there was now an open doorway leading into gaping darkness.

CHAPTER
TWENTY-EIGHT

"A secret door!" Theo exclaimed with wonder. "This is so cool!"

Livy shrank back until she was almost behind Theo's wheel-chair. "It looks scary. What's in there?"

"Only one way to find out." Theo's eyes gleamed with excitement.

I tugged my phone free from my pocket and switched on the flashlight app. Then I directed the light into the darkness beyond the secret door.

"There's a staircase," I told the others. "A short one. Then another door."

Wary of potential spiders and cobwebs, I stepped through the opening and onto the top stair.

"Don't go, Auntie Em," Livy pleaded.

I turned back. "I'm just going to have a peek," I said. "You wait here with Theo."

"I'll come with you," Wyatt said, stepping into the phone booth.

I led the way down the short staircase, shining my light around, noting that the dust on the stairs had been recently disturbed.

I half expected the door at the bottom of the staircase to be locked, but it opened easily when I put my hand on the knob. The door let out an ominous creak as it opened into a long, low-ceilinged room. The beam from my flashlight app danced over a light switch on the wall to my left. I flicked it on, not knowing if it would work, but sconces on the wall flickered to life, casting a warm glow over the room. I shut off the light on my phone.

"Don't leave us in suspense!" Theo called from out in the corridor.

I glanced at Wyatt, and he nodded. We retraced our steps to find Livy and Theo peering into the phone booth.

"Well?" Theo demanded as soon as Wyatt and I came into view.

"You've got to see what's down there," I said, unable to keep a note of excitement out of my voice. "It's a secret room."

"Is it scary?" Livy asked.

"Not at all," I assured her.

Theo frowned at the entrance to the phone booth. "My chair won't fit. Then there's the stairs." Her frown transformed into a smile as she looked up at Wyatt. "You look strong."

It took only a few seconds for Theo to get on Wyatt's back, with her arms around his neck and his arms looped under her legs. Livy took my hand, and we led the way down the short stairway and into the long room.

As soon as we crossed the threshold, Livy slipped her hand out of mine and wandered away, curiosity apparently replacing her apprehension.

"Whoa," Theo said as she and Wyatt entered the room.

I was just as awestruck. Before finding the light switch, I'd thought maybe we'd stumbled upon a dirty old cellar, the kind where no one but serial killers would hang out. I most definitely hadn't expected this.

Three of the room's four walls were exposed brick. Red-and-black damask wallpaper covered the fourth wall. In the corner to the right of the door was a small platform, which I suspected had been used as a stage. At the far end of the room, rickety-looking wooden stools lined a bar. The shelves on the brick wall behind the bar held dusty bottles in a variety of shapes, sizes, and colors.

As I walked slowly toward the bar, I took in the sight of photographs hanging crooked on the papered wall. Several showed dancers in this very room in 1920s outfits, and one depicted a three-piece band playing on the stage in the corner. The female singer wore a dazzling flapper dress and headband, with her hair styled in finger waves.

"Is this what I think it is?" I asked as I turned around.

Theo's eyes were wide behind her glasses as she gazed around from her vantage point on Wyatt's back.

"A speakeasy." She said the words almost reverently.

Livy climbed up onto one of the creaky barstools. "What's a speakeasy?"

"It's a place where people would go to drink alcohol and dance back when alcohol wasn't allowed," I explained.

"Alcohol? Like beer?"

"Beer and other drinks."

Livy wrinkled her nose. "I don't like the smell of beer."

"You can set me down," Theo said to Wyatt when they reached the bar.

"On one of the stools?" he asked.

"Maybe the chair." She indicated one of two chairs tucked beneath the nearest of a half dozen small round tables.

He carefully lowered her to the floor and then guided her into the chair.

"Do you think Freddie knew about this place?" she asked.

"Someone's been here recently," I said. "There were footprints on the stairs before we came down."

Wyatt let out a low whistle. He was behind the bar now, facing the bottles on the shelves, his back to the rest of us.

"What is it?" Theo asked eagerly.

"Someone might have been here recently, but this place must have been forgotten for a long time," he said.

I joined him behind the bar. "Why do you say that?"

"These bottles. They date back to the 1920s. Some even earlier."

"Maybe someone knew about them but didn't bother to get rid of them," Theo said.

"Maybe, if they didn't know what they were looking at," Wyatt conceded. "But some of these would be worth a lot of money these days." He tapped a brown bottle. "Like this whiskey. I wouldn't be surprised if someone would pay a few thousand dollars for it."

"Seriously?" I said with surprise.

Livy popped up between me and the shelves. "Look at this, Auntie Em."

She held up a small wicker basket. Inside was a vintage fountain pen, a lone pearl earring, and a single elbow-length glove.

"Where'd you find that?" I asked her.

She pointed to the lowest shelf. "Right there."

"The speakeasy's lost and found maybe?" I speculated.

"Can I see?" Theo called from the other side of the bar.

Livy scurried around to share her finds.

When I turned my attention back to the shelves of booze, I noticed something that gave me pause. I put a hand to Wyatt's arm, but when the warmth of his body reached my fingertips through the fabric of his jacket, I snatched my hand away again.

"Check this out." I pointed at a spot on the lowest shelf.

"What is it?" Theo asked.

"Circles," Wyatt answered, as he studied what I'd pointed out. "Six of them. Without dust."

"Somebody took six of the bottles!" Theo exclaimed.

"And not very long ago," I added.

I turned around and met Theo's gleaming eyes.

"You know what this means, right?" she asked.

I glanced at Livy, who was at the other end of the room now, looking at the photos on the wall.

I lowered my voice so my niece wouldn't hear me. "We might have found a motive for murder."

CHAPTER
TWENTY-NINE

"So you really do think Hoffman could be the killer?" Jemma asked me the next morning.

I settled into the reclining chair at one of the hair-washing stations at the salon where she worked. The salon wouldn't open for another hour, so we had the place to ourselves, which meant we could talk freely.

"The evidence is hard to ignore," I said.

Jemma wrapped a towel around my shoulders and eased me back into the neck rest, making sure that my hair hung down into the sink instead of getting trapped beneath me. "I knew he was a first-class turd, but a murderer? I didn't see that coming. Not until we watched the surveillance video, anyway."

"Same."

I'd already shared the previous day's discoveries with Jemma as she fluffed out my hair, studying it from all angles as she always did before starting a cut, even if it was simply a trim like I wanted today.

Now she turned on the water. "So, what are you going to do?"

"I have to take what I know to the police," I said without enthusiasm. "Hoffman will know I snitched on him and will hold it against me forever. I probably didn't have much chance of getting my money back from him before, but if I did, I can kiss that chance goodbye now."

"Not necessarily." Jemma aimed the spray of warm water at my hair. "You should tell the cops about the theft too."

"What's the point? It didn't do any good when I reported it before," I said. "Hoffman was too sneaky, routing the money through an offshore account. Probably through multiple accounts. I couldn't prove it was him. Plus, the officer I talked to basically told me the theft was my fault because I didn't keep my password secret enough. But you know I can't remember passwords. If I didn't write them down, I'd be locked out of everything."

Jemma massaged shampoo into my hair. "I still think you should bring it up."

I sighed and closed my eyes. "Maybe I will."

"But now for the most important part." She turned on the sprayer again and washed away the suds. "How was investigating with Wyatt?"

I couldn't see her face, but I could hear the eyebrow waggle in her voice.

"It was . . . interesting?" I tried to keep at bay the memories that wanted to rush to the front of my mind. The dumbwaiter incident was best left undiscussed.

"That's all you've got for me?"

Who was I kidding? I wanted to tell my bestie everything.

"Okay, so a hell of a lot more than interesting," I confessed.

Jemma drew in a sharp breath. "Emersyn Gray, are you holding out on me?"

"We kissed. And I'm not talking a chaste peck on the lips."

She let out a squeal and dropped the sprayer. Water shot up into the air and rained down on my face.

"Jemma!" I raised my head and grabbed the towel from around my neck to wipe my face.

I had my eyes closed when she grabbed my hand and yanked

me up out of the reclined chair, pulling me into a bone-crushing—and slightly damp—hug.

"Water's going everywhere!"

"It can be cleaned up." She gave me another squeeze, nearly snapping my ribs, before she released me. Then she shut off the water and grabbed another towel. She wiped it over the seat and shoved me back down into the chair. "Tell me everything. Every detail. How hot was it?"

"On a scale of chili peppers?" I settled back into the neck rest. "We're talking habanero hot."

Jemma squealed again. I scrunched my eyes shut, but this time she maintained control of the sprayer and kept the water aimed solely at my hair. "I'm so happy for you, Emersyn!"

"Don't get too excited," I cautioned. "It's not like it's going to happen again."

I silently sobbed inside at that thought.

"What?!" Jemma shut off the water. "Have you lost your ever-loving mind?"

"The opposite, actually. I can't deny the attraction, and I can't deny that he's a freaking amazing kisser." Even that was an understatement. "But there's nothing else between us. It's purely physical. No emotional connection."

"So?"

I heard the squirt of the bottle a second before she began massaging conditioner into my hair.

I tried to figure out how to explain my jumbled thoughts and feelings. "That's not what I'm looking for at this stage in my life. I'm not even looking for a relationship, but if I'm going to have one, I want it to be meaningful. I want it to have a chance of really going somewhere."

"Maybe there will be an emotional connection if you give him a chance."

"I don't know, Jem. We're from completely different worlds. I'm not a country club kind of girl. Hobnobbing with the Tiffanys of the world? No, thanks."

"Not all rich people are like Hoffman's latest target," Jemma pointed out.

"No," I agreed, "but I'd never fit into that world. I'm not sure I'd even want to."

Jemma rinsed the conditioner from my hair. "Maybe he's not even all that rich. Maybe he's just got lots of debt from keeping up his image."

"Then I'd want to date him even less. I don't need a financially imprudent guy in my life."

"Okay, fair enough."

I thought she might drop the subject there, but I should have known better.

"How did the kiss rank in the history of all your kisses?" she asked, a note of eagerness in her voice.

I stayed silent as she continued to rinse my hair.

"Emersyn," she pressed.

I wasn't entirely sure why I was so reluctant to admit the truth, but I knew Jemma wouldn't let me get away with anything less.

"Number one. By a long shot."

"Oh my God! If he's that good at kissing, imagine what he's like—"

"Stop!" I shouted.

"The water's too hot?" She shut it off.

"It's the conversation that's too hot. Please, let's not go there."

My thoughts had already strayed in that direction more than once and definitely didn't need more encouragement.

She gently wrung the water out of my hair. "Oh, I really think you *should* go there."

"Jemma! I don't even know his last name. Who knows what kind of secrets he's hiding? For all I know, he could have killed Freddie."

"Why would he have killed Freddie?"

"I don't know," I admitted. "But he was at the Mirage that day, and he's trying to be part of my investigation, maybe to make sure I don't get too close to the truth."

My stomach clenched at the thought. I really didn't want that to be the case.

"The only reason he visited the Mirage that day was to return your phone, which he picked up after meeting you by chance in Connecticut," Jemma pointed out. "It seems pretty far-fetched to suspect him of killing Freddie."

"True," I said with relief.

"And why don't you ask him for his last name?"

"Maybe I will." I sat up, and Jemma adjusted the towel that hung around my shoulders. "But at the moment, I've got more important things to worry about."

"Talk to the cops," Jemma advised, leading me to her styling station. "Get that over with, and then we can focus on you and Wyatt."

"Or not."

From the way Jemma laughed, I knew that was a battle I was doomed to lose.

Even though I left the salon feeling fabulous—thanks to Jemma first trimming my hair and then styling it into glossy waves that I could never achieve on my own—the mood didn't last long. By the time I stood outside the front doors to the police station, I was ready to throw up from nerves. I had to make sure I didn't get myself in trouble when I spoke to the cops. They couldn't know that I'd been in Hoffman's apartment without his knowledge, even if I had used a key.

Hopefully the fact that Hoffman was caught on the Mirage's surveillance camera around the time of the murder would be enough to get the police to focus their investigation on him.

Maybe they'd even get a search warrant and find the label with the broken glass on their own. If Hoffman hadn't already thrown it away. But if he'd wanted it enough to take it from the crime scene, there was a good chance he still had it in his possession.

Ten minutes later, I sat in a small room containing a table and four chairs. An interview room for witnesses rather than suspects, I figured. It wasn't exactly cozy, but it resembled a basic office more than the type of interview room I usually saw on TV shows. Not that those were necessarily realistic, but maybe they were? I really had no idea.

After another ten minutes of fidgeting in my seat and losing games on my phone, Thor—Detective Callahan—joined me in the room. I gave him the spiel that Jemma and I had discussed previously. Basically, I said that something had bothered me about the photo he'd shown us, and I thought maybe I did recognize the person after all, but could I see the video to be sure?

As the detective called up the relevant video file on his tablet, I voiced a question I hadn't meant to ask.

"You know Wyatt? The guy who was at the Mirage when Freddie's body was found?"

Callahan barely glanced up from the tablet. "The man who responded to Ms. Gao's screams at the same time you did?"

"Right," I confirmed. "I just wondered . . . is he a suspect?"

The detective regarded me with his piercing eyes before responding. "Traffic cam footage confirmed what he told us; namely, that he arrived at the Deco Mirage less than five minutes before you met up with him. We believe the victim was already dead when he got there."

"Oh." As those words sank in, a surge of relief allowed me to breathe easier. My relief, however, didn't overshadow my curiosity. "Do you happen to know Wyatt's full name?"

Again, Detective Callahan turned his discerning gaze on me. Then, without answering my question, he angled his tablet toward me and played the relevant clip of video footage.

I sighed, realizing that the subject of Wyatt was now closed. I turned my focus to the video playing on the screen and pointed out the orange Apple Watch strap on Hoffman's wrist. I also explained how I recognized his loping stride.

The detective wrote down Hoffman's name as well as his address and phone number when I provided them. I told him about the speakeasy, and the fact that some bottles appeared to have been removed from behind the bar recently. I didn't mention the label I'd seen in Hoffman's apartment, but I gathered up my courage and told Detective Callahan about the fact that my ex had logged into my online banking account when we were still dating and had transferred out the bulk of my savings without my consent.

"Did you report it at the time?" Callahan's ice-blue eyes bore into me as if he could see straight into my thoughts.

I tried not to shrink back in my chair. The detective's gaze intimidated me, and the way Hoffman had taken me for a fool still filled me with shame. Between the two things, it took great effort to maintain a confident air about me.

"Yes," I replied, "but I was told there wasn't enough evidence to charge him."

The detective stared at me, and I thought I detected a hint of suspicion in his otherwise impassive expression. Did he think I was making up stories?

I shifted uncomfortably in my seat. "Even though he wasn't charged, I thought you should know that he can be unscrupulous."

Callahan glanced down at his notebook. "What can you tell me about your relationship with Frederick Hanover?"

"What?" The question took me by surprise. Weren't we supposed to be talking about Hoffman?

"Frederick Hanover, the murder victim."

"I know who he is," I said, unable to help sounding a tad grumpy. "I didn't have a relationship with him. He was the building's super. That's it."

"But he wasn't a stranger to you."

A distinct feeling of unease slithered over my skin. "No. I saw him around the building."

"But you weren't friends?"

His line of questioning had me puzzled and increasingly nervous. I tried to slow my accelerating heart rate without letting on that I was anything but calm.

"Not friends," I said, choosing my words carefully. "But not enemies either. Just acquaintances, really."

"You never had any disputes with him?"

"Nothing serious."

"Did you ever argue with him?"

My relatively unruffled exterior cracked. "Why are you asking me these questions?"

His relentless blue gaze never strayed from my face. "Please answer."

I stifled a huff of annoyance. "No disputes and no arguments. I barely knew the guy."

"Then perhaps you can explain to me why a witness recently came forward to tell us that they overheard you arguing with Mr. Hanover. In fact, you were overheard telling him"—the detective flipped back a few pages in his notebook as if to consult an earlier entry—"to 'drop dead, sleazebag.'"

A frosty chill crept through my body, freezing every organ one by one. I was turning into an ice statue. The cops would need a forklift to move me to the jail cell. If I didn't shatter first, because that felt like a distinct possibility.

"Who told you about that?" The question came out hushed with shock and fear.

I wrapped my arms around myself and clenched my jaw to keep my teeth from chattering. I'd thought Freddie and I were the only ones who knew about that conversation. I hadn't even told Jemma, because I was afraid that she'd push me to report Freddie to the landlord, and I suspected that wouldn't have helped.

"I'm not at liberty to disclose the identity of the witness." Callahan's cool demeanor lowered the room's temperature another two degrees.

I stared at Detective Callahan.

He stared back. "Did you say those words to Mr. Hanover?"

"Yes," I confessed. Then I sat up straighter, not ready to be completely cowed by the detective. "He really was a sleazebag. I approached him about fixing a leaky pipe in my unit. He cornered me in his office and threatened to have me and my niece evicted if I didn't do some favors for him, and not of the building-maintenance variety."

"Did you report the incident?"

"No."

"Why's that?"

"What would have been the point? If he'd found out that I'd ratted on him to the landlord, it would have made the situation worse." My increasing frustration had the benefit of raising my body temperature to a more comfortable level. "Do you really think I might have killed Freddie over that incident?"

He remained as cool and impassive as ever. "Did you?"

"No!"

"It must have made you angry," Callahan said. "A lowlife like him threatening to toss you and your niece out on the street."

I rested my forearms on the table and leaned forward. "Detective, if I killed every male who's ever sexually harassed me in any way, I'd have a whole trail of bodies behind me, starting with Troy Nestor in sixth grade."

The detective seemed unmoved by that statement.

But of course he was unmoved. He was a man, after all, and therefore had no clue what it was like to be a girl or woman in this world.

"Ms. Gray, can you please tell me where you were at the time of Freddie Hanover's death?"

The question made my stomach churn in a worrisome way.

"Out buying groceries."

"Where?"

I rattled off the name and location of the store. Surely, they'd have surveillance footage that would back up my claim. Although I'd stopped at the park for a while to enjoy the sunshine. Callahan might think there was plenty of time unaccounted for before I arrived at the grocery store.

"Do I need a lawyer?" I asked with an edge to my voice.

"That's entirely up to you."

"Am I free to leave?"

The detective leaned back in his chair and set his pen next to his notebook. "Any time you like."

I stood up so abruptly that my chair almost toppled over backward. "You know, if you want innocent citizens to feel comfortable enough to come forward with potentially relevant information, treating them like criminals isn't a great strategy."

With those parting words, I stormed out of the interview room and down the hallway to the right.

I stopped short after a few paces. I didn't know if I was going the right way. Had I turned right or left to get into the interview room?

I couldn't bear the thought of turning back and having Detective Callahan see me pass by him, so I continued onward. Maybe it should have come as a relief when I realized I'd gone the correct way, but all I felt was queasiness in my stomach and a lightheaded sensation that had me worried I might faint.

CHAPTER
THIRTY

I'd never been so happy to come home to the Deco Mirage. For a while there, I thought I'd be spending the night—or maybe the rest of my life—behind bars, wearing an orange jumpsuit. So to be in my own apartment, even if it did have crumbling plaster and cracks in the walls, was as good as staying at the Ritz-Carlton.

Yet despite my relief at being home and away from Callahan's piercing gaze, I wasn't free of worries. The detective hadn't arrested me, but I had no doubt that I was on his suspect list. I wished I could, in retaliation, put his name on *my* suspect list, but of course that was ridiculous. I had absolutely no foundation for suspecting him of killing Freddie. Just of barking up the wrong tree.

At least I didn't have to put Wyatt's name on Theo's murder board. Just my own instead. I probably should have set up the board and decided what to do next investigation-wise now that I seemed to be in hot water right along with Mr. Nagy.

Mr. Nagy!

My brain finally made a connection that it might have identified earlier if I weren't so frazzled and distracted by all the things going on in my life.

The cops had arrested my neighbor, so why would they look at me as a suspect?

I dashed out into the hall, knocking on the door to the next apartment. Mrs. Nagy answered, her face breaking into a smile when she saw me.

"Emersyn, dear, come in." She ushered me into the apartment.

I was about to ask about her husband, but then I spotted him sitting in his worn and faded armchair.

"Mr. Nagy!" I exclaimed. "You're home!"

"And it's so good to be here," he said with a smile.

"So the police finally realized that you're innocent?" I asked.

His smile faded. "No. Not yet."

"He's out on bail," his wife explained. "Because of his age and his health problems."

"My bad heart is finally good for something." Mr. Nagy tried to inject his words with humor, but fell short.

"He's on house arrest," Mrs. Nagy added.

Her husband tugged up one pant leg to reveal an ankle monitor.

"I had to pledge all of our savings," she continued. "And my cousin had to help out by putting her house on the line."

They exchanged a worried glance, and my excitement fizzled away. I sank down onto the sofa while Mrs. Nagy brought me a cup of tea. Her husband already had one, and hers sat on the coffee table, half empty.

"The detective was questioning me like I'm a suspect, so when I saw you here, I thought surely . . ." I trailed off, confused as to what Detective Callahan might be thinking.

"You're a suspect?" Mrs. Nagy asked, shocked. She perched on the sofa next to me.

"An imbecile, that's what the detective must be," Mr. Nagy declared. "You're such a nice young lady. You'd never harm anyone."

I thanked him, not bothering to mention that I'd nearly clobbered a diner with a cocktail glass on my last day on the job at the restaurant.

"Maybe he has his doubts about you though," I said to Mr. Nagy. "Otherwise, why treat me like a suspect?"

"There is some doubt," he said.

"That's what our lawyer tells us," Mrs. Nagy added.

Their words gave me a double dose of relief. "I'm glad you've got a lawyer."

Mr. Nagy took a sip of his tea. "A public defender. We can't afford anything else."

"Leona gave us the contact information for a friend of hers," Mrs. Nagy said. "But we never called him."

"He's a lawyer?" I asked, wondering if I might need to retain his services.

Mrs. Nagy was only partially successful at stifling a smile. "No, but years ago he played one on television."

That got a smile out of me too.

"Do you know why the police now have doubts about your guilt, Mr. Nagy?" I asked after sampling my tea. Creamy and sweet, just the way I liked it.

"They determined that Freddie was struck by a right-handed assailant," he replied.

"And you're left-handed?"

"Right-handed," he said, causing me some confusion.

"But Zoltán's had weakness on his right side ever since he had a stroke three years ago," Mrs. Nagy explained. "The police are no longer so sure he had the strength to inflict Freddie's head wound."

"That's good news," I said, though that was likely why Detective Callahan was now looking at another suspect—me.

"It is, although the charges haven't been dropped." Mrs. Nagy patted my knee. "If you're a suspect, you should get a lawyer."

My stomach shriveled at the thought. I couldn't afford a lawyer. Probably not even a fake one like Leona's actor friend.

"Zita tells me you're a private investigator now and working on the case," Mr. Nagy said, saving me from responding to his wife's advice.

"I'm not exactly a private investigator, but I am trying to figure out who really killed Freddie."

"With the help of a very handsome young man," Mrs. Nagy added, a twinkle in her eyes.

I busied myself with drinking my tea so I wouldn't need to comment on that detail.

Mrs. Nagy turned the conversation to the subject of Livy, and I stayed and chatted for a few more minutes before returning to my own apartment. I'd been back for only a minute or two when someone knocked on my door.

When I opened it, my heart did a little cheerleading dance in my chest.

I stared at Wyatt, suddenly not sure what to do or say. "How did you get in the building?" I asked in an effort to prevent a potentially awkward silence from stretching between us.

"Agnes buzzed me in. I wanted to check in and see how the new security system was working at the bakery."

My brain froze. What was I supposed to do? Or say? Did he regret our kiss? Want another one? He wasn't giving me any hints, but he did seem to be waiting for me to speak, so I scrambled to think of something to say.

"I've been thinking about our . . ." I tried to keep a grasp on my vague train of thought, but Wyatt was so darn distracting, standing there looking absurdly good in his faded jeans and dark blue button-down shirt with the sleeves rolled up.

"About our kiss?" he guessed, his slow grin heating me from the inside out.

"Yes. Wait—what? No!" I desperately backpedaled. "Our investigation! Not our . . ."

Überhot, super steamy, totally unforgettable kiss? my brain supplied.

Wyatt's grin widened, and panic shot through me.

"Did I say that out loud?" I didn't think I had, but my brain was crazy distracted, and the amusement with a dash of heat in his eyes had me worried.

"Whatever it was, I wish you had," he said, "but I think I have an idea of what you were thinking, anyway."

I really, *really* hoped not.

"You're a mind reader now?" I grumbled, feeling snippy for some unknown reason. Maybe because I didn't like the thought of being transparent to him when he was still mostly a mystery to me.

"Just observant. Especially when it comes to you."

Some of my frostiness melted away. "What did you observe?" I couldn't keep the question to myself, even though I sensed I was straying into dangerous territory. But it was a hot and magnetic kind of danger. Irresistible, like the man standing before me.

His eyes traveled down to my lips, and any ice left inside of me melted away, replaced by hot sparks ready to ignite into a full-fledged fire at any moment.

He met my gaze again before speaking. "I observed that you—"

"Beep beep!"

I nearly jumped out of my skin when Theo spoke from behind him. I hadn't even noticed her arrive.

Wyatt stepped into the apartment to make room for Theo. His hand brushed mine as he moved past me, and he took hold of my fingers for a fleeting moment, giving them the gentlest of squeezes before letting them slip out of his hand.

The sweetness of the gesture took my breath away.

I wanted to send a text to Jemma saying, *I'm done for! Completely done for! Help!* But it didn't seem like the time to rush off to send a message in private, and I didn't need Theo—who'd just sailed into my apartment like she owned the place—catching on to my thoughts.

Suddenly worried I was late to meet Livy, I checked the time on my phone. School wouldn't let out for a while yet. Relieved, I set my phone back on the kitchen counter.

"Shouldn't you be doing schoolwork?" I asked Theo.

"It's already done," she replied. "Schoolwork's a breeze."

I wished I could have said the same when I was in school.

"It's good you're both here," Theo continued. "If you're not too busy making goo-goo eyes at each other, we can get down to business."

"We're not making goo-goo eyes at each other!" I shot back.

"Sure." She drew out the word. "Where's the murder board?"

"I'll go get it," I said in a rush.

I darted into my bedroom and hauled the whiteboard out from under my bed, along with the packages of magnets and pens.

"We should hang it on the wall," Theo said when I returned to the living area.

Wyatt immediately relieved me of the cumbersome board.

"We can't leave it out in the open," I said. "I don't want Livy to see it."

"Fine. Set it on that desk then." Theo nodded toward the small desk pushed up against one wall.

It hardly got used except for storage, since Livy usually did her homework at the kitchen table and I mostly used my laptop on the couch.

Wyatt did as Theo had directed, and I ripped open the packages and dumped the pens and magnets onto the surface of the desk.

"Maybe we should do this another time," I said, tossing the empty packaging into the recycling bin by the door. "I'm not sure I'm up to investigating right now. It's been a rough day."

I gave them a condensed version of what had transpired at the police station.

"All the more reason for us to solve this murder," Theo declared. "The police obviously don't know what they're doing."

"And we need to clear Emersyn's name," Wyatt added, earning him a grateful smile from me.

"That too," Theo conceded, though not, I thought, with sufficient fervor.

I sank down onto the couch. "I can't believe the police think I might have killed Freddie. Can my life seriously get any worse?"

I really should have known better than to taunt the universe like that.

CHAPTER
THIRTY-ONE

My mom peeked in through the door, which I'd neglected to shut. "Oh. Are we interrupting?"

My dad appeared behind her. My mom didn't hesitate to join us in the living room, but my dad hovered in the entryway.

"Not really," I said as I slowly got to my feet, wariness tensing my muscles.

"Your neighbor let us into the building as she was leaving," my dad said. He could have meant Mrs. Nagy or any other female Mirage resident.

"What brings you by?" I asked. "I wasn't expecting you."

"You're not the only one to be taken by surprise today," my mom said, the edge to her voice setting off clanging alarm bells in my head.

"Susan . . ." my dad began in his peacemaker voice.

My mom paid him no heed. "Your father had an appointment in the city this morning. We thought it would be nice to have lunch at the restaurant where you work."

Oh, shit.

My insides turned to sludge.

My mom pinned me with her piercing, pale blue gaze. "Imagine our surprise when we mentioned to the waitress that you're our daughter and she told us that it was a shame you no longer work there."

"I can explain." My voice came out strained, barely rising above a whisper.

"Please do." Her words were as sharp and cold as icy knife blades. "How can you provide stability for Olivia when you don't even have a job? How can you be a good example for her?"

"I . . ." My voice abandoned me. So did my brain. I couldn't think of a single thing to say in my defense.

Theo spoke up, surprising me. "She has a job." She wheeled over to my mom and held out a shiny, uncreased Wyatt Investigations business card.

How many of those things did she have?

My mom read the card as my dad peeked over her shoulder. "Wyatt Investigations?"

Wyatt stepped forward. "I'm Wyatt. Of Wyatt Investigations."

He offered his hand, and my dad shook it, looking a little bemused.

My mom barely glanced at Wyatt before shooting her gaze back to me. "You're working as a private investigator?" She made it sound like the most undesirable job on the planet. "Taking photos of sleazy, cheating husbands in compromising positions?"

"No!" I choked out.

"Wyatt Investigations takes on a varied caseload," Theo said, entirely calm and collected, the exact opposite of what I was feeling in that moment. "And Emersyn works in a primarily administrative capacity," she added.

I bit back a protest. Now was not the time to refute that claim.

"Administrative?" my mom echoed in a questioning and skeptical tone.

"Booking client appointments, making phone calls, doing research," Theo said.

"That's not so bad, right?" I sounded desperate, but that's because

I was. Desperate to lighten my mom's mood, to gain her approval, to keep her from campaigning to take Livy away from me.

"I suppose," my mom conceded grudgingly.

"She's a real asset to the agency," Wyatt said.

I shot him a grateful smile.

"It's true," Theo agreed, and I could have hugged her in that moment.

"And you are?" my mom asked her.

"Theo Harris. I'm job shadowing Emersyn. It's a school credit thing."

It was a little scary how easily and smoothly the kid could lie.

"Well . . . we'll let you get on with it then," my dad said, putting an arm around my mom's shoulders and attempting to steer her toward the door. "We didn't mean to interrupt you during business hours."

"Emersyn," my mom said over her shoulder, "the next time you have news, perhaps you could share it with us, so we're not taken by surprise."

"Sure. Sorry," I babbled. "It slipped my mind the last time we talked."

My dad swept my mom out the door, and I had to force myself not to run over and slam it shut behind them. Instead, I speed-walked and closed it quietly.

"Thank you, thank you, thank you," I said to Theo and Wyatt as I sagged against the door. "You really saved my bacon." I met Wyatt's gaze. "Again."

One corner of his mouth crooked up. "Your mother seems like a force of nature."

And I'm a natural disaster, I thought. *At least in her eyes.*

Out loud, I said, "With a habit of pelting me with hail."

"You just need to know what you're doing when dealing with parents like that," Theo said, as if it were the simplest thing in the world. "Then it's not much of a problem."

"Clearly, I *don't* know what I'm doing."

Theo shrugged. "My life coaching costs extra. And right now we've got a murder to solve."

"Wait. We're paying you?" I said, confused. "We're not making any money here."

"Not yet." She headed for the door. "My grandma was taking a lemon cake out of the oven when I left the apartment. We need fuel, so I'll go grab us some slices while you get the murder board set up."

She zipped out into the hallway without waiting for either of us to agree to her plan.

As I shut the door behind her, my phone chimed, so I picked it up and read the new text message. It was from my mom.

We still need to discuss Olivia's new living arrangements.

My stomach twisted into knots.

"I really can't do this," I said. "Not today."

"What's wrong?" Wyatt asked with concern. "Did you get some bad news?"

"Not news, just . . . more family drama." I set aside my phone. "With that and the police interrogation, I need some time to myself."

"That's okay," he assured me. "I'll text Theo and tell her we're leaving our meeting for another time."

"Maybe tomorrow." Leaving it any later would probably put me on Theo's bad side, which was a slightly terrifying thought.

"Is there anything else I can do to help?" he asked.

I tried to muster a smile as I shook my head. "I'll be okay." An ache of gratitude cut through my chest. "But thank you."

He nodded, his gaze searching my face, as if he were trying to make sure that I really was okay. His eyes were so full of compassion that my throat constricted and my eyes burned, but I was determined not to cry.

"I'll walk you out," I said quickly, darting around him to get to the door. I needed to get out from under his direct scrutiny, to give myself a moment to fight off the threat of tears.

Out in the hall, I led the way to the stairwell. Sharing an elevator with Wyatt struck me as a very bad idea, especially given my current state of emotional fragility and vulnerability. I took the stairs at a jog, and Wyatt followed without a word. Once in the lobby, we slowed our pace.

I took in the sight of the rainy afternoon through the front door. The dreariness of the day matched my mood.

Wyatt opened the door but then paused, his gaze meeting mine. "I'll see you soon, Emersyn."

I wasn't convinced that it was a good idea for me to see him again, especially after that kiss we'd shared. But even though the prudent part of my brain—which seemed to be a very small part—told me I should cut all ties with him, that didn't quell my curiosity.

Even if I did wisely decide not to see him again, there was something I wanted to know.

"Hey, Wyatt?"

He paused, halfway out the door.

"You still haven't told me your last name," I said.

He gave me a ghost of a grin as a shadow passed across his face. "Who says I have one?"

I caught one last glimpse of his almost-grin as he continued out into the gray and blustery afternoon.

CHAPTER
THIRTY-TWO

Theo was waiting for me when I returned to the Mirage the next afternoon after picking Livy up from school.

"Hi, Theo!" Livy ran up to her and gave her a hug.

My heart swelled at the sight, especially when Theo gave her an affectionate squeeze in return.

I stepped aside as a muscular white man with longish, slicked-back brown hair emerged from the hallway to my right and strode toward the front door. I didn't know his name, but I recognized him as Bitty's godson. I smiled at him, but he didn't so much as glance my way.

"Can we play hide-and-seek again?" Livy asked as the man disappeared out the door. She was bubbling with excitement at the prospect.

I didn't get a chance to reply before the door to one of the old-fashioned phone booths opened, distracting me. Detective Callahan stepped out of the booth. When he spotted the three of us, his blue eyes zeroed in on me. My heart dropped through the floor, right down to the creepy basement.

"Detective," I said with grave apprehension as he headed our way.

"Ladies," he replied, his blue gaze passing over Theo and Livy before landing on me again.

It took effort, but I managed not to squirm.

"Did you search the speakeasy?" Theo asked.

Callahan stared at me for another second before turning his attention to her. "I had a team in there yesterday after Ms. Gray told me about its existence."

"Then why were you in there just now?"

I loved that Theo wasn't afraid to voice whatever question was on her mind. At least, I loved it at that moment, since it wasn't directed at me.

"Just doing my job."

Theo watched him with narrowed eyes. "Livy," she said without looking away from the detective, "can you go press the button for the elevator?"

Livy looked to me, uncertainty clear on her face. She might not understand why the detective was there, but she most definitely sensed the tension that had filled the lobby.

I gave her an encouraging nod. "Go ahead. We'll be there in a moment."

She adjusted her backpack on her shoulders and headed for the elevator.

Theo lowered her voice so Livy wouldn't overhear. "Is it your job to investigate Emersyn when you've already arrested a man for the murder?"

"Theo!" I admonished, worried she was pushing too hard.

She acted like she hadn't heard me, which was par for the course, really.

"The case isn't yet closed," Callahan replied, apparently unfazed by Theo's grilling. "Enjoy your afternoon."

Theo and I watched him stride out the front door.

"Are you coming now?" Livy asked with dramatic impatience. She had sagged against the elevator doors to hold them open.

"He really thinks you did it," Theo said quietly, wheeling toward the elevator.

I hurried along at her side. "What? No way."

"Then why was he sniffing around here?"

"Because he thinks Hoffman might be guilty?" I voiced that possibility with more hope than conviction.

Theo sent me a sidelong, pitying glance before boarding the elevator.

I followed after her with heavy steps, each one seeming to pound out the word *doom*.

Mrs. Nagy opened her door when she heard us out in the hallway. She looked a little tired, but she smiled when she saw my niece.

"I thought it might be you, Livy," she said. "Would you like to come over and help me bake some cookies?"

"Yes!" Livy bounced with excitement as she turned her pleading eyes on me. "Please, Auntie Em?"

"Are you sure it's not too much?" I asked my neighbor. "You know, with everything that's going on?"

"The distraction would do me good," she assured me. "And spending time with Livy brings me such joy."

"It makes me happy too," Livy said, giving Mrs. Nagy a gap-toothed smile.

I could practically see the elderly woman's heart melt at the sight. My own heart did the same. I truly believed that her husband was innocent, that they were exactly what they seemed: a kind and generous elderly couple who adored Livy. I'd never doubted for a second that my niece would be safe in their care.

"All right," I said to Livy, sliding her backpack off her shoulders. "But don't spoil your dinner by eating all the cookies."

"I won't eat all of them," she said, following Mrs. Nagy into her apartment. "Only half."

"Save the other half for me!" Theo called after her.

The sound of Livy's giggle lifted my spirits and gave me a surge of energy and renewed determination. Mr. Nagy and I would have our names cleared in no time.

I checked my phone and wished I hadn't.

Can we meet today? Wyatt had texted.

"Let's get a move on," Theo urged.

I tucked my phone away. I could always respond to Wyatt later, once I'd figured out what to say.

I let us into my apartment and dropped Livy's backpack on a kitchen chair. Then I fetched the murder board from my bedroom. Even though it was still blank, I'd returned the board to its hiding place under my bed the day before. I carried it out into the living room and set it on the desk, letting it lean against the wall.

Theo dug through her backpack and pulled out a manila folder.

"Is my file in there?" I asked, trying to get a peek inside when she opened the folder.

She made no attempt to hide the contents from me. "Personnel files are kept in a secure location. This is just murder board stuff."

I frowned with disappointment—I really wanted to know what she'd written in my file and, more importantly, in Wyatt's file—but I accepted the pictures she handed me. One for each of our three murder suspects. They were home-printed and consisted of a candid photograph of Minnie, one of Hoffman's selfies from social media, and a generic silhouette of a man from the shoulders up.

"How did you get this one?" I asked as I studied the candid shot of Minnie checking her mailbox in the lobby.

"With my phone."

"But not with Minnie's consent." I was pretty sure she had no idea she'd been photographed.

"You want me to announce to people that I'm taking their picture to put on our murder board?"

Well, when she put it that way . . .

"Never mind." I stuck each photo up on the board with the help of a magnet.

Theo handed me a pen, and I wrote Hoffman's and Minnie's names below their photos. I added an x under the man's silhouette. Then I stepped back to survey what we had.

"So, we've got Hoffman and Minnie and Wyatt's unknown mystery man from the pub as our suspects." My thoughts strayed away from the investigation. "Of course, Wyatt's a bit of a mystery man himself."

"Not really," Theo said.

"He won't even tell me his last name."

"You let a little thing like that stop you?" Theo shook her head. "You need to get some investigative chops if you want to make it in this business."

I was about to tell her that I didn't have any intention of trying to make it in the private investigation business, but I had a more important thought to follow. "Are you saying you know his last name?"

"I know a lot of things."

I planted my hands on my hips. "Did he tell you his surname?"

"I didn't need him to." Theo produced a package of Twizzlers from her bag. She pulled one out and took a bite. "Google told me all I need to know."

"But if you just type 'Wyatt' into the search bar, you get eleventy billion results that have nothing to do with him." I knew that for a fact, since I'd tried googling him the other day. Even adding the name of the country club hadn't elicited any relevant results.

"Haven't you heard of image searching?" She offered me the package of candy.

I took one of the Twizzlers. "Sure, but I don't have a photo . . ." My gaze snapped to Minnie's picture on the murder board. Then I whirled around to face Theo again. "You took a picture of Wyatt and used it to find him online."

Theo raised her eyes to the ceiling. "Finally, she gets it."

I pointed my floppy rope of candy at her. "Okay, dish. Who is he? What's his secret? Why doesn't he want us to know his last name?"

She lifted her chin. "I can only share details about the agency's employees on a need-to-know basis."

"But I really, *really* need to know."

She sized me up, and her wicked smile made an appearance. "You've got it bad."

"Just tell me. *Please*." I wasn't above begging, not when my curiosity was about to kill me.

Finally, Theo relented. "His name is Wyatt Quintal Alessi."

I took a moment to absorb her words. "Quintal Alessi." I rolled the names around in my mouth, testing them out. A light bulb went off in my head. I repeated Wyatt's last words to me. "'Who says I have one?'" I slapped a hand to my forehead and groaned. "He has two last names, not one."

It was probably best that Wyatt wasn't there with us, because in that moment I was sorely tempted to throttle him. Far more than I wanted to kiss him. Because I didn't want to kiss him at all.

Liar, liar, pants on fire! the traitorous voice in my head yelled.

I practically dove at the coffee table, where I'd left my phone. I typed Wyatt's full name into the search bar, my thumbs moving so fast they were little more than a blur.

"Oh. My. God." My eyes nearly popped out of my head when I scanned what came up on the page.

I clicked on the image results, and my jaw dropped. Numerous photos of Wyatt looking smoking hot filled my screen. In some he was dressed casually; in others he wore a designer suit or a tux. A few photos featured him alone, but in others he was pictured alongside a striking woman who had glowing brown skin, sharp cheekbones, and gleaming black hair. She looked vaguely familiar, and it didn't take more than a second or two to figure out why.

"Holy shit!"

"Right?" Theo said with a grin, coming over to join me by the coffee table. "He's the son of Rosângela Quintal, former Brazilian supermodel and megarich businesswoman."

"That explains the car and country club membership." My voice sounded faint. "But she looks more like his older sister than his mother. What's her secret?"

There was a knock on the door a split second, and then it opened. Jemma breezed in before I could even make a move toward the entryway.

"Maybe you shouldn't barge right in," Theo said to her. "Emersyn and Wyatt could be doing some *very private* investigating."

"As much as I wish that were true, Livy's usually home at this time of day." Jemma glanced around. "Where is the little Livysaurus?"

"Next door baking cookies with Mrs. Nagy," I replied.

Jemma put her hands to her hips. "Then why aren't you doing some *very private* investigating with Wyatt?"

"Because we're supposed to be investigating Freddie's murder," I reminded her. "You know, to keep Mr. Nagy and me out of jail."

I'd already told her via text messages about my status as a suspect.

Jemma dropped her purse on a kitchen chair and came closer to check out the whiteboard. "No reason why you can't mix business with pleasure."

"Can we focus, please?" I pleaded.

"We need to figure out if Minnie has an alibi for the time of the murder," Theo said.

"Excellent idea." One I could definitely get behind.

Theo started toward the door. "Let's go talk to her now."

"All of us?" I asked, no longer so sure of the merits of the plan. "We don't want her realizing that we suspect her."

"She won't suspect anything if we act casual." Theo zoomed out into the hallway.

Jemma practically pushed me out of the apartment.

I hurried to lock the door behind us. "What, exactly, are we supposed to say? If we ask where she was at the time of the murder, it'll be obvious that we suspect her."

"Don't worry," Theo said, boarding the elevator. "I've got an idea."

Somehow that worried me more than ever.

CHAPTER
THIRTY-THREE

Theo knocked on the door to Minnie and Yolanda's second-floor apartment.

"What's the plan?" I whispered.

"Just follow my lead," she said.

I sent an uneasy glance at Jemma, but she appeared unconcerned.

The door opened before I had a chance to voice any misgivings.

"Yes?" Yolanda took in the sight of the three of us. She was a tall and wiry woman with fair but weathered skin, short brown hair, and brown eyes. She didn't smile at us, but I wasn't sure I'd ever seen her smile. While Minnie was friendly and talkative, Yolanda—in my experience—liked to keep to herself.

I forced a smile and tried to come up with a greeting, but whatever words I might have settled on dried up in my throat. There was something about Yolanda's penetrating stare that I found intimidating.

"Hi, Yolanda," Theo said, sounding completely natural and casual. "Is Minnie in?"

"Not right now," she replied, her words clipped.

"Do you know where we can find her?"

Yolanda's eyes narrowed. "What's this about?"

"We have some questions about art," Theo said.

"On Livy's behalf," I said at the same time that Theo added, "I'm writing a paper on art history."

I bit my lip as Theo flicked a glare in my direction.

She melded our lies together. "I'm writing a paper on art history, *and* Livy is working on a multimedia project. We were hoping Minnie could give us some ideas."

Yolanda's gaze slid to Jemma.

"I'm just along for the ride," my bestie said with a smile.

Yolanda stared at the three of us for another two seconds before speaking again. "She's at the gym. She won't be home until this evening."

"Emersyn's thinking of joining a gym," Jemma piped up.

"I am?"

My friend discreetly jabbed an elbow into my ribs.

"Yes," I amended quickly. "I am."

"Which gym does Minnie use?" Jemma asked.

Yolanda's eye twitched. "Ultimate Beast."

Jemma nudged my arm. "I've heard good things. You should try it, Emersyn."

"Ha!" I cut off my burst of laughter and tried to adopt a serious expression. "Right. Maybe I will."

"Thanks, Yolanda," Theo said.

Yolanda appraised us with her brown eyes once again before shutting the door.

"So, I guess we wait till this evening to talk to Minnie," I said as we headed for the elevator.

"Where's your sense of urgency?" Theo asked. "Do you want to end up in jail?"

"Minnie's not here," I reminded her.

"So go to her." She said it like it was the most obvious idea in the world.

To me, it seemed like a flawed plan. "Wouldn't it be weird for me to track her down at her gym and start grilling her?"

"Not if it seems like you're there for another reason," Jemma said, earning a nod from Theo.

"What reason would I possibly have for showing up at a gym called Ultimate Beast?" I asked as we reached the elevator.

Jemma and Theo exchanged a look before fixing their eyes on me.

"Oh, no. No way!" I crossed my arms over my chest, taking a firm stand. "I am absolutely not going to work out at Ultimate Beast."

UNLEASH YOUR INNER BEAST MODE!

The slogan plastered across the front window of the fitness center practically screamed at me as I stood on the sidewalk staring at the gym's façade.

"This is a bad idea," I said to Jemma.

She took me by the elbow and dragged me toward the gym's front door. "Get a move on. Mrs. Nagy can only babysit Livy for another two hours."

"But how can you work out with me when you don't have any gear?"

I'd only agreed to the plan—if caving to Theo and Jemma's combined pressure could be considered agreeing—because Jemma promised to come with me. She'd raided my closet before leaving the Mirage and had cajoled me into changing into burgundy leggings with a matching burgundy-and-pink sports bra that I'd bought more than a year ago when I thought I'd give yoga a try. I lasted exactly one class and hadn't worn the clothes since. Now I stood shivering, huddled in the cute but inadequate jacket I wore over the outfit.

Jemma waved off my question with a flick of her hand. "I can buy something to wear. These places always sell branded clothing and fitness accessories."

As soon as we stepped into the lobby, I saw that she was right.

To our left was a small store area with everything from T-shirts and leggings to water bottles and resistance bands. Straight ahead, a highly toned and perky woman with flawless sienna skin and a swishy black ponytail stood behind a sleek desk, wearing a wireless earpiece with a small microphone attached. Emblazoned on the wall behind her was the slogan TRAIN LIKE A BEAST. BECOME THE ULTIMATE YOU.

"I so do not belong here," I whispered to Jemma.

The perky woman smiled at us as Jemma pushed me forward. "Welcome to Ultimate Beast. Can I help you with anything?"

I took a step backward. "Actually, we're in the wrong—"

Jemma took my arm and propelled me closer to the desk, speaking over me. "We're interested in becoming members, but we want to try things out first."

"Of course!" The name tag on the woman's hot-pink sports bra said JAZZ. "We have guest passes available. For one day, one week, or one month."

"Let's start with one day," Jemma said. "Do you have any brochures?"

"Right here." Jazz gestured at a display of brochures like she was channeling Vanna White.

Jemma snatched one up. "I'll take a quick look."

As she opened the shiny pamphlet—adorned with fit, toned people with gleaming white smiles—she wandered away. A hallway led deeper into the building, and in the lobby there were two large interior windows, one looking into a weight room and another with a view of a large area filled with stationary bikes. A dozen or so sweaty but gorgeous men and women were in the middle of a spin class. Every single one of them could have worked as a fitness model. Maybe some of them did.

I really didn't belong here.

"I'll need you to fill out a form." Jazz tapped a small sign. "If you scan this QR code, the form will come up on your phone. Otherwise, I can get you a paper one."

"Digital is fine." I scanned the code and glanced over at Jemma as I filled out the form on my phone.

She'd wandered first into the store area, but now she stood by the window with a view of the weight room.

The phone on the desk rang, so Jazz excused herself and answered it.

With the form half filled out, I crossed the lobby to join Jemma.

"You need to get in the weight room," she whispered. "Isn't that Minnie over there?"

I took a closer look. Sure enough, my petite neighbor was working out on one of the rowing machines, clad in baby blue leggings and a matching racerback tank top.

"Why don't we wait until she's on her way out?" I suggested, loving the idea. "We can say we're just arriving."

"But who knows how long she's going to be working out for? Time is ticking." Jemma nodded at my phone. "Have you got that filled out yet?"

I went back to adding all my information. Meanwhile, Jemma returned to the desk, where Jazz had finished her phone call. When I'd completed the form, I hit the SUBMIT button at the bottom of the page. Jemma and Jazz were deep in conversation, and I wondered if it was a good idea to let my best friend speak with the woman alone. I hurried over that way.

To my relief, they were talking about their favorite nail salons.

"You're all set," Jazz said to me when I joined them.

"I am?" I looked to Jemma. "What about you?"

She gestured at her outfit of snug black pants, an equally snug top, and three-inch heels. "I can't work out in these clothes."

I took her arm and pulled her a few feet away from the desk. "You were going to buy an outfit," I reminded her.

"Have you seen the prices on their stuff?" She slid my jacket off my shoulders.

I clutched her arm. "Jemma, you cannot abandon me."

"I'd never do that." She peeled my fingers from her arm. "I'll be here cheering you on the whole time."

"That's not—"

"You'll do great." She spoke over me in what I guessed was meant to be an encouraging voice.

To me, her words sounded like a death knell.

She freed her arm from my trembling grip and whispered, "Go get 'em, Sherlock."

Then she shoved me toward the Hallway of Doom.

CHAPTER
THIRTY-FOUR

I started out with a series of stretches, doing my best to look confident, like I worked out all the time. As I leaned down to touch my toes, I cast a glance at Minnie. She'd moved from the rowing machine to a treadmill by the time I'd entered the room, and she now stared out the window at the busy street, running with the same intensity she'd applied to her rowing.

I looked over at the interior window, where Jemma stood watching on the other side of the glass. She pointed at Minnie and mouthed, *Get on the treadmill!*

I heaved a resigned sigh and climbed onto the empty machine to the right of Minnie.

"Hey, Minnie," I said, hoping I'd get to question her without ever turning on the treadmill.

She kept staring straight ahead, a mixture of concentration and determination on her face.

I tried again to get her attention. "Minnie?"

She still didn't react.

I finally noticed the earbuds she had in.

I glanced over at the window to the lobby, shrugging at Jemma, only to find that my friend had disappeared. If she was off getting a massage or lounging in the sauna . . . well, I didn't know what I'd do, but there would be consequences.

"Are you done?" a voice boomed from behind me, making me jump.

Minnie didn't even blink.

A blond man with bulging muscles and a crew cut stood behind my treadmill, staring at me.

"Sorry?" I asked.

"The treadmill." His stare morphed into a glower. "If you're done, let someone else use it."

I glanced around and realized that all the other treadmills were occupied.

"I'm just getting started," I said, not ready to give up on questioning Minnie.

"Then get on with it," he grumbled before storming off to the bench press.

Not eager to incur anyone else's wrath, I turned on the machine and punched a few of the many other buttons on the control panel. After a bit of lurching and stumbling, I got the treadmill going at what I hoped would be a gentle jogging pace. I gave myself a minute to get settled into a rhythm, and a smile slowly took shape on my face.

This wasn't so bad. It actually felt pretty good.

Emboldened by my newfound treadmill confidence, I waved at Minnie, hoping to catch her attention. The movement disrupted my balance just enough to trip me up. I made a grab for the handrails but missed. Before I even knew it was happening, I flew off the back of the machine and ended up in a heap on the floor.

"Now are you done?" a voice boomed from above me.

I looked up to see the man with the crew cut glaring down at me.

I nodded, having no desire to step back on the machine.

Without offering to help me up or so much as asking if I was okay, the guy hopped on the treadmill.

I struggled to my feet, feeling a twinge in one ankle.

Jazz materialized by my side. "Emersyn! Are you all right?"

"I'm fine," I assured her, but I winced when I put weight on my sore ankle.

Jazz produced an exercise ball, seemingly out of nowhere, and slid it behind me. "Why don't you sit down a minute?"

I did as she suggested, sinking down onto the soft, bouncy ball. The pain in my ankle eased.

"I'm sorry," Jazz said, pointing at her headset. "I've got a call coming in."

"No problem. I'm fine, really."

She smiled with relief. "Hang in there." She hurried toward the lobby.

"Oh, hey, Emersyn," a familiar voice said.

Minnie.

She was off the treadmill now, a towel flung around her shoulders as she chugged water from a reusable bottle emblazoned with the words GRUB TUBZ. By the time I realized it was her who'd greeted me, she was already across the room and disappearing out the door.

I knew I should follow her and strike up a conversation, but that would have required my ankle to support my weight. I tested it by starting to stand, but a zing of pain sent me sinking back onto the ball.

Maybe when Minnie was on her way out of the gym, Jemma would intercept her. I checked the interior window again. Jemma hadn't reappeared.

I closed my eyes for a moment, concentrating solely on calming my growing frustration.

"Emersyn? I didn't know you worked out here."

My eyes flew open. Bodie stood in front of me.

I shot to my feet, and the exercise ball rolled away. A man doing dumbbell lunges nearly tripped over it, saving himself at the very last second. He glared across the room at me.

I cringed as I hopped on one foot. "I'm so sorry!"

With a scowl, the man went back to his exercises.

Meanwhile, Bodie had jogged across the room and snatched up the exercise ball. He set it in a bin in the corner, where it apparently belonged.

"Are you okay?" Bodie asked when he came back over my way. "Did you hurt yourself?" He put a hand to my elbow, helping to hold me steady.

"I twisted my ankle. It's my first time here," I confessed. "And I'm really not Ultimate Beast material."

Bodie laughed, but not in a disparaging way. "I think you're Ultimate Beast material. Maybe your own style of beast, though."

"You are a kind, kind man."

"Just an honest one."

"We'll leave that debate for another time."

"Probably a good idea," he said with a grin that held no trace of derision. "Can I give you a ride home?"

My eyes must have lit up like stars when he said those words. If Jemma really had abandoned me, I would have to hobble to the subway. "You drove here?"

"Sure. The bar where I work is around the corner, so I've got a pass for the parking garage down the street." He gave me a once-over. "How about I bring the car around to the front door after I shower and change? You can sit in the lobby while you wait."

"Sounds good. Thank you." I barely managed to stop myself from telling him he was my hero.

When I limped out into the lobby a minute later, Jazz shot me a sympathetic smile.

"How are you feeling?" she asked.

"A little better, thanks," I replied.

"Glad to hear it!" She produced my jacket from beneath the desk. "Your friend asked me to hold this for you."

"Where did she go?" I still harbored suspicions that she was getting a massage somewhere in the depths of the building.

"She said something about a work emergency?" The phone on the desk rang, and Jazz reached up to tap a button on her headset.

"I haven't paid for my pass yet," I said quickly. Not with money, anyway. My ankle had paid a price. My dignity too.

"Your friend took care of all that. Excuse me."

Jazz answered the call, and I limped over to a padded bench and dropped down onto it with a whimper. I wrapped my jacket around me and fished my phone out of the pocket. Jemma had texted me, apologizing profusely that she had to run to the salon to style a client's hair for a last-minute event. I grumbled a few choice words before stuffing my phone back in my pocket.

The next time my bestie had a bright idea, I would run for the hills.

CHAPTER
THIRTY-FIVE

Ten minutes later, Bodie—his hair damp from his shower—passed through the lobby and assured me he wouldn't be long getting the car. Sure enough, he soon pulled up to the curb in his black sports car.

I sighed when I settled into the leather seat. "Nice car."

The engine purred as Bodie joined the stream of traffic with minimal honking from other drivers.

"Thanks. The lease payments are a bitch but . . ."

"Totally worth it?" I guessed.

He smiled. "Yep." He flipped a switch on the console. "You look like you could use the heated seat."

"I'm not that cold, but . . ." Warmth seeped into my back and legs. "Oh . . ."

"Right?" Bodie grinned.

I sighed again and wriggled deeper into the seat.

"How are things going with your quest to clear Mr. Nagy's name?" Bodie asked a moment later.

I forced myself to stay awake even though the warm seat was trying to lull me to sleep. "You know about that?"

"I think the whole building does." Bodie changed lanes, prompting a chorus of angry honks from other drivers. "Bitty told me about it when I was getting my mail the other day."

"The Mirage's rumor mill isn't always the most accurate source of information."

"So, you're not in the middle of a steamy romance with your investigative partner?"

I sat up straighter, suddenly wide awake. "What? Who said that?"

"Actually, no one, to my knowledge." He gave me a sheepish smile. "I was teasing."

I relaxed, but my words came out grumbly when I said, "Well, good."

"But it's true?"

"No! Absolutely not." The memory of kissing Wyatt flashed in my mind. I did my best to kick it to the curb.

"Glad to hear it."

I glanced his way. "Yeah?"

He smiled, flicking his eyes to meet mine before turning them back to the road.

A hint of warmth touched my cheeks, unrelated to the heated seat.

"I'm glad you're helping Mr. Nagy," Bodie said.

"Well, I'm *trying* to help him." I thought of my failed attempt to get information out of Minnie. "But I'm not really detective material."

Bodie rubbed at the scruff on his jaw before settling his hand back on the steering wheel. "I have some suspicions."

"Really?" I perked up, my curiosity awakened.

"First of all, I suspect that you're not giving yourself enough credit."

I sank deeper into the seat. "Thanks, but I haven't even been able to figure out if Minnie has an alibi."

"Minnie Yang?" His incredulity was understandable. "You think she might have killed Freddie?"

"It's possible. She hated the guy."

His forehead scrunched up as he absorbed my words. "But she's so . . . small. Her name suits her."

"Have you seen her working out at the gym?"

"Okay, yeah, I have. You're right. She's a beast. But a murderous beast?"

"I hope not." I stifled a yawn, tempted to close my eyes and sink even deeper into the deliciously warm seat. "I'd much rather the culprit be the mystery man."

"What mystery man?"

"Apparently, Freddie met with an unidentified man at Shanahan's Suds a few days before he died," I explained. "The mystery man might not have anything to do with the murder, but it would be nice to know who he was."

"I'm friends with Mike, the owner of the pub," Bodie said, flicking on his turn signal. "He might still have security footage from that day. You could get a picture of the guy to show around. Maybe Mike even knows his name."

"Do you think he'd talk to me?"

"Sure. Tell him I sent you. If he wants to confirm that, he can text me. Actually, you know what? I'll text him to let him know you're coming. I'd go with you, but I need a nap before tonight's gig."

"Gig?" I usually heard him describe an evening's work of bartending as a shift.

"Sometimes on my nights off from the bar, I work for a catering company. There's this fancy shindig in Manhattan tonight. A charity gala. Lots of rich folks."

"Does that mean good tips?"

Bodie laughed. "In my experience, most rich people aren't great tippers."

"Maybe that's how they get rich. By being stingy."

"Could be. I wouldn't really know. Serving drinks is the closest I get to any rich people."

"That's closer than I get."

Except that wasn't entirely true. I was recently very up close and personal with Wyatt in the dumbwaiter shaft. I pushed that thought aside. I didn't want to be thinking about Wyatt, especially when I was sitting next to another hot guy, one who seemed much more relatable and not quite so far out of my league.

"Thanks, Bodie," I said, trying to get my mind back on track. "Talking with Mike might be the break I need."

"No problem. I want to help any way I can."

He stopped the car in the middle of the road, right in front of the Mirage. Parked cars lined the street, bumper to bumper.

"I'll drop you off here, so you don't have to walk from the garage."

I thanked him as I undid my seatbelt and opened the door.

"Emersyn, wait."

I stopped with one leg out of the vehicle.

"Check the glove compartment. There's something in there for Livy."

I opened it, and a plastic bag tumbled out into my hands. It held about half a dozen drink umbrellas in a variety of colors.

"I promised I'd get her some," he explained.

"You remembered?"

He'd mentioned it more than a week ago, when Livy found out that he made "fancy drinks" for a living.

"Of course. She's a great kid."

I smiled, fighting an unexpected prickle of tears. "She is. How much do I owe you?"

"Emersyn, I don't think my boss even paid a penny a piece for those things."

"You won't get in trouble?" I asked, wanting to be sure.

"No one even knows they're gone. Even if they did, they wouldn't care. They're all yours. Well, Livy's."

"She'll love them. Thanks, Bodie." The gesture triggered a flurry of butterflies in my chest and warmed me more thoroughly than the luxurious heated seat.

I tucked the umbrellas into my coat pocket and gingerly extricated myself from the car, waving as Bodie drove off toward the parking garage around the corner. I missed the heated seat by the time I reached the curb. The damp autumn wind cut through my coat and thin leggings, sending icy shivers through me. On top of that, I was parched and beyond ready to chug a tall glass of water, followed by a chilled can of apple Bubly.

I stopped outside the Mirage's front door, my keys dangling from my fingers. My thoughts had meandered back to the brand name I'd seen on Minnie's reusable water bottle. I'd seen that name before. In Freddie's apartment.

Was that significant?

I rolled that possibility around in my head.

It likely didn't mean anything, I decided. Maybe it was a popular brand, though I'd never heard of it until recently.

I filed the information about Grub Tubz away in my mind and got myself out of the blustery wind. Stairs were a definite no for me in my current condition, so I limped straight for the elevator. While riding it up to the third floor, I tugged the packet of drink umbrellas out of my pocket and smiled at them. They might not be worth much money, but they would put a smile on Livy's face. To me, that was priceless.

CHAPTER
THIRTY-SIX

I spent the next morning applying for jobs and doing an interview via video conference. I thought it went all right, so I treated myself to a can of apple Bubly afterward. Whether I landed the job or not, at least the process had helped to distract me on a challenging day. I didn't want to think too much about the fact that it was Ethan's birthday, because I didn't want to end up in tears, but the significance of the date still weighed heavily on me.

On my way to pick up Livy from school, I stopped at the store to buy some butter and chocolate. I was very conscious of every dollar that left my bank account lately, but it was worth the extra expense to bring my niece some comfort.

As Livy washed her hands in preparation to help me bake, I decided to drown out the melancholy thoughts trying to seep into my head.

"Why don't we turn on some music?" I suggested. "It'll be like a cake-baking birthday party."

Livy bounced up and down, water droplets spraying off her wet hands. "Taylor Swift! Taylor Swift!"

I handed her a towel and brought up a playlist on my phone. Once we had the music going, we measured out the ingredients for the cake, pausing now and again to dance along to our favorite songs. Fortunately, my ankle had recovered while I slept the night before, so I could dance with abandon.

After I put the cake in the oven, I collapsed onto the couch, exhausted.

"That was like a cardio baking routine," I said.

Livy threw herself onto the couch—and me—with a giggle.

"It's going to be the best cake ever!" she said as she wrapped her arms around me. "Daddy would love it."

I gave her a gentle squeeze. "He would."

"When can we eat it?"

I laughed at that. "I thought you wanted chocolate frosting?"

"I do! Lots and lots of frosting!"

"Then we have to wait for the cake to bake and cool."

Livy let go of me and flopped onto her back. "That'll take forever."

"In the meantime, let's get some dinner." I pushed myself up off the couch, ignoring the fatigue in my limbs.

"Can't we have cake for dinner?" Livy asked, hopeful.

I ruffled her hair. "Nice try, sweet pea."

Later, as I slathered chocolate frosting onto the cooled cake, I silently wished Ethan a happy birthday. The heavy weight of grief in my chest intensified, but then I looked at Livy, who was licking frosting off the hand mixer's beaters, and I smiled.

"Can we show the cake to Grandma and Granddad?" she asked as I smeared on the last bit of frosting and handed her the spatula to lick.

"Let me just check if they're home," I said.

Really, I wanted to warn my parents about why Livy had asked to FaceTime with them. If they didn't feel up to talking about Ethan's birthday—or didn't think they could do it without breaking down—I wanted to give them a chance to decline.

As I typed out a text message to my dad, I wondered if my mom's recent stance on Livy's custody had anything to do with Ethan's birthday. It was the first one since he'd died. Maybe, as the day had approached, her need to cling to Livy—all she had left of her only son—had become heightened. I could understand that. And if that was the case, would she back off on the custody issue once we all got through this day?

My dad replied to my text within minutes, and soon Livy was chatting away with my parents on FaceTime, showing them the cake and telling them all about how we'd baked it.

I could tell my mom was blinking away tears at one point, but for the most part, the call seemed to have a positive effect on her and my dad.

After saying goodbye to my parents, we finally ate a slice of cake each. Buoyed up by the sugar, Livy had another dance party, solo this time, while I watched from the couch. Then, finally, she crashed.

As she wriggled into bed that night, she hugged her dinosaur stuffie to her. "Do you think Daddy could taste the cake from heaven?" she asked.

"Absolutely," I replied as I tucked the blankets around her.

She burrowed down deeper. "Auntie Emersyn?"

"Yes, Livysaurus?"

"Is it okay to be happy and sad at the same time?"

I stroked her hair away from her face. "Of course it is, sweetie. Feelings are complicated like that. And it's perfectly okay."

Her eyes appeared luminous in the dim light from her bedside lamp. "I really miss my daddy."

My heart cracked. "I know you do, hon."

"But I'm really glad I've got you."

I fought against a wave of tears and forced my voice to remain steady. "Back at you, sweetie. I'm the luckiest auntie in the world."

No matter what might go wrong in my life, I knew that was the truth.

CHAPTER
THIRTY-SEVEN

I decided the next day to focus my investigation on someone other than Minnie for a while. Hopefully I'd have a chance to talk with her soon so I could find out if she had an alibi, but after my previous attempt to question her, I didn't feel ready to try to track her down again.

Hopefully, the police were taking a good look at Hoffman as a suspect. Thor, aka Callahan, might think I was trying to throw my ex under the bus, but I wanted to believe that he'd at least look into the claims I'd made. After all, Hoffman was caught on the Mirage's security camera, so I had that to back me up.

With Minnie and Hoffman on the back burner of my investigation, that left the mystery man. I'd received word that the job I'd interviewed for the day before had been given to another candidate, so I spent an hour or so looking at more online job postings, until I felt like my soul was bleeding out through my eyes. At that point, I gave up for the day. Much of the morning had passed, and I decided it was the perfect time to stop by the pub. Not that I could afford to be eating out, but maybe a soft drink and an appetizer wouldn't break my bank account.

As I walked to Shanahan's Suds, I pulled out my phone and checked my messages.

Everything OK? Can we meet?

Wyatt had sent the message while I was immersed in my job search.

I'd respond later, I decided, when I'd hopefully have something to show for my investigative efforts. I'd never replied to his previous message, and that set off little flickers of guilt inside of me, but I wasn't sure that I was ready to talk to him. Maybe it was petty, but I was ticked off at him for keeping his identity a secret. Did he think I was untrustworthy? Did he think I'd fangirl all over him if I knew he was related to someone famous? If so, he really didn't know me at all. I'd only fangirl over someone crazy-awesome famous, like Taylor Swift. Rosângela Quintal might have been a supermodel back in the day, but Tay Tay she was not.

By the time I reached Shanahan's, the damp breeze had me wishing I'd worn a coat over my pale pink sweater. I was on the brink of shivering when I entered the pub, where deliciously warm, food-scented air greeted me. The place was fairly quiet, probably because it wasn't yet noon, but a man and woman sat eating at the bar together, half watching the football game playing on three different television screens, and a handful of other diners sat scattered around the restaurant.

Nobody was at the hostess station, which had a sign asking customers to PLEASE WAIT TO BE SEATED, so I took a few steps farther into the pub, glancing around. Hopefully Mike would be willing to share the security footage with me, but I figured I should probably establish myself as a paying customer before asking for any favors.

I turned in a slow circle, hoping to spot someone who could direct me to a table. I'd only made it forty-five degrees when I came to a halt, my eyes narrowing.

Wyatt spotted me at the same time. He raised a hand in greeting and then pointed to the empty bench across the table from him.

I took him up on the offer, marching over and sliding into the booth. He had a soft drink in front of him but no food.

"What are you doing here?" I demanded.

Unfazed, he took a sip of his drink before setting it down again. "Hello to you too. I'm doing great, thanks. How about you?"

I ignored the fact that he was pointing out my rudeness. "What you're *doing* is investigating without me, right?"

He regarded me with those entrancing eyes of his. "I didn't realize being partners meant we had to be joined at the hip."

"We aren't partners," I reminded him, my voice terse. "We're just working together. Temporarily. Under the banner of *my* agency."

"Okay." He sat back, resting one arm along the top of the booth. "I didn't know that working together meant I had to report my every move to you. Besides, I did try to involve you, but you've been ghosting me."

My gaze drifted to the arm he had draped over the back of the booth. I absolutely did not wonder what it would feel like to be sitting snuggly next to him and have that arm settle around my shoulders.

"I'm not ghosting you," I grumbled. "I've just been busy."

"Investigating without me?"

I clamped my mouth shut.

He flashed me a triumphant smile. "And why are *you* here?"

I wanted to kiss that smile right off his face. Wipe it off! Wipe, not kiss!

Focus, Emersyn!

"For your information, I've got a good lead." I let a hint of smugness creep into my voice. "I've got a connection to the owner of this pub, which means there's a good chance I'll get to look at the security footage and maybe even get a photo of our mystery man."

Wyatt nodded, as if seriously pondering my words. "By the owner of this pub, you mean Mike?"

I gaped at him. "How do you know his name?"

"We had a chat a few minutes ago. And we took a look at the

footage. He emailed me the relevant clips, and he's printing out a few stills for me as we speak."

A waitress appeared at our table, bearing a plate of food, which she set in front of Wyatt with a smile. The delicious aromas wafted across the table to me, and my stomach growled like an angry crocodile.

"Oh," the waitress said, only then noticing me. "Can I get you anything?"

I looked at the menu and had to bite back a groan of disappointment when I saw the prices listed next to the appetizers. I dug deep into my reservoir of willpower and set the menu aside.

"Just ice water, please." I eyed Wyatt's clubhouse sandwich and fries and nearly whimpered.

The waitress frowned with disapproval. "Nothing to eat?"

"No, thanks. I'm fine."

She shot daggers at me with her eyes before turning a beaming smile on Wyatt. "Let me know if you need anything."

She winked—seriously winked!—at him before flouncing off, her ponytail swinging behind her.

I felt a flicker of satisfaction when Wyatt didn't watch her walk away, despite the way she was swinging her hips in her tight black skirt.

"So, what other leads have you got?" he asked as he picked up half of his sandwich.

I glared at him, irrationally annoyed that he'd asked me that question since, of course, I had zero other leads.

I grabbed a fry off his plate and chomped on it.

Wyatt stopped eating to take a sip of his drink. "I thought you weren't hungry."

I made short work of the fry and then sat back, crossing my arms. "I'm not."

My stomach chose that moment to let out a thunderous growl.

From the amusement on Wyatt's face, I could tell he'd heard it. My cheeks flushed.

"Why don't you order some food?" he suggested.

"I'm fine," I grumbled.

As the son of a supermodel, he'd most likely never had to worry about the price of anything. I wasn't about to share my financial difficulties with him. He wouldn't understand and would probably judge me. I was doing enough of that on my own and really didn't need any assistance.

"Are you annoyed with me?" Wyatt asked before finishing off the first half of his clubhouse sandwich.

That was probably sourdough bread. My favorite.

My fingers twitched, longing to reach across the table and grab the remaining half of the sandwich.

"Emersyn?" Wyatt prodded, and I realized I'd been staring at his food.

"Why would I be annoyed?" I wasn't about to answer his question. Not truthfully, anyway. I didn't yet want to show my cards by letting him know I was irked by the fact that he'd kept me in the dark about his identity.

I wanted to know if he would voluntarily share his full name with me in time.

"So, you weren't ghosting me, and yet you didn't invite me along on your investigative mission today," he said before starting in on the second half of his sandwich.

"I could handle it on my own. Besides, I'm sure you have a hundred better things to do than investigate a murder with someone like me."

He quirked an eyebrow in a totally unsexy way.

(Okay, so it was super sexy, but I needed to pretend it wasn't.)

"Someone like you?" He sounded confused.

"Let's face it," I said, deciding to dish out a slice of honesty. "I'm a hot mess."

He set his sandwich down. "That's not what I see. I see a beautiful, intelligent, kindhearted, and capable woman."

His words warmed me, even though I knew I shouldn't let them.

"You only say that because you hardly know me."

One corner of his mouth curved upward. "I know more than you might think."

"Such as?" I asked, equal parts curious and apprehensive.

He leaned back in his seat. "Let's see . . . You spend a lot of time with your niece, you like bright colors, and you have an affinity for apple Bubly."

I tried to mask my surprise. "You can't possibly know about the Bubly."

"And yet I do."

I narrowed my eyes. "Someone must have told you. Jemma?"

"Nope."

"Theo?"

He shook his head.

"Livy?"

"Nobody."

I scrutinized him from across the table, radiating suspicion. He held my gaze for a good three seconds before a grin crept onto his face.

"There were several empty cans in the recycling bin by your door," he said.

"Hmm," I conceded. At least he hadn't been snooping around my apartment without my knowledge. I glanced down at my pale pink sweater. "Bright colors?"

That darned twinkle appeared in his eyes. "Maybe not always on the outside."

The memory of him draped in my colorful underwear came rushing back.

"Oh, no, you don't!" I admonished.

The twinkle was full-on dancing now. "Don't what?"

I leaned forward and practically hissed my next words. "Refer to that . . . *incident*. It never happened and will never be mentioned again."

He grinned, slow and sexy. "You don't want me to mention your unmentionables?"

"Yes! No! Argh!" I took a deep breath in an attempt to get myself unflustered. "That's correct," I said more calmly, and maybe a little primly. "Never again. Is that clear?"

"Crystal clear." He picked up a fry from his plate. "In fact, as transparent as that sheer fuchsia number that—"

I lunged across the table to cover his mouth with my hand, nearly knocking over his drink. "Shush!"

My eyes locked with his, and my heart thumped. I was close enough to breathe in his enticing, outdoorsy scent. The temperature of my blood immediately shot up a degree or two. I finally realized that I had my fingertips pressed to his lips and snatched my hand away as if I'd been shocked.

I sank back down into my seat and adjusted my sweater as I tried to recover a shred of dignity. "And it's translucent, not transparent."

"I stand corrected."

I glared at him.

He remained unfazed.

My stomach gave another loud growl, and I grabbed three more of his fries.

"Why don't you order something?" he asked.

I tucked my hands into the sleeves of my sweater and shrank into my seat. "Because I just needed a few fries."

He studied me for a moment, a little too perceptibly for my comfort. "I can get you—"

"No!" I realized I'd spoken a lot louder than I'd meant to. "No, thank you," I amended at a lower volume. "I'm fine."

I didn't need to accept charity from him. It wasn't like I was going to starve. As soon as I got home, I could make myself a meal of . . . crackers and peanut butter. And chocolate cake.

To my relief, a man came up to our table, holding papers in his hand and diverting Wyatt's attention away from me.

"Hey, Wyatt," the man said in greeting. Then he nodded at me before handing the papers to my companion. "I got those stills you asked for."

"These are great," Wyatt said, taking a quick look at the two sheets. "Thank you."

"I'm sorry I can't help you with the guy's name, but if he shows up here again, I'll text you."

"Thanks, Mike."

"Enjoy your meal," he said with a nod at both of us.

As Mike walked away, I realized that the waitress had never brought my ice water. I sighed and averted my gaze from Wyatt's glass, which was still half full of soda.

Wyatt set the papers on the table and slid them toward me. "Our mystery man."

I picked up the two sheets. Each one showed a grainy photo of a white man with brown hair who appeared to be in his thirties. Although the pictures weren't sharp, they were clear enough.

"I've seen this guy before," I said. "At the Mirage."

Wyatt was about to take a drink but now set down his glass. "Does he live there?"

"Nope, but he visits someone who does." I tapped the photo that showed the closest view of the man's face. "This is Bitty Dover's godson."

CHAPTER
THIRTY-EIGHT

I appeased my growling stomach by eating a few more of Wyatt's fries—only because he swore that he wasn't going to eat them all. I didn't know if I really believed that, but the fries were delicious—perfectly salted and seasoned—and my stomach was ready to devour itself from the inside out.

"Should we go talk to the godmother now?" Wyatt asked when we left the pub a short while later.

"Sounds like a plan," I agreed.

Wyatt pulled his phone from his pocket and checked the time. He slowed his pace. "I didn't realize how late it was. I'm sorry, Emersyn. I promised I'd meet up with my mom this afternoon."

"No worries," I assured him. "I'll talk to Bitty and let you know how it goes."

"Really?" he asked, stopping on the sidewalk. "You won't ghost me again?"

I stopped too, so abruptly that a man in a suit had to dodge around me. He scowled, but I barely noticed.

"I didn't ghost you," I said to Wyatt. "I was just . . . busy."

"Are you sure? It's not because our kiss made you uncomfortable?"

"What? No! The kiss was great. I mean, not great, but . . ." I floundered.

"Incredible?" Wyatt suggested. "Mind-blowing?"

Yes, yes, yes! the candid part of me wanted to yell. My stomach flipped at the thought that *he* might believe those adjectives described our kiss.

Then I remembered how he'd kept his surname a secret from me. He still was, really. Hoffman had burned me so badly that trusting no longer came so easily to me. Secrets scared me, because I knew they could leave scars.

Since Wyatt had steered the conversation in a dangerous direction, I decided to do the mature thing and change the subject.

"I'll talk to Bitty and text you if I learn anything."

He searched my eyes with his own, as if trying to find the words I'd left unspoken. I hoped I kept them well hidden.

"All right," he said finally.

I turned and walked off down the street. I could feel his eyes on me still, but I never looked back.

After a snack of crackers and peanut butter, I savored my last remaining can of apple Bubly—that one hundred percent did not make me think of Wyatt. I enjoyed every last drop, knowing I wouldn't be buying more until I had a real paying job. I tossed the empty can into the recycling bin and then cut a chunk of cake and set it on a paper plate. Livy and I had barely made a dent in the dessert, and we needed help to finish the rest. I took the big piece of cake, probably equal to four average slices, and delivered it to Mr. and Mrs. Nagy.

The gesture delighted them, and I was glad I'd thought of it. The elderly couple had been so good to me and Livy. It was nice to have a chance to return even just a little kindness.

After a short chat with the Nagys, I paid a visit to Bitty's apartment on the ground floor. When Bitty let me into her unit, I found Leona lounging on the couch with a martini in hand. She wore a sparkly green dress and several necklaces, and rings adorned nearly all her fingers. As usual, her garishly reddish-orange hair was styled into large curls. She'd overdone the smoky-eye look, and her bright red lipstick had smeared at the corner of her mouth.

I wondered how many martinis she'd already consumed.

"Emersyn, darling," Leona trilled before taking a long sip of her cocktail. "How delightful."

"Can I get you a martini, dear?" Bitty offered, heading for the kitchen.

"No, thank you," I said. "I won't keep you long. I just came to ask about your godson."

"Vincent?" Bitty retrieved her martini from the kitchen counter and joined us in the living area. "What do you want to know about him?"

"No offense to young Vincent," Leona said, "but why would you be interested in him when you've already got two hunky hunks of burning love to play with?"

"Sorry?" Had she really said *hunky hunks of burning love*?

"Elvis was 'a hunk, a hunk of burning love,' not 'a hunky hunk of burning love,'" Bitty corrected.

Leona flicked a hand. "Phht. He was both!"

Bitty conceded that point with a tip of her head to the side.

"I'm sorry," I said, feeling like I'd suddenly landed on a different planet. "I'm not sure what you're talking about."

Actually, I did have a sneaking suspicion.

"No need to play coy," Leona said as she tucked her feet up on the couch and took another sip of her martini. "The building's all abuzz with the news of your steamy affairs with Wyatt the stud muffin and hot stuff Bodie."

My suspicion was well-founded, but I was oh-so-wishing I'd never come to Bitty's apartment.

I didn't know if I should react first to Leona's use of the phrase *stud muffin* or to the erroneous nature of the so-called news.

In the end, I went with the latter.

"There's no steamy affair. With any guy."

Leona brushed off my denial. "Oh, don't worry, darling. I get it. You don't want people to know you're sleeping with your boss."

"Boss?" Where did she get that idea? "Wyatt is definitely not my boss."

"But the two of you are investigating Freddie's murder," Bitty said, making herself comfortable in one of two matching armchairs. She gestured for me to take the vacant one.

I remained standing. "Not in any official capacity. And, if anything, Wyatt works for me."

Bitty appeared confused. "But then why is his name on the business card?" She picked up one of the offending cards from the coffee table and held it up for me to see.

"How did you get that?" I asked.

Bitty shrugged and dropped the card back on the coffee table before sipping from her martini glass. "Agnes gave it to me."

I stifled a groan. Just how many cards had I dropped out on the front steps? Whatever the number, it was clearly too many.

Leona leaned toward me. "So, you're having a little trouble in the love department?"

"What?" I sputtered. "No!"

She waved a bejeweled hand in the air. "It's all right, dear. Sometimes I forget that not everyone is a starlet. I had to fend off gorgeous men in my youth. Still do." She let out a tinkling laugh.

Bitty sat forward in her seat. "We can help you. Between us we must have over a century's experience with men."

Leona nodded. "I have *so* much experience." She almost purred the words.

I fought off a shudder. "I really don't need help with my love life." I decided it was time to get the conversation back on track, but before I could speak again, Bitty beat me to it.

"You should really start with your appearance," she said, appraising me from her seat. "I always look to my dear cousin Princess

Diana for inspiration. Now, there's a woman who never looked anything other than elegant."

"No need to look beyond the grave for guidance when I'm right here," Leona cut in, a sharp edge to her voice.

"Pearls." Bitty stood up and set her drink on the coffee table, acting as if she hadn't heard Leona. "A string of pearls always elevates an outfit and adds sophistication."

"I don't even own any pearls," I said out loud, while on the inside I shouted, *How did I get on this roller coaster, and how do I get off?*

"Fortunately, I do." Bitty made her way across the living area. "I've got the real deal and a set of fake ones. I can lend you the fake ones." She disappeared into her bedroom before I could stop her.

I sank down into the nearest armchair, my head spinning.

Leona downed the last of her drink before fixing her glassy eyes on me. "Now, if you need some tips for the bedroom . . ."

I shot back to my feet. "No!" I lowered the volume of my voice a notch. "No, thank you."

Bitty returned empty-handed and looking bewildered. "Oh dear," she said, glancing around the apartment. "I can't seem to find my pearls."

"The fake ones or the real ones?" Leona asked.

"They've both gone missing." Bitty's hands fluttered. "Oh dear. And my doctor was telling me the other day that my mind is as sharp as a tack." She let out a jittery little laugh. "Silly me. I must have misplaced them. Just like my brooch and my cameo necklace."

A pang of sympathy kept me from fleeing the apartment. "When did you last see your pearls?"

She put a hand to her throat, as if reaching for one of the missing necklaces. "I wore the real ones to the cocktail party. The one Yolanda and Minnie held for Freddie." Her face crumpled in confusion. "I could have sworn I put them back in my jewelry box."

"I'm sure they'll turn up," I said in what I hoped was a comforting voice.

"Yes. Of course they will," Bitty said, but she didn't sound at all sure.

Leona lifted her friend's martini up off the coffee table. "Darling, have a drink. It'll help clear your mind."

I wasn't so sure about that, but Bitty accepted the drink and downed a large gulp. Then she sank into the armchair in a rather wobbly fashion.

"Now, where were we?" Leona said. "The key to keeping a man coming back for more—"

"Vincent!" I practically shouted. "I came to ask about Vincent." I directed my next words at Bitty. "Did he know Freddie?"

"Oh." She thought for a moment. "I suppose he might have. After all, he visits me here quite often. He probably ran into Freddie from time to time."

"But they weren't friends?" I asked.

"Not that I'm aware of."

"Business associates?" I suggested.

"I don't see how they could have been," Bitty said. "Freddie was a building superintendent. Vincent owns a store."

I latched on to that last statement. "A store?"

"On East Fordham Road."

"What kind of store?"

"He sells a little of everything." Bitty emptied her glass with a gulp. "Now, who would like another martini?"

Leona waved her empty glass in the air, light glinting off the jewels on her fingers. "I'd never turn down an offer like that." She fixed her eyes on me. "You know, Emersyn, back when I was on *Passion City,* I filmed many passionate love scenes. The steamiest one of all was when my character and her evil twin's husband—who'd recently returned from the dead—encountered each other, quite by accident, while skinny-dipping in a hot spring beneath the full moon. The best part was when I wrapped—"

I made a break for it. "Thank you, ladies! Have a nice day!"

I fled from the unit, letting the door slam shut behind me.

CHAPTER
THIRTY-NINE

I ran down the hall like a streak of lightning.

When I burst out into the lobby, I nearly collided with Bodie.

"Hey, where's the fire?" he asked, putting a hand on my arm to steady me. He held a paper bag in his other hand, and delicious aromas wafted up from it.

I glanced over my shoulder. Leona and Bitty hadn't followed me, much to my relief.

"No fire," I said. "Just some very unwanted advice from Leona and Bitty."

He grinned. "That definitely requires a high-speed escape." He punched the button for the elevator. "Better get on quick in case they decide they want to share some more pearls of wisdom."

The doors parted, and he gestured for me to go ahead of him. When he joined me, I got a stronger whiff of the delicious food smells.

"How was the fancy shindig?" I asked as I pressed the buttons for the third and fifth floors.

"The pay was good, and the people were bearable. Plus, the tips were better than expected." He held up the paper bag. "That's why I'm treating myself to pizza rolls from Massimo's."

I nearly groaned with longing. "Massimo's. No wonder it smells so good."

Massimo's was a tiny pizza joint located a short walk away from the Mirage. Massimo and his son Luca made the best pizza rolls.

"Are you hungry?" Bodie asked. "Because I've got plenty."

Even though I'd had some of Wyatt's fries and a few crackers with peanut butter, my stomach still rumbled.

Bodie chuckled at the sound, and my cheeks warmed.

"I'm happy to share." He met my eyes with his gorgeous blue ones. "Even happier to have your company."

The doors opened to the third floor.

I hit the button to close them again. "Thank you."

A few seconds later, the elevator deposited us on the fifth floor.

"Oh, hey." With his free hand, Bodie fished something out of his pocket as we walked down the hallway. "I got this coupon for a free ice cream cone. I thought you might like it for Livy."

Touched, I accepted the coupon. Bodie's fingers brushed against mine, setting off a flutter in my stomach.

"She'll love that," I said, hoping I didn't sound breathless. "Thank you." I tucked it into my pocket. "You're always so considerate."

He smiled. "I like helping out my neighbors." He held my gaze. "Especially my favorite ones."

A heady warmth glowed in me as we stopped outside his door.

Once we were inside Bodie's apartment, he set the pizza rolls out on the coffee table along with two different dipping sauces.

"How are you recovering from your Ultimate Beast workout?" he asked, fetching two plates from a cupboard and two glass bottles of soda from the fridge.

"I'm surviving, and my ankle is better." I sank down onto the couch, not bothering to mention that it hadn't been much of a workout.

"Gentle stretching might help if you're stiff." Bodie sat next to me and handed me one of the plates and a drink. "Or maybe book a massage."

"A massage isn't really in my budget these days." Nothing much was.

"I hear you." He nudged the box of pizza rolls along the coffee table until they were within my reach. Then he popped the top off his bottle of cola. "My car is pretty much my one luxury. Any other extra money goes into my savings."

I bit into a roll and gasped as hot cheese and sauce seared my tongue. "Ow, ow, ow!" I fanned my mouth. I swallowed quickly, hoping to save my tongue but scorching my throat in the process.

"Too hot?" Bodie pressed his opened drink into my hand. "Quick. Take a sip."

I chugged half the bottle, sighing as the pain receded.

As I handed the drink back, our fingers overlapped. We went still, neither of us releasing the drink. Bodie's gaze drifted down to my lips.

My breath caught as he used the thumb of his free hand to gently nudge a spot just below my lip.

"Missed a drop," he whispered.

My tongue darted out, touching a hint of sweetness as well as the roughness of the pad of Bodie's thumb. My heart thumped, and my blood warmed.

I released my hold on the bottle and grabbed the unopened one. I swapped the two, careful not to brush my skin against his again.

"We should trade now that I drank half of yours." Avoiding his eyes, I took a quick sip of soda before biting carefully into my cooled pizza roll. I savored the delicious flavors as the tension in the air slowly dissipated. "Are you saving up for something particular?" I asked, hoping my voice didn't sound unnatural as I tried to get back to our conversation.

Bodie shrugged, suddenly looking a tad bashful. It was both cute and sexy on him.

"I'm thinking of going back to college." He said it like a confession. "I dropped out last time, halfway through my sophomore year. I thought I had better things to do with my life. Like backpacking across Europe."

"That does sound amazing." I'd never been to Europe. The only time I'd ever left the country was on a road trip to Canada when I was twelve.

"I was so broke that some nights I slept under the stars," he continued. "But, yeah, it was amazing."

"I'd love to go to Europe one day," I said with a sigh, knowing any sort of travel was out of my reach for the foreseeable future.

"You'll get there." Bodie nudged a dipping sauce closer to me. "You've got to try the ranch."

I did, and it was heavenly.

"I think it's really great what you're doing, by the way," Bodie said as he grabbed a third roll for himself.

I dipped my second pizza roll in the ranch sauce and sent him a sidelong glance laced with incredulity. "Pretending to be a detective while I'm unemployed?"

He shook his head, taking a moment to swallow before clarifying. "Raising your niece. It can't be easy, suddenly becoming a single parent when you've never had kids before."

"It's not easy," I admitted as I wiped my fingers on a paper napkin. "Well, Livy makes it as easy as it possibly could be. It's just . . ."

"A major adjustment?"

I offered him a ghost of a smile. "You could say that. But, honestly, looking after Livy has actually helped me."

"With the loss of your brother?"

I looked at him with surprise. I'd never mentioned Ethan to him before.

He gave me a sheepish smile tinged with sadness. "Our neighbors like to talk."

I didn't really mind. Not this time, anyway.

"Yes, with losing my brother." A lump rose in my throat. I swallowed hard to suppress it.

Bodie looked down at his hands, empty now that he'd finished eating. "I think I can see how it would." He let out a breath before continuing. "My kid sister died when she was twenty-one. Hit by a drunk driver."

My heart plummeted. "Oh my God. Bodie, I'm so sorry."

"Thanks. She wasn't married, or even thinking about having kids at that age, but sometimes I wonder if she'd had a few more years, if she'd left behind a son or daughter, maybe it would be like . . ." He shrugged and looked away from me.

"Like there was a little piece of her still here with you?" I asked, my voice soft and a little shaky.

He met my gaze and swallowed hard, like he too had a lump of emotion rising up in his throat. "Yeah."

I rested a hand on his arm. He covered it with one of his own.

As we shared a long look of understanding, I sensed a gossamer thread spilling out from me and winding around his fingers, his wrist, his arm. Tears filled my eyes, but I didn't want to cry, so I gave Bodie's arm a gentle squeeze and released it, averting my gaze and gathering up the remains of our meal.

"Don't worry about that," Bodie said. "I'll get it."

I stacked our plates but left the rest and stood up.

"What's next for you today?" Bodie asked as he got to his feet.

I appreciated the return to normal conversation. As much as I valued that moment of connection we'd shared, I wanted the chance to wrestle my emotions back under control.

"I want to talk to Bitty's godson, Vincent," I said. "He knew Freddie, at least to some degree."

"You mean Vinny? That guy who hangs around here sometimes?"

"That's him. Apparently, he runs a shop on East Fordham Road. I'm hoping to find him there."

Bodie's forehead creased, and his eyes filled with concern. "Yeah, I know his shop. You're not planning on going there alone, are you?"

"Why?"

"He runs a pawnshop. A sketchy one."

Bitty hadn't mentioned that part.

"Aren't all pawnshops sketchy?" I asked as a shiver of unease ran along my spine.

"Maybe. Vinny's definitely is." Bodie carried the plates and leftover pizza rolls into the kitchen. "I'd go with you, but I've got to be at work soon."

"Don't worry about it."

"Promise me you won't go there on your own?"

I gave him what I hoped was a reassuring smile. "I'm sure I can get someone to go with me."

He stashed the leftover food in the fridge. "I don't know Vinny well, but he might not take kindly to being questioned about the murder."

"I'll be discreet," I said. "Other than asking a few innocent-sounding, casual questions, I'll blend in with the crowd. Or the merchandise, if there isn't a crowd."

Bodie came out of the kitchen and stopped in front of me. "You, blend in? I doubt it. I bet you turn heads every time you enter a room."

"I'm pretty sure I don't."

"Then the world is full of fools." He lifted a lock of my hair and let it fall back to my shoulder. His blue eyes met mine. "Emersyn?"

"Mmm?" I couldn't seem to breathe well enough to get an actual word out.

"I'd like to see you again really soon."

I couldn't look away from his entrancing blue eyes. "You will."

He took hold of the fingers of my left hand, his skin warm against mine. "Of course, I'd like it even better if you didn't leave."

"I thought you had to go to work," I said, my voice barely above a whisper, even though I hadn't intended to speak so quietly.

A hint of a grin touched his lips, drawing my attention to them.

"Not quite yet," he whispered as he leaned in.

My breath hitched, and my eyes closed.

A burst of jarring music jolted us apart.

Chagrined, Bodie released my hand and grabbed his phone off the kitchen counter.

"Shit," he said when he saw the screen. "Sorry. It's my boss. It could be about my shift."

"It's okay," I assured him, already opening the door. "Take it. I'll see you around."

"Emersyn?" When I stopped, he said, "Really soon, I hope."

We shared the briefest of smiles. Then I closed the door as he answered his call.

CHAPTER
FORTY

My thoughts spun in my head like a frantic dust devil. As soon as I stepped on the elevator, I typed out a text to Jemma.

HALP! So confused!

I sent the message and tried some deep breathing. It didn't do much good. I really needed my best friend to talk me out of my confusion. Bodie had nearly kissed me, and I'd wanted him to. Yet, in that moment when our lips had almost touched, I'd felt a tiny ping of guilt about Wyatt. Which was crazy, because Bodie was smoking hot and—even better—we had an emotional connection. And I still wasn't convinced that it was the right time in my life for a romantic entanglement with either Bodie or Wyatt.

"There she is!" someone exclaimed as I stepped off the elevator.

Carmen and Agnes hovered outside the door to my apartment. Carmen held a silver-headed cane, and Agnes had a Tasty Buns box in her hands.

"We've come for an update on the case," Agnes announced as I got closer. "We don't want Zita and Zoltán suffering anymore."

"And that detective was sniffing around the building," Carmen added.

I stopped a few feet away from them. "Again? When?"

"He was knocking on your door not five minutes ago," Carmen replied.

My heart sank. Here I was worried about men and relationships when what I needed to be worried about was keeping myself and Mr. Nagy out of jail.

Priorities, Emersyn! Come on!

Apprehension crept along my skin. "Did he mention why he wanted to talk to me?"

"We didn't ask," Agnes said. "We watched from around the corner." She pointed over her shoulder, down the hallway.

"So?" Carmen cut in. "How's the investigation going?"

I jangled my keys in my hand. "I've got a person of interest I want to speak with."

"Who is it?" Agnes asked.

I unlocked the door to my apartment. "Well, I don't want this getting back to Bitty . . ."

"You don't have to worry about that," Agnes assured me. "Our lips are sealed. Right, Carmen?"

"I never engage in gossip," Carmen said, her posture as regal as always. "You can confide in us."

The ladies followed me into my apartment, and Agnes shut the door.

She handed me the box and nudged her glasses up higher on her nose. "An assortment of day-old goodies from my bakery. You need to keep your strength up."

I peeked inside, and my mouth watered at the sight of the éclairs and the rolled lace cookies filled with mocha cream. "Thank you, Agnes."

"The person of interest?" Carmen prompted as I tucked the box in the fridge.

"Freddie was seen talking to Bitty's godson, Vincent, in the days before his death," I said. "Apparently, Vincent owns a pawnshop, and I have reason to believe that Freddie may have been quietly trying to sell some expensive whiskey from the early twentieth century."

Carmen nodded with understanding. "And you think Vincent was his fence."

"Ooh! Fence!" Agnes exclaimed with delight. She nudged Carmen with her elbow. "Look at you with all the fancy lingo." She turned her eager eyes on me. "So, where is this pawnshop?"

"East Fordham Road," I said.

Carmen's gaze sharpened. "Vinny's Pawnshop? Is that the one?"

"Apparently."

"You can't go there alone," Carmen said. "All sorts of questionable characters go in there."

"Bodie warned me about that."

Carmen nodded with approval. "He's a good man. You could do far worse. Although juggling two men isn't something I recommend doing for long."

Agnes nodded sagely. "It rarely turns out well."

"I'm not juggling two men," I said.

Agnes's eyes widened. "Is there a third? You've been busier than we thought."

"No!" I rushed to correct her. "I'm not juggling any men! I'm not in a relationship with Bodie or Wyatt or anyone else."

Carmen and Agnes exchanged a look.

Then Agnes tapped the side of her nose. "We understand. You don't want them getting wind of each other."

I was about to correct her again when Carmen opened the door.

"Let's get a move on," she said. "There's no time like the present."

"Get a move on?" I echoed with surprise.

"To the pawnshop," Carmen said with obvious impatience. She used her cane to herd Agnes and me out the door.

"But I don't have anyone to accompany me," I protested as I snatched my keys from the entryway table where I'd dropped them moments before.

"What are we? Invisible?" Carmen groused as I locked the door. "That's what happens when you become a senior citizen. Everyone looks right past you, thinks you're good for nothing."

"I didn't mean that!" I hurried to assure her. "I just thought that you ladies would have better things to do." Or that I should take someone stronger and more imposing with me. I decided it was best to keep that thought to myself.

"Better than solving a murder and helping our beloved neighbors?" Agnes said with surprise. "What could be more important than that?"

I didn't have a good answer for her.

"Yoo-hoo!" Leona called as she hurried along the hall toward us. She staggered slightly but got herself back on course. "What's happening?"

"We're going to question a murder suspect!" Agnes said with excitement.

"Speak with a person of interest," I corrected.

"How exciting!" Leona said as she wrapped a green feather boa around her neck. "It's a good thing I caught you then."

"Why's that?" I asked, not sure I wanted to hear the answer.

Leona lifted her chin. "It's not like any of *you* have experience playing a detective on television."

"And you do?" Agnes asked with genuine curiosity.

"Well, I never *played* a detective," Leona admitted. "But on *Passion City* I certainly played *with* one. If you know what I mean." She gave us an exaggerated wink.

Oh, dear heaven.

I sent a longing glance at my apartment door. I was wondering if I could somehow sneak back inside when Carmen put a hand to my back and propelled me down the hall.

"Come on," she said, setting a brisk pace. "I'm driving."

CHAPTER
FORTY-ONE

I seriously questioned my sanity minutes later when Carmen took a corner so fast that the back end of her white 1983 Lincoln Continental skidded across the road with a squeal from the tires. If not for my seatbelt, I would have tumbled across the red-velour-covered back seat and right into Leona's lap.

Judging by the rust around the wheel wells and the black smoke belching out from the exhaust pipe, I suspected that Carmen didn't own the vehicle because she was a classic car connoisseur. I had a hunch that she'd been driving this thing since the '80s. Although how it could have survived that long in her possession, I didn't know. She drove like a maniac. A maniac with a serious case of road rage.

"The light's green, you moron!" she yelled at the yellow Volkswagen Beetle in front of us as she leaned on the horn. "What are you waiting for? Christmas?"

The other car slowly began moving into the intersection. Carmen stomped on the gas pedal, sending the Lincoln lurching forward and nearly giving me whiplash. She swerved around the Volkswagen, two wheels going up on the sidewalk. A woman laden with shopping bags dove into a recessed shop doorway for safety.

I grabbed onto the edge of my seat when Carmen removed one hand from the steering wheel to give the driver of the Beetle the finger as we zoomed past the smaller car.

"Carmen!" I said, shocked and scandalized.

"He had it coming." She swerved around a delivery van and screeched to a halt behind a line of traffic backed up at a red light.

"Oh, this is nothing," Agnes said over her shoulder from the front passenger seat. "You should see her when she's late for bingo."

If I survived to have that chance, I'd avoid it at all costs. This ride was hazardous enough for me.

I glanced over at Leona, who, like Agnes, didn't appear at all fazed by Carmen's crazy driving. Before leaving the Mirage for the nearby parking garage, Leona had insisted that we stop at her apartment, where she'd grabbed her handbag and donned a gray fedora. She still had the boa and sparkly green dress on, and I detected a slight whiff of alcohol emanating from her. I was probably better off not knowing how many martinis she'd consumed at Bitty's place.

Again, I questioned my sanity for going along with this plan. When Bodie warned me to take someone with me to Vinny's Pawnshop, this bunch probably wasn't what he had in mind.

After a few minutes—each one spent with my heart in my throat—Carmen snagged a coveted parking spot. Stole it, really. Another vehicle was about to back into the space by the curb when Carmen darted into it nose-first. When the driver of the other vehicle shouted some choice words out his window, Carmen lowered hers and did the same.

I slid down in the back seat as she cursed like a sailor.

The other guy drove off, and Carmen parked the Lincoln crookedly, with the bumper kissing the back of the car in front of it. I slipped out of the car and scurried a few feet away, not wanting to be associated with the poorly parked Lincoln or its driver. By the time Carmen reached the sidewalk, she was back to her elegant-looking self. She held her cane in one hand and a handbag in the other. She hooked the bag over her arm, patted down her short gray hair, and led the way down the sidewalk at a lively pace.

We rounded a corner and walked for a block and a half before Carmen pointed out a tiny storefront with bars over the window. The building next door had a FOR LEASE sign hanging on the metal grille that covered the front door and windows. Graffiti adorned the brick edifices, and a piece of trash tumbled along the sidewalk in the breeze.

Even without going inside Vinny's Pawnshop, I could see why Bodie had warned me not to come here on my own. The area gave me sketchy vibes, even in broad daylight.

"So, what's our cover story?" Agnes asked as we approached the door to the pawnshop.

"Pretend you're shopping for a birthday gift," I suggested. "You know, on a budget."

"What should our code names be?" Leona asked.

I was relieved that she wasn't slurring her words, despite the martini fest at Bitty's apartment. She did, however, stumble slightly.

I put a hand to her arm to steady her on her high heels. "We don't need code names."

She and Agnes looked disappointed.

"But," I said, hoping to raise their spirits, "if we need to make a quick getaway for any reason, one of us should say the word 'pizza.'"

All three ladies nodded at that suggestion. Leona's and Agnes's eyes gleamed with anticipation, and Carmen's glinted with steely determination. I wondered, not for the first time, if I'd made a mistake by coming with the three ladies. Maybe I should have waited until Jemma was available. Or pushed my pride aside and called Wyatt. But I was here now. There was no point in having second thoughts.

Squaring my shoulders, I led the way into the store. As soon as I stepped inside, I was hit with the smells of old wood, leather, mustiness, and something else. Grease maybe?

The shop was narrow, with only two aisles. From just inside the door, I could already see that the place was crammed with a wide array of items, from an air fryer to an old gramophone, bicycle parts to furniture. Grimy oil paintings and musical instruments hung from one brick wall. On the other side of the store stood a long glass display case full of jewelry. The four of us headed in that direction, our heads swiveling to take in the sight of the incredible amount of merchandise.

A man emerged from the back, coming through a door behind the jewelry display case. He was a big, beefy guy, with bulging muscles and tattoos all over his arms. He had longish, wavy brown hair that was slicked back from his face with a generous amount of gel.

I recognized him right away.

Vincent, the man we'd come to see.

"What can I do for you today, ladies?" he asked, sounding jovial enough. He did a double take and squinted at Carmen. "Have we met before?"

Carmen gave him a regal nod, one hand resting on the silver head of her cane. "Indeed, we have. I live in the same building as your godmother."

Vinny grinned, revealing a gold tooth. "Right. I thought so." He gestured at the display of goods in front of him. "Are you looking for anything in particular?"

"A gift," I said. "For my grandmother."

"Are you thinking jewelry?"

"Oh, definitely," Agnes said. "She loves jewelry."

Leona pressed a hand to her chest. "A woman after my own heart."

Agnes, Leona, and Carmen pointed out some necklaces that caught their attention, and Vinny removed them from the display case one at a time. I wandered farther along the case, waiting for the right moment to casually bring up Freddie's murder.

"Oh, this is lovely," Agnes said, holding a sapphire necklace up to her throat.

Carmen appraised her with critical eyes. "You'd look better with emeralds."

"We're shopping for my grandmother, remember?" I said, hoping the reminder would keep them on track.

"No reason we can't look for ourselves as well," Leona countered before addressing Vinny. "Oh, darling, I simply must get a closer look at that cuff bracelet."

While Leona slid the bracelet onto her wrist and Vinny rattled off some details about it, I tamped down my impatience. I couldn't exactly interrupt him with talk of the murder if I wanted to sound casual, but I also couldn't stay here all day waiting for the right moment.

I wandered a little farther and then stopped, leaning in closer to peer through the glass at a delicate hummingbird brooch made up of tiny, colorful stones. I'd seen the brooch before. Attached to Bitty's sweater the day after the murder. It was the brooch that Bitty thought she'd misplaced.

My jaw nearly dropped as I put two and two together.

"What's caught your eye?" Carmen asked, coming over to join me. "Oh my stars," she said when she spotted the brooch.

I could tell that she'd made the same connection that I had.

Agnes scooted over to get a look for herself. "What is it?"

Leona joined us as well.

Carmen fixed a steely glare on Vinny. "Why, you thieving slubberdegullion!"

"Slubberde—what?" Vinny asked, baffled.

Agnes, too, had recognized the brooch. "Villain, fiend, louse!" she seethed at Vinny.

Leona pointed an accusing finger at him. "You're a crook!"

Vinny's eyes grew hard. "Hold on, ladies. You don't want to be accusing me of anything."

"The evidence is right in front of us." I stabbed a finger at the glass top of the display case. "That brooch belongs to Bitty. She thinks she misplaced it, but you've had it all along."

Carmen had moved farther along the case and now pointed at another item. "Those are probably Bitty's pearls!" She took two more steps and pointed again. "And her cameo necklace!"

Vinny glared at us through narrowed eyes. "You can't prove that."

I snapped photos of the offending items with my phone. "Bitty will identify them."

"We'll take the photos to the cops if we have to," Agnes added.

Carmen stared at him with steely eyes, her hand gripping her cane. "If you don't want to end up in the slammer, you'd better return every single thing you took from Bitty."

"Yeah?" Vinny sneered at her. "And who's gonna make me?"

Leona elbowed us aside as she tugged her fedora down over her forehead. She grabbed the collar of Vinny's shirt and yanked him down to her level, so they were nose to nose over the display case. "Pipe this, noodlehead," she said, sounding like she was trying to imitate Humphrey Bogart's voice.

"Noodlehead?" Vinny echoed.

Leona ignored his interruption. "We didn't make this trip for biscuits. We're gonna brace ya, put the screws on ya, and if you don't sing like a bird, we're gonna fill ya with daylight. Savvy?"

Vinny yanked back out of Leona's reach, his T-shirt rumpled and his eyes wide. "Are you batshit crazy?!"

"You bet we are!" Agnes chimed in. She put up her dukes and danced around like a boxer ready to fight. "And if you don't do as we say, we're going to flay you up so bad!"

"Flay me?" Vinny backed up a step. "You ladies belong in the nuthouse."

Agnes punched at the air. Vinny flinched, and so did I. This was getting way out of hand.

"Pizza!" I yelled. "Who wants pizza?"

Everyone ignored me.

Leona planted her palms on the top of the display case. "You've been dealing in more than just oyster fruit."

"Oyster what?" Vinny backed up another step.

"Pearls, you buffoon," Carmen said, poking him in the chest with the end of her cane. "We know you iced Freddie Hanover."

Vinny put his hands up. "Hey, whoa. No way. I didn't kill nobody!"

"But you knew him," I said, no longer so eager to flee now that the conversation was back on track, even if it was a crazy, out-of-control roller coaster track.

"Okay, yeah, sure," Vinny admitted, "but that's not a crime."

"Being a fence is," I said.

He shook his head, anger replacing his fear. "Nah. Don't go throwing accusations at me. You won't like what happens next."

Carmen poked him in the chest with her cane again. "Don't threaten her."

"Yeah, buster. Pipe that." Leona produced a pearl-handled pistol from her handbag. The kind you'd see a femme fatale wield in an old hard-boiled detective film.

Vinny's eyes widened as Leona pointed the weapon at him. Mine did too.

"You bet I brought my beanshooter," Leona said, still channeling Bogart. "If you don't want to get yerself a Chicago overcoat, you'd better start singing."

"Yeah!" Agnes bounced and punched the air again, making Vinny cringe. "Sing like a canary! Whistle like the wind! Hiss like a snake!" She herself let out a long and violent hiss.

Vinny recoiled.

"Or you'll find yourself in cement shoes," Carmen added, getting into the noir spirit.

"I didn't kill Freddie!" Vinny yelled. "I'll return Bitty's stuff! What else do you want me to say?"

"Did you sell some old-timey whiskey for Freddie?" I asked.

"No."

Leona aimed her pistol more precisely. "Want to taste lead, buster?"

Vinny raised his hands in surrender and plastered his back against the wall. "Okay, okay! Freddie contacted me, wanted to meet. And we did. He wanted to know if I could find a buyer for a stash of whiskey he'd found. Good stuff. I said I thought I knew a guy, but I'd have to get back to him. Next thing I heard, Freddie was dead."

"Did he ever bring you the booze?" I asked.

"Just one bottle, to that first meeting. You know, like a sample of the merchandise."

"Maybe you decided you didn't want to be the middleman," I said, thinking on my feet. "Maybe you thought you'd steal the stash of booze and sell it yourself."

"I don't even know where to find the stash," Vinny protested. "Freddie never told me."

Carmen reached her cane over the display case and pinned him to the wall with it. "You could have followed him."

"But I didn't! I swear!"

Vinny was a lowlife and a crook, but was he a killer? I wasn't sure. Maybe he was telling the truth about Freddie. I had a hunch that he was. But I didn't exactly have the best judgment when it came to people, especially men.

When Carmen pulled back her cane, Vinny took a step forward and reached beneath the display case.

In a flash, he whipped out a baseball bat and brandished it in the air. "Get out of my shop, you crazy old bats!"

"I'm twenty-eight!" I objected.

"And still as nutty as a fruitcake!" he shot back.

Leona held her pistol steady. "We ain't leaving without Bitty's jewelry."

She and Vinny stared at each other. I could almost hear Wild West showdown music playing in the background.

Vinny broke first. "Fine!" Keeping hold of the baseball bat, he used his free hand to grab items out of the case. He slammed the brooch, pearls, necklace, and three rings onto the counter. "Take them and get the hell out of here."

Carmen swept the jewelry into her handbag and snapped it shut. She leveled a glare at Vinny. "Your mother must be ashamed of you. Bitty certainly will be."

Vinny raised the bat and came running out from behind the display case.

"Pizza!" I screamed, shoving Agnes and Carmen in the direction of the door. I grabbed Leona's arm and dragged her along with me. "Pizza! Pizza! Pizza!"

We burst out the door and onto the sidewalk, stumbling into one another.

For one terrified second, I thought Vinny would follow us out onto the street with his bat. Instead, he yanked the door shut and locked it.

Emboldened by the glass door between us, Agnes stuck out her tongue at him.

Vinny glowered at us and raised the bat again.

I grabbed Agnes's arm and ran off down the street.

CHAPTER
FORTY-TWO

"I think I've aged ten years this week," I said to Bodie as I slouched on a barstool.

I'd stopped by his place of employment after leaving the pawnshop, driven by a powerful need to see him again. Maybe I should have ignored that desire, but I was getting tired of denying my feelings.

"Turn around." He gestured for me to spin on the stool.

I shot him a suspicious glance but did as instructed.

From across the bar, he touched each lock of my hair, one by one.

I craned my neck, trying to see what he was up to. "What are you doing?"

"Still no gray hairs." He dropped my hair and patted my shoulder. "You're good."

"Well, that's something, at least," I said, turning to face him again.

That gave me a perfect view of his grin.

My stomach flipped at the sight.

"You sure know how to keep life interesting, Emersyn," he said.

I'd already told him about the pawnshop escapade. He'd laughed so hard that he'd drawn the attention of a few nearby patrons. Thankfully, they'd since gone back to minding their own business.

"But," he continued, "when I asked you to take someone with you to Vinny's place, I wasn't talking about senior citizens."

I sighed. "Sometimes you've just got to work with what you've got."

"And you do," he said, his magnetic gaze locking on mine. "Work it, I mean."

The room temperature spiked as electricity sizzled in the air between us.

Without breaking eye contact, Bodie tipped his head to the side, indicating a door marked STAFF ONLY. "Come on. There's something I want to show you."

Intrigued, I slid off the stool.

"Hey, Gina," Bodie called to the lone server working the floor. "I'm taking five."

He came out from behind the bar and took my hand, leading the way through the door.

My skin buzzed, especially where his hand held mine.

As the door swung shut behind us, Bodie stopped. I did a quick visual sweep of our surroundings before focusing my attention on him.

"This is what you wanted to show me?" I asked. "A dimly lit corridor with unsightly stains on the floor?"

"Not the ideal atmosphere, I admit. And it's not what I wanted to show you."

"Then what?"

He took both of my hands in his. "I want to show you how I feel about you, Emersyn."

The hum of electricity running along my skin intensified as he held my gaze.

He let go of one of my hands so he could cup my cheek. He searched my eyes, as if looking for permission.

I drew in a sharp breath, my lips parting.

His eyes darkened with desire.

Then his mouth was on mine, gentle at first, then hungry, more insistent.

I rose up onto my toes, leaning into the kiss, seeking the tipping point that would send me over the brink.

A nearby thud snapped me back to our surroundings.

We broke apart a split second before the door to the alley opened. A guy dressed in jeans and a black T-shirt wheeled in a keg on a dolly.

"Hey, Benny," Bodie said, barely able to take his eyes off me.

I inched toward the other door. "I'll see you later, Bodie."

He looked like he wanted to say something to me, like he wanted to reach for my hand, but Benny started chatting with him, so I slipped out into the bar.

Gina blocked my path before I could turn for the front door. She sized me up as she leaned an elbow on the bar, chomping on a wad of gum. "So, are you, like, dating Bodie?" she asked, her hazel eyes lacking any warmth.

"We're just friends," I said, her hostile gaze setting me on edge. The memory of Bodie's tongue sliding over mine prompted me to elaborate. "And neighbors."

Okay, so maybe that didn't sum up our relationship either.

Gina scrutinized me in silence for another three seconds before she seemed to dismiss me as potential competition. I wasn't sure how I felt about that.

"You live in the building where that guy was killed?" she asked.

"You've heard about the murder?"

She shrugged one shoulder. "Sure, a detective came by. Super hot. Wanted to know if Bodie was here when the victim was killed."

"They've been checking the whereabouts of pretty much everyone in the building," I said, feeling the need to defend Bodie in some small way.

She blew a bubble with her gum and popped it. "Makes sense."

"Someone confirmed his alibi, right?" He'd told me as much, but I figured a prudent detective would double-check.

"The assistant manager, Alex. They were here together that morning. Then I came in at eleven. Bodie was here all day."

"That's good. I mean, that the police were able to confirm that." I tried to rein myself in from the edge of babbling as I inched my way around Gina. "Anyway, I'd better run. Nice talking to you."

I caught a glimpse of disinterest in her eyes before I scurried out the door.

Once on the street, I dashed off to the nearest subway station.

I was in desperate need of a chat with my bestie.

CHAPTER
FORTY-THREE

"It's been a day," I said to Jemma when I arrived at the salon where she worked.

"I know the feeling," she sympathized as she led me through the busy salon and into the employee break room in the back.

We had the small room to ourselves. Jemma shut the door, giving us even more privacy.

"I love most of my clients," she whispered, "but somehow I ended up with three of my most difficult ladies all in one day."

"Which is why I brought you this." I held out the plastic container I'd brought from home. I'd made a quick stop there on my way to visit my friend. "I thought you might need it."

Jemma had texted moments after I'd left the bar, telling me that she was ready to explode, thanks to crabby, overly picky, and downright unpleasant clients.

She peeked into the container and then looked up with grateful eyes. "Aw, Em. Is this from Ethan's cake?"

I'd told her about the cake on my brother's birthday, after she'd sent me a text to make sure I was doing okay.

"Yes, and it's delicious, if I do say so myself."

She grabbed a fork from the kitchenette and sank it into the slice of cake. "How's Livy doing?"

"She amazes me with her resilience," I said, sitting at the room's small table. "I think our little birthday party was good for her."

Jemma sat across from me and scooped up another forkful of cake. "What about you? Are you still hanging in there?"

"I'm doing okay," I said. "It helps that I've had some major distractions."

I proceeded to tell her about the visit to the pawnshop.

Jemma laughed so hard that she got me laughing too.

"I needed to hear that story as much as I needed this cake," she said after I wrapped up the tale. "Thank you, Em."

"I'm glad the ordeal was good for something." I crossed my arms over my chest. "But I'm still mad at you for ditching me at the gym the other day."

"I'm so sorry," Jemma said, her brown eyes full of remorse. "It was Cindy Lafayette who texted with a hair emergency. She's one of my best tippers, so how could I refuse her plea for help?" She whipped a crisp bill out of her pocket and waved it in front of my face. "See?"

I grabbed her hand so I could read the number on the bill. "She gave you a hundred bucks as a *tip?*"

"Yep." Jemma grinned like the cat that got the canary. "And because I'm super-duper sorry that I abandoned you—"

"In a torture chamber with a murder suspect," I cut in to remind her.

"I'm spending this tip money on dinner for you, me, and Livy," she finished.

I perked up a little at that. "Really?"

"Of course. You're my bestie, and Livy's my favorite kid in the whole world. And I really, *really* don't want you to be mad at me."

I unfolded my arms. "Oh, you know I can't stay mad at you for long."

She threw her arms around me. "Thank you! And I'm so sorry."

I gave her a squeeze in return. "You're forgiven."

"Now," Jemma said as she released me, "let's get out of here."

"You're done for the day?" I asked with surprise.

"So done, thanks to a cancellation." She handed the plastic container back to me, empty now except for a few smears of chocolate frosting. "I'll come with you to pick up Livy."

We rode the subway to the Mirage, where I dropped off the empty container before we walked over to Livy's school.

"Now you can update me on your investigation," she said on the way, "and whatever happened with Bodie."

I'd refused to talk about either subject while on the train with strangers all around us. Out here on the street, we had at least a semblance of privacy.

After the *HALP!* text I'd sent her, I'd told her only that an encounter with Bodie had prompted it and that I'd give her the details in person.

I'd just started in on that story when we reached the school. The bell rang, and the doors burst open, spilling children out onto the playground. Livy spotted Jemma and me and came running our way, her two braids flying out behind her.

She latched on to me first, squeezing me around my waist with an excited, "Auntie Em!" Then she tackle-hugged Jemma. "Hi, Jemma!"

My best friend hugged her back. "Hi, sweetie pie. Guess what the three of us are doing this evening."

"What? What?" Livy bounced up and down, jostling her backpack.

"Going out for dinner!"

Livy cheered and bounced around some more.

The sight made my heart soar while simultaneously sending a stab of guilt through me. If I were a competent adult with a steady paycheck, I could treat Livy more often, without having to rely on my best friend to do so.

I didn't have a chance to dwell on my guilt, and that was probably for the best. Livy skipped along ahead of us, so Jemma urged me to get back to our conversation.

Keeping my voice low enough that Livy wouldn't overhear, I told Jemma all about my latest encounter with Bodie. Her jaw dropped, and she grabbed my arm when I got to the bit about the kiss.

"Oh my God, Emersyn! You've got two major hotties interested in you! This is the best!"

"No, it's not!" I disagreed. "It's confusing!"

"What is there to be confused about?"

I told her about my mixed feelings, how I felt an emotional connection with Bodie, but how my attraction to Wyatt was stronger, to the point that I'd thought of him when Bodie kissed me. Yep, a superhot guy kissed me passionately, and I thought of someone else. I'd expected more of a spark, maybe even full-on fireworks, but I'd searched the kiss for a flame, even an ember, and came up empty.

Jemma squealed with happiness. "That means you've got it bad for Wyatt."

"That's not a good thing!"

"How could it not be?"

"Have you forgotten everything I told you the other day?" I asked.

On the way to Ultimate Beast, I'd filled Jemma in on how, thanks to Theo, I'd finally learned Wyatt's full name and looked him up on the Internet.

Jemma stopped me in the middle of the sidewalk. "Em, listen up. You are absolutely good enough for Wyatt. More than good enough, no matter how much money he has and no matter how famous his mom might be."

"It's not just that," I said as we resumed walking. "I know we only met recently, but the fact that he's secretive is a major red flag for me."

Jemma tucked her arm through mine. "I know. After what Hoffman did to you, trusting isn't easy."

"It really isn't. And I have to be extra careful now with Livy in my care."

"Speaking of that," Jemma said, talking even more quietly now, "how's the situation with your mom?"

"I haven't heard anything more from her about Livy's guardianship. That's good, right?" That's what I told myself at night so I could fall asleep instead of staring at the ceiling for hours and hours.

"I sure hope so," Jemma said. "Now, back to Wyatt."

I groaned. "If—and that's a big if—I were going to pursue a relationship with someone, Bodie is the far better choice."

"But there's no real spark there, and you can't get Wyatt off your mind."

Perhaps, I realized in that moment, the thought of forming a strong emotional connection with Wyatt scared me a little. Probably because something told me that he had the potential to really break my heart. Like, shatter it to pieces.

"Maybe," Jemma said, shaking me out of my introspection, "what you need is to have a fling with Wyatt to get him out of your system. Then maybe you'll find a spark with Bodie. Or another guy."

My shoulders slumped. "You know I can't do casual flings. Even if I tried, I'd get attached. And getting attached leads to getting hurt."

"Okay, true," Jemma conceded. "Separating the emotional from the physical has never been you."

Ahead of us, Livy bunny-hopped her way up the front steps of the Mirage. When she reached the top, she ran back down to fetch the front door key from me. I handed it over, and she hopped up the stairs again.

"I just need to never see Wyatt again," I whispered to Jemma as we followed Livy up the steps. "I'll tell him we're done investigating together, and that will be that. Once I've had time to forget about him, I'll be fine. I just really, *really* need to steer clear of him."

Livy hauled the door open and ran inside. We followed her and stepped into the lobby in time to hear her call out with delight, "Wyatt! Hi!"

I stopped so abruptly that Jemma bumped into me.

Wyatt stood in the middle of the lobby, looking dangerously hot in jeans, a T-shirt, and that darned military-style jacket that fit him like a bespoke glove.

Why, oh, why did the universe hate me so much?

CHAPTER
FORTY-FOUR

"Look who's here, Auntie Em!" Livy called out.

She spun in circles, a big smile on her face.

I warily met Wyatt's gaze.

Yep, as I'd feared, those freaking butterflies woke up and fluttered around inside me.

"I need a number for a good pest control company," I said to Jemma out of the corner of my mouth.

She glanced around fearfully, as if expecting to see cockroaches skittering across the floor. "What kind of pests are we talking about?"

"Butterflies," I whispered. "Unwanted, very active butterflies."

The fear left her eyes as she caught on. "Ooh, but you know what follows butterflies."

"Heartbreak," I said, my voice flat as I tried but failed to avert my gaze from Wyatt's.

"Fireworks," she countered.

I shook my head and approached Wyatt.

"Hey," he said. "Thanks for the text about Bitty's godson. I get the feeling you left out some details, though."

"Almost all of them, actually." I'd provided only the bare minimum information, with no reference to the crazy shenanigans.

"And you definitely want to hear the whole story," Jemma said with a smile.

Wyatt turned his gaze back to me. "Maybe you can fill me in? Then we can come up with a plan of action."

I wished his obsidian eyes didn't hold such sway over me. They sent my heart thudding in a way that couldn't be healthy. "I've already had more than enough action, thank you."

A spurt of laughter burst out of Jemma before she stifled the rest of it.

I shot a glare in her direction.

She transformed her expression into a mask of innocence.

Wyatt waited for a further response from me.

I sighed, realizing that he wasn't about to walk away and disappear from my life. "I might need a stiff drink before I tell you about Vinny. And anyway, I think it's time to focus on Hoffman again."

Doing that would not only help the investigation—hopefully—but it would also serve as a good reminder that romantic liaisons did not lead to happily ever after. Not for me, anyway. Clearly, I needed that reminder, because my heart was still galloping and my fingertips itched to run down his T-shirt-covered pecs. Well, uncovered pecs would be even better, though maybe not in the middle of the lobby.

Focus! I scolded myself silently.

"If you need a drink, we should raid the speakeasy," Jemma suggested with an excited gleam in her eyes.

"Too late," Wyatt said. "I just took a look in there. The cops must have cleared out all the booze."

Jemma frowned with disappointment. "Darn."

"Why are you talking about booze?" Livy asked as she skipped and hopped over our way.

"No reason, sweetie." I undid and refastened the loose hair tie at the end of one of her braids.

"I have umbrellas." She looked at us in turn with blue eyes that were so much like her dad's. "You know, for fancy drinks. You can all have one, if you want."

Jemma put her arm around my niece and gave her a squeeze. "Thank you, sweet pea."

Livy bounced up and down. "Can I go out in the courtyard?"

"Okay," I said, "but only for a few minutes."

She slid her arms free of her backpack and let it fall to the floor at my feet. Then she took off at a run.

I wished I had even half of her energy.

It didn't seem like I was getting my drink, and I wasn't getting rid of Wyatt until I shared what information I had, so I gave him the condensed version of what had happened at the pawnshop.

"So, Freddie took one bottle to his meeting with Vinny," Wyatt said once I'd finished the tale and he'd had a chance to shake his head over the antics of my older partners in crime.

"And he had one in his apartment," I added. "Partially empty. And another in his office that ended up broken."

"Sampling some of the wares himself," Jemma said with a nod. "That doesn't surprise me."

Wyatt tucked his hands in the pockets of his jeans. "That accounts for three of the missing bottles."

I thought back to what we'd observed in the speakeasy. "But, judging by the clear circles in the dust, there were six bottles missing."

"So maybe Hoffman found out about the speakeasy and fought with Freddie," Jemma theorized. "A bottle broke during the tussle. Then, after killing Freddie with the croquet mallet that was sitting in the office, Hoffman took some bottles from the speakeasy."

"But then why would he have taken the label off the broken bottle?" I asked, unconvinced.

She reconsidered her theory. "Okay. Maybe he took the label, did some research, and then came back and took some bottles from the speakeasy on another day?"

"I don't know. We should ask Theo if she can find him on the security footage any time after the murder." I looked around. "Where is Theo, anyway?"

Jemma shrugged. "She doesn't actually live here, right? Maybe she's at home."

I tapped out a quick text message to the teen. *Where u @?*

Not that I needed Theo around to run my life.

Okay, maybe I did.

I tried to stay focused. "For now, I'm going to see if Hoffman's been up to anything fishy, like trying to sell old bottles of booze. Can I use your car for a stakeout, Jemma?"

"You could, but it's at home, remember?"

Wyatt spoke up: "I've got my car right here."

"There! That's the perfect solution," Jemma declared.

"No, it's not!" I shot her a glare before forcing a smile for Wyatt. "Thank you, but I don't need your car."

"But I'd like to be part of the stakeout," he said, "so why not go in my car?"

"And I'll help out by babysitting Livy," Jemma offered, as if it were the best idea ever.

"That's not helping, Jemma. It's really not."

"You don't want to go on the stakeout with me," Wyatt surmised, studying me with those coal-black eyes of his.

"That's not what I said."

"You claim that you're not avoiding me, and yet you don't seem to want anything to do with me."

"She's avoiding you," my friend said.

"Jemma!" I seethed. I flashed my fake smile at Wyatt again. "I'm not avoiding you."

"Oh, she is." My traitorous BFF lowered her voice to a stage whisper. "Because of the kiss."

Wyatt glanced from her to me. "You told me the kiss didn't make you uncomfortable."

"That's not the issue," Jemma said. "The issue is that the kiss was sizzling."

"Jemma!" I was seriously considering trading her in for a new BFF. I took her arm and dragged her off to the side. "I was just telling you how I need to not be around Wyatt."

"But maybe you do," she countered. "See how you feel after you spend hours with him in his car. He's bound to have some disgusting habits that will completely turn you off. And then, hey, presto! Your problem is solved!"

I considered that. "You might have a point. Maybe his car is full of fast-food wrappers."

"And mouse droppings."

"Ew! I'm not sitting in a car with rodent poop."

"Okay, no mouse droppings," Jemma said. "But he'll probably sit there belching, talking about himself nonstop, chewing gum with smacking, wet mouth noises."

I shuddered. "I just can't with wet mouth noises."

"Exactly."

She pushed me back toward Wyatt and smiled brightly at him. "Emersyn would like to graciously accept your offer to accompany her on the stakeout in your vehicle."

Wyatt looked to me. "For real?"

"For real," I said, hoping I wouldn't regret it.

Livy reappeared, spinning in circles on her way toward us. "When are we going out for dinner? I'm already hungry."

"Slight change of plans, sweet pea," Jemma told her. "It's just you and me tonight. Do you know what that means?"

"What?" Livy stopped spinning and stood in one spot, swaying slightly.

Jemma waved her hundred-dollar bill in the air. "We get to spend all of this on the two of us."

"Yes!" Livy danced around with excitement.

"Should we leave now?" Wyatt asked me.

"We can't," I said. "We're not prepared."

Jemma nudged me with her elbow and whispered in my ear, "Maybe he is."

"Jemma!" With my cheeks flaming, I made a beeline for the elevator. I hit the button and then whirled around.

Wyatt, midstride, came to a halt.

I opened my mouth, then shut it again. I'd almost told him to wait in the lobby, but as soon as I met his eyes, I knew I couldn't do that. Well, I *could,* but I wouldn't feel good about it.

"Come on," I said. "I just need a few minutes to get ready."

The elevator doors parted. I swept Jemma and Livy on board ahead of me and waited for Wyatt to follow us before I hit the button to close the doors. Once they'd shut, I slumped against the back wall. Despite Jemma's master plan to get me to lose my attraction to Wyatt, I looked ahead to our stakeout with dread.

"What's wrong, Auntie Emersyn?" Livy asked, looking up at me with her innocent blue eyes.

I rested a hand on her head. "Oh, nothing, sweetie."

"Think happy thoughts," she advised. "They'll turn your frown upside down!"

I couldn't help but smile at that. "Thanks, Livysaurus. You're right."

As we disembarked from the elevator on the third floor, I cast around in my head for happy thoughts. The only one I could latch on to in that moment was the fact that Theo hadn't been present in the lobby. I liked the kid, there was no denying that, but having her and Jemma double-team me there in front of Wyatt . . . that would have been way too much.

I decided to thank the universe for small mercies.

Even if the universe didn't have a habit of playing nice with me.

CHAPTER
FORTY-FIVE

"I cannot believe you got me into this," I whispered to Jemma once I had Livy set up at the kitchen table with a snack of apple slices and string cheese.

Wyatt sat at the table with my niece, chatting about dinosaurs.

"I'm giving you a helping hand," Jemma said.

"More like pushing me off a bridge," I grumbled.

"Now you're being overdramatic. This could be exactly what you need to get over Wyatt."

"It had better work."

I made a mad dash for my bedroom and ensured that I shut the door securely. I did not need any more underwear incidents of any kind happening in my life. After sweeping my hair into a ponytail, I swapped out my pink sweater for a long-sleeved black T-shirt and the same black hoodie I'd worn when sneaking into Hoffman's apartment. Hopefully that would make me less visible when spying on my ex from Wyatt's car.

When I emerged from my bedroom, Wyatt was standing near the door while Jemma helped Livy into her coat.

"Auntie Em," my niece said, "Jemma's taking me to the mall, and then we're going out for dinner and ice cream."

"That sounds amazing, sweetie." I kissed the top of her head. "Have fun."

While Livy did up the zipper on her jacket, I mouthed, *Thank you,* to Jemma.

She gave me a quick hug, whispering in my ear, "Good luck."

When the door shut behind them, I hurried into the kitchen and opened the fridge door. "Shoot." Nothing in there tickled my fancy.

"What's wrong?" Wyatt asked.

Oh, let me list the things, I thought. *Number one: the seriously hot man in my living room who I need to somehow forget about. Number two: a police detective who possibly suspects me of murder. Number three: family drama that could lead to me losing guardianship of my precious niece. Oh, and number four: I can't find a freaking job!*

Out loud, I simply said, "How can we have a stakeout without decent snacks?"

"Why don't we hit a convenience store on the way?" Wyatt suggested.

I heard the siren call of chocolate in the distance.

"Good plan." I slammed the fridge shut and grabbed my phone off the end of the kitchen counter. "I think I'm ready to go."

It wasn't until the elevator doors closed on us that I realized we should have taken the stairs. Even though Wyatt stood several inches away from me, I felt like he was taking up the entire elevator, and all the oxygen inside of it. It wasn't that he was hogging the space; it was more like his presence filled every corner and wrapped around me.

If the stakeout didn't expose any disgusting habits of his, I was in big, big trouble.

To keep myself from fidgeting, I checked my phone and noticed a new text message.

From my mom.

I've contacted a lawyer about transferring Livy's guardianship.

My stomach lurched.

The elevator floor tilted beneath my feet.

Hurt and anger and panic rumbled inside of me. I was a volcano of emotion, ready to erupt. Then grief punched me in the gut so swiftly and with such force that I gasped, and my phone fell from my hand, clattering to the floor.

"Emersyn?" Wyatt's voice seemed to come from far away, even though I could have reached out and touched him.

I tried to hold it back, but a sob broke free, one that seemed to come from the depths of my soul, wrenching its way out of me. I missed my brother so much in that moment that I thought the pain might split me in two.

I sank to my knees, trying to grab my phone from the floor, but tears blurred my vision, and I came up empty.

"Emersyn? What's wrong?" Wyatt put an arm around me and helped me to my feet.

He pressed my phone into my hand, and I clutched the device to my chest.

I was vaguely aware of the elevator doors opening, but Wyatt didn't make a move to disembark, and I couldn't. I didn't think I could even move my feet.

The tears were coming fast and furious now, with sob after sob racking my body. "I'm sorry," I choked out. "I'm so sorry."

Wyatt kept a hand on my elbow, as if afraid I might fall to the floor again. "Can you tell me what's wrong? I'm really worried, Emersyn."

The elevator doors closed. I leaned against the back wall and slid down until I was sitting on the floor. I wiped my sleeve across my face, but my vision remained blurred.

"I miss my brother, Ethan," I managed to say as my sobs lost some of their ferocity. My voice sounded as raw as my insides felt. "He died of cancer last year."

And I'm trying so hard to take care of Livy, but I can't get my life together, I added, only in my head.

Maybe my mom was right. Maybe I wasn't cut out to be a parent. But I didn't want to lose Livy from my daily life, and I'd promised Ethan I'd take care of her. That I'd raise her. It was a literal deathbed promise. What kind of sister would I be if I broke it?

I drew up my knees and hid my face in my hands. I heard rather than saw Wyatt sit down next to me. I felt his presence close beside me, steady and soothing.

He rested a hand on my back, sending comforting warmth seeping through my hoodie. The gentle pressure of his hand acted like an anchor, tethering me enough to allow me to breathe less raggedly.

"I'm so sorry, Emersyn," he said, his voice resonating with compassion. "That's got to be devastating."

More tears trickled out of my eyes as I raised my head. "I'm sorry too. I didn't mean to fall apart in front of you. It just hit me so hard out of the blue."

His thumb moved in comforting circles on my back. "You have nothing to apologize for. Grief is like that. You think you're doing fine, and then it sucker punches you."

I looked at him through bleary eyes. There was an undercurrent to his words and a shadow in his eyes that told me he spoke from experience.

I woke up my phone and passed it to him. "My mom doesn't think I'm fit to raise Livy. And maybe she's right. I'd be letting my brother down if I didn't take good care of his daughter like I promised, but maybe I'm also letting him down by keeping Livy from a better life with my parents."

Wyatt read the text message and gently placed my phone back in my hand. "I didn't realize that Livy lived with you full-time."

"I'm her legal guardian. It's what Ethan wanted. Partly because Livy and I have always been close, but also because my dad had a heart attack three years ago. Ethan wanted him to have a stress-free retirement. Livy's an easy kid to look after, but . . ."

"Parenting is still a lot?"

I nodded. "So I've learned. But I wouldn't trade it, not for any-thing. Except maybe for Livy's well-being. I want what's best for her, and what's best for my dad's health. But I don't know what's truly best anymore."

"I know we just met recently," Wyatt said, his voice so kind that my soul ached at the sound, "but Livy looks like she's as happy and as healthy as she could be in her circumstances. You're doing great, Emersyn."

I let out a humorless laugh. "I don't even have a job. Not a real one."

"That's a temporary situation. One you can change. One you *will* change."

"I've tried." The bleakness behind my words was an echo of what resonated inside of me.

Wyatt rested a hand on my arm. "Keep trying."

I nodded and fought off a fresh onslaught of tears.

I had to keep trying. For Ethan and for Livy.

I sniffled and wiped the tears off my cheeks. I'd finally stopped crying, but my eyelids felt puffy, and an immense weariness spread through my body. Embarrassment rode along with the wave of exhaustion. Wyatt was the last person I wanted to see me at my worst, but he had a front row seat, and I had nowhere to hide.

I stood up, trying to ignore the aching of my heart. Somehow, I had to keep going, like I'd been doing since Ethan died.

"Is it all right if I give you a hug?" Wyatt asked as he stood up too.

Tears blurred my eyes again as I nodded. In that moment, I needed a hug even more than I needed to forget the gorgeous man standing before me.

He stepped closer and wrapped his strong arms around me in the gentlest way. I leaned against him, resting my head below his collarbone, listening to the steady beat of his heart and letting myself soak in the comfort he was offering. It was like I'd finally found shelter after battling through a fierce storm. I relaxed against his strong frame, letting myself simply exist in the moment, with no worries about what I might have to face in the future.

The embrace was so different from the one we'd shared in the dumbwaiter shaft. Yet, somehow, it was no less intimate, no less profound. I felt safe in his arms, protected. He exuded a warmth that was more than just body heat, more than just our crazy chemistry.

I didn't want to let go.

And that was dangerous.

I gathered up what little shreds of strength I could find and stepped back out of his embrace. "Thank you," I said with genuine gratitude. "I'm all right now."

He searched my face, as if he were trying to make sure that I really was okay. His eyes were so full of compassion that my throat constricted and my eyes burned, but I was determined not to cry anymore that day.

"I totally get it if you want to call off the stakeout," I said, trying to give him an out.

"If I do?" He seemed surprised by my words. "I understand if you're not feeling up to it now, but I'm game."

"I just cried in front of you, broke down in front of you. You're supposed to run away." In my experience, that's what most men would want to do.

"I'm not running anywhere, Emersyn," he said, never breaking eye contact. "Especially not when you need a friend."

I tucked my hands up inside the sleeves of my hoodie. "Are we friends?" I didn't mean for the question to come out sounding so tentative and vulnerable.

"I'd like to think so. New friends and business partners with lots of potential."

The words *lots of potential* woke up the butterflies in my chest.

I chose the safest way to respond.

"Associates. Not partners. It's my agency, remember?"

A flicker of a grin made a fleeting appearance on his face. "My name's on the card."

"How many times are you going to remind me of that?"

This time his grin stayed a little longer. "As many times as it takes."

With a trembling finger, I punched the button to open the elevator doors. I was like a ball of electric emotions, bouncing all over the place and on the verge of short-circuiting. Stepping into the lobby, getting more space, brought me a sliver of relief, but I craved fresh air.

I made it three steps before Wyatt put a hand on my arm to stop me.

"Emersyn? I still want to do the stakeout, but if you need to cancel or postpone, I totally understand."

Part of me wanted to crawl into bed and disappear under a pile of blankets, but I also dreaded the thought of returning to my empty apartment and waiting all on my own until Jemma returned with Livy.

"No," I said, making up my mind. "I need the distraction. And . . ." I felt like I was about to take a dangerous step off a cliff. "And the company."

His gaze seemed to reach for my soul when he said, "You've got it."

CHAPTER
FORTY-SIX

I slid into the passenger seat of Wyatt's BMW with a sigh. If I ever managed to own a car in the future, it would likely be a second-hand clunker, never anything as new and eye-catching as this BMW. The cognac-and-black interior was almost as gorgeous as the metallic green exterior. The seats were comfy, and there was a hint of new-car smell.

I took in my surroundings while waiting for Wyatt to circle around and get into the driver's seat. The car was pristine. So much for fast-food wrappers and unpleasant smells.

He could still have other gross habits, I reminded myself.

The night was young, after all. Heck, it wasn't even five o'clock.

We didn't talk much as I directed Wyatt to Hoffman's apartment building in Longwood. I appreciated the time to gather myself. The fact that my mom had booked an appointment with a lawyer still sent a myriad of emotions—including abject fear—roiling through me every time I thought of it, but I did my best to push that problem to the back of my mind.

Sometime this week, I'd speak to my dad. That was the only plan of action I could come up with. My mom tended to plow through people with hurricane force whenever she had a bee in her bonnet, and my dad typically rode along with the storm. I didn't want to drag him into the middle of a fight, especially considering his health issues, but I had to at least talk to him. Even if I decided that Livy was better off with my parents, I didn't want to be railroaded. I had a voice, and I intended to use it to advocate for Livy, whatever that meant in the end.

"I guess we could be sitting here for nothing if Hoffman's already sold the whiskey," I said once Wyatt had found a parking space down the street from Hoffman's building. "If he even stole the booze in the first place."

At least we knew, thanks to his recent social media post, that he was hanging out at home. Or had been an hour earlier, anyway. The chance that he would decide to do something incriminating while we happened to be watching was slim, but I didn't know how else to find out if he was Freddie's killer.

"How long did you two date?" Wyatt asked as we kept an eye on the front entrance of the three-story brick building.

I sighed, wishing I'd never crossed paths with Hoffman at the pub trivia night where we'd met. "Eight months. Which was eight months too long. Not that I realized that until it was too late."

Just as I was about to dive into the box of Milk Duds I'd bought at the convenience store, the door to Hoffman's building opened. It was the third time that had happened since we'd arrived. Still, I couldn't believe our luck. While I'd hoped that Hoffman would make an appearance, I didn't think he actually would. I thought we would end up sitting there in Wyatt's car until we were half frozen, with no evidence and no leads.

Maybe the universe didn't hate me after all. Not completely, anyway.

Then again . . .

"Fudge muffins!" I slid down in the passenger seat until I was below the window.

Hoffman was walking our way, the strap of a slightly bulging messenger bag slung over one shoulder.

"Fudge muffins?" Wyatt echoed with obvious amusement.

"Hide your face!"

Hoffman had met Wyatt only the one time, but Wyatt's face wasn't easy to forget. Not for me, anyway.

Wyatt turned his head slightly to the side and looked down at his phone, as if engrossed in whatever was on the screen.

"I'm trying to train myself not to swear in front of Livy," I explained in a whisper. "Fudge muffins might not have as much impact as an F-bomb, but it'll have to do."

"It has impact," Wyatt countered, not doing a very good job of fighting the grin that was trying to appear on his face. "Maybe just not of the same variety."

"Is he gone?" I whispered, ignoring his teasing. And the effect his grin had on my stomach.

Wyatt flicked his gaze toward the passenger-side window. "Nope. He slowed down. I think he likes my car."

I groaned. "I was afraid of that."

My left leg threatened to cramp as I waited for Hoffman to peer in the window and catch me hiding in the footwell. That would have been so on-brand for my life at the moment.

Instead, something actually went right for a change.

"He's gone," Wyatt said.

I wriggled my way back onto the passenger seat and twisted around until I spotted Hoffman disappearing around the corner.

"Let's go," I said.

I had the presence of mind to grab the box of Milk Duds and shove it in my hoodie pocket before scrambling out of the car.

Wyatt and I jogged to the end of the street and peered around the brick building on the corner. Hoffman was still in sight. We followed him at a brisk walk, me with the hood of my sweatshirt pulled up. An unnecessary precaution, as it turned out, because Hoffman never looked back.

We followed him to the nearest subway station and hung back

while he waited on the platform. I noticed that he had wireless earbuds in his ears, probably playing music. Hopefully that made him less likely to realize we were tailing him.

"How many bottles of booze do you think he could have in that bag?" I asked.

"One or two."

The train pulled into the station, and Wyatt and I hurried through the crowd of bodies to board the same car as Hoffman, but through a different door. I had a panicky moment when he turned my way, but I managed to put my back to him. Wyatt assured me seconds later that Hoffman remained oblivious to our presence.

We nearly lost him when he changed trains a while later, but we managed to get him back in our sights. Wyatt and I didn't want to draw attention to ourselves, so we mostly stayed quiet. Boredom set in quickly, and the trip seemed to stretch on forever, but Hoffman finally left the train in the Sunset Park area of Brooklyn and hoofed it toward the waterfront.

"Any idea why he'd be in this area?" Wyatt asked as we followed at a safe distance behind Hoffman's loping form.

"Not a clue."

As we drew closer to the waterfront, the area changed from a mix of residential and commercial to mainly industrial, with warehouses on both sides of the street. Aside from parked cars and some slightly recessed doorways, we didn't have much cover. Fortunately, Hoffman kept up his trend of not looking back.

We passed a warehouse-turned-gym, which triggered flashbacks to my time at Ultimate Beast. I suppressed a shudder and kept walking, ready to dart behind a parked car at any moment if our target glanced back.

When Hoffman stopped, my heart took a leap, and I crouched down behind a dark sedan. Wyatt stepped into a recessed doorway. I peeked around the car to see Hoffman open the door to a brick warehouse and disappear inside.

I straightened up, and Wyatt and I approached the building. I swept the hood of my sweatshirt off my head on the way.

"What the heck is he doing here?" I wondered.

I scrutinized the building. It had a brick exterior, with graffiti-splattered, corrugated metal doors over the loading bays and bars over the second-story windows. The only windows. So much for peeking inside to see what Hoffman was up to. Nothing on the outside of the building gave any clue as to what might be going on inside.

"Is there an alley?" I asked, wondering if there might be lower windows around back.

Wyatt pulled out his phone and typed the building's address into a map app.

"No alley," he said as he zoomed in on a satellite map. "And all the entrances are out here in the front."

"Great." I crossed my arms and sized up the distance from the ground to the high windows.

Was I ready to channel Spider-Man?

CHAPTER
FORTY-SEVEN

The answer was no.

I definitely wasn't ready to attempt to scale the building.

I wasn't that crazy. Not yet, anyway.

Besides, it was still light out, and the area was quiet but not deserted. The last thing I needed was for the cops to show up and arrest me for whatever crime fit the harebrained scheme I had wisely scrapped almost as soon as it crossed my mind.

"Maybe we should watch from across the street," Wyatt suggested as I continued to stare at the warehouse.

I agreed with that plan. At least from that position we could duck behind the row of parked cars if Hoffman made a sudden reappearance. We waited for a van to pass, and then we darted across the street and leaned against the wall of another warehouse.

"I don't suppose you have infrared binoculars," I said, stuffing my hands into the pockets of my hoodie. As soon as my fingers touched the box of Milk Duds, my mouth watered.

"Damn. I left them in my car with all the rest of my spy gear."

"Ha ha." I rolled my eyes and tore open the box.

"I said I had a background in security, not that I'm 007."

I poured a couple of Milk Duds into my palm. "I just thought—"

"That I must have every tool and toy under the sun?" Wyatt

shifted and shoved his hands into the pockets of his jeans. "I guess the fact that we met at the country club kind of gave it away."

"That you've got money?" I asked. When he nodded, I added, "If it hadn't, the car would have."

One corner of his mouth turned up in a short-lived grin. "I do love my car."

I offered him the box of candy. "What about the country club?"

"Not so much." He poured a few Milk Duds into his hand. "The amenities are great. The company is hit-or-miss."

We fell silent, enjoying our chewy, chocolate-coated caramels while watching the warehouse across the street. His answer intrigued me and left me with the feeling that he was more than just some hot rich guy. Maybe I'd sensed that all along.

I glanced his way as I finished the last of my Milk Duds. I flattened the empty box and shoved it into the pocket of my hoodie.

"I have been avoiding you lately," I confessed, suddenly feeling the need to offer up at least a bit of honesty. "Somewhat, anyway. There's a lot going on in my head."

"So it's nothing to do with me, specifically?"

I tried to figure out how to answer that. "You confuse me. I like you, but I'm wary. I don't want to get burned, even as friends, but I really don't know you, so how can I trust you?"

Wyatt stayed silent while we watched the building across the street. Nobody came in or out. Nobody even walked by. Now that daylight had begun to fade, due in part to the darkening clouds overhead, I detected a glow of light emanating from the high, bar-covered windows. But as for what was happening inside the building, we remained clueless.

I crossed my arms over my chest, trying to stay warm. I should have brought a jacket, especially since the clouds looked ready to open up and pour rain down upon us. At least they were holding off for the moment, but I didn't trust my luck to continue for long.

As Wyatt's silence stretched on, I couldn't help but fidget. Maybe I'd offered up too much honesty too soon. Even though I knew I'd likely be better off if I scared him out of my life, I didn't actually want to run him off.

I'd never claimed to be sensible.

Out of the corner of my eye, I saw Wyatt take out his wallet and remove something.

My gaze flicked down when he held a plastic card out to me.

His driver's license.

I opened my hand, and he placed the license on my palm.

The name on it wasn't new to me, thanks to Theo's revelation, but the card still felt weighty in my hand. It was the importance of the gesture that gave it that heft. It had taken him a while, but he'd shared his identity of his own accord.

"Wyatt Quintal Alessi," I read. "A March baby. Three years, one month, and two days older than me." I passed the card back. "Thank you."

He tucked it away in his wallet. "I wasn't trying to be—"

"Secretive?" I offered.

"I was going to say a jerk."

I smiled at that, just a little. "You didn't want me putting two and two together."

"Have you now?"

"In keeping with the spirit of honesty and openness, I already had, thanks to Theo."

That took him by surprise. "She knows my full name?"

"I'm pretty sure she knows everything about both of us," I said.

"Should I be worried?"

I didn't need time to consider my answer. "Most likely."

We shared the briefest of smiles before turning our eyes back to the warehouse across the street.

"You thought if I knew about your famous mother, I'd . . . what?" I asked. "Go all fangirl? Morph into a gold digger?"

He was silent for a moment before responding.

"My mom grew up in Brazil," he said. "Her family was dirt poor. She got pregnant with me when she was fifteen. Her family knew that they couldn't look after me—they were already struggling—so I was given up for adoption."

My gaze snapped to him. I hadn't expected that. He kept his eyes trained on the warehouse.

"At the time, my birth mother had no idea that she'd get discovered by an agent and shoot to fame as a supermodel two years after I was born."

I opened my mouth to say something but then closed it again when words eluded me.

I'd never known Rosângela Quintal's background. She was just a familiar face I saw in commercials and print ads. She'd enjoyed the height of her fame when I was a kid, but she had her own fashion and cosmetic lines that remained popular to this day.

"An American couple adopted me," Wyatt continued. "Lorenzo and Emilia Alessi. I grew up in Syracuse in a middle-class neighborhood with a middle-class life. And it was great."

"I sense a but," I said quietly.

"An *until*."

Even in the waning light, I didn't miss the shadow of pain that passed across his face.

He stared across the street. "Until my parents were both killed in a car crash when I was fourteen."

"Oh my God. Wyatt." My heart broke for him.

He plowed on, as if determined to finish the story. "I ended up in the foster system and bounced around from placement to placement for about three years. Until my birth mother tracked me down. She took me in, and we became close. Became family. I've never wanted for money since, but I know what it's like to lose everything, to have nothing and no one. There's a lot more to my story than country clubs, cars, and a famous parent. But that's the stuff people see first, and most don't bother to look any further."

"Like me?" I whispered, my regret and heartache mingling together.

"I didn't mean you," he said with nothing but kindness in his eyes.

Kindness that I didn't deserve.

"But I did," I insisted, turning to face him. "I did judge you. I figured you couldn't know what it's like to struggle, to worry about money. I thought a rich guy like you could never truly understand someone like me." I looked him straight in the eye, hoping to convey the depth and sincerity of my remorse. "I'm sorry, Wyatt."

He shook his head. "You couldn't have known. Like you said, you hardly know me."

"But I thought I knew enough to put you in a box. I really am sorry. And I'm sorry you went through all that. I can't imagine how awful it must have been to lose your parents at such a young age. I can't even handle losing my brother as an adult."

Facing me now, Wyatt touched a hand to my arm. "You're handling it better than you think."

"Maybe on the outside."

His eyes held fathomless understanding and compassion. "There's no timeline for grief. That's one thing I know for sure."

I looked up at him, realizing only then how close we stood to one another. An invisible tether bound us together in that moment. He felt it too. I could see it in his eyes. I could sense it in the gentle, reverent way he brushed his thumb across my cheek. As he lowered his hand, he let a lock of my hair slide through his fingers.

I grasped fistfuls of his open jacket, below the lapels. His inky eyes held mine like magnets, and the air around us buzzed with a heady, electric energy. Or maybe the buzzing was inside of me. All I knew was that every breath of space between us was too much.

"Wyatt."

The whisper had barely left my lips when his mouth was on mine.

The kiss started out soft, gentle. Then one of Wyatt's hands skimmed down to the small of my back, anchoring there, the warm pressure a flash point for the heat that flared through me. I slid my arms around him and pressed in closer, the taste of him only fueling my need for more.

Wyatt eased up and pulled back, just long enough to tug a yearning gasp from me, just far enough to allow me a glimpse of his heat-hazed eyes. Then we dove back in, and I fell into the dizzying depths of the kiss.

A rough burst of laughter rang out, startling us apart.

Dazed, I took a second to realize that Hoffman had emerged from the warehouse across the street, his phone to his ear.

"Yeah, I know," he said into the phone. He turned his head our way, his gaze skipping past us before snapping back to home in on me.

"Oh, shit," I said.

So much for going unnoticed.

CHAPTER
FORTY-EIGHT

Hoffman lowered his phone, then put it back to his ear. "I've got to go," he said before ending the call.

He strode across the street.

I took a step back and bumped into the brick wall behind me.

"It'll be fine," Wyatt said, quietly enough so only I would hear.

I shot him a look of incredulity before facing my ex.

"Did you follow me here?" Hoffman demanded, his muddy brown eyes sparking with fury.

"Yes." I didn't see any point in lying. What else would I be doing there?

Hoffman took in the sight of Wyatt standing next to me. "You and your detective," he said with a heavy dose of disdain. "You're never going to prove that I stole anything from you."

"Maybe not," I conceded with a fake sweet smile, "but I'm betting we can prove that you murdered Freddie Hanover."

"You're the one who sicced the cops on me?" Hoffman shook his head with disgust. "I should've known." He stepped right up into my personal space, trying to intimidate me. "You really think you'll get away with this?"

Wyatt put a hand to Hoffman's chest, exerting just enough pressure to send him back a step.

My ex glared at him. "Get your hands off me."

Wyatt didn't move a muscle. "Only if you stay back."

The two men engaged in a brief staring contest. Rage still contorted Hoffman's face, but he blinked first and took another step back.

"Why the hell would I kill some guy I didn't even know?" he asked, returning his attention to me.

"You were at the Mirage on the day of the murder," I said. "You were caught on camera."

"I came to bring you flowers. Then I changed my mind. That's not a crime."

"Why would you bring me flowers?" I asked, momentarily distracted by the question that had bothered me ever since seeing him on the Mirage's security footage.

"I thought we could get back together. Then I came to my senses."

Beside me, Wyatt shifted but didn't speak.

"You mean you were trying to butter me up so I'd call off my private detective." I didn't believe for a second that he still harbored any positive feelings toward me. If he ever did. "Does Tiffany know you bought roses for another woman?"

"Don't you dare tell her." He tried to take a step closer, but Wyatt's hand landed on his chest again. He glared down at it but stayed in place, even after Wyatt removed his hand.

I decided to get back on track. "You know what? It doesn't matter. What matters is the murder."

"I had nothing to do with that."

"Then why were you in the building so long after you dumped the roses?" Wyatt asked.

"That's none of your business."

"I think you saw Freddie disappear into the vintage phone booth," I said. "I bet you waited until Freddie was out of the way, and then you discovered the speakeasy and all the old booze. You wanted to make some money by selling it, so you took a bottle. But

Freddie caught you and tried to take the liquor back. The bottle broke during the struggle. Then you hit him over the head with the croquet mallet that was in Freddie's office."

The scenario played out with unpleasant clarity in my head.

Hoffman's face flushed. "I don't know what you're talking about."

I didn't believe that for a second. "You're lying. What's in the bag you brought here?"

He didn't have it on him at the moment.

"A bottle of water and a script."

"No booze?"

His face contorted.

"Hello, Emersyn!" a familiar voice called out.

I was so engrossed in the fight with my ex that it took me a good three seconds to realize that Leona Lavish stood across the street, holding a reusable water bottle. Her presence took me so much by surprise that I momentarily forgot about Hoffman.

I crossed the road. "Leona? What are you doing here?"

"I could ask you the same thing, darling." She gestured at the warehouse behind her with a languid hand. "I teach acting classes here."

"In the warehouse?" That struck me as odd.

"It's been converted into studio spaces. All sorts of classes are taught here. Stained glass, pottery, drama, you name it." She glided a step closer to me. "If you want to sign up for one of my classes, I could give you the friends and family discount. Five percent off."

"That's sweet," I said as Wyatt joined us on the sidewalk. "But I don't think acting is my thing."

"You never know until you try it." Leona took a sip of her water.

I peered closely at the reusable bottle. It had the words GRUB TUBZ printed on it.

"Is that the same brand of water bottle that Minnie has?" I asked, even though I knew the answer.

"She gave it to me as a sample product." Leona screwed the cap back on. "I think she's hoping I'll like it enough to buy more Grub Tubz containers."

"Minnie sells the products?" I glanced Wyatt's way and could tell he was wondering why I was so interested.

"It's a side hustle," Leona explained.

"Did she ever sell some to Freddie?" I asked, ignoring Hoffman as he sidled up to us.

"I don't know, but she might have. Or maybe she gave him a sample too. Before he ended up on her bad side, that is. She's given samples to several people in the building. It's a good way to drum up business." She addressed Hoffman next. "Break's over in two minutes." She smiled at me. "See you at the Mirage, Emersyn." She wiggled her fingers in a wave as she disappeared back inside the warehouse.

"Hold on." I swung around to face Hoffman. "You're taking acting lessons?"

Hoffman shrugged one shoulder. "I'm thinking of moving to Hollywood."

I felt sorry for Hollywood but happy for myself and the rest of New York City. Except . . .

"You won't be going anywhere other than to jail," I said, not at all sorry that I might be bursting his bubble.

His eyes filled with scorn. "I didn't kill anyone. And if you ever try spying on me again, I'm going to call the police and tell them you're harassing me."

He turned on his heel and stormed into the warehouse, slamming the door shut behind him.

"He's a nasty piece of work," Wyatt remarked once we were alone.

"If only I'd realized that much sooner," I said with a sigh of regret.

But Hoffman could be charming when he wanted to be, and I'd so wanted to believe that he was as crazy about me as he'd pretended to be.

I stared at the brick exterior of the warehouse, my thoughts swirling.

"What are you thinking?" Wyatt asked.

"Minnie told me that she never talked to Freddie, except maybe to say hello, but he had a Grub Tubz flyer in his apartment."

"And he probably got it from Minnie."

I nodded. "She must have talked to him more than she admitted to."

Wyatt drew the same conclusion as I had. "So she lied."

"And why do that if she had nothing to hide?"

CHAPTER
FORTY-NINE

I ended up taking the subway home. Wyatt wanted to drive me from Longwood, where he'd left his car, but I declined the offer. My brain felt like a pinball machine, with my thoughts shooting here, there, and everywhere. One second, I was thinking about the murder and the next about the kiss. Then my thoughts jumped to the story Wyatt had shared about his background before hopping to Livy's guardianship and then back to the kiss again. It was exhausting and distracting, and I needed some time to settle the whirring in my head.

I arrived home—just barely beating the rain—to find Livy hyped up from ice cream, leftover chocolate cake, and a lip-synch battle with Jemma. By the time she'd had a shower and dressed in her pajamas, she'd settled down enough that I could at least hope she'd fall asleep without much trouble.

Jemma wanted a detailed account of the stakeout as soon as I arrived home, but I made her wait until Livy was asleep. She grumbled a bit but gave in and scrolled through her social media feeds while I tucked my niece into bed.

"Did you have fun with Jemma?" I asked Livy as I sat on the edge of her mattress.

She nodded, hugging her dinosaur stuffie with one arm and a

plush turtle with the other. "I love Jemma. I want to make her a friendship bracelet."

"That's sweet. She'd love it."

Livy's forehead scrunched up with worry. "I don't have the stuff I need to make a friendship bracelet."

"We'll get some," I assured her, mentally working out how much money I had left in my bank account. "Just . . . maybe in a week or two, okay?"

She nodded. "I want to make a bracelet for you too, Auntie Em."

Her words, and the pure love behind them, set off a warm glow inside my chest.

"Thank you, sweet pea." I kissed her head. "I'd wear it every day."

"Can I make one for Daddy too?"

I smiled through the sudden ache that cleaved my heart. "Of course you can."

Her forehead scrunched again. "He can't wear it in heaven, can he?"

"Maybe not," I said, choosing my words carefully, "but I bet he'll know that you made it for him. And he'll love it so much."

She considered that before looking into my eyes. "Do you want to make one for him too?"

I smiled, even though it hurt to do so. "I'd like that very much."

"But if he was your brother, does that mean he wasn't your friend?"

I fought to keep my smile from trembling. "He was both." My eyes stung from the tears I refused to let fall. "My brother and my friend."

Maybe that hadn't been true when we were younger, when I made a pastime out of pestering him and he was always striving to gross me out, but by the time I finished high school, that had changed for the better.

Livy yawned, her eyelids growing heavy.

I kissed her head again and switched off the bedside lamp.

"Sweet dreams, Livysaurus," I said when I reached the door.

"Night night, Auntie Emersyn," she said sleepily.

As I eased out of her bedroom, I heard her whisper, "Night night, Daddy."

I pressed a hand to my chest to help me hold back a sob.

Jemma jumped up from the couch when she saw the tears that had finally broken free to tumble silently down my cheeks.

"Oh, Em." She gave me a quick hug. "Are you okay?"

I wiped away my tears and nodded. "I'm fine. I've got lots to tell you."

She eyed me with concern but didn't press the issue. I appreciated that. The day had left me emotionally wrung out, and I didn't want to cry and exhaust myself further. Instead, I gave Jemma a lighthearted play-by-play of everything that had transpired during the stakeout. She squealed when I got to the part about the kiss. I tried to downplay it, but my bestie saw right through me.

Eventually, Jemma left and, once alone, I sat on my bed staring at my phone for a long time. My stomach tied itself up in tighter and tighter knots with every passing minute. I couldn't sleep, not with so much on my mind. Maybe I'd regret my next move, but I needed to try to take the reins in my life.

Not letting myself chicken out, I called my mom, bracing myself for an argument or at least for her not to listen to a word I had to say.

"Emersyn, hon?" she said when she picked up. "It's late for a call. Is everything all right?"

The genuine concern in her voice cracked me open. Tears spilled down my cheeks.

"Everything's okay," I assured her through quiet sobs.

"But you're crying. Something must be wrong."

I clutched a pillow to me, holding on like it was a life preserver. "I miss Ethan, Mom," I said, emotion pouring out of me, through my tears and my words. "So much that it hurts. *Physically hurts.* I know you miss him too. And I don't want us fighting. We both love Livy. We both want what's best for her. Please, can't you give me a chance to prove that I can be a good parent to her?"

My sobs intensified after I finished talking. I didn't know if my mom had even been able to understand my words.

Silence stretched between us. My breath hitched as I tried to get my sobs under control. I was about to ask my mom if she was still there when she finally spoke, her voice thick with emotion.

"I do know what you mean, Emersyn. It hurts every day. And Livy is all I've got left of Ethan. It's hard to let her go at the end of our visits."

I wiped at my tears. "I know it is, and if you want to spend more time with her, I'm fine with that. She loves visiting you. But I don't think uprooting her is in her best interest."

Another long pause followed.

"You might be right," my mom finally conceded. "But I worry about your financial and employment stability. I worry about it for Livy's sake, and I worry about it for your sake."

"I'm getting things back on track," I said, hoping that was true. "Please, Mom, give me a chance."

The next pause stretched on so long that I almost gave up hope of ever getting a response.

Then, finally, my mom spoke quietly.

"I can do that. But, Emersyn, when it comes down to it, I have to put Livy's needs first."

"Always," I agreed, hoping desperately that I wouldn't blow this chance.

CHAPTER
FIFTY

I awoke the next morning feeling like I'd gone through a wringer, with every bit of emotional energy squeezed out of me. Theo had texted the night before to say that she'd been at aqua therapy yesterday. She asked—dictated, really—for us to meet this afternoon. Somehow, I found her demand comforting. Maybe because it was a glimmer of normalcy in the midst of my emotional turmoil. I didn't dwell on the fact that I now considered investigating a murder and taking orders from a teenager as normal.

Spurred on by the chance my mom had given me, I spent the morning job hunting. My spirits lifted around midday, when I received invitations to interviews for two jobs I'd applied for previously. One was for a copywriting job and the other was for a position at the local clothing store. That job was part-time and paid minimum wage, but it was better than nothing.

Livy had a playdate at a friend's house, so I was waiting on my own in the Mirage's lobby when Theo rolled in the front door.

The sun had made an appearance that afternoon, so we sat out in the courtyard while I brought Theo up to speed on everything. Well, everything except the kiss and the issue of Livy's guardianship. I didn't want to think about either of those topics.

I counted myself lucky that she snickered only a couple of times while I related the story of my torture session at Ultimate Beast. She laughed harder at the tale of my visit to Vinny's Pawnshop with my unintended sidekicks.

"We need to get back into the speakeasy," Theo declared once I'd finished debriefing her.

"But the cops have already searched it," I reminded her.

"We might still find some fingerprints, and if we find Hoffman's prints, that'll be proof that he knew about the speakeasy."

I was about to ask how she planned to search for fingerprints when she pulled a black plastic case out of her backpack. I read the label as she handed it to me.

"A fingerprinting kit," I said. "Seriously, do your parents let you loose with their credit cards?"

"Gift cards," Theo said. "I get them for Christmas and my birthday. I really wanted to order a portable biometric scanner, but those are out of my price range."

"Is it even legal for the average citizen to own one of those things?"

Theo shrugged. "Does it matter?"

She wheeled across the courtyard, heading for the door. "Come on," she said. "My chair won't fit through the secret door, so you'll have to dust for prints."

Once inside the building, Theo gave me a quick lesson on how to use the fingerprinting kit. Then she sent me through the secret door, calling out some final instructions before adding that she was heading upstairs to grab some cookies from her grandparents' apartment. Left in peace, I dusted the bar, the shelves behind it, and a few other surfaces. It probably would have been best to dust the bottles of liquor, but the police had cleared them all out, leaving nothing but dust bunnies, dead flies, and clear circles on the shelves where the bottles had once stood.

The police had already dusted for prints, as evidenced by the black, powdery film left behind. That made me wonder if there was much point in me doing the same. I didn't want to voice that thought to Theo, though, so I found a few clear spaces to dust and lifted two partials and one full print. At one point I thought I heard a muffled noise from somewhere not far off, but I held still and waited and heard nothing more.

As I packed up the kit, the lost and found basket that Livy had shown me before caught my eye and got me thinking. Had Freddie found the art deco cuff links in the basket and helped himself? Probably. The cocktail shaker disguised as a trophy was likely from the speakeasy too.

I grabbed the kit and decided it was time to leave, but I paused when I reached the display of photos hanging on the wall. I loved 1920s women's fashion, so I took the time to admire the flapper dresses the women wore in the pictures. As I moved along the wall, something twitched in my memory before quickly slithering out of my grasp. I felt like I was missing something, but no matter how many times I looked at each photo, I couldn't figure out what that might be.

"What's taking so long?" Theo yelled, clearly back from her short trip upstairs.

I hurried up the steps and joined her out in the hallway, where she handed me a chocolate chip cookie.

"How do you propose we get fingerprints for comparison?" I asked before taking a bite of the delicious, chewy homemade cookie.

"We'll get Freddie's—for elimination purposes—from his office or apartment. As for Hoffman's, you can use your key to get into his place again."

She made it sound like a walk in the park, not an endeavor that required breaking the law and risking time in the pokey.

I finished off the cookie in two more bites and tried the door to Freddie's office, now free of police tape. I expected to find it locked, but it swung open easily. So easily that it couldn't have been latched properly.

"Take a look at this." I pointed at the damaged doorjamb and corresponding scratches and splintering on the door itself.

Theo drew the same conclusion as I had. "Someone broke in."

I peeked into the office. It was empty, so I entered the room, with Theo right behind me. All the drawers of the filing cabinet had been left partially open, and the same was true of the desk drawers.

"They were looking for something," I surmised.

Theo approached the desk. "And probably found it. Come and look."

I rounded the desk. She pointed into the bottom drawer, which was the deepest one. It was empty, save for a thin layer of dust on the bottom. Two circles of disturbed dust were visible, the same size as the clear circles on the shelves in the speakeasy.

"Freddie had a couple of bottles stashed here," I said.

"And whoever broke in probably found them and took them."

"The camera in the lobby doesn't cover the entrance to the office."

"But it might show someone entering the building through the front door," Theo said. "Someone who doesn't belong here."

"It's worth checking," I agreed.

Even if the person didn't have a key to the building, they could always ring a bunch of units until someone buzzed them in. That was probably how Hoffman got in on the day of the murder.

We left the office and turned toward the lobby. A small poster caught my eye as I paused by the bulletin board on the wall outside Freddie's office door.

"Hey," I said, "Minnie's having an art show."

Theo studied the poster. "Maybe we should go."

Theo's grandma stepped off the elevator, carrying a full garbage bag in one hand.

"Hello, girls," she said with a kind smile. "What are you up to?"

Theo zipped up her backpack, hiding the fingerprinting kit. "Just hanging out."

"Mrs. Harris, can I take that for you?" I asked, gesturing at the garbage bag that was almost dragging on the floor.

"Oh, I'm just taking it out to the dumpster," she said.

"I can do that."

She beamed at me. "That's very kind of you."

I relieved her of the bag.

"Thank you, dear." To her granddaughter she added, "Homework all done, honey?"

"Of course," Theo replied.

With another smile, Mrs. Harris got back on the elevator. "Come up for more cookies if you get hungry," she said as the doors closed.

"I'll be right back," I said to Theo, already heading down the hall.

I passed through the courtyard and into the back wing of the building. I pushed open the door to the alley and kicked down the doorstop before stepping outside.

The bag of garbage slipped from my hand and slumped to the ground.

Then I screamed.

CHAPTER
FIFTY-ONE

"Is he dead?" Theo asked, more curious than worried.

I, on the other hand, was definitely worried. And horrified. And feeling sick.

"I'm scared to check," I admitted.

"Nudge him with your foot," she suggested.

Hoffman was my ex, and a total jerk, but I couldn't bring myself to treat him like the bag of garbage at my feet. Theo, who'd ended up following me toward the back of the building, had cruised outside when she heard my scream. Judging by the lack of looky-loos, nobody else had heard me, or everyone who had was pretending they hadn't.

I cautiously approached Hoffman where he lay sprawled face down by the dumpster. His brown hair was matted with blood, and red splatters decorated the shoulder and hood of his heather gray sweatshirt. His messenger bag lay next to him, too flat to contain any bottles.

I crouched down and reluctantly pressed two fingers to the side of Hoffman's neck.

I stood up and backed away. "He's alive." I tugged my phone out of my pocket. "I'd better call for help."

"Not yet," Theo said, unzipping her backpack. "Take his fingerprints first."

"Are you kidding me?"

"Don't you want to compare his prints to the ones in the speakeasy?"

"I need to call an ambulance. And the police. Someone clearly attacked him."

"Another thirty seconds won't kill him."

This was one time I wouldn't be swayed by Theo.

She crossed her arms and glared at me while I called 911. When I hung up a minute later, she tried again.

"We've probably got a couple of minutes before anyone shows up. You could still get his prints."

"And how would I explain to the cops why he's got black ink on his fingers?" I asked, standing firm.

Theo patted the backpack on her lap. "I've got wet wipes in here. My mom makes me carry them."

Thankfully, the wail of a siren reached our ears. That wasn't exactly an uncommon sound in the city, so I wasn't sure if it was heading for the alley until the firetruck turned off the street and cut its siren.

Theo and I waited off to the side while the firefighters tended to Hoffman and then spoke with the paramedics and cops who arrived on the scene within the next couple of minutes. By the time the paramedics had Hoffman on a stretcher, he had regained consciousness. When he caught sight of me, he pointed an accusing finger my way. "Did you do this to me?"

"Of course not!" I planted my hands on my hips. "Why are you accusing me?"

"Someone hit me from behind."

"It wasn't me. I'm the one who called 911. You're welcome," I added acerbically when he showed no signs of gratitude.

"Where's the whiskey you stole?" Theo called out from her spot by the building's back door.

Hoffman scowled as the paramedics loaded him into the ambulance, but he said nothing further. As annoying as that was, I figured I already knew the answer. Whoever had attacked Hoffman had taken the booze he'd most likely stolen from Freddie's office.

"Code four," Theo said under her breath as I joined her by the door.

At least, that's what I thought she said.

"What's a code four?" I asked, confused.

"*Thor*, not four!" she corrected in a harsh whisper.

Detective Callahan strode past, giving us a suspicious glance on his way to the ambulance.

"Oh, great," I said as he climbed inside to talk to Hoffman.

Theo and I spoke separately with a uniformed police officer, outlining how we'd found Hoffman in the alley. There wasn't much to tell, so it didn't take long, and we'd already finished by the time the detective hopped down from the back of the ambulance.

I silently warned my knees not to tremble when the detective fixed his ice-blue eyes on me. Theo returned to my side as Callahan approached.

He didn't bother with a greeting. "It's interesting that you were the one to find your ex out here," he said, never blinking as he studied me.

I crossed my arms, then uncrossed them when I realized I'd taken on a defensive posture. "I'm not the one who attacked him."

Callahan's eyes narrowed by a hair. "I didn't say you were."

My arms hung awkwardly at my sides, like they didn't belong there. The right one twitched, and I gave in to the urge to cross them over my chest again. "You were insinuating. I know Hoffman accused me, but I didn't do it."

Theo spoke up in my defense. "She's been with me for the past hour. Well, for most of it, anyway."

Oh, fantastic.

Way to help me out, Theo, I wanted to say, but instead I gritted my teeth.

Callahan's blue eyes shifted to Theo and then returned to me. I got the feeling he was mentally fitting me for an orange jumpsuit.

"I checked the video surveillance footage from the grocery store," he said, causing a weight to settle in my stomach. "It's a seven-minute walk from this building to the store, and yet, on the day of the murder, you didn't get there until nearly twenty minutes after leaving the Mirage."

I knew what he'd left unsaid: That gave me plenty of time to sneak back into the Mirage through a side or back door, murder Freddie, flee the building, and then continue to the grocery store.

"I have shorter legs than you," I pointed out, relieved to find that my voice wasn't trembling like my knees were. "Plus, I stopped at the park for a few minutes to enjoy the sunshine."

"Did anyone see you there?"

"Nobody who knows me," I said, the weight in my stomach growing heavier.

His eyes still on me, Detective Callahan flicked open his notebook. He finally looked down to write a line or two, and I sucked in a breath, glad to be momentarily free of his intense scrutiny.

Then he hit me with the full force of his blue gaze again. "I'd appreciate it if the two of you left the scene now." He gestured toward the open door and gave us a pointed stare.

I huffed out a sigh, and Theo rolled her eyes, but we obeyed.

"Thank you for giving me an alibi with a gaping hole in it," I grumbled to Theo once the door had closed behind us.

"Yeah, I guess I shouldn't have gone on that cookie run," she said. "You know, Emersyn, you could be in big trouble."

And orange was so not my color.

CHAPTER
FIFTY-TWO

Minnie's art show turned out to be a swanky affair. Fortunately, my friends and I had dressed for the occasion. I hoped that meant we would blend in with the crowd, because we didn't want anyone knowing our true purpose for attending the event.

"Please tell me we have a plan," I whispered to my companions as I adjusted the strap of my emerald green dress.

A black-clad waitress carrying a tray of filled champagne flutes stopped in front of us. I plucked one of the glasses off the tray with a thank-you, and Jemma and Wyatt did the same. Theo—wearing a purple jumpsuit under a black blazer—let out a sigh but didn't comment on being left out.

"We find Minnie and get her to tell us if she has an alibi for the murder," Theo said as we made our way deeper into the gallery hosting the art exhibition.

Minnie was one of three artists being featured at the event, and we were far from the first attendees to arrive.

I searched the sea of bodies around us. "Easier said than done."

"Let's split up," Theo suggested.

A crafty smile appeared on Jemma's face. "Good idea. Theo, you come with me. Em and Wyatt, you go that way." She pointed to the left with a red nail that matched her bodycon dress. Then she strode off in the opposite direction, Theo following her.

"Subtle," I said to their retreating backs.

I took a gulp of champagne and walked off to the left, trying not to look at Wyatt too much, even though his presence at my side was like a powerful magnet. He wore a charcoal three-piece suit with a midnight blue tie, and Wyatt in a waistcoat wasn't a sight I'd been prepared for. Fortunately, we hadn't found ourselves alone, until now. Well, we were as alone as we could be in a crowd of champagne-drinking art lovers, which definitely wasn't alone enough for blazing hot kisses and tearing each other's clothes off. Not that I was thinking about either of those things.

Nope.

Not at all.

I took another gulp of champagne, leaving me with no more than a sip or two in the bottom of my glass.

I zeroed in on a petite, dark-haired woman in a black dress.

Not Minnie after all.

I was about to keep walking when Wyatt put a hand to my arm and tugged me gently off to the side. I moved with him, behind a large metal sculpture and into a shadowy alcove.

"Oh," I said when I realized we had a modicum of privacy. My fingers itched to reach for the buttons on his waistcoat, so I gripped my champagne flute more tightly and curled my free hand into a fist.

"Sorry." Wyatt's fingers ghosted down my arm, leaving goose-bumps in their wake.

When his hand reached mine, my fist unfurled and our fingers twined together. My blood buzzed and my head spun. Neither had anything to do with the champagne.

His ember-hot gaze sent sparks of heat simmering along my skin.

"You look incredible." The way he said that with both his words and his eyes allowed me to believe that he was speaking the truth.

"Thank you. You do too."

My heart gave a little leap, as if it were trying to get closer to his. I'd told Jemma that Wyatt and I had only a physical connection, not an emotional one. That wasn't the case anymore. Not since our talk outside the warehouse. There was so much to this man beyond money and ridiculously good looks.

I wanted desperately to kiss him, but it wasn't the time or place. We didn't have nearly enough privacy for the way I wanted to kiss him.

I caught sight of Jemma and Theo across the room. When Jemma spotted us, she waved me over with an urgency that quickened my pace. I slipped around a group of people who were admiring a six-foot-tall oil painting and joined my friends. Wyatt followed right behind me. I could sense him there, even without looking over my shoulder.

"Code Thor!" Theo said under her breath before I could ask what was up.

This time I heard her correctly. I followed her line of sight and spotted Detective Callahan across the room. As if he sensed our eyes on him, he turned and focused his laser-like blue gaze on us. He stared at us for a long moment before disappearing into the adjoining room.

"Why is he here?" I asked with a quiver of anxiety.

"Keeping an eye on his suspects, probably," Wyatt said.

"Mr. Nagy's not here. Neither is Hoffman. That leaves Emersyn," Theo so helpfully pointed out.

"I'm doomed." I downed the last of my champagne and placed the empty glass on a passing waiter's tray.

Wyatt did the same with his. Jemma, who'd already ditched her empty glass at some point, grabbed a full flute before the waiter disappeared into the crowd.

"We've got your back," she assured me before taking a sip of champagne.

Her promise did nothing to stop my knees from quaking as Detective Callahan walked over my way.

CHAPTER
FIFTY-THREE

"Ms. Gray," the detective said in a cool voice. "How convenient to see you here."

"Is it?" My voice sounded unnaturally high.

"I understand that Ms. Gao sometimes brings you day-old goods from her bakery."

"Um . . . so?" I asked, thrown off by the question. "What do Agnes's baked goods have to do with anything?"

I glanced at my friends, but they appeared to be just as puzzled as me.

"Some of the desserts she sells are decorated with gold leaf," Callahan explained.

Oh.

I'd never made that connection.

Did that mean Agnes belonged on my suspect list?

"Is that the case with any food she's given you recently?" the detective asked.

"Not that I can think of." That was the truth, but the way he stared at me made me wonder if Agnes had answered a similar question in the affirmative.

"I'd like you to stop by the station tomorrow so we can have a chat."

Champagne churned in my stomach.

"Not without a lawyer present," Wyatt said, stepping up to stand at my side.

He put a hand to my back, and comforting warmth radiated through the fabric of my dress, easing my trembling slightly.

Callahan's eyes never left my face. "Then I'll see you and your lawyer tomorrow morning. Shall we say ten o'clock?"

I nodded, because I couldn't get my voice to work in that moment.

Callahan strode away.

"I can't afford a lawyer," I whispered once I found my voice.

"I'll take care of that," Wyatt said, removing his hand from my back.

I immediately missed his touch.

"I can't let you pay for my lawyer," I protested.

Jemma nudged me with her elbow. "Em, accept the offer. Please. I don't want to be visiting you in jail."

I pictured myself trying to hug Livy through iron bars.

I raised my gaze to meet Wyatt's. "Thank you."

"I've got Minnie in my sights," Theo announced. She gave a discreet nod to the side.

Sure enough, Minnie stood surrounded by several stylishly dressed men and women, ranging in age from about forty-five to seventy-five.

"Oh my God," I said as the light glinted off an oil painting on display beyond Minnie and those chatting with her.

The painting depicted a close-up view of a plume of feathers in shades of blue, purple, and gold.

"What is it?" Wyatt asked as he moved closer to me.

I tried to ignore the way my skin tingled in response to his nearness.

"Gold leaf. On the painting." I thought back to the cocktail party/wake held at Minnie and Yolanda's apartment. I landed on a memory of a piece of art on the wall. "I've seen gold leaf on one of Minnie's other paintings as well."

"And there was gold leaf on Freddie's body," Theo added.

"She's our killer." Jemma stared hard at Minnie.

Theo's eyes gleamed behind her glasses. "We should get her to confess."

"But she's the lady of the hour," Jemma pointed out. "It might be hard to get her alone."

"Leave that to me," Theo said.

Before we could ask her what she had up her sleeve, she shot off toward Minnie's admirers. She nearly ran into two of them before slowing down.

"Excuse me. Sorry. I'd really like to see that painting." She nodded at the picture of the feathers.

Minnie and the others stood between her and the work of art, but they scattered as Theo started moving her wheelchair again, putting their toes in serious danger of getting run over.

Suddenly alone, Minnie was about to turn away when I swooped in and tucked my arm through hers. "Minnie, this is a fabulous exhibition."

She beamed at me. "Thank you, Emersyn. And thank you for coming." She looked around as Jemma, Theo, and Wyatt closed in on us.

"There's something we need to talk to you about," I said, leading her into the alcove that Wyatt and I had vacated mere minutes earlier. The others followed, crowding into the small space with us.

"Oh?" Minnie said, clearly unsure of what exactly was happening. "What's that?"

"Freddie's murder," Theo said in a matter-of-fact tone.

Minnie's left hand fluttered and landed near the base of her throat. "What about it?"

"Where were you at the time of the murder?" I asked, releasing my gentle hold on her right arm.

Her eyes widened with surprise and—I thought—fear. "Why are you asking me that?"

"We're trying to find out the location of everyone who lives in the building," Wyatt said smoothly. "We're wondering if you or your neighbors saw or heard anything that day that might be helpful in solving the crime."

Wyatt's charm put Minnie at ease, and she lowered her hand from her throat. "I was in and out for the first part of the morning, loading a few of my pieces into a van so they could be transported here to the gallery."

"You work at home?" I asked with surprise. I didn't think their one-bedroom apartment had room to accommodate an art studio. I certainly hadn't seen any signs of one while I was at the cocktail party.

"Not usually," Minnie replied. "Sometimes on small pieces. And I had a couple that were hanging on the wall in the apartment. The gallery sent a van to pick up all my work, both from home and from my studio. It parked in the alley while we moved everything downstairs."

"Did you see anybody while you were loading the van?" Jemma asked.

"The driver, of course, but either Yolanda or I was with him the entire time," Minnie said. "I don't recall seeing anyone else."

I thought that over. "What about Yolanda? Did she see anyone?"

"Not that I'm aware of."

"And once all the pieces were loaded into the van?" I prodded.

"The driver brought them here to the gallery. I went back upstairs to my apartment."

"What time was that?" Wyatt asked.

"I'm not entirely sure, but it was maybe an hour later that I heard all the sirens and realized that something had happened."

I put the next question to her. "Was Yolanda with you during that hour?"

Minnie's gaze skittered about. "Not the entire time."

"Can anyone else vouch for your whereabouts?" Jemma asked.

Minnie's hand fluttered back to the base of her throat. "I . . . No . . . But . . ."

Theo jumped back into the interrogation. "You told us that you only ever spoke to Freddie to say hello, but he had a Grub Tubz flyer, and you're a sales rep."

Minnie shook her head, her eyes unmistakably lit with fear now. "I don't sell the Grub Tubz products."

"Leona said that she got her water bottle from you," Wyatt said before I had a chance.

"I gave it to her as a sample. I thought if I did that, maybe she'd want to buy some."

"But you said you're not a sales rep," Jemma reminded her.

"I'm not," Minnie maintained.

"She's telling the truth."

Our heads turned in unison toward the new voice.

Yolanda stood just outside the alcove, glaring at us.

She crossed her wiry arms over her chest before adding, "I'm the one who gave Freddie the flyer."

I fought the urge to shrink away from her. She stood several inches taller than me, and the way she glowered at us suggested that she wouldn't mind wringing our necks.

She stepped into the alcove and put a protective arm around her petite partner. "Why are you interrogating Minnie?"

Theo seemed unfazed by Yolanda's annoyance. "She had reason to be angry with Freddie. Plus, there was gold leaf on Freddie's body, and Minnie uses gold leaf in her artwork."

"Sometimes I do," Minnie admitted. "But I didn't kill Freddie. I got rid of my anger by playing darts with Rosario. After that, I was fine."

"Then maybe you killed him because of the whiskey," Jemma said.

Minnie seemed truly baffled. "What whiskey?"

"From the speakeasy," I explained.

Rage sparked in Yolanda's eyes. "Nobody should have touched that whiskey!"

"You know about the speakeasy?" I asked with surprise.

The light glinted off something on the sleeve of Yolanda's black shirt.

I drew in a sharp breath. "Gold leaf." I raised my eyes to meet her angry brown ones. "It was you, Yolanda. You killed Freddie."

Minnie cried out as Yolanda lunged for my neck.

CHAPTER
FIFTY-FOUR

A blur of charcoal gray flashed in front of me.

I expected to feel Yolanda's hands close around my throat, but suddenly, somehow, she was on the floor.

Wyatt knelt next to her, pinning her arms behind her back.

"Stop accusing us!" Yolanda yelled as Detective Callahan darted around the sculpture that partially hid the alcove from the rest of the room.

There was a great hullabaloo as Wyatt and Callahan got Yolanda to her feet and Minnie sobbed. A man I'd never seen before, but who seemed to be with Detective Callahan, quickly cleared away the crowd that was squeezing in toward the alcove to see what was happening. A plainclothes police officer most likely, I thought.

When things quieted down, we quickly brought Callahan up to speed.

"I'm so sorry," Minnie said through a sob after I'd finished.

A cloud of emotion flitted across Yolanda's stormy eyes, and her shoulders slumped. Then her eyes hardened again as she spoke to the detective. "I didn't mean to kill Freddie."

We all stared at her in shock, and Minnie let out a strangled noise of despair.

"Was it because of the whiskey?" I asked. "You wanted the money it would bring in a sale to the right buyer?"

Yolanda scowled at me. "I don't care about money. I care about the speakeasy. My grandfather's the one who ran it back in the twenties."

"But, except for the missing bottles, the place looks like it hasn't been touched in decades," Jemma pointed out.

"And that's how I wanted it to stay!" Yolanda tried to wrestle her arm from Callahan's grip without success. "I didn't want anyone to know about it. I didn't want anything to change. It's my grandfather's speakeasy. Sometimes I go in there to feel close to him again."

Minnie cried harder, and Yolanda's tough exterior cracked again, just for a split second.

"How did you realize that Freddie knew about the speakeasy?" Theo asked in a rush, as if afraid she'd run out of time to get her questions answered. "Did you see him sneaking in there?"

"I didn't catch him in the act, but I was in his apartment, trying to sell him some Grub Tubz," Yolanda explained. "I saw the trophy on a shelf."

"The one that converts to a cocktail shaker," I said. I shot a quick glance at Callahan, worried he'd wonder how I knew about the trophy, but he remained focused on Yolanda as she spoke again.

"I knew he'd stolen it from the speakeasy. And then I saw the bottle of whiskey. None of it was his to take!"

"We can finish this conversation down at the station," the detective said.

Minnie reached a hand out to Yolanda, but Callahan hauled her away, telling her she was under arrest for Freddie's murder.

Jemma put an arm around Minnie, who had her face in her hands.

Maybe I should have felt elated that we'd found Freddie's killer.

Instead, a heavy weight of sadness pressed down on me, and all I wanted to do was go home.

CHAPTER
FIFTY-FIVE

"I wish this party wasn't happening," I confessed as Jemma and I approached the open door to Rosario's apartment.

"Everyone wants to show their appreciation," my friend said. "Plus, Agnes's bakery is supplying the food, so we definitely don't want to miss out."

She took my arm and propelled me into the apartment, where big band music played and several of my neighbors had already gathered.

With Yolanda under arrest for Freddie's murder, Mr. Nagy and I were both in the clear. Callahan had canceled my visit to the police station, and with Livy at a friend's house, I was free to mix and mingle. Yet, despite my relief at no longer being a murder suspect, I didn't feel at all in a partying mood.

"Emersyn!" Agnes exclaimed when she saw me.

She grabbed my hand and pulled me farther into the room, alerting the others to my arrival. The next thing I knew, Mrs. Nagy had wrapped me in an embrace.

I returned the hug, pouring all my love and gratitude into it. This woman had done so much for me and Livy. I hadn't done nearly enough to repay her.

"Thank you, Emersyn," she said. "Thank you for helping my Zoltán."

I blinked away tears as I stepped back. "I'm not sure how much I really helped, but I'm glad his name is cleared."

"It's such a weight off his shoulders." She smiled lovingly across the room at her husband, who was over in the kitchen, chatting and laughing with Rosario and Carmen.

The counter had been turned into a makeshift bar. As at the previous party in the building, Bodie mixed and shook cocktails, keeping everyone's glasses full. Jemma was already there, talking with Bodie while he prepared a drink for her.

I chatted with Mrs. Nagy and Agnes for another minute or two, and then Jemma came over to join me, carrying two peachy-colored drinks. She handed one to me.

I thanked her, relieved that I didn't need to approach Bodie myself. My feelings for Wyatt might still be in a jumble, but I knew now that they were stronger than what I felt for the hot bartender. At some point, I'd have to tell Bodie that I had no intention of taking our relationship any further, but this was so not the time or place.

Not that telling him that would mean I was ready to move forward with Wyatt. I still suspected that staying single was the wisest option for me at the moment.

Jemma might not agree, but I wanted clarity and stability in my life, not confusion and the potential for heartbreak. Then there was the whole guardianship dispute with my mother. That would require my full attention going forward. My mom had granted me a reprieve of sorts, but I was basically on probation. One wrong step, and she'd take up her crusade again.

Jemma and I sampled some of the food from Agnes's bakery and chatted with the building's residents. The whole time, I kept glancing toward the door. I knew Agnes had invited Wyatt to the party, but he'd yet to make an appearance. Despite my confused feelings, I really wanted to see him.

During one such glance at the entrance, I spotted Minnie out in the hallway, hovering with a haunted expression on her face.

The petit four I'd eaten sat heavily in my stomach.

I excused myself from my current conversation and stepped out into the hall.

"Minnie ..." I started, trying to find a way to put my feelings into words. "I'm so sorry. This wasn't the outcome I was hoping for."

Minnie's eyes were bloodshot, with dark rings beneath them. "Yolanda didn't do it. She couldn't have." She blinked back tears. "She must have confessed because she thinks I did it and she wants to protect me."

"You really think she believes you could have killed Freddie?" I asked.

I suspected that Yolanda had confessed so readily to prevent any further wrongful accusations against Minnie, but I didn't doubt the veracity of the confession.

"I didn't tell the entire truth when I said playing darts cured me of my anger," Minnie said, wringing her hands. "I got angry all over again when Yolanda told me about Freddie taking the trophy from the speakeasy."

"So you knew about the secret room too."

She nodded. "I never paid any attention to the liquor behind the bar, but the speakeasy and everything in it means so much to Yolanda. She knows I was angry on her behalf. She must think that I killed Freddie, so she confessed to protect me."

"But she was angry too," I said as gently as I could. "And the gold leaf on Freddie's body must have transferred from Yolanda. She probably got it on her when she was moving your artwork that day."

She shook her head, unwilling to accept my theory. "We were never apart for more than fifteen minutes. Wouldn't she have had blood on her?"

I didn't know what else to say, so I repeated my earlier words. "I'm so sorry."

Minnie patted my arm. "I know you were just trying to help Mr. Nagy, Emersyn."

Her forgiveness and understanding left me feeling worse than before.

She gave me a weak smile and wandered off down the hall, looking a little lost.

I returned to Rosario's apartment, even less in the mood for a party now.

"This is delicious," Bitty said as she sipped at her peachy cocktail.

"You might want to be careful," Carmen advised. "There's a lot of vodka in that thing."

"Like my dear cousin Princess Diana once said, 'Vodka is kind of a hobby.'" Bitty giggled and took another sip of her drink as she swayed off to talk to Mrs. Nagy.

"Wasn't it Betty White who said that?" Jemma asked.

"It certainly was." Leona joined our group, a red cocktail in hand. "Did I ever tell you about the time I gave Betty a ride to the airport when her—"

"Yes," Carmen broke in loudly. "Many, many times."

"What's that cocktail you've got there?" I asked Leona in a desperate bid to keep the peace. She looked ready to gouge Carmen's eyes out.

Fortunately, my attempt at distracting her worked.

"Bodie called it a sour cherry gin sling." She took a sip. "It's delicious. You should try one."

Jemma elbowed me in the ribs. "Yes, Emersyn, go ask Bodie to make you one." She lowered her voice to a whisper. "And maybe ask for a little something more too."

I rolled my eyes and didn't budge.

"I'm popping back down to your place to use the washroom," Jemma said.

"I'm sure you could use Rosario's." I glanced in that direction.

"Someone just went in there. I won't be long." Jemma set aside her empty glass and headed out of the apartment.

When I turned my attention back to my neighbors, the cherry garnish in Leona's glass grabbed my attention.

The cherry shimmered with gold.

"Gold leaf?" My voice sounded vague, probably because my thoughts were so busy spinning.

Leona held up her glass so it caught the light streaming in through the nearby window. "Bodie said he uses it all the time when he works for that fancy catering company. People like bling in their cocktails. He sneaked a little bit home for us. Wasn't that sweet?"

Her dangly diamond earrings sparkled in a beam of sunlight.

Two memories surfaced and clicked together.

I looked over Bodie's way. He smiled at something Bitty said to him and then reached for his cocktail shaker. His gaze met mine from across the room. It took half a second, but then he grinned at me before getting back to mixing drinks.

I set my half-empty glass on a side table and slipped out of the apartment. My heart beat so fast that I felt dizzy and lightheaded. I leaned against the wall in the hallway to ensure I didn't fall over.

When would Jemma get back?

And what about Wyatt?

He still hadn't shown up.

I pushed off from the wall and hurried to the elevator on shaky legs.

I needed to check something.

I needed to be sure.

I clutched my phone tightly as the elevator deposited me in the lobby. I hurried across the deserted space, my footsteps loud against the marble floor. I slipped into the vintage phone booth and opened the secret door to the speakeasy.

My heart continued to pound like the galloping hooves of a runaway horse.

Breathe, Emersyn, I reminded myself as another wave of light-headedness swept over me.

I nearly tripped down the steps but made it safely to the wall of photographs. I found the one of the band playing on the small stage in the corner. Peering closely at the picture, I saw that I was right.

My heart sank.

The earring I'd found in Bodie's apartment was a match for the one the singer wore in the photograph.

It didn't belong to his ex-girlfriend.

He must have found it here in the speakeasy. Probably in the lost and found basket.

Which meant he knew about the secret room and the booze.

Bodie knew his liquor. He probably realized right away that the old bottles would fetch a good price when sold to the right buyer.

The gold leaf on Freddie's body hadn't come from Yolanda. It had come from Bodie. He used gold leaf in his work. Some must have stuck to his clothes or skin, and when he fought with Freddie over the old liquor . . .

I needed to talk to Detective Callahan.

I rushed up the steps to the secret door.

And crashed right into Bodie.

CHAPTER
FIFTY-SIX

"Hey, Bodie." I tried my best to sound casual, but my voice came out a little higher and more breathless than normal. "I didn't realize you knew about this place."

He had his hands on my upper arms, as if to steady me after our collision, but instead of letting me go, he tightened his grip until I almost yelped.

"What was it that clued you in?" His blue eyes had gone hard.

The sight sent shards of ice into my blood.

I fought to keep the fear off my face. "About what?"

He smirked and hauled me out of the phone booth.

The hallway and lobby were both deserted.

"You know what?" He wrenched my phone from my hand and tossed it into the booth. "I don't even care. I know you put things together, and that's enough."

"I don't know what you're talking about," I lied, even though it was likely pointless.

My gaze skipped to my phone, but Bodie kicked the booth's door shut and dragged me toward the elevator.

"Bodie! Let me go!" I tried to stand my ground, but my high-heeled shoes had no traction on the marble floor. "Help!" I yelled, hoping that somebody somewhere in the building would hear me.

Bodie clamped a hand over my mouth and yanked me on board the elevator. I flailed and struggled, desperate to get away before the doors closed. He held me in place with ease and kept his hand over my mouth. Until he flung me against the elevator's side wall. I gasped in pain when my hip smacked against the handrail and my head bounced off the faux wood paneling.

I lunged for the doors as they closed, but Bodie caught me and locked an arm around my neck. The doors shut.

It felt like they were sealing my fate.

Bodie hit the button for the top floor.

"I'm sorry to say we're not going back to the party," he said, as if I hadn't already guessed that. "They'll have to mix their own drinks."

The elevator climbed up and up. I needed to get away, but Bodie was ridiculously strong—from way too many hours spent at Ultimate Beast—and panic had scattered my mind.

I fought through the haze of fear and remembered a self-defense move I'd learned back in high school. I raised up one foot and stomped down, grazing the inside of Bodie's leg before smashing the heel of my shoe into his foot.

At least, that's what I meant to do. He moved his foot out of the way just in the nick of time.

"Don't make this harder than it needs to be," he said. "You're no match for me. I saw you at the gym. You're pathetic. Cute, but pathetic."

A sparking-hot cloud of rage built inside of me, muffling some of my fear.

He was a murderer and a liar, and he was calling *me* pathetic?

He thought he was going to take me away from Livy?

At the thought of my beautiful, sweet niece, my rage morphed into something hard and solid.

Livy wasn't losing another loved one.

Not if I had anything to do with it.

I wanted to talk to Bodie, to distract him while I came up with a plan to save myself, but he'd clamped his hand over my mouth again. I tried to bite his fingers, but he managed to keep them curved enough that I couldn't sink my teeth into his flesh. When the doors opened to the fifth floor, he dragged me off the elevator.

I couldn't move my head much, but I glanced up and down the hall, trying to will someone to appear. Someone who could help me.

The corridor remained empty.

Bodie half dragged and half carried me to a door that led to a narrow staircase.

I knew where we were going. And I knew why.

I struggled and flailed again.

Bodie shifted from cold calm to red-hot anger in a flash.

He slammed me against the wall of the stairwell and pressed a forearm against my throat so that I could hardly breathe.

"Bodie! Stop!" I wheezed in a faint voice that sounded nothing like me.

He brought his face right up to mine. "You want *me* to stop? You're the one trying to ruin everything. All I needed was some money. I'm drowning in debt, and my car's about to get seized. Those bottles of whiskey were my ticket to an easier life, but then people had to get in my way. First Freddie, then that dude with the messenger bag, and now you. I don't want to hurt you, Emersyn, but you've brought this on yourself."

Tears pricked at my eyes as black splotches blotted out my vision. "What would your sister think?" I rasped. "If she could see you now?"

"My sister is alive and well and living her perfect life in Boston. I didn't want to lie to you, Emersyn, but I needed you to trust me so you wouldn't poke holes in my alibi."

"Alibi . . ." I couldn't get enough oxygen to say more.

"Yeah. Alex, the assistant manager at the bar? She has a thing for me and was more than happy to lie to the cops. I didn't want you figuring that out."

I tried to absorb his words, but my mind grew fuzzy as my vision darkened further.

Just as I was about to slip into oblivion, Bodie eased up the pressure on my throat and hauled me up the stairs.

I tried to scream while I had the chance, while he didn't have my mouth covered or my airway blocked, but I was still trying to catch my breath and my throat felt so bruised. When I tried to yell, I ended up coughing. By the time I stopped sputtering, Bodie had dragged me out the door and onto the roof.

The wind whipped through my tangled hair and stung my tear-filled eyes. I grabbed at the corner of the rooftop enclosure. Bodie yanked me away.

I cried out as the stucco scraped the skin off my fingertips.

I kicked and flailed so fiercely that Bodie had to use both arms to restrain me, leaving my mouth uncovered.

"Help!" I screamed, over and over. The wind whipped my words away, up into the sky where no one would hear them.

Bodie dragged me to the edge of the roof. I scratched at his face with my fingernails, drawing a trickle of blood from his cheek. He reared back and smacked my face. My head rang from the impact, and little pinpricks of silver light flashed in my vision.

"I'm sorry, Emersyn."

He sounded genuinely remorseful, but then he took advantage of my momentary shock to heave me up and over the four-foot barrier at the edge of the roof.

"No!" I screamed into the wind.

I thrashed about and pummeled my fists against any part of him that I could reach. My legs dangled over the edge. One of my shoes slipped off and fell away. I kicked up one leg and managed to hook it over the barrier. Latching on to Bodie's shoulder and wrenching him down toward me, I used him as leverage to swing myself up and over the wall. He grabbed for my shoulder as I tumbled to the floor of the roof. His fingers caught the strap of my dress. With a ripping of stitches, the strap broke away, leaving him with nothing but fabric in his grasp. I crawled away from him, losing my other shoe in the process. I clambered to my feet and ran for the door.

Bodie tackled me to the floor, right by the bench where I'd sat with Mr. Nagy. Pain split through my knee and elbow. I screamed with the fierce power of combined fear and frustration.

He jammed his knee into my back, pinning me down. My cheek pressed against the gritty rooftop, tiny pebbles cutting into my skin.

I saw Livy's smiling face so clearly in my mind.

A sob broke out of me.

"I can't go to jail, Emersyn. I really am sorry."

"Help!" I screamed again, but my voice had gone hoarse.

Bodie grabbed me by the shoulders.

Then the door to the stairway flew open.

Wyatt and Jemma burst through it, a gaggle of seniors behind them.

I felt more than saw Bodie's hesitation.

I reached under the bench, and my hand closed around cool glass. I whipped out Mr. Nagy's bottle of pálinka and twisted around, smashing the bottle against the back of Bodie's head.

The glass shattered.

Bodie crumpled.

The pungent, fruity smell of pálinka burned my nose.

I scrambled up and away from Bodie, scared he might rise again at any second.

Tears blurred my vision. I blinked.

When I could see again, Wyatt had a barely conscious Bodie pinned to the floor.

Jemma threw her arms around me, almost knocking me off my feet. "Oh my God! Emersyn! Are you okay?"

My neighbors swarmed around me, everyone exclaiming and chattering all at once.

I was safe, I realized.

Alive and safe.

I sank into Jemma's arms and let my tears fall.

CHAPTER
FIFTY-SEVEN

I huddled in my cozy sweater as I sat on a bench in the courtyard, watching with a glowing heart as Livy danced around the rim of the old fountain.

She had no idea what had transpired on the Mirage's roof three days earlier while she was at a friend's house. She thought my scrapes and bruises resulted from a simple tumble, and I'd explained Bodie's absence from the building by saying that he'd moved out. Which wasn't entirely untrue. He was currently housed in a jail cell and would—hopefully—remain behind bars for a long, long time.

Jemma sat on my left with her arm tucked through mine.

"I talked to Detective Callahan this morning," I told her.

"Did he have anything to share?" Jemma asked.

"He confirmed that Minnie's guess was right. Yolanda thought Minnie killed Freddie out of a double dose of anger—because of how he'd humiliated her and how he'd desecrated the speakeasy—so Yolanda confessed to protect her."

"Misguided, but a little bit sweet," Jemma said, sharing my sentiment on the matter.

"Bodie's been formally charged with the assault on Hoffman," I added, "as well as with murder and attempted murder."

Sparks of anger danced in Jemma's brown eyes. "I hope he rots in jail."

Weariness weighed down my next words. "Me too."

"Why did Bodie attack Hoffman? Did Thor say anything about that?"

"Bodie didn't realize that the police knew about the speakeasy and had cleared out the liquor. Neither did Hoffman, but he found two bottles in Freddie's office. Bottles that the cops didn't take when they searched the office right after the murder."

"Because they didn't know they had any significance at the time," Jemma surmised.

I nodded. "When Bodie caught Hoffman slipping the bottles into his bag, he knocked Hoff out and dumped his body in the alley, taking the bottles for himself, probably mere moments before Theo and I showed up in the lobby."

"Hoffman should be in jail too," Jemma grumbled.

I didn't disagree.

"I don't think we were far off with our theory about Hoff," I continued. "He didn't kill anyone, but I'm pretty sure Freddie caught him taking a bottle of whiskey from the speakeasy. They must have fought, and the bottle broke. Hoffman grabbed the label before he took off, probably so he could find out the value of the whiskey so he'd know if it would be worth coming back for more."

"That must have happened right before the murder," Jemma said.

"That's what I figure," I agreed, "since Freddie never had a chance to clean up the spilled booze." I paused for a moment before sharing what else I'd learned from Detective Callahan. "Bodie's the one who told the cops about Freddie threatening to evict me. He overheard our conversation."

Jemma made a face. "Ugh! He heard what the sleazeball was saying to you and just stood there listening?"

"Not such a surprise, now that I know what type of person Bodie really is."

"I never would have guessed that Bodie was an even bigger creep than Freddie."

"You and me both." I held back a shudder.

"What about the gold leaf the cops found in the Nagys' apartment?" Jemma asked.

"I talked to Mrs. Nagy about that," I replied. "She figures it came from some petits fours that Agnes brought over for tea the day before the murder. They were decorated with gold leaf. Mrs. Nagy couldn't think of how else it would have ended up in her kitchen."

The door to the building opened, and Wyatt stepped out into the courtyard.

"Look who's here." Jemma smiled, a little slyly, I thought.

Wyatt's eyes found mine, and a pleasant zing shot through me. A chaotic tangle of emotions rode in on its wake. I didn't know what to think or feel about Wyatt, but I decided that was a problem for another time. Or maybe not. There was a good chance I'd never see him again after today.

Despite the little whimper of disappointment from my heart at the thought, it was likely for the best. Bodie had left me bruised on the outside, but he'd also deepened the scars I already had on the inside. I thought he was a good guy, that we had a real connection. And I was oh so wrong.

I could be wrong about Wyatt too.

Nevertheless, I could set aside my wariness for an hour or so.

"I should go," Jemma whispered.

I clutched her arm, holding her in place. "No, don't."

She gave in, probably only because she was still getting over the scare she'd had when she'd raced back to Rosario's apartment in time to see my shoe fall past the window. I'd texted her in the elevator on my way down to the speakeasy, sharing my suspicions about Bodie. When she realized that he was gone from the party too, she gathered up a posse of my senior neighbors and Wyatt—who'd just shown up—and rushed up to the roof. Luckily, she'd correctly guessed that my shoe must have fallen from there.

I could tell I surprised Jemma when I stood up from the bench. "I'll just be a moment."

I met Wyatt on a sunny patch of grass, far enough away from Jemma and Livy that we had a semblance of privacy.

"How are you doing?" he asked, his eyes tracing a path from the bruises on my face to the ones on my neck.

I could feel his gaze like a physical touch, gentle, intoxicating. I had to take a steadying breath before I could speak.

"I'm okay," I said, my voice quieter than I'd intended. "And I'm glad you're here."

A corner of his mouth quirked up. "That's a nice change."

"I know I haven't always been welcoming," I admitted. "But I want you to know that I truly appreciate the way you helped up on the roof."

His grin disappeared, and his eyes darkened. His fingertips skimmed my cheek, near an angry red scrape and purple bruise. Beneath his touch, my blood warmed. A hum traveled through my bones, electric yet comforting at the same time. It was unlike anything I'd ever felt before.

He brushed a strand of hair off my face and tucked it behind my ear with such tenderness that I had to blink back tears. When he dropped his hand, the absence of his touch set off a hollow, echoing ache inside me.

Wyatt's coal-black eyes burned with regret and something hotter, more volatile. "I wish I'd made it to the roof faster."

I threw caution to the wind and took his hand in mine. Our fingers twined perfectly together.

"I'm told you moved as fast as humanly possible," I said. "In fact, I think some residents of the building suspect you're actually superhuman."

A faint smile touched his lips, weighed down by remorse. "Definitely only human. But I was a scared-as-hell human when I realized you were in trouble."

Tears burned in my eyes as I smiled at him. "Sit with us?"

As my hand slid out of his, he caught two of my fingers and gave them the gentlest of squeezes before releasing them.

I had to tear my gaze from his and remind myself to breathe.

I led the way back to the bench and sat next to Jemma. She gave me a knowing look, but I just patted the empty spot on my other side, an invitation for Wyatt. He accepted, sitting close enough that his arm brushed against mine. I tried not to breathe too deeply, but I still caught a heady whiff of his outdoorsy scent.

"I owe you both my life," I said, glancing first at Jemma, then at Wyatt. "You and the Senior Squad."

"Ooh, that's a good name," Jemma said with delight. "We should get them badges."

"Or not," I countered. "That was definitely a one-time thing." I knocked on the wooden seat of the bench, in case the universe was getting any cruel ideas.

The door opened for the second time in two minutes, and Theo sailed out into the courtyard. Livy jumped down from the edge of the fountain and ran to greet her. They spoke for a moment, and then Livy bounced off to practice cartwheels on the grass while Theo came over to join us by the bench.

"I've been wanting to talk to you," I said, pinning her with my most disapproving glare. "I checked my bank account this morning and—funny thing—Hoffman transferred back the exact amount he stole from me."

"Our plan worked?" Jemma exclaimed with triumph. "I can't believe it!"

"I'm not sure I *do* believe it." I kept my narrowed eyes fixed on Theo. "Please tell me you didn't hack into his account after I asked you not to."

"I promise I didn't hack his bank account," Theo said, unfazed by my glare. "And I didn't transfer the money. He did that himself."

"Why would he do that?" Wyatt asked before I had the chance. "I mean, it's great that he did, but he didn't strike me as the type to have an attack of conscience."

Theo tried for a casual shrug. "Maybe you misjudged him?"

"Theodosia Harris," I said in my best mom voice. "What did you do?"

She glanced aside, then huffed and rolled her eyes. "Fine. I hacked into his phone and had a look around."

I put my hands to my face. "We agreed—"

"That I wouldn't hack into his bank account. And I didn't. But I did find out that he'd been chatting with several women on dating apps. I sent him an anonymous message, letting him know that screenshots of those chats would be sent to Tiffany if he didn't return your money within forty-eight hours."

"Nice one," Jemma said, impressed.

I groaned. "Theo, blackmail is also against the law."

"He's not going to turn us in for that," she said without any doubt. "It's way more important to him to keep Tiffany financing his life."

She was probably right about that.

"So, the money is really mine again?" I hadn't yet allowed myself to believe that.

Jemma put an arm around my shoulders. "It was always yours."

"And I think you've seen the last of Hoffman," Theo added.

"And if not," Wyatt said, "we've all got your back."

I smiled as relief, gratitude, and affection all bloomed in my chest, bringing tears to my eyes.

"Anyway," Theo said, taking charge of the conversation, "change your passwords, if you haven't already. Just in case. And I hope you're ready for your next job."

I blinked away my tears. "You mean at the clothing store?" I asked with confusion.

My interview had taken place the day before, and I'd just found out an hour ago that I'd landed the job. It was only part-time at minimum wage and would barely cover my rent, but it was a step in the right direction, and hopefully a sign that my fortunes were changing for the better.

"For Wyatt Investigations," Theo explained.

"I'm pretty sure I've already mentioned that the agency doesn't actually exist," I said.

"Then why do you have a paying client?" Theo asked.

"Paying . . ." I echoed faintly.

"Client?" Jemma finished for me.

"Since when?" Wyatt asked, sounding a little too interested, if you asked me.

"Since a woman contacted us through our website last night. She's hired the two of you to find out if her soon-to-be ex-husband is lying about the fact that he's too injured to work and needs alimony."

"Okay, but we aren't actually detectives," I pointed out, because—clearly—she needed the reminder.

"You just solved a murder case," she countered.

"Well, sort of . . ."

"She's already agreed to our rates," Theo said, unmoved by my protestations.

"We have rates?" I glanced at Wyatt.

He shrugged.

Theo handed me her phone. It displayed a string of messages, including one where Theo told the woman the cost of hiring Wyatt Investigations.

My eyes widened when I saw the figure. "She seriously agreed to that?"

"We'll take the case, right?" Wyatt said to me.

"You're not actually part of the agency, you know."

"Then why is my name on the business card?" Before I could answer that question—again—he continued, "And why does the HR department have a file on me?"

"He's got a point," Jemma said.

Theo nodded her agreement.

My exasperation intensified. "No, he doesn't! And there is no HR department!"

Everyone looked at me and waited.

I held out for a good three seconds before caving.

"Ugh! Okay, fine. Just this one case."

After all, it sounded straightforward enough, and I wasn't exactly in a position to say no to the money. The savings Hoffman had returned gave me a cushion, but I still needed to earn a living.

"Can you set up a meeting with the client?" Wyatt asked Theo.

She smiled, clearly pleased with herself. "Already done. Tomorrow afternoon at one o'clock."

I didn't know what lay ahead with Livy's guardianship, and I really didn't know how I was supposed to ignore the crazy, off-the-charts chemistry between me and Wyatt if we were going to be working together again.

I also didn't know how I was going to get my life fully back on track.

All I knew for sure was that I was definitely not a detective.

My gaze slid back to the dollar amount displayed on Theo's phone.

Maybe.

ACKNOWLEDGMENTS

Creating this book has been such an adventurous and fun-filled journey, and I've enjoyed every step. Several wonderful people have traveled this road with me, and this book wouldn't exist without their support, insight, and expertise. Special thanks to my agent, Jessica Faust, for championing this project, and to my editor, Alicia Clancy, for your enthusiasm, guidance, and belief in this story and its characters. Thanks also to Jean Slaughter, Abby Duval, Saige Francis, Katie Zilberman, Brandon Hopkins, Jean-Michel Perchet, Carlos Beltran, Alexis Flynn, the entire team at Bantam Dell. I might not have a Senior Squad, but you're my Story Squad. ♥

SARAH FOX is the author of the *USA Today* bestselling Pancake House Mysteries, as well as the Music Lover's Mysteries, the Literary Pub Mysteries, the True Confections Mysteries, and the Magical Menagerie Mysteries. She was born and raised in Vancouver, British Columbia, where she developed a love for mysteries at a young age. When not plotting (fictional) murders or doling out sardines to her mini panther (black cat), she is often reading her way through a stack of books or spending time outdoors with her English springer spaniel.

authorsarahfox.com
Instagram: @the_write_fox
Facebook.com/authorsarahfox

ABOUT
THE TYPE

This book was set in Caslon, a typeface first designed in 1722 by William Caslon (1692–1766). Its widespread use by most English printers in the early eighteenth century soon supplanted the Dutch typefaces that had formerly prevailed. The roman is considered a "workhorse" typeface due to its pleasant, open appearance, while the italic is exceedingly decorative.